Sharon Kendrick once won a national writing competition by describing her ideal date: being flown to an exotic island by a gorgeous and powerful man. Little did she realise that she'd just wandered into her dream job! Today she writes for Mills & Boon, and her books feature often stubborn but always *to-die-for* heroes and the women who bring them to their knees. She believes that the best books are those you never want to end. Just like life…

Louise Fuller was a tomboy who hated pink and always wanted to be the Prince—not the Princess! Now she enjoys creating heroines who aren't pretty push-overs but are strong, believable women. Before writing for Mills & Boon she studied literature and philosophy at university, and then worked as a reporter on her local newspaper. She lives in Tunbridge Wells, with her impossibly handsome husband, Patrick, and their six children.

THE ITALIAN'S CHRISTMAS HOUSEKEEPER

SHARON KENDRICK

REVENGE AT THE ALTAR

LOUISE FULLER

MILLS & BOON

First Published in Great Britain 2018
by Mills & Boon, an imprint of HarperCollins*Publishers*
1 London Bridge Street, London, SE1 9GF

The Italian's Christmas Housekeeper © 2018 by Sharon Kendrick

Revenge at the Altar © 2018 by Louise Fuller

ISBN: 978-0-263-93554-7

MIX
Paper from
responsible sources
FSC® C007454

Printed and bound in Spain
by CPI, Barcelona

THE ITALIAN'S CHRISTMAS HOUSEKEEPER

SHARON KENDRICK

To Maura Sabatino, who is funny and beautiful
and whose help for this book was invaluable.

Grazie mille for bringing Naples alive with
your words—and for helping me to create
a Neapolitan Christmas!

CHAPTER ONE

SALVIO DE GENNARO stared at the lights as he rounded the headland. Flickering lights from the tall candles which gleamed in the window of the big old house. They made him think of Christmas and he didn't want to think about it—not with still six weeks left to go. Yet here in England the shops were already full with trees and tinsel and the kind of gifts surely no sane person would want for themselves.

His mouth hardened as the dark waters of the Atlantic crashed dangerously on the rocks beneath him.

Christmas. The *least* wonderful time of the year in his opinion. No contest.

He slowed his pace to a steady jog as dusk fell around him like a misty grey curtain. The rain was heavier now and large drops of water had started to lash against his body but he was oblivious to them, even though his bare legs were spattered with mud and his muscles were hot with the strain of exertion. He ran because he had to. Because he'd been taught to. Tough, physical exercise woven into the fabric of his day, no matter where in the world he was. A discipline which was as much a part of him as breathing and which made him hard and strong. He barely noticed that his wet singlet was now clinging to his torso or that his shorts were plastered to his rocky thighs.

He thought about the evening ahead and, not for the first time, wondered why he had bothered coming. He was here because he wanted to buy a prime piece of land from his aristocratic host and was convinced the deal could be concluded more quickly in an informal setting. The man he was dealing with was notoriously difficult to pin down—a fact which Salvio's assistant had remarked on, when she'd enquired whether she should accept the surprise invitation for dinner and an overnight stay.

Salvio gave a grim smile. Perhaps he should have been grateful to have been granted access to Lord Avery's magnificent Cornish house, which stood overlooking the fierce midwinter lash of the ocean. But gratitude was a quality which didn't come easily to him, despite his huge wealth and all the luxury it afforded him. He wasn't particularly looking forward to dinner tonight. Not with a hostess who'd been eying him up from the moment he'd arrived—her eyes lit with a predatory hunger which was by no means unusual, although it was an attitude he inevitably found tedious. Married women intent on seduction could be curiously unattractive, he thought disdainfully.

Inhaling a lungful of sea air, he grew closer to the house, reminding himself to instruct his assistant to add a couple of names to the guest list for his annual Christmas party in the Cotswolds, the count-down to

which had already begun. He sighed. His yearly holiday celebration—which always took place in his honey-
stone manor house—was one of the most lusted-after
invitations on the social calendar, though he would have
happily avoided it, given the opportunity. But he owed
plenty of people hospitality and you couldn't avoid
Christmas, no matter how much the idea appealed.

He'd learnt to tolerate the festival and conceal his
aversion behind a lavish display of generosity. He
bought expensive gifts for his family and staff and in-
jected yet more cash into the charitable arm of his vast
property empire. He took a trip to his native Naples to
visit his family, because that was what every good Neapolitan boy did, no matter how old or successful he
was. He went back to the city which he avoided as much
as possible because it was the home of his shattered
dreams—and who liked to be reminded of those? For
him, home would always be the place where he had been
broken—and the man who had emerged from the debris
of that time had been a different man. A man whose
heart had been wiped clean of emotion. A man who
was thankfully no longer at the mercy of his feelings.

He increased his pace to a last-minute sprint as he
thought about Naples and the inevitable litany of questions about why he hadn't brought home a nice girl to
marry, nor produced a clutch of bonny, black-haired
babies for his mother to make a fuss of. He would be
forced to meet the wistful question in her eyes and bite
back the disclosure that he never intended to marry.
Never. Why disillusion her?

He slowed his pace as he reached the huge house,

glad he had declined his hostess's invitation to accompany her and her husband to the local village that afternoon, where a performance of Cinderella was taking place. Salvio's lips curved into a cynical smile. Amateur dramatics in the company of a married woman with the hots for him? Not in this lifetime. Instead, he intending making the most of the unexpected respite by trying to relax. He would grab a glass of water and go to his room. Listen to the soothing soundtrack of the ocean lashing hard against the rocks and maybe read a book. More likely still, he would chase up that elusive site in New Mexico which he was itching to develop.

But first he needed to dry off.

Sinking her teeth into a large and very moist slice of chocolate cake, Molly gave a small moan of pleasure as she got her first hit from the sugary treat. She was starving. Absolutely starving. She hadn't eaten a thing since that bowl of porridge she'd grabbed on the run first thing. Unfortunately the porridge had been lumpy and disappointing, mainly because the unpredictable oven had started playing up halfway through making it. Not for the first time, she wondered why her bosses couldn't just have the kind of oven you simply switched on, instead of a great beast of a thing which lurked in the corner like a brooding animal and was always going wrong. She'd been working like crazy all morning, cleaning the house with even more vigour than usual because Lady Avery had been in such a state about their overnight guest.

'He's Italian,' her employer had bit out. 'And you know how fussy they are about cleanliness.'

Molly didn't know, actually. But more worrying still was Lady Avery's inference that she wasn't working hard enough. Which was why Molly dusted the chandeliers with extra care and fastidiously vacuumed behind the heavy pieces of antique furniture. At one point she even got down on her hands and knees to scrub the back door porch—even if she did manage to make her hands red raw in the process. She'd put a big copper vase of scented eucalyptus and dark roses in the guest bedroom and had been baking biscuits and cakes all morning, so that the house smelt all homely and fragrant.

The Averys rarely used their Cornish house—which was one of the reasons why Molly considered being their resident housekeeper the perfect job. It meant she could live on a limited budget and use the lion's share of her wages to pay off her brother's debt and the frightening amount of interest it seemed to accrue. It was the reason she endured the isolated location and demanding attitude of her employer, instead of spreading her wings and finding somewhere more lively.

But the winter had made her isolation all the more noticeable and it was funny how the approach of Christmas always reminded you of the things you didn't have. This year she was really missing her brother and trying not to worry about what he was doing in Australia. But deep down she knew she had to let go. She *had* to. For both their sakes. Robbie was probably having the time of his life on that great big sunny continent—and maybe she should count her blessings.

She took another bite of chocolate cake and did exactly that, reminding herself that most people would revel in the fact that when the Averys *were* around, they entertained all kinds of amazing people. Guests Molly actually got to meet—even if it was only in the context of turning down their beds at night or offering them a home-made scone. Politicians who worked with Lord Avery in the Palace of Westminster, and famous actors who spouted Shakespearean sonnets from the stages of London's theatres. There were business people, too—and sometimes even members of the royal family, whose bodyguards lurked around the kitchen and kept asking for cups of tea.

But Molly had never heard Lady Avery make such a fuss about anyone as she'd done about the impending arrival of Salvio De Gennaro, who was apparently some hotshot property developer who lived mostly in London. Earlier that day she had been summoned into her boss's office, where the walls were decked with misty photos of Lady Avery wearing pearls and a dreamy expression, in those far-off days before she'd decided to have a load of extensive work done on her face. A bad idea, in Molly's opinion—though of course she would never have said so. Lady Avery's plump lips had been coated in a startling shade of pink and her expression had been unnaturally smooth as she'd gazed at Molly. Only the hectic flicker in her pale eyes had hinted how excited she was by the impending visit of the Italian tycoon.

'Everything is prepared for our guest's arrival?' The words were clipped out like tiny beads of crystal.

'Yes, Lady Avery.'

'Make sure that Signor De Gennaro's bed linen is scented with lavender, will you?' continued her boss. 'And be sure to use the monogrammed sheets.'

'Yes, Lady Avery.'

'In fact...' A thoughtful pause had followed. 'Perhaps you'd better go into town and buy a new duvet.'

'What, *now*, Your Ladyship?'

'Yes. Right now.' A varnished scarlet fingernail began tracing a circle on the sheet of blotting paper on the desk and an odd, trembling note had crept into her employer's aristocratic voice. 'We don't want Signor De Gennaro complaining about the cold, do we?'

'We certainly don't, Lady Avery.'

The last-minute purchase of the new duvet had been the reason why Molly hadn't been on hand to greet the Italian tycoon when he'd arrived. And when she'd returned from her shopping expedition—gasping under the bulky dimensions of a high-tog goose-down duvet—there had been no sign of him. Only his open suitcase and a few clothes strewn around his room indicated he was somewhere in the vicinity, although he was nowhere to be seen in the house. Which at least meant Molly had been able to make up his bed in peace—though her heart had started racing when she'd spotted the faded denims slung carelessly over a stool. And when she'd picked up the dark sweater which lay crumpled beside it, she had been startled by the softness of the cashmere as she'd automatically started to fold it. Briefly, her fingertips had caressed the fine wool before she had taken herself downstairs for tea and some restorative cake and she was just on her third mouthful when the kitchen door opened then slammed shut with a rush of icy air and Molly looked up to see a man framed in the doorway who could only be the Italian billionaire.

Her heart crashed against her ribcage.

The most perfect man she could have imagined.

Her mouth opened slightly but she clamped it shut and the chocolate fudge cake she'd been eating suddenly tasted like glue against the roof of her mouth.

Mud-spattered and windswept, he was standing perfectly still—his singlet and shorts surely the craziest choice of clothes he could have selected for the bitter winter day, although a fleecy top was knotted around his narrow hips. His olive skin was silky-smooth and his body was... Molly tried not to shake her head in disbelief but it took some doing, because his body was sensational—and she was certainly not the kind of woman who spent her time analysing men's bodies. In fact, her interest had never really been sparked by anyone.

Until now.

She swallowed, the cake she was holding suddenly forgotten. It took a lot for Molly to disregard the sugar craving which had always been the bane of her life, but she forgot it now. Because she'd never seen a man like this. Not someone with a rocky torso against which his wet top clung to every sinew, as if it had been painted on with a fine-tipped brush. Nor such narrow hips and sculpted thighs whose glorious flesh was exposed by the shorts he seemed to wear so comfortably. Her eyes moved up to his face. To eyes as black as one of those moonless nights when you couldn't ever imagine seeing daylight again. And his lips. Molly swallowed again.

Oh, those lips. Sensual and full, they were hard and un-smiling as they looked at her with something it took a moment for her to recognise. Was it...*disdain*? Her heart pounded uncomfortably. Yes, of course it was. Men with whiplike bodies which didn't carry an ounce of extra weight would be unlikely to approve of an overabundant female who was bulging out of her ugly uniform and stuffing a great big fix of carbohydrate into her mouth.

Flushing to the roots of her hair, she put down the half-eaten cake and rose to her feet, wondering why the ground beneath them suddenly felt as if it were shifting, the way she'd always imagined standing on quicksand might feel. 'I'm...' She blinked at him before trying again. 'I'm so sorry. I wasn't expecting anyone...'

His voice was sardonic as his gaze met hers for one heart-stopping moment, before dropping briefly to the crumb-laden plate. 'Clearly not.'

'You must be...' *A dark angel who has suddenly fallen into my kitchen? The most gorgeous man I've ever seen?* Her chest felt tight. 'You must be Signor De Gennaro?'

'Indeed I am. Forgive me.' Jet eyebrows were raised as he unknotted the warm top from his hips and pulled it over his head before shaking out his damp, dark curls. 'I seem to have disturbed your snack.'

Her *snack*? Although his English was faultless, his richly accented voice was nearly as distracting as his body and Molly opened her mouth to say it was actu-ally a late lunch because she'd been rushing around all morning preparing for *his* arrival, but something stopped her. As if someone like Salvio De Gennaro

would be interested in her defence! As if he would believe her making out she was a stranger to cake when
her curvy body told an entirely different story. Smoothing her uniform down over her generous hips, she tried
to adopt an expression of professional interest, rather
than the shame of being caught out doing something
she shouldn't. And he was still staring at her. Making
her aware of every pulsing atom of her body in a way
which was making her feel extremely self-conscious…
but strangely enough, in a *good* way.

'Can I get you anything, Signor De Gennaro?' she
questioned politely. 'I'm afraid Lord and Lady Avery
have gone to the village pantomime and won't be back
until later.'

'I know,' he said coolly. 'Perhaps some water. And
a coffee, if you have one.'

'Of course. How do you take your coffee?'

He flickered her a smile. 'Black, short, no sugar.
Grazie.'

Of course not, thought Molly. No sugar for someone
like him. He looked as if he'd never been near anything
sweet in his life. She wished he'd go. Before he noticed
that her brow had grown clammy, or that her nipples
had started to push distractingly against the unflatter-
ing navy-blue uniform Lady Avery insisted she wore.
'I'll do that right away,' she said briskly. 'And bring
them up to your room.'

'No need for that. I'll wait here,' he said.

She wanted to tell him he was making her feel awkward by standing there, like some kind of brooding,
dark statue—just *staring* at her. As if he had read her

thoughts, he strolled over towards the window and she became aware of an almost imperceptible limp in his right leg. Had he injured himself when out running and should she ask him whether he needed a bandage or something? Perhaps not. Someone with his confidence would be bound to ask for one.

She could feel a stray strand of hair tickling the back of her neck and wished she'd had time to fix it. Or had been sitting reading some novel which might have made her look interesting, instead of scoffing cake and emphasising the fact that she was heavy and ungainly.

'I'll try to be as quick as I can,' she said, reaching up into one of the cupboards for a clean glass.

'I'm in no hurry,' he said lazily.

Because that much was true. Salvio had decided that he was enjoying himself though he wasn't quite sure why. Maybe it was the novelty factor of being with the kind of woman he didn't come across very often—at least, not any more. Not since he'd left behind the backstreets of Naples, along with those women whose curves defined fecundity and into whose generous flesh a man could sink after a long, hard day. Women like this one, who blushed alluringly if they caught you looking at them.

He had waited for a moment to see if she would recognise him. If she knew who he was—or, rather, who he *had* been. But no. He was familiar with recognition in all its forms—from greedy delight right through to feigned ignorance—but there had been no trace of any of those on her face. And why should there be? She was much younger than him and from a different country.

How would she have known that in his native Italy he had once been famous?

He watched her busying herself, her curvy silhouette reminding him of the bottles of Verdicchio which used to line the shelves of the city bar he'd swept as a boy, before the talent scouts had discovered him and ended his childhood. She turned to switch on the coffee maker and a sudden dryness turned his throat to dust because…her breasts. He swallowed. *Madonna mia*—what breasts! He was glad when she turned away to open the fridge door because his erection was pressing uncomfortably against his shorts, though, when she did, he then became mesmerised by her shapely bottom. He was just fantasising about what her shiny brown hair would look like loose when she turned around and surveyed him with eyes as grey as the Santissima Annunziata Maggiore—that beautiful church in Naples, which had once been an orphanage.

Their gazes clashed and mingled and something unspoken fizzled in the air as Salvio felt a leap of something he couldn't define. The hardness in his groin was familiar but the sudden clench of his heart was not. Was it lust? His mouth twisted. Of course it was lust—for what else could it be? It just happened to be more powerful than usual because it had taken him by surprise.

Yet there was no answering hunger in her quiet, grey gaze—something which perplexed him, for when *didn't* a woman look at him with desire in her eyes? She was wary, he found himself thinking, with a flicker of amusement. Almost as if she were silently reproaching him for his insolent appraisal—and maybe that senti-

ment was richly deserved. What *was* he doing survey-
ing her curvy body, like a boy from a single-sex school
who was meeting a beautiful woman for the first time?

'You're the cook?' he questioned, trying to redeem
himself with a safe, if rather banal question.

She nodded. 'Sort of. Officially, I'm the housekeeper
but I do a bit of everything. Answer the door to guests
and make sure their rooms are serviced, that sort of
thing.' She pushed the coffee towards him. 'Will there
be anything else, Signor De Gennaro?'

He smiled. 'Salvio. And you are?'

She looked taken aback, as if people didn't ask her
name very often. 'It's Molly,' she answered shyly, in a
voice so soft it felt like silk lingerie brushing against
his skin. 'Molly Miller.'

Molly Miller. He found himself wanting to repeat it,
but the conversation—such as it was—was terminated
by the sudden sweep of car headlights arcing powerfully
across the room. As he heard the sound of a large car
swishing over gravel, Salvio saw the way she flinched
and automatically tugged at her drab dress so that it
hung more uniformly over her wide hips.

'That's the Averys.'

'I thought it must be.'

'You'd better… You'd better go,' she said, unable to
keep the waver of urgency from her voice. 'I'm supposed to be preparing dinner and Lady Avery won't
like finding a guest in the kitchen.'

Salvio was tempted to tell her that he didn't give
a damn what Lady Avery would or wouldn't like but
he could see the fear which had darkened her soft

grey eyes. With a flicker of irritation he picked up his espresso and water and headed for the door. *'Grazie mille,'* he said, leaving the warm and steamy kitchen and walking rapidly towards the staircase, reluctant to be around when the Averys burst into the hallway.

But once back in his own room, he was irritated to discover that the low burn of desire was refusing to leave him. So that instead of the hot shower he'd promised himself, Salvio found himself standing beneath jets of punishingly cold water as he tried to push the curves of the sweet little housekeeper from the forefront of his mind and to quell the exquisite hardness which throbbed at his groin.

CHAPTER TWO

'MOLLY, THESE POTATOES are frightful. We can't possibly ask Signor De Gennaro to eat them. Have they even *seen* an oven? They're like rocks!'

Molly could feel herself flushing to the roots of her hair as she met Lady Avery's accusing stare. Were they? She blinked. Surely she'd blasted them for the required time, carefully basting them with goose fat to make them all golden and crispy? But no. Now she stopped to look at them properly—they were definitely on the anaemic side.

She could feel her cheeks growing even pinker as she reached towards the table to pick up the dish. 'I'm so sorry, Lady Avery. I'll pop them back in the—'

'Don't bother!' snapped her employer. 'It will be midnight before they're fit to eat and I don't intend going to bed on a full stomach. And I'm sure Salvio won't want to either.'

Was it Molly's imagination, or did Lady Avery shoot the Italian a complicit smile from the other side of the table? The way she said his name sounded unmistakably predatory and the look she was giving him was enough to make Molly's stomach turn. Surely the aristocrat wasn't hinting that she intended ending up in bed with him, not with her husband sitting only a few feet away?

Yet it had struck her as odd when Sarah Avery had come down for dinner wearing the tightest and lowest-cut dress imaginable, so that the priceless blaze of the Avery diamonds dazzled like stars against her aging skin. She'd been flirting outrageously with the Italian businessman ever since Molly had served pre-dinner drinks and showed no sign of stopping. And meanwhile, her husband—two decades older and already a quarter of the way through his second bottle of burgundy—seemed oblivious to the undercurrents which had been swirling around the dinner table ever since they'd sat down.

The meal had been a disaster from the moment she'd put the starters on the table and Molly couldn't understand why. She was a good cook. She knew that. Hadn't she spent years cooking for her mother and little brother, trying to produce tasty food on a shoestring budget? And hadn't part of her job interview for Lady Avery consisted of producing a full afternoon tea—including a rich and rather heavy fruit cake—within the space of just two hours…a feat she had managed with ease? A simple meal for just three people should have been a breeze, but Molly hadn't factored in Salvio De Gennaro, or the effect his brooding presence would have on her employer. Or, if she was being honest, on her.

After he'd swept out of the kitchen earlier that afternoon, it had taken ages for her heart to stop thumping and to be able to concentrate on what she was supposed to be doing. She'd felt all giddy and stupidly... *excited*. She remembered the way he had looked into her eyes with that dark and piercing gaze and wondered if she'd imagined the pulsing crackle of electricity between them before telling herself that, yes, of course she had. Unless she really thought a man who could have his pick of any woman on the planet would have the slightest interest in a naïve country girl who was carrying far too much weight around her hips.

In her dreams!

But there was no doubt that Salvio's unexpected trip to the kitchen had rocked Molly's equilibrium and after he'd gone, all the light had seemed to disappear from the room. She'd sat down at the table feeling flat, which was unusual for her because she'd always tried to be an optimist, no matter what life threw at her. She was what was known as a glass-half-full type of person rather than one who regarded the glass as half empty. So why had she spent the rest of the afternoon mooching around the kitchen in a way which was completely out of character?

'Molly? Are you listening to a word I'm saying?'

Molly stiffened as she saw the fury in Lady Avery's eyes—but not before she'd noticed Salvio De Gennaro's face darken with an expression she couldn't work out. Was he wondering why on earth the wife of a famous peer bothered employing such a hapless housekeeper?

'I'm so sorry,' said Molly quickly. 'I was a bit distracted.'

'You seem to have been distracted all afternoon!' snapped Lady Avery. 'The meat is overcooked and the hors d'oeuvres were fridge-cold!'

'Come on, Sarah. It's no big deal,' said Salvio softly. 'Give the girl a break.'

Molly's head jerked up and as she met the understanding gleam of Salvio De Gennaro's ebony eyes, she felt something warm and comforting wash over her. It was like sitting beside a fire when snow was falling outside. Like being wrapped in a soft, cashmere blanket. She saw Lady Avery appear momentarily disconcerted and she wondered if Salvio De Gennaro's silky intervention had made her decide that giving her housekeeper a public dressing-down wouldn't reflect very well on *her*. Was that why she flashed her a rather terrifying smile?

'Of course. You're quite right, Salvio. It's no big deal. After all, it's not as if we're short of food, is it? Molly always makes sure we're very well fed, but—as you can tell—she's very fond of her food!' She gave a bright, high laugh and nodded her head towards the snoring form of her husband, who had now worked his way through the entire bottle of wine and whose head was slumped on his chest as he snored softly. 'Molly, I'm going to wake Lord Avery and guide him to bed and then Signor De Gennaro and I will go and sit by the fire in the library. Perhaps you'd like to bring us something on a tray to take the place of dinner. Nothing too fussy. Finger food will do.' She flashed another toothy smile. 'And bring us another bottle of the Château Lafite, will you?'

'Yes, Lady Avery.'

Salvio's knuckles tightened as he watched Molly scuttle from the room, though he made no further comment as his hostess moved round the table to rouse her sleeping husband and then rather impatiently ushered him from the room. But he couldn't shake off the feeling of injustice he had experienced when he'd seen how the aristocrat treated the blushing housekeeper. Or the powerful feeling of identification which had gripped him as he'd witnessed it. Was it because he'd known exactly how she would be feeling? His mouth hardened. Because he'd been where she had been. He knew what it was like to be at the bottom of the food chain. To have people treat you as if you were a machine, rather than a person.

He splayed his fingers over the rigid tautness of his thighs. He would wait until his hostess returned. Force himself to have a quick drink since she'd asked for one of the world's most expensive wines to be opened, then retire to his room. He glanced at his watch. It was too late to go back to London tonight but he would leave at first light, before the house was awake. All in all it had been a wasted journey, with Lord Avery too inebriated to talk business before dinner. He hadn't even been able to work because the damned Internet kept going down and because his thoughts kept straying to the forbidden… And the forbidden had proved shockingly difficult to erase from his mind. He sighed. How crazy was it that the wholesome housekeeper had inexplicably set his senses on fire, so that he could think of little but her?

He'd walked into the orangery before dinner to see her standing with a tray of champagne in her hands. She had changed into a simple black dress which hugged her body and emphasised every voluptuous curve. With her shiny brown hair caught back at the nape of her neck, his attention had been caught by those grey eyes, half concealed by lashes like dark feathers, which were modestly lowered as she offered him a drink. Even that was a turn-on. Or maybe especially that. He wasn't used to modesty. To women reluctant to meet his gaze, whose cheeks turned the colour of summer roses. He'd found himself wanting to stand there studying her and it had taken a monumental effort to tear his eyes away. To try to make conversation with a host who seemed to be having a love affair with the bottle, and his disenchanted wife who was almost spilling out of a dress much too young for a woman her age.

'Salvio!' Sarah Avery was back, a look of determination on her face as she picked her way across the Persian rug on her spiky black heels. 'Sorry about that. I'm afraid that sometimes Philip simply can't hold his drink. Some men can't, you know—with predictable effects, I'm afraid.' She flashed him a megawatt smile. 'Let's go to the library for a drink, shall we?'

There had been many reasons why Salvio had left Naples to make his life in England and he had absorbed the attitudes of his adopted country with the tenacity he applied to every new challenge which came his way. These days he considered himself urbane and sophisticated—but in reality the traditional values of his Neapolitan upbringing were never far from the surface. And in his world, a woman never criticised her husband to another person. Particularly a stranger.

'Just one drink,' he said, disapproval making his words harsher than he intended. 'I have a busy schedule tomorrow and I'll be leaving first thing.'

'But you've only just arrived!'

'And I have back-to-back meetings in London, from midday onwards,' he countered smoothly.

'Oh! Can't you cancel them?' she wheedled. 'I mean, I've heard that you're a complete workaholic, but surely even powerhouses like you are allowed to slow down a little. And this is a beautiful part of the world. You haven't really seen any of it.'

With an effort, Salvio forced a smile because he found her attitude intensely intrusive, as well as irritating. 'I like to honour my commitments,' he observed coolly as he followed her into the firelit library, where Molly was putting cheese and wine on a table, the stiff set of her shoulders showing her tension. He wasn't surprised. Imagine being stuck out here, working for someone as rude and demanding as Sarah Avery. He sank into one of the armchairs, and watched as his hostess went to stand by the mantelpiece in a pose he suspected was intended to make him appreciate her carefully preserved body. She ran one slow finger over the gleaming curve of an ancient-looking vase, and smiled.

'Are you looking forward to Christmas, Salvio?' she questioned.

He was immediately wary—recoiling from the thought that some unwanted invitation might soon be heading his way. 'I am away for most of it—in Naples,' he said, accepting a glass of wine from Molly—ridiculously pleased to capture her blushing gaze before she quickly turned away. 'I'm always glad to see my family but, to be honest, I'm equally glad when the holiday is over. The world shuts down and business suffers as a result.'

'Oh, you men!' Sarah Avery slunk back across the room to perch on a nearby chair, her bony knees clamped tightly together. 'You're all the same!'

Salvio managed not to wince, trying to steer the conversation onto a more neutral footing as he sipped his wine, though all he could think about was Molly hovering nervously in the background, the black dress clinging to her curvaceous figure and a stray strand of glossy brown hair dangling alluringly against her pink cheek. He cleared his throat. 'How are you and your husband planning to spend Christmas?' he questioned politely.

This was obviously the opportunity Sarah Avery had been waiting for and she let him have the answer in full, telling him how much Philip's adult children hated her and blamed her for ending their parents' marriage. 'I mean, I certainly didn't set out to get him, but I was his secretary and these things happen.' She gave a helpless shrug. 'Philip told me he couldn't help falling in love with me. That no power on earth could have stopped it. How was I supposed to know his wife was pregnant at the time?' She sipped a mouthful of wine, leaving a thin red stain above the line of her lip gloss. 'I mean, I really don't care if his wretched kids won't see me—it's Philip I'm concerned about—and I really think they need to be mindful of their inheritance. He'll cut them off if they're not careful!'

Salvio forced himself to endure several minutes more of her malicious chatter, his old-fashioned sensibilities outraged by her total lack of shame. But eventually he could stand no more and rose to his feet and, despite all her cajoling, she finally seemed to get the message that he was going to bed. Alone. Like a child, she pouted, but he paid her sulky expression no heed. He felt like someone who'd just been released from the cage of a prowling she-cat by the time he escaped to the quietness of the guest corridor and closed the door of his room behind him.

A sigh of relief left his lips as he looked around. A fire had been lit and red and golden lights from the flames were dancing across the walls. He'd been in these grand houses before and often found them unbearably cold, but this high-ceilinged room was deliciously warm. Over by the window was a polished antique cabinet on which stood an array of glittering crystal decanters, filled with liquor which glinted in the moonlight. He studied the walls, which were studded with paintings, including some beautiful landscapes by well-known artists. Salvio's mouth twisted. It was ironic really. This house contained pictures which would have been given pride of place in a national gallery—yet a trip to the bathroom required a walk along an icy corridor, because the idea of en-suite was still an alien concept to some members of the aristocracy.

He yawned but didn't go straight to bed, preferring to half pack his small suitcase so he was ready to leave first thing. Outside he could see dark clouds scudding across the sky and partially obscuring the moon, turning the churning ocean silver and black. It was stark and it was beautiful but he was unable to appreciate it because he was restless and didn't know why.

Loosening his tie and undoing the top button of his shirt, Salvio braved the chilly corridor to the bathroom and was on his way back when he heard a sound from the floor above. A sound which at first he didn't recognise. He stilled as he listened and there it was again. His eyes narrowed as he realised what it was. A faint gasp for breath, followed by a snuffle.

Someone was crying?

He told himself it was none of his business. He was leaving first thing and it made sense to go straight to bed. But something tugged at his... He frowned. His conscience? Because he knew that the person crying must be the little housekeeper? He didn't question what made him start walking towards the sound and soon found himself mounting a narrow staircase at the far end of the corridor.

The sound grew louder. Definitely tears. His foot creaked on a step and an anxious voice called out.

'Who's there?'

'It's me. Salvio.'

He heard footsteps scurrying across the room and as the door was pulled open, there stood Molly. She was still wearing her black uniform although she had taken down her hair and removed her sturdy shoes. It spilled over her shoulders in a glorious tumble which fell almost to her waist and Salvio was reminded of a painting he'd once seen of a woman sitting in a boat, with fear written all over her features. He could see fear now, in soft grey eyes which were rimmed with red. And suddenly all the lust he'd felt from the moment he'd set eyes on her was replaced by a powerful sense of compassion.

'What's happened?' he demanded. 'Are you hurt?'

'Nothing's happened and, no, I'm not hurt.' Quickly, she blotted her cheeks with her fingertips. 'Did you want something?' she asked, a familiar note of duty creeping into her voice. 'I hope… I mean, is everything in your room to your satisfaction, Signor De Gennaro?'

'Everything in my room is fine and I thought I told you to call me Salvio,' he said impatiently. 'I want to know why you were crying.'

She shook her head. 'I wasn't crying.'

'Yes, you were. You know damned well you were.'

An unexpected streak of defiance made her tilt her chin upwards. 'Surely I'm allowed to cry in the privacy of my own room.'

'And surely I'm allowed to ask why, if it's keeping me awake.'

Her grey eyes widened. 'Was it?'

He allowed himself the flicker of a smile. 'Well, no—now you come to mention it. Not really. I hadn't actually gone to bed but it's not a sound anyone particularly wants to hear.'

'That's because nobody was supposed to. Look, I'm really sorry to have disturbed you, but I'm fine now. See.' This time she gritted her teeth into a parody of a smile. 'It won't happen again.'

But Salvio's interest was piqued and the fact that she was trying to get rid of him intrigued him. He glanced over her shoulder at her room, which was small. He hadn't seen a bedroom that small for a long time. A narrow, unfriendly bed and thin drapes at the window, but very little else. Suddenly he became aware of the icy temperature—an observation which was reinforced by the almost imperceptible shiver she gave, despite the thickness of her black dress. He thought about the fire in his own bedroom with the blazing applewood logs which she must have lit herself.

'You're cold,' he observed.

'Only a bit. I'm used to it. You know what these old houses are like. The heating is terrible up here.'

'You don't say?' He narrowed his eyes speculatively. 'Look, why don't you come and sit by my fire for a while? Have a nightcap, perhaps.'

She narrowed her eyes. 'A nightcap?'

He slanted her a mocking smile. 'You know. The drink traditionally supposed to warm people up.'

He saw her hesitate before shaking her head.

'Look, it's very kind of you to offer, but I can't possibly accept.'

'Why not?'

'Because...' She shrugged. 'You know why not.'

'Not unless you tell me, I don't.'

'Because Lady Avery would hit the roof if she caught me socialising with one of the guests.'

'And how's she going to find out?' he questioned with soft complicity. 'I won't tell if you won't. Come on, Molly. You're shivering. What harm will it do?'

Molly hesitated because she *was* tempted—more tempted than she should have been. Maybe it was because she was feeling so cold—both inside and out. A coldness she'd been unable to shift after the telling off she'd just been given by Lady Avery, who had arrived in the kitchen in an evil temper, shaking with rage as she'd shouted at Molly. She'd told her she was clumsy and incompetent. That she'd never been so ashamed in her life and no wonder Signor De Gennaro had cut short the evening so unexpectedly.

Yet now that same man was standing in the doorway of her humble room, asking her to have a drink with him. He had removed his tie and undone the top button of his shirt, giving him a curiously relaxed and accessible air. It was easy to see why Lady Avery had made a fool of herself over him during dinner. Who wouldn't fall for his olive-dark skin and gleaming ebony eyes?

Yet despite his sexy appearance, he had looked at her understandingly when she'd messed up during dinner. He'd come to her rescue—and there was that same sense of concern on his face now. He had an unexpected streak of kindness, she thought, and kindness was hard to resist. Especially when you weren't expecting it. An icy blast of wind rushed in through the gap in the window frame and once again Molly shivered. The days ahead didn't exactly fill her with joy and her worries about Robbie were never far from the surface. Couldn't she loosen up for once in her life? Break out of the lonely mould she'd created for herself by having a drink with the Italian tycoon?

She gave a tentative shrug. 'Okay, then. I will. Just

a quick one, mind. And thank you,' she added, as she slipped her feet back into the sensible brogues she'd just kicked off. 'Thank you very much.'

He gave a brief nod, as if her agreement was something he'd expected all along, and Molly tried to tell herself that this meant nothing special—at least, not to him. But as he turned his back and began to walk she realised her heart was racing and Molly was filled with an unfamiliar kind of excitement as she followed Salvio De Gennaro along the narrow corridor towards his grand bedroom on the floor below.

CHAPTER THREE

'HERE.'

'Thanks.' Molly took the brandy Salvio was offering her, wondering if she'd been crazy to accept his invitation to have a drink with him, because now she was in his room she felt hopelessly embarrassed and out of place. She noticed his half-packed open suitcase lying on the far side of the room and, for some stupid reason, her heart sank. He obviously couldn't wait to get away from here. Awkwardly, she shifted from one foot to the other.

'Why don't you sit down over there, beside the fire?' he suggested.

Lowering herself into the chair he'd indicated, Molly thought how weird it was to find herself in the role of visitor to a room she had cleaned so many times. Just this morning she'd been in here, fluffing up the new duvet and making sure the monogrammed pillowcases were all neatly facing in the right direction. Over there were the neat stack of freshly ironed newspapers Lady Avery had insisted on, and the jug of water with the little lace cover on top. Yet it was funny how quickly you could get used to the dramatic change from servant to guest. The soft leather of the armchair felt deliciously soft as it sank beneath her weight and the warmth of the fire licked her skin. She took a tentative sip from her glass, recoiling a little as the powerful fumes wafted upwards.

'Not much of a drinker?' observed Salvio wryly, as he poured his own drink.

'Not really.' But even that minuscule amount of liquor had started to dissolve the tight knot of tension in the pit of her stomach, sending a warm glow flooding through her body. Molly stared out of the windows where clouds were racing across the silvery face of the moon. Outside the temperature had plummeted but in here it felt cosy—in fact, she might even go so far as to say she was starting to feel relaxed. Yet here she was in a strange man's bedroom in her black uniform and heavy-duty shoes as if she had every right to be there. What on earth would Lady Avery say if she happened to walk in? Anxiety rippled through her as she glanced at Salvio, who was replacing the heavy stopper in the bottle. 'I really shouldn't be here,' she fretted.

'So you said,' he drawled, his tinge of boredom implying that he found repetition tedious. 'But you are here. And you still haven't told me why you were crying.'

'I…' She took another sip of brandy before putting the glass down on a nearby table. 'No reason really.'

'Now, why don't I believe you, Molly Miller?' he challenged softly. 'What happened? Did you get into more trouble about dinner?'

Her startled expression told Salvio his guess was correct. 'I deserved it,' she said flatly as she met his gaze. 'The meal was rubbish.'

Briefly he acknowledged her loyalty. She would have been perfectly justified in moaning about her employer but she hadn't. She was a curious creature, he thought, his gaze flickering over her dispassionately. Totally without artifice, she didn't seem to care that the way she was sitting wasn't the most flattering angle she could have chosen. Yet her abundant hair glowed like copper in the firelight and as she crossed one ankle over the other he was surprised by how unexpectedly erotic that simple movement seemed. But he hadn't brought her here to seduce her, he reminded himself sternly. Tonight he had cast himself in the role of the good Samaritan, that was all. 'And that's the only reason for your tears?'

Molly gave an awkward wriggle of her shoulders. 'Maybe I was feeling sorry for myself,' she admitted, shifting beneath his probing gaze. Because no way was she going to tell him the real reason. He wouldn't be interested in her wayward brother or his habit of accumulating debt, but more than that—she was afraid of saying the words out loud. As if saying them would make them even more real. She didn't want to wonder why Robbie had rung up just an hour ago, asking her if she had any spare cash for a 'temporary' loan, despite his promises to find himself some sort of job. Why hadn't he got any money of his own? Why was he asking her for more, after all his tearful promises that from now on he was going to live his life independently and free of debt? She swallowed. She couldn't bear to think that he'd got himself into that terrible spiral yet again—of playing poker and losing. Of owing money to hard-faced men who wouldn't think twice about scarring his pretty young face...

'Call it a touch of self-pity,' she said, meeting the black fire in his eyes and realising he was still waiting for an answer. 'Not something I imagine you have much experience of.'

Salvio gave a mirthless smile. How touching her faith in him! Did she think that because he was wealthy and successful, he had never known pain or despair, when he had been on intimate terms with both those things? His mouth hardened. When his life had imploded and he'd lost everything, he remembered the darkness which had descended on him, sending him hurtling into a deep and never-ending hole. And even though he'd dragged himself out of the quagmire and forced himself to start over—you never forgot an experience like that. It marked you. Changed you. Turned you into someone different. A stranger to yourself as well as to those around you. It was why he had left Naples—because he couldn't bear to be reminded of his own failure. 'Why do you stay here?' he questioned quietly.

'It's a very well-paid job.'

'Even though you get spoken to like that?'

She shook her head, her long hair swaying like a glossy curtain. 'It's not usually as bad as it was tonight.'

'Your loyalty is touching, *signorina*.'

'I'm paid to be loyal,' she said doggedly.

'I'm sure you are. But even taking all that into account, this place is very *isolato*...isolated.' He gave a flicker of a smile, as if begging her to forgive his sudden lapse into his native tongue. 'I can't imagine many people your age living nearby.'

'Maybe that's one of the reasons I like it.'

He raised his eyebrows. 'You don't like to socialise?'

Molly hesitated. Should she tell him that she always felt out of place around people her own age? That she didn't really do the relaxed stuff, or the fun stuff, or the wild stuff. She'd spent too many years caring for her mother and then trying to keep her brother from going off the rails—and that kind of sensible role could become so much a part of you that it was difficult to relinquish it. And wouldn't that kind of admission bring reality crashing into the room? Wouldn't it puncture the slightly unreal atmosphere which had descended on her ever since she'd walked in here and settled down by the fireside, allowing herself to forget for a short while that she was Molly the housekeeper—so that for once she'd felt like a person in her own right?

'I can take people or leave them,' she said. 'Anyway, socialising is expensive and I'm saving up. I'm intending to put my brother through college and it isn't cheap. He's in Australia at the moment,' she explained, in answer to the fractional rise of his dark brows. 'Doing a kind of...gap year.'

He frowned. 'So you're here—working hard—while he has fun in the sun? That's a very admirable sacrifice for a sister to make.'

'Anyone would do it.'

'Not anyone, no. He's lucky to have you.'

Molly picked up her glass again and took another sip of brandy. Would Salvio De Gennaro be shocked if he knew the truth? That Robbie hadn't actually got a place at college yet, because he was still 'thinking about it', in spite of all her entreaties to get himself a proper education and not end up like her. She licked her lips, which tasted of brandy. She didn't want to think about Robbie. Surely she could have a night off for once? A night when she could feel young and carefree and revel in the fact that she was alone with a gorgeous man like Salvio—even if he had only invited her here because he felt sorry for her.

Putting her glass down, she stared at him and her heart gave a sudden lurch of yearning. He hadn't moved from his spot by the window and his powerful body was starkly outlined by the moonlight.

'What about you?' she questioned suddenly. 'What brought you here?'

He shrugged. 'I was supposed to be discussing a deal with Philip Avery.' He twisted his lips into a wry smile. 'But that doesn't look like it's going to happen.'

'He'll be much more receptive in the morning,' said Molly diplomatically.

'It'll be too late by then,' he said. 'I'm leaving as soon as it's light.'

Molly was aware of a crushing sense of disappointment. She'd wanted... She stared very hard at her brandy glass as if the dark amber liquid would provide the answer. What had she wanted? To see him at breakfast—their eyes meeting in a moment of shared complicity as they remembered this illicit, night-time drink?

'Oh, that's a shame,' she said, sounding genuinely disappointed.

He smiled, as if her earnestness had amused him. 'You know, you're far too sweet to be hiding yourself away somewhere like this, Molly.'

Sweet. Molly knew it was a compliment yet for some reason it offended her. It made her sound like the cake he'd caught her eating. Because sweet wasn't sexy, was it? Just as *she* wasn't sexy. 'Am I?' she questioned tonelessly.

He nodded, walking over to the desk and writing something on the back of a business card before crossing the room and handing it to her. 'Here. Take this. It will get you straight through to my assistant. If ever you decide you want a change, then give her a ring. She knows plenty of people, and domestic staff are always in short supply.' He met her eyes. 'You could always find something better than this, you know.'

'Despite dinner being such a disaster?' She tried to sound jokey even if she didn't feel it, because she realised she was being dismissed. Getting up from the comfort of her fireside seat, Molly took the card and slid it into the hip pocket of her dress.

'Despite that,' he agreed, his words suddenly trailing away as his gaze followed the movement of her hand.

Molly became aware of a subtle alteration in the atmosphere as Salvio lifted his eyes to her face. She'd wondered if the attraction which had sizzled between them earlier had been wishful thinking, but maybe it hadn't. Maybe it had been real. As real as the sudden thrust of her nipples against the soft fabric of her dress and the distracting heat between her thighs. She held her breath, waiting, instinct telling her that he was going to touch her. Despite him being who he was and her being just Molly. And he did. Lifting his hand, he ran the tips of his fingers experimentally over her hair.

'*E capelli tuoi so comme a seta,*' he said, and when she looked at him in confusion, he translated. 'Your hair is like silk.'

It was the most beautiful thing anyone had ever said to her and when she heard it in Italian it made her want to melt. Was that why he did it, knowing it would push her a little further beneath his powerful spell? Molly told herself to move away. She should thank him for the drink, for his kindness and for giving her his card and then hurry back to her little room to mull over her memories and hug them to her like a hot-water bottle. But she didn't move. She just carried on gazing up into the rugged perfection of his looks, praying he would kiss her and make the fairy tale complete—even if that was all she was ever going to have to remember him by. 'Is—is it?' she questioned.

Salvio smiled, letting his thumb drift from the fire-warmed strands, to hover over the unmistakable tremble of her lips. He felt a tightness in his throat as he realised what he was about to do. He had invited her here because he sensed she was lonely and unhappy—not because he intended to seduce her. Because there were rules and usually he followed them. He no longer took physical comfort just because it was available—because it was pretty much always available to a man like him. Just as he no longer used sex to blot out his pain, or his anger.

But the little housekeeper had touched a part of him

he'd thought had died a long time ago. She had stirred a compassion in his soul and now she was stirring his body in a way which was all too obvious, if only to him. He could feel the aching hardness at his groin, but the urge to kiss her was even more overwhelming than the need to bury himself deep inside her body. He told himself he should resist—gently shoo her out of the door and send her on her way. And maybe he would have done—had she not chosen that moment to expel a shaky breath of air, the warmth of it shuddering softly against his thumb.

How could something as insignificant as a breath be so potent? he marvelled as he stared down into her wide grey eyes. 'I want to kiss you,' he said softly. 'But if that happens I will want to make love to you and I'm not sure that's such a good idea. Do you understand what I'm saying, Molly?'

Wordlessly, she nodded.

'And the only thing which will stop me, is you,' he continued, his voice a deep silken purr. 'So stop me, Molly. Turn away and walk out right now and do us both a favour, because something tells me this is a bad idea.'

He was giving her the opportunity to leave but Molly knew she wasn't going to take it—because when did things like this ever happen to people like her? She wasn't like most women her age. She'd never had sex. Never come even close, despite her few forays onto a dating website, which had all ended in disaster. Yet now a man she barely knew was proposing seduction and suddenly she was up for it, and she didn't care if it was *bad*. Hadn't she spent her whole life trying to be good? And where had it got her?

Her heart was crashing against her ribcage as she stared up into his rugged features and greedily drank them in. 'I don't care if it's a bad idea,' she whispered. 'Maybe I want it as much as you do.'

Her response made him tense. She saw his eyes narrow and heard him utter something which sounded more like despair than joy before pulling her almost roughly into his arms. He smoothed the hair away from her cheeks and lowered his head and the moment their lips met, she knew there would be no turning back.

At first his kiss was slow. As if he was exploring her mouth by touch alone. And just when she was starting to get used to the sheer dreaminess of it, it became hard. Urgent. It fuelled the hunger which was building inside her. He levered her up against him, so that her breasts were thrusting eagerly against his torso and she could feel the rock-hard cradle of his pelvis. She should have been daunted by the unmistakable bulk of his erection but she wasn't, because her hungry senses were controlling her now and she didn't feel like good, rule-following Molly any more. She felt like wanton Molly—a victim of her own desire.

And it felt good.

More than good.

His laugh was unsteady as he splayed his fingers over one of her breasts, the nipple instantly hardening against his palm. 'You are very passionate,' he murmured.

Molly gave a small gurgle of pleasure as he found the side zip of her dress because suddenly she *felt* passionate. As if she had been waiting all her life to feel this way. 'Am I?'

'I don't think you need any reassurance on that score, *bedda mia*.'

He was wrong, of course—but he wasn't to know that and Molly certainly wasn't going to tell him. She felt breathless as he peeled the plain black dress away from her body and let it fall to the ground before stepping back to survey her. And wasn't it funny how a look of admiration in a man's eyes could be powerful enough to dispel all a woman's instinctive insecurities? Because for once Molly wasn't thinking that her tummy was too plump or her breasts unfashionably massive. Or even that her bra didn't match her rather functional pants. Instead she was revelling in the look of naked hunger which made his eyes resemble black fire as they blazed over her.

And then he picked her up. Picked her up! She could hardly believe it. He was carrying chunky Molly Miller towards the bed as if she weighed no more than a balloon at a child's birthday party, before whipping back the brand-new duvet she'd purchased that very morning and depositing her beneath it. It was the most delicious sensation in the world, sinking into the mattress and lying beneath the warmth of the bedding, her body sizzling with a growing excitement—while Salvio De Gennaro began to undress. She swallowed, completely hypnotised as she watched him. The shoes and socks were first to go and then he unbuttoned his shirt, baring his magnificent chest before turning his attention to the zip of his trousers. But when he hooked his thumb inside the waistband of his boxers, Molly squeezed her eyes tightly closed.

'No. Not like that. Open your eyes. Look at me,' he instructed softly and she was too much in thrall to disobey him.

Molly swallowed. She couldn't deny that it was slightly daunting to see just how aroused he was and as she bit her lip, he smiled.

'Me fai asci pazzo,' he said, as if that explained everything.

'Wh-what does that mean?'

'It means you make me crazy.'

'I love it when you talk Italian to me,' she said shyly.

'Not Italian,' he said sternly as he slipped into bed beside her. 'Neapolitan.'

She blinked. 'It's different?'

'It's dialect,' he said and she noticed he was placing several foil packets on the antique chest of drawers beside the bed. 'And yes, it's very different.'

The appearance of condoms somehow punctured some of the romance, but by then he was naked beside her and Molly was discovering that the sensation of skin touching skin was like nothing she'd ever known. It was *heaven*. Better than chocolate cake. Better than… well, anything really.

'Salvio,' she breathed, trying out his name for the first time.

'Sì, bedda mia? Want me to kiss you again?'

'Yes, please,' she said fervently, and he laughed.

His kisses were deep. It felt as if he were drugging her with them, making her body receptive to the caress of his fingers. And, oh, those fingers—what magic they worked as he tiptoed them over her shivering flesh. He massaged her peaking nipples until she was writhing with pleasure, and when he slid his hand between her thighs and discovered how wet she was, he had to silence her instinctive gasp with another kiss.

And because she didn't want to be passive, Molly stroked him back. At first she was cautious—concentrating on his chest and ribcage, before daring to explore a belly which was far flatter than her own. But when she plucked up the courage to touch the unfamiliar hardness which kept brushing against her quivering thigh, he stopped her with a stern look. 'No.'

She didn't ask him why. She didn't dare. She was afraid of doing anything which would shatter the mood or show how inexperienced she really was. Which might make Salvio De Gennaro bolt upright in bed and incredulously question what the hell he was doing, being intimate with a humble housekeeper. But he didn't. In fact, he seemed just as in tune with her body as she was with his. Like greedy animals, they rolled uninhibitedly around on the bed, biting and nipping and stroking and moaning and there was only the briefest hiatus when Salvio reached for one of the foil packets.

'Want to put this on for me?' he questioned provocatively. 'Since my hands are shaking so much I'm beginning to wonder if I can manage to do it myself.'

Some of Molly's composure left her. Should she say something?

Salvio, I've only ever seen a condom in a biology class at school. I've never actually used one for real.

Mightn't learning that send him hurtling out of bed in horror? Yes, he might be as aroused as she imagined any man *could* be, but even so…mightn't it be a bit heavy if she burdened him with a piece of knowledge which wasn't really relevant? After all, it wasn't as if she was expecting this…interlude to actually go anywhere.

And maybe he read her thoughts because he brought his face up close to hers and surveyed her with smoky eyes. 'You know that I—'

'Yes, I know. You're leaving in the morning,' she said. 'And that's okay.'

'You're sure?'

'Quite sure. I just want…'

'What do you want, Molly?' he questioned, almost gently.

'I just want tonight,' she breathed. 'That's all.'

Salvio frowned as he stroked on a condom. Was she for real, or just too good to be true? He kissed her again, wanting to explode with hunger but forcing himself to move as slowly as possible as he pushed inside her molten heat, because he was big. He'd been told that often enough in the past but he had never felt bigger than he did tonight.

But size had nothing to do with her next reaction. The tensing of her body and her brief grimace of pain told their own unbelievable story. Confusion swirled his thoughts and made him momentarily still. With an almighty effort he prepared to withdraw, but somehow her tight muscles clamped themselves around him in a way which was shockingly new and exciting, making him dangerously close to coming straight away.

He sucked in a raw breath, trying desperately to claw back control. Trying to concentrate on not giving in to his orgasm, rather than on the unbelievable fact that the housekeeper was a virgin. Or rather, she *had* been.

But stopping himself from coming was the hardest sexual test he'd ever set himself. Maybe it was her tightness which felt so delicious. Or the uninhibited way she was responding to him. She was a stranger to all the games usually played in the bedroom, he realised—and her naivety made her an unmatchable lover, because she was a natural. She hadn't learnt any tricks or manoeuvres. The things she was doing she hadn't done with any other man before and somehow that turned him on. He revelled in the way she squirmed those fleshy hips as he drove into her. The way she thrust her breast towards his lips, so that he could tease the pointing nipple with first his tongue and then his teeth. He sensed the change in her—the moment when her orgasm became inevitable—and he watched her closely, seeing her dark eyelashes flutter to a close. Triumph washed over him as she made that first disbelieving choke of pleasure and a rosy flush began to blossom over her breasts. And only when the last of her violent spasms had died away did he give in to his own need, unprepared for the power of what was happening to him. It felt like the first time, he thought dazedly. Or maybe the only time.

And then he fell asleep.

CHAPTER FOUR

IT WAS STILL dark when Salvio awoke next morning—the illuminated dial of his wristwatch informing him it was just past six. He waited a moment until his eyes became adjusted to the shadows in the bedroom. In the heat of that frantic sexual encounter which had taken him almost by surprise last night, he hadn't bothered to close the drapes and outside it was still dark—but then, sunrise came late to this part of the world in the depths of an English winter.

He glanced across at the sleeping woman beside him, sucking in a slow lungful of air as he tried to get his head around what had happened. Trying to justify the fact that he'd had sex with the innocent housekeeper, when deep down he knew there could be no justification. Yet she had wanted it, he reminded himself grimly. She had wanted it as much as him.

They had been intimate again during the night—several times, as it happened. His stretching leg had encountered the voluptuous softness of her warm flesh, making him instantly aroused. There had been a stack of questions he'd been meaning to ask, but somehow her touch had wiped them from his mind. The second time had been amazing—and so had the third. She was so easy to please. So grateful for the pleasure he gave her. He'd expected her to start bringing up tricky topics after orgasm number five, but his expectations hadn't materialised. She hadn't demanded to know if he had changed his mind about seeing her again, which was fortunate really, because he hadn't. His eyes narrowed. He couldn't. She was too sweet. Too naïve. She wouldn't last a minute in his world and his own cynical nature would destroy all that naïve enthusiasm of hers in an instant.

Leaning over, he shook her bare shoulder—resisting the desire to slip his hand beneath the duvet and begin massaging one of those magnificent breasts.

'Molly,' he murmured. 'Wake up. It's morning.'

It was a shock for Molly to open her eyes and realise she was staring up at the magnificent chandelier which hung from the ceiling of the guest bedroom. In this faint light it twinkled like the fading stars outside the window and she forced herself to remember that in several hours' time she would be attacking it with her feather duster, not lying beneath the priceless shards of crystal, with the warm body of a naked man beside her.

A shiver ran through her as she turned her head to look at Salvio, her heart punching out a violent beat as she realised what she'd done. She swallowed. What *hadn't* she done? She had let him undress her and explore every inch of her body, with his tongue and his fingers and a whole lot more beside. When he'd been deep inside her body, she had choked out his name over and over again as he had awoken an appetite she hadn't realised she possessed. Somehow he had waved a magic wand and turned her into someone she didn't really recognise and she had gone from being inexperienced Molly Miller, to an eager woman who couldn't get enough of him. Briefly she closed her eyes.

And she wasn't going to regret a single second of it. Because you couldn't turn the clock back—and even if you could, who would want to?

She yawned, stretching her arms above her head and registering the unfamiliar aching of her body. How many times had he made love to her? she wondered dazedly, as she recalled his seemingly insatiable appetite and her own eager response.

She forced herself to ask the question she didn't really want to ask. 'What time is it?'

'Just after six.' There was a pause. His eyes became hooded. 'Molly—'

'Well, you'd better get going, hadn't you?' Her breezy interjection forestalled him because she'd guessed what he was about to say—the heaviness of his tone warning her that this was the Big Goodbye. And he didn't need to. He had to go and she was okay with that. Why ruin everything by demanding more than he'd ever intended to give? She pinned an efficient smile to her lips. 'You did say you wanted to get away early.'

He frowned, as if her response wasn't what he'd been expecting, but Molly knew there was only one way to deal with a situation like this, and that was by being sensible, the way she'd been all her life. She had to face facts, not mould them to suit her fantasies. She knew there could be no future between her and the billionaire tycoon because their lives were too different. Last night the boundaries had become blurred—but one night of bliss didn't change the fundamentals, did it? She was employed as a housekeeper—and lying in an honoured guest's bed was the very last place she should be.

'You're sure you're okay?' he growled.

She wondered where the rogue thought came from. The one which made her want to say, *Not really, no. I wish you could take me with you wherever you're going and make love to me the way you did last night.*

But fortunately, the practical side of her character was the dominant one. As if Salvio De Gennaro would want to take her away with him! She tried to imagine cramming herself into that low-slung sports car— why, her weight would probably disable the suspension! 'Why wouldn't I be okay?' she questioned breezily. 'It was great. At least, I think it was.' For the first time, a trace of insecurity crept into her voice as she looked at him with a question in her eyes.

'Oh, it was more than "great",' he affirmed, reaching out to trace the tip of his finger over the quiver of her bottom lip. 'In fact, it was so good that I want to do it all over again.'

Once again Molly felt her stomach clench with desire and a rush of heat tugged deep inside her. 'But...' she whispered as he moved closer.

'But what, *mia bedda*?'

'There isn't...' She swallowed. 'There isn't time.'

'Says who?'

He slipped his hand between her legs. Molly wondered what had happened to the sensible part of her now. Forgotten, that was what. Banished by the first lazy stroke of his finger over her slick heat. 'Salvio,' she moaned, as his dark head moved down and his tongue found her nipple.

He lifted his head from her breast, dark eyes gleaming in the half-light. 'You want me to stop?'

'You know I don't,' she gasped.

'So why don't you show me what you *would* like?'

Maybe it was the knowledge that this was the last time which made her so adventurous, because Molly suddenly found her hand drifting over his taut belly to capture the rocky erection which was pressing so insistently against her thigh. 'This,' she said shakily. 'This is what I want.'

'And where do you want it?'

'In me,' she breathed boldly. 'Inside me.'

'Me, too,' he purred, reaching out to grab a condom from the sadly diminished pile on the bedside cabinet.

Molly was aware of being warm and sticky as he moved over her. Of her hair all mussed and her teeth unbrushed—but somehow none of that seemed to matter because Salvio was touching her as if she were some kind of goddess. His fingers were sure and seeking and goosebumps rippled over her skin in response as he smoothed his hand over her belly. She felt as if she were *soaring* as she wrapped her thighs around his hips and gave herself up to the exquisite sensation of that first sweet thrust and then the deepening movements which followed.

She loved the way they moved in time. The way she

felt as if she were on a fast shuttle to paradise when another orgasm took her over the top. And she loved his almost helpless expression as his face darkened and he pumped his seed inside her. The way his tousled head collapsed onto her shoulder afterwards as he uttered something intently in what she presumed was more Neapolitan dialect. His breathing was warm and even against her neck and, terrified he would fall asleep and delay his departure, she shook him. 'Salvio,' she whispered. 'Don't go to sleep. You'd better go. Before anyone wakes up.'

'Then you'd better get out of here, too,' he instructed, pushing aside the rumpled duvet. 'Right now. Before anyone sees you.'

For some reason his remark dispirited her and brought her crashing back to earth, allowing reality to puncture her little bubble of happiness. But despite the insecurities which were bubbling up inside her, Molly managed to retain her cheery smile, enjoying the sight of Salvio pulling on his jeans and sweater and quietly opening the door as he headed for the bathroom.

Once he'd gone she got out of bed and pulled on her discarded underclothes—pulling a face as she smoothed her crumpled work dress over her hips and rolled her black tights into a little ball, which she gripped in her hand. She'd be able to do something with her appearance once Salvio had left, she reasoned—glancing up as the door opened as he came back into the bedroom, his dark hair glittering with tiny drops of water from the shower.

In silence he dressed before snapping his overnight

case closed, his expression very serious as he walked towards her. For a moment he just stood in front of her, his gaze sweeping over her like a dark spotlight, as if he were seeing her for the first time.

'So why?' he questioned simply. 'Why me?

Molly expelled a shuddered breath, because in a way she'd been waiting for this question. He hadn't asked her last night and she'd been glad, because she hadn't wanted the mundane to spoil what had been the most fantastic night of her life. In a way, she would have preferred it if he hadn't brought it up now—but he had, and she needed to answer in a way designed to keep it light. Because she didn't want a single thing to tarnish the memory of how glorious it had been. She shrugged. She even managed a smile. 'I don't meet many men in this line of work,' she said. 'And certainly none like you. And you're...you're a very attractive man, Salvio—as I expect you've been told on many occasions.'

He frowned, as if her honesty troubled him. 'I want you to know that I didn't invite you in here in order to seduce you,' he said slowly. 'I'm not saying the thought hadn't crossed my mind earlier, but that wasn't my intention.'

She nodded. 'I know it wasn't. You were being kind, that's all. Maybe that's why I agreed to have a drink with you.'

He gave an odd kind of laugh. 'You had a very profound effect on me, Molly.'

There was an expression in his dark eyes which Molly couldn't work out but maybe it was best that way. She didn't want him telling her it had been an

inexplicable thing he'd done. She wanted to hang onto
what had happened between them—to treat it as you
would one of those precious baubles you hung on the
tree at Christmas. She didn't want to let the memory
slip from her fingers and see it shatter into a million
pieces.

'I'm glad,' she said, holding onto her composure only
by a thread, her heart pounding frantically beneath her
breast. 'But time's getting on. You'd better go.'

He nodded, as if being encouraged to leave a bedroom was a novel experience for him, but suddenly he
turned and walked towards the bedroom door without
another word, and Molly's heart twisted painfully as he
closed it quietly behind him. She stood there framed in
the window, watching as he emerged from the house,
his dark figure silhouetted against the crashing ocean,
and for a second he looked up, his black gaze capturing
hers. She waited for him to smile, or wave, or something—and she told herself it was best he didn't, for
who knew who else might be watching?

Throwing his bag inside, he slipped into the driver's
seat, the closing door blotting out her last sight of him.
His powerful car started up in a small cloud of gravel
before sweeping down towards the coastal road and she
watched until it was just a faint black dot in the distance.
As sunrise touched the dark clouds with the first hint
of red, Molly wondered if Salvio's life was a series of
exits, with women gazing longingly out of windows as
they watched him go.

Her cheeks were hot as she whipped the bottom sheet
from the bed and removed the duvet cover. She would

come back later to collect the linen and clean the room from top to bottom. But first she needed a hot shower. The Averys had plenty of events coming up and Molly had a long list of things to do today. Perhaps it was good that the weeks ahead were busy during the run-up to Christmas. It would certainly stop her from dwelling on the fact she would never see Salvio again. Never feel his lips on hers or his powerful arms holding her tight. Because this was what happened in the grown-up world, she told herself fiercely. People had fun with each other. Fun without expectations, or commitment. They had sex and then they just walked away.

Quietly, she closed the guest-room door behind her and was creeping along the corridor with the exaggerated care of a cartoon thief, when she became aware of someone watching her. Her heart lurched with fear. A shadowed figure was standing perfectly still at the far end of the guest corridor.

Not just anyone.

Lady Avery.

Molly's footsteps slowed, her heart crashing frantically against her ribcage as she met the accusing look in her boss's pale eyes.

'So, Molly,' Lady Avery said, in a voice she'd never heard her use before. 'Did you sleep well?'

There was a terrible pause and Molly's throat constricted, because what could she say? It would be adding insult to injury if she made some lame excuse about why she was creeping out of Salvio's room at this time in the morning, carrying a balled-up pair of tights. And now she would be sacked. She'd be jobless and homeless at the worst possible time of year. She swallowed. There was only one thing she *could* say. 'I'm sorry, Lady Avery.'

Her aristocratic employer shook her head in disbelief. 'I can't believe it!' she said. 'Why someone like him could have been interested in someone like you, when he could have had...'

Her words trailed away and Molly didn't dare fill the awkward silence which followed. Because how could Lady Avery possibly finish her own sentence without losing face or dignity? How could she possibly admit that *she* had been hoping to end up in Salvio's bed, when she was a married woman and her husband was in the house?

Molly's cheeks grew hot as she acknowledged the shameful progression of her thoughts. Behaving as if the Neapolitan tycoon were some kind of prize they'd both been competing over! Had the loneliness of her job made her completely indiscriminate, so that she had been prepared to leap into bed with the first man who had ever shown her any real affection? 'I can only apologise,' she repeated woodenly.

Once again, Lady Avery shook her head. 'Just get back to work, will you?' she ordered sharply.

'Work?' echoed Molly cautiously.

'Well, what else did you think you'd be doing? We have ten people coming for dinner tonight, in case you'd forgotten. And since this time I'm assuming you won't be obsessing about one of the guests, at least the meat won't arrive at the table cremated.' She gave Molly an arch look. 'Unless no man is now safe from your clutches. I must say you're the most unlikely candidate to be a *femme fatale*. Just get back to work, will you, Molly, before I change my mind?'

'Y-yes, Lady Avery.'

Unable to believe she hadn't been fired on the spot, Molly spent the next few weeks working harder than she'd ever worked before. She went above and beyond the call of duty as Christmas approached and she tried to make amends for her unprofessional behaviour. She attempted ambitious culinary experiments, which thankfully all turned out brilliantly. She baked, prodded, steamed and whipped—to the fervent admiration of the stream of guests which passed through the mistletoe-festooned hallway of the house. And if Lady Avery made a few sarcastic digs about Molly hanging around hopefully beneath the sprigs of white berries, Molly was mature enough not to respond. Maybe her boss's anger was justified, she reasoned. Maybe she would have said the same if the situation had been reversed.

And it didn't matter how busy she was—it was never enough to stop her thoughts from spinning in an unwanted direction. She found herself thinking about Salvio and that was the last thing she needed. She didn't want to remember all the things he'd done to her. The way he'd stroked her face and lips and body, before pushing open her thighs to enter her. Just as she didn't want to think about the way he'd whispered *'bedda mia'* and *'nicuzza'* in that haunting dialect when they'd both woken in the middle of the night. Because remembering that stuff was dangerous. It made it all too easy to imagine that it mattered. And it didn't. Not to him. He'd been able to walk away without a second glance and Molly had told him she was able to do the same.

So do it.

Stop yearning.

Stop wishing for the impossible.

It was four days before Christmas when two bomb-shells fell in rapid succession. Molly had just been about to drive to the village, when she came across Lady Avery standing in the hallway—a full-length fur coat swamping her fine-boned frame. Her face looked cold. As cold as the wintry wind which was whistling outside the big house and bringing with it the first few flakes of snow.

'Molly, don't bother going to the shops right now,' she said, without preamble.

Molly blinked. She'd made the pudding and cake and mince pies, but she still had to pick up the turkey and the vegetables. And hadn't they run out of satsumas? She looked at her boss helpfully. 'Is there something else you would rather I was doing?'

'Indeed there is. You can go upstairs and pack your things.'

Molly stared at her boss in confusion. 'Pack my things?' she echoed stupidly. 'I don't understand.'

'Don't you? It's really quite simple. Surely there's no need for me to spell it out for you. We no longer re-quire your services.'

'But…'

'But what, Molly?' Lady Avery took a step closer and

now Molly could see that all the rage she'd been bottling up since Salvio's departure was about to come spilling out. 'I hope you aren't going to ask me why I haven't given you more notice, because I really don't think the normal rules apply when you've abused your position as outrageously as you have done. I really don't think that *sleeping with the guests* ever made it into your job description, do you?'

'But it's just before Christmas!' Molly burst out, unable to stop herself. 'And this…this is my home.'

Lady Avery gave a shrill laugh. 'I don't think so. Why don't you go running to your boyfriend and ask if he wants you over the holiday period? *Because it's not going to happen, that's why.* Salvio will have moved on to the kind of women he's more usually associated with by now.' Her pale eyes drilled into Molly. 'Do you know, they say there isn't a supermodel on the planet he hasn't dated?'

'But why…why wait until now?' questioned Molly in a low voice. 'Why didn't you just fire me straight away?'

'With wall-to-wall engagements planned and Christmas just over the horizon?' Lady Avery looked at her incredulously. 'I was hardly going to dispense with your services and leave myself without a housekeeper at such a busy time, now, was I? That's what's known as cutting off your nose to spite your face.' There was a pause. 'You'll find you've been paid up to the end of the month, which is more generous than you deserve. Philip and I have decided to fly to Barbados tomorrow for a last-minute holiday and we're going out for the rest of the day. Just make sure you're gone by the time we return, will you, Molly?'

'But…but where will I go tonight?'

'You really think I care? There's a cheap B&B in the village. You can go there—*if* they'll take you.' Lady Avery's mouth had curved into a cruel smile. 'Just make sure you leave your car and house keys on the hall table before you go.'

And that was that. Molly could hardly believe it was happening. Except that she could. Her heart clenched as her old friend Fear re-entered her life without fanfare and suddenly she was back in that familiar situation of being in a fix. Only this time she couldn't blame her brother, or the vagaries of fate which had made her mother so ill throughout her childhood. This time it was all down to her.

Biting her lip, she thought desperately about where she could go and what she could do, but no instant solution sprang to mind. She had no relatives. No local friends who could provide her with a roof over her head until she found herself another live-in job. Her mind buzzed frantically as some of Lady Avery's words came flooding into her mind. How would Salvio react if she called him up and told him she'd been fired as a result of their crazy liaison? Would he do the decent thing and offer her a place to stay? Yet, despite recoiling at the thought of throwing herself on the mercy of a man who'd made it clear he wanted nothing but a one-night stand, it was growing increasingly clear that she might *have* to. Because the second bombshell was hovering overhead ready to explode, no matter how hard she tried to block it from her mind.

Telling herself it was stress which had made her period so late, she pushed the thought away as she remembered the card Salvio had given her—the one with a direct line to his assistant. What had he said? That his assistant knew plenty of people and could help her find a domestic role if ever she needed one. Molly licked her lips. She didn't want to do it but what choice did she have? Where would she even *start* looking for a new job and a home at this time of year?

Quickly, she packed her clothes, trying not to give in to the tears which were pricking at the backs of her eyes. Carefully she wedged in the framed photo of her mother and the one of Robbie in his school uniform, the cute image giving no hint of the gimlet-eyed teenager he would become. And only when she was standing in her threadbare winter coat, with a hand-knitted scarf knotted tightly around her neck, did she dial the number on the card with a shaking finger.

Salvio's assistant was called Gina and she didn't just sound friendly—she sounded *relieved* when Molly gave her name and explained why she was ringing.

'I can't believe it,' she said fervently. '*You* are the answer to my prayers, Molly Miller.'

'Me?' said Molly doubtfully.

'Yes, you.' Gina's voice softened. 'Are you free now? I mean, as of right now?'

'I am,' answered Molly cautiously. 'Why?'

'Because Salvio is having his annual pre-Christmas party in the Cotswolds tomorrow, just before he flies to Naples—and the housekeeper we'd hired has called to say her mother has fallen downstairs and broken her wrist, and she's had to cancel. If you can step in and take over at the last minute I can make it very worth your while.'

Molly pushed out the words from between suddenly frozen lips. 'That's very bad news—about the broken wrist, I mean, but I don't think I—'

But the tycoon's assistant was breezing on as if she hadn't spoken.

'Salvio must rate you very highly to have given you my number,' Gina continued. 'Why, it's almost like fate. I won't even have to bother telling him about the change. He doesn't like to be bogged down with domestic trivia and he's always so busy.'

Molly bit her lip so hard it hurt. This was fast becoming a nightmare, but what else could she do? How could she possibly turn down this opportunity just because she'd had sex with the man who would now unwittingly be employing her? She would just blend into the background and pray that the Neapolitan tycoon would be too busying partying to pay her any attention. And if the worst came to the worst and he discovered her identity—then she would shrug her shoulders and tell him it was no big deal.

Realistically, what could go wrong?

But being rumbled by Salvio wasn't the worst thing which could happen, was it? Not by a long way. The fear which had been nagging at her for days came flooding into her mind and this time would not be silenced, because all her excuses about stress and anxiety were rapidly fading. Because she wasn't sure if anxiety was capable of making your breasts ache and feel much bigger than usual. Or whether it could sap your normally voracious appetite.

She stared at her pale reflection in the hall mirror and saw the terror written in her own eyes. Because what if she was pregnant with Salvio De Gennaro's baby?

CHAPTER FIVE

VISIBILITY WAS POOR—in fact, it was almost non-existent. Salvio's fingers tightened around the soft leather of the steering wheel. Eyes narrowed, he stared straight ahead but all he could see was an all-enveloping whiteness swirling in front of the car windscreen. Every couple of seconds, the wipers dispelled the thick layer of snow which had settled, only to be rapidly replaced by another.

Frustrated, he glanced at the gold watch at his wrist, cursing the unpredictability of the weather. His journey from central London to the Cotswold countryside had been excruciatingly slow and in an ideal world he would have cancelled his annual party. But you couldn't really cancel something this close to Christmas, no matter how preoccupied you were feeling. And he *was* feeling preoccupied, no doubt about it—even though the reason for that was disconcertingly bizarre. An impatient sigh escaped his lungs as he watched another flurry of snow. Because he couldn't stop thinking about the curvy little housekeeper with the big grey eyes, with those luscious breasts, whose tips had fitted perfectly into his hungry mouth. Most of all, he couldn't stop remembering her purity. Her innocence.

Which he had taken. Without thought. Without knowledge. But certainly not without feeling.

Memories of how it had felt to penetrate her beautiful tightness flooded his mind and Salvio swallowed as he touched his foot against the brake pedal. Would he have bedded her so willingly if he'd known she was a virgin? Of course he wouldn't. His desire for the housekeeper had been completely out of character and he still couldn't quite fathom it. He usually enjoyed women who were, if not quite his equal, then certainly closer on the social scale than Molly Miller would ever be.

He thought about Beatriz—the Brazilian beauty with whom he'd been enjoying a long-distance flirtation for the past few months. He had been attracted to her because she'd played hard to get and he'd convinced himself that a woman who wouldn't tumble straight into his arms was exactly what he needed. But as her attitude towards him had thawed, so had his interest waned— and the memory of Molly had completely wiped her from his mind. And although Beatriz had made it clear she would be happy to share his bed after his Christmas party, the idea had left him cold, despite the fact that most men lusted after her statuesque beauty. He had been wondering about the most tactful way to convey his sudden change of heart, when she'd rung last night to say her plane had been delayed in Honolulu and she didn't think she was going to make his party. And hadn't he been struck by an overwhelming feeling of *relief*?

'*No importa*. Don't worry about it,' he had responded quickly—probably too quickly.

A pause. 'But I'm hoping we can see each other some other time, Salvio.'

'I'm hoping so too, but I'm flying out to Naples for Christmas and I'm not sure when I'll be back.' His response had been smooth and seasoned. And distinctly dismissive. 'I'll call you.'

He could tell from her sharp intake of breath that she understood the underlying message and her good-bye had been clipped and cold. She hadn't even wished him a happy Christmas and he supposed he couldn't blame her.

But his mind had soon moved on to other things and, infuriatingly, he kept recalling the sweet sensation of a naked Molly in his arms. He swallowed. The way her soft lips had pressed into his neck and her fleshy thighs had opened so accommodatingly. There were a million reasons why he shouldn't be thinking about her but she was proving a distractingly difficult image to shift. Was that because she hadn't put any demands on him? Because she'd been okay about him walking out of her life? Most women hung on in there, but Molly Miller was not among their number. And hadn't that intrigued him? Made him wonder what it might be like to see her in a more normal setting. Perhaps even take her out to dinner to see how long it would take for her allure to fade.

He'd thought a few times about contacting her—but what could he say, without falsely raising her hopes? No. He was doing her a favour by leaving her alone—

that was what he needed to remember. Breaking hearts was his default mechanism—and no way would he wish that kind of pain on the passionate little housekeeper.

It was the most beautiful house Molly had ever seen. Pressing her nose against the icy-cold glass, she peered out through the taxi window at the sprawling manor house, whose gardens were a clever combination of wild and formal and seemed to go on for ever. Although the sky was pewter-grey, the light was bright with snow and everything was covered in white. Fat flakes tumbled like giant feathers from the sky, so that the scene in front of her looked like one of those old-fashioned Christmas cards you couldn't seem to buy any more.

But Molly's emotions were in turmoil as the cab inched its way up the snowy drive. She had underestimated the impact of leaving Cornwall because even though the job had left a lot to be desired, it had still been her home and her security for the last two years. More than that, her departure had been forced upon her in the most dramatic and shameful of ways. Suddenly she felt rudderless—like a leaf caught up by a gust of wind being swirled towards an unknown destination.

But even worse than her near-homelessness was the confirmation of her worst fears. That it hadn't been stress or anxiety which had made her period so late. That the weird tugs of mood and emotion—like wanting to burst into tears or go to sleep at the most inopportune times—hadn't been down to the *worry* of getting pregnant. She couldn't even blame the sudden shock of losing her live-in job, or the corresponding jolt to her confidence. No, the reason had been made perfectly clear when she'd done not one, but two pregnancy tests in the overcrowded bathroom of the little boarding house she'd stayed in last night. With growing horror and a kind of numb disbelief she had sat back on her heels and stared at the unmistakable blue line, shaking with the shock of realising that she was pregnant with Salvio's baby.

And wondering what the hell she was going to do about it.

But she couldn't afford to think about that right now. The only thing she needed to concentrate on was doing her job—and as good a job as possible. She was going to have to tell him, yes, but not yet. Not right before his party and the arrival of his presumably high-powered guests.

She paid the driver and stepped out of the cab onto a soft blanket of snow. There were no other tyre marks on the drive and the only sign of life was a little robin hopping around as she made her way to the ancient oak front door, which looked like something out of a fairy tale. She knocked loudly, just in case—but there was no answer and so she let herself in with the keys she'd picked up from Salvio's assistant, along with a great big wodge of cash for expenses.

Inside, everything was silent except for the loud ticking of a grandfather clock, which echoed through the spacious hallway, and the interior was even more beautiful than the outside had suggested. It spoke of elegance and money and taste. Gleaming panelled walls carved with acorns and unicorns. Huge marble fireplaces and dark floorboards scattered with silk rugs were illuminated by the sharp blue light which filtered in through the windows. Yet the beauty and the splendour were wasted on Molly. She felt like an outsider. Like the spectre who had arrived at the feast bearing a terrible secret nobody would want to hear. She felt like curling up in a ball and howling, but what was the point of that? Instead she forced herself to walk around the house to get her bearings, just as she would with any new job.

A quick tour reassured her that the cupboards and fridge were well stocked with everything she could possibly need, the beds all made up with fresh linen and the fires laid. She lit the fires, washed her hands and started working her way through the to-do list. Barring bad weather cancellations, twenty-five guests would be arriving at seven. Gina had informed her that there were plenty of bedrooms if bad weather prevented some of the city guests getting back to London, but Salvio would prefer it if they left.

'He's a man who likes his own company,' she'd said.

'Does he?' Molly had questioned nervously, as an image shot into her head of a crying baby. How would he ever be able to deal with *that*?

Maybe he wouldn't want to.

Maybe he would tell her that he had no desire for an unplanned baby in his life. Had she thought about *that*?

A local catering company were providing a hot-buffet supper at around nine and wine waiters would take care of the drinks. All Molly had to do was make sure everything ran smoothly and supervise the local waitresses who were being ferried in from the nearby village. How difficult could it be? Her gaze scanned down to the bottom of the list.

And please don't forget to decorate the Christmas tree!

Molly had seen the tree the moment she'd walked in—a giant beast of a conifer whose tip almost touched the tall ceiling, beside which were stacked piles of cardboard boxes. Opening one, she discovered neat rows of glittering baubles—brand-new and obviously very expensive. And suddenly she found herself thinking about Christmases past. About the little pine tree she and Robbie used to drag in from the garden every year, and the hand-made decorations which their mother had knitted before the cruel illness robbed her of the ability to do even that. It had been hard for all of them to watch her fading away but especially tough for her little brother, who had refused to believe his beloved mother was going to die. And Molly hadn't been able to do anything to stop it, had she? It had been her first lesson in powerlessness. Of realising that sometimes you had to sit back and watch awful things happen—and that for once she couldn't protect the little boy she'd spent her life protecting.

Didn't she feel that same sense of powerlessness now as she thought of the cells multiplying in her womb? Knowing that outwardly she looked exactly the same as before, while inside she was carrying the Neapolitan's baby.

Her fingers were trembling as she draped the tree with fairy lights and hung the first bauble—watching it spin in the fractured light from the mullioned window. And then it happened—right out of nowhere, although if she'd thought about it she should have been expecting it. If she hadn't been singing 'In The Bleak Midwinter' at the top of her voice she might have heard the front door slam, or registered the momentary pause which followed. But she wasn't aware of anything until something alerted her to the fact that someone else was in the room. Slowly she turned her head to see Salvio standing there.

Her heart clenched tightly and then began to pound. He was wearing a dark cashmere overcoat over faded jeans and snowflakes were melting in the luxuriant blackness of his hair. She thought how tall and how powerful he looked. How his muscular physique dominated the space around him. All these thoughts registered in the back of her mind but the one which was at the forefront was the expression of disbelief darkening his olive-skinned features.

'You,' he said, staring at her from between narrowed eyes.

Molly wondered if the shock of seeing her had made him forget her name, or whether he had forgotten it anyway. In either case, he needed reminding—or this situation could prove even more embarrassing than it was already threatening to be. 'Yes, me,' she echoed, her throat dry with nerves. 'Molly. Molly Miller.'

'I know your name!' he snapped, in a way which made her wonder if perhaps he was protesting too much. 'What I want to know is what the hell you're doing here.'

His face had hardened with suspicion. It certainly wasn't the ecstatic greeting Molly might have hoped for—if she'd dared to hope for anything. But hope was a waste of time—she'd learnt that a long time ago. And at least a life spent working as a servant and having to keep her emotions hidden meant she was able to present a face which was perfectly calm. The only outward sign of her embarrassment was the hot colour which came rushing into her cheeks, making her think how unattractive she must look with her apron digging into her waist and her hair spilling untidily out of its ponytail. 'I'm just decorating the Christmas tree—'

'I can see that for myself,' he interrupted impatiently. 'I want to know *why*. What are you doing here, Molly?'

The accusation which had made his mouth twist with anger was unmistakable and Molly stiffened. Did he think she was stalking him, like one of those crazed ex-lovers who sometimes featured in the tabloids? Women who had, against all the odds, come into contact with a wealthy man and then been reluctant to let him—or the lifestyle—go.

'You gave me your assistant's card, remember?' she reminded him. 'And told me to ring her if I needed to find work.'

'But you already have a job,' he pointed out. 'You work for the Averys.'

Molly shook her head and found herself wishing she didn't have to say this. Because wasn't it a humiliating thing to have to admit—that she had been kicked out of her job just before Christmas? 'Not any more, I don't,' she said. She met the question which was glittering from his black eyes. 'Lady Avery caught me leaving your bedroom.'

His eyes narrowed. 'And she *sacked* you because of that?'

Molly's colour increased. 'I'm afraid so.'

Beneath his breath, Salvio uttered some of the words he'd learnt in the backstreets of Naples during his poverty-stricken childhood. Words he hadn't spoken in a long time but which seemed appropriate now as remorse clawed at his gut. It was his fault. Of course it was. Was that why she was looking at him with those big grey eyes, like some wounded animal you discovered hiding in the woods? Because she blamed him and held him responsible for what had happened? And it never *should* have happened, he told himself bitterly. He should never have invited her into his room for a drink, despite the fact that she'd been crying. He'd tried very hard to justify his actions. He'd told himself he'd been motivated by compassion rather than lust, but perhaps he had been deluding himself. Because ultimately he was a man and she was a woman and the chemistry between them had been as powerful as anything he'd ever experienced. Surely he wasn't going to deny *that*.

His eyes narrowed as he studied her. Despite her initial innocence, had she subsequently recognised the sexual power she had wielded over him? It wasn't inconceivable that her sacking had come about as a result of her own ego. She might easily have made a big show of leaving his room, with that dreamy look of sexual satisfaction which made a woman look more beautiful than fancy clothes ever could. And mightn't that have provoked Sarah Avery, whose advances he had most definitely rejected?

Suddenly he felt as if he was back on familiar territory, as he recalled the behaviour of women during his playing days, and one woman in particular. He remembered the dollar signs which had lit up in their eyes when they'd realised how much his contract had been worth. These days he might no longer be one of Italy's best-paid sportsmen, but in reality he was even wealthier. Was that why Molly Miller was here—prettily decorating his tree—just waiting to hit him with some kind of clumsy demand for recompense?

'So why exactly did Gina offer you this job?' he questioned.

She bit her lip. 'Because the woman who was supposed to be doing it had to suddenly go and look after her mother. And I didn't let on that I…' Her words faltered. 'That I *knew* you, if that's what you're worried about. Gina doesn't have a clue about what went on between us. There was a slot to fill, that's all—and I just happened to be in the right place at the right time.'

Or the wrong place at the wrong time. Just like the last time they'd met.

The thoughts rushed into Salvio's head before he could stop them and he felt his body tense as he worked out how best to handle this. Because now he found himself in a difficult situation. He frowned. The amazing night he'd shared with her had haunted him ever since, but nobody was going to deny that it had been a fool-hardy action on so many levels. Did she think it was going to happen again? he wondered. Was she expecting to resume her position in his bed? That once all his guests had left, he would be introducing her to another night of bliss?

He raked his gaze over her, unable to suppress the hunger which instantly fired up his blood but resenting it all the same. He shouldn't feel this way about her. He shouldn't still want her. That night had been a mistake and one which definitely shouldn't be repeated. Yet desire was spiralling up inside him with an intensity which took him by surprise and despite his best efforts he was failing to dampen it. With her fleshy curves accentuated by the waistband of an apron, she looked the antithesis of the glamour he'd always regarded as a prerequisite for his lovers. She looked *wholesome* and plain and yet somehow incredibly sexy.

Suddenly he felt a powerful urge to take her in his arms and lie her down beside the Christmas tree. To pull down her mismatched panties and kiss between those generous thighs, before losing his tongue and then his body in all that tight, molten heat. He wondered how she would react if he did. With the same breathtaking eagerness she had shown before—or would she push him away this time? His mouth hardened and so uncomfortably did his groin and, although he was unbearably tempted to test out the idea, he drew himself up, wondering if he'd taken leave of his senses.

He was her boss, for heaven's sake!

Shaking his head, he walked over to the window and

stared out at the thick white layer which was coating the lawns and bare branches of the trees. The light was fading from the sky, intensifying the monochrome colours of the garden so that all he noticed was the diamond-bright glitter of the ice-encrusted snow.

His mouth hardened. He'd thought tonight would just be another evening to get through, before flying out to Naples for a family Christmas. Slowly, he turned around. But suddenly everything had changed—and all because of this pink-faced woman who was standing in front of him, nervously chewing her lip.

'How long are you supposed to be working here?' he demanded.

'Just for tonight. And tomorrow I have to supervise the clean-up after the party.'

'And after that?' he probed. 'What then?'

She rubbed the tip of her ugly shoe over the Persian rug as if she were polishing it. 'I don't know yet. I'll just have to find something else.'

'Including accommodation, I suppose?'

She moved her shoulders awkwardly, as if he had reminded her of something she would prefer to forget, and when she looked up, her grey eyes were almost defiant. 'Well, yes. The jobs I take are always live-in.'

His eyes narrowed. 'And how easy will that be?'

Her attempt to look nonchalant failed and for the first time Salvio saw a trace of vulnerability on her face.

'Not very easy at this time of the year, I imagine.'

Salvio felt the flicker of a heavy pulse at his temple as another unwanted streak of conscience hit him and he recognised he couldn't just abandon her to the wolves.

He had bedded her and she had lost her job as a result of that—so it stood to reason he must take some of the responsibility. He nodded. 'Very well. Tomorrow, I'll have a word with Gina. See if we can't find you something more permanent.' He saw her face brighten and wondered if he had falsely raised her hopes. 'Not with me, of course,' he continued hastily. 'That isn't going to happen. The night we shared was many things, Molly, but it certainly didn't lay down a suitable foundation for any kind of working relationship between us.'

Molly flinched. She had thought him kind and that his behaviour towards her in the past had been thoughtful. But he wasn't kind, not really. He'd made it clear she couldn't ever work for him, not now she had been his lover—so, in effect, wasn't he patronising her just as much as Lady Avery had done? Before she thought she'd seen consideration in his face but that had been replaced by a flinty kind of calculation. Because Salvio De Gennaro could be utterly ruthless, she recognised— her heart sinking as she tried to imagine how he was going to react to her unwelcome news.

'Do you understand what I'm saying, Molly?' he continued remorselessly.

'Of course I do,' she said. 'I wasn't expecting to get a job with you. So please don't worry about it, Salv— Signor De Gennaro,' she amended, unable to hide her sudden flash of sarcasm. 'I won't bother you. You won't even know I'm here.'

The look on his face told her he didn't believe her and, despite her inexperience, Molly could understand why. Because how could they remain indifferent to each other when the atmosphere around them was still charged with that potent chemistry which had led to her downfall before? And wasn't she longing for him to touch her again? To trace his fingertip along the edges of her trembling lips, before replacing them with his mouth and kissing her until she capitulated to his every need.

Well, that would be insane.

Molly swallowed as she picked another bauble from its soft nest of tissue paper and the Neapolitan turned away.

'I need to get showered and changed before the party,' he said roughly. 'Just get on with your work, will you, Molly?'

CHAPTER SIX

SHE WISHED HE would stop staring at her.

Liar. Molly shivered as she picked up an empty wine glass and put it on her tray. *Admit it. You like it when he stares at you. Even though his face looks all dark and savage, as if he hates himself for doing it.*

And how much more savage will he look when he discovers the truth? she wondered.

It was the end of a long evening and only a few die-hard guests remained. Contrary to predictions the snow had stopped falling, allowing the chauffeur-driven cars to take the giggling London guests safely back to the capital. Vintage champagne had flowed, delicious food had been eaten and there hadn't been a single crisis in the kitchen, much to Molly's relief. A group of local singers had trudged through the snow and treated the partygoers to an emotional medley of Christmas carols, before being given mulled wine and hot mince pies and sent on their way with a huge donation to rebuild the roof of the village hall. And now Salvio was standing talking to a dark-suited man in the far corner of the huge drawing room—someone had whispered that he was a sheikh—but every time she looked up, Molly could see the hooded black eyes of the Neapolitan trained on her.

She hurried down to the kitchen where at least she was safe from that devastating gaze and the ongoing concern of how exactly she was going to break her momentous news. At least when you were helping stack clean plates and showing the hired help where to put all the silver cutlery, it was easy to forget your own problems, if only for a while. But at twenty past midnight the last of the staff departed and only the sheikh who had dominated Salvio's company for much of the evening was left, the two men deep in conversation as they sat by the fireside.

Molly was in the basement kitchen drying the final crystal glass when she heard a deafening chatter outside and peered out to see a helicopter alighting on the snowy lawn. Moments later the sheikh, now swathed in a dark overcoat, his black head bent against the flattening wind, began to run towards it. She could see the glint of a royal crest on the side of the craft as the door closed and it began its swaying ascent into the sky. Her hands were shaking as she suddenly realised she was alone in the house with Salvio and she wondered what she should do. She put the glass down. She should behave as she normally would in these circumstances— even if this felt anything like normal.

Taking off her damp apron and smoothing down her black dress, she went upstairs to find Salvio still sitting beside the fire, his stance fixed and unmoving as he gazed into the flickering flames. His long legs were stretched out before him and the rugged perfection of his profile looked coppery in the firelight. Never had he seemed more devastating or more remote and never had she felt so humble and disconnected. How crazy was it that this man had briefly been her lover and would soon be the father of her child?

Molly cleared her throat. 'Excuse me.'

He looked up then, his eyes narrowing as if he couldn't quite remember who she was, or why she was here.

'*Sì*, what is it?' he questioned abruptly.

'I didn't mean to disturb you, but I wondered if there was anything else you'd like?'

Salvio felt his heart slam hard against his chest. If it had been any other former lover asking that question, it would have been coated in innuendo. But Molly's words weren't delivered suggestively, or provocatively. Her big grey eyes weren't slanting out an unspoken invitation. She simply looked anxious to please, which only reinforced the differences between them. Once again he cursed his hot-headedness in taking the curvy housekeeper to his bed.

Even though he could understand exactly why he'd done it.

He'd spent this evening watching her, despite his best intentions. He'd told himself she was strictly off-limits and he should concentrate on his guests, but it had been Molly's wide-hipped sway which had captured his gaze and Molly's determined face as she had scurried around with trays of drinks and food which had captivated his imagination. He had seen the natural sparkle of her grey eyes and had remembered the healthy glow of her cheeks when she had romped enthusiastically in his arms. But her face was pale now, he noted. Deathly pale—as if all the colour had been leeched from it.

'No, I don't think there is,' he said slowly, forcing himself to treat her as he would any other member of staff. 'Thank you for all your hard work tonight, Molly. The party went very well. Even the Sheikh of Razrastan stayed far longer than he intended.'

'You're very welcome,' she said.

'I'm sure we can think about a generous bonus for you.'

'There's no need for that,' she said stiffly.

'I think I'll be the judge of that.' He gave her a benign smile. 'And I haven't forgotten my promise to try to find you some work. Or, rather, to ask Gina to help.' His words were tantamount to dismissal but she didn't move. Salvio saw the faint criss-crossing of a frown over the smooth expanse of her brow and something— he never knew what it was—compelled him to ask a question he usually avoided like the plague. 'Is everything okay?'

Her hands began twisting at the plain fabric of her work dress and he could see the indecision which made her frown deepen.

'Y-yes.'

'You don't sound very sure.'

'I wasn't going to tell you until tomorrow,' she said, her knuckles whitening.

Instinct made Salvio sit upright, his body tensing. 'Tell me *what*?' he questioned dangerously.

Molly licked her lips. She'd thought that a good night's

sleep and the addition of daylight might take some of the emotional sting out of her disclosure. But now she could see that any idea of sleep was a non-starter, especially with the thought of Salvio in bed nearby and the heavy realisation that he'd only ever wanted her that one time. But more than that, the news was bubbling inside her, wanting to get out. She needed to tell someone—and who else was she going to confide in?

'I'm pregnant,' she said bluntly.

There was a moment of silence—a weird and intense kind of silence. It was as if every sound in the room had been amplified to an almost deafening level. The crackle and spit of the fire. The loud thunder of her heart. The sudden intake of her own shuddered breath. And now there was shadow too, as Salvio rose from his chair—tall and intimidating—his powerful frame blocking out the firelight and seeming to fill the room with darkness.

'You can't be,' he said flatly. 'That is, if you're trying to tell me it's mine?'

She met the unyielding expression which had hardened his face and Molly's heart contracted with pain. Did he really think she'd lost her virginity to him and then rushed out to find herself another lover—as if trying to make up for lost time? Or was he just trying to run from his own responsibility? She stared at him reproachfully. 'You know it is.'

'I used contraception,' he bit out. 'You know I did.'

She felt blood rush into her cheeks. 'Maybe you weren't—'

'Careful?' He cut across her words with a bitter

laugh. 'I think that's a given, don't you? Reckless might be closer to the mark. On all counts.'

'Don't,' she said quickly.

His eyebrows shot up imperiously, as if he couldn't quite believe she was telling him what to do. *'What?'*

'Please don't,' she whispered. 'Don't make it any worse than it already is by saying things which will be difficult to forget afterwards.'

His eyes narrowed but he nodded, as if acknowledging the sense of her words. 'Are you sure?' he demanded. 'Or is it just a fear?'

She shook her head. 'I'm certain. I did a test.'

Another silence. 'I see.'

Molly's lips were dry and her heart was racing. 'I just want to make it clear that I'm only telling you because I feel duty-bound to tell you.'

'And not because you're after a slice of my fortune?'

Hurt now, she stared at him. 'You think that's what this is all about?'

His lips curved. 'Is it such a bizarre conclusion? Think about it, *mia bedda*. I'm rich and you're poor. What is it they say in the States?' He flicked the fingers of both hands, miming the sudden spill of money from a cash register. 'Ker-*ching*!'

Molly made to move away but his reflexes were lightning-fast and quicker than hers. He reached out to curl his fingers around her arm before pulling her towards him, like an expert angler reeling in their catch of the day. The movement made her breathless but it also made her hungry for him in a way she didn't want to be. Just one touch and her senses had started jangling, as she felt that now familiar desire washing over her. Meeting the gleam of his black eyes, she prayed she would find the strength to pull away from him and resist him. 'What do you think you're doing?' she demanded.

'I'm doing about the only thing which could possibly make me feel good right now,' he grated and brought his mouth down hard on hers.

Molly willed herself not to respond. She didn't have to do this—especially not after those insults he'd just hurled her way, making out she was some kind of gold-digger. But the trouble was that she *wanted* to kiss him. She wanted that more than anything else in the world right then. It was as if the beauty of his touch was making her realise how she'd got herself into this predicament in the first place. His kiss had been the first step to seduction and even now she found it irresistible. Closing her eyes, she let him plunder her lips until there was no oxygen left in her lungs and she had to draw back to suck in a breath of air. She shook her head distractedly. 'Salvio,' she whispered, but he shook his head.

'Don't say anything,' he warned, before scooping her up in his arms and carrying her out of the room.

Molly blinked in confusion because his hands were underneath her bottom and they were caressing it in a way which was making her want to squirm. As if in some kind of unbelievable dream he was carrying her up that sweeping staircase as if she were Scarlett O'Hara and he were Rhett Butler. And she was letting him.

So stop him. Make him put you down.

But she couldn't. Because *this* was powerlessness,

she realised—this feeling of breathy expectation bubbling up inside her as he kicked open the door of the
master bedroom. The heavy oak door swung open as
if it had been made of matchsticks as he carried her effortlessly across silken Persian rugs before depositing
her on the huge bed.

And even though Molly could see no real affection
on his proud Neapolitan features—nothing but sexual
hunger glittering from his dark eyes—that didn't stop
her from reciprocating. Was it the delicious memory
of his lovemaking which made her open her arms to
him and close them around him tightly? Or was it more
basic than that? As he peeled her dress, shoes and underclothes from her body before impatiently removing
his own clothes she began to wonder if there was some
deep-rooted need to connect physically with the man
whose seed was multiplying inside her.

Or at least, that was her excuse for what was about
to happen.

'Salvio,' she gasped as his finger stroked a slow circle around the exquisitely aroused peak of her now bare
nipple. *'Oh!'*

His naked body was warm against hers. 'Shh…'

It was more of a command than an entreaty but Molly
heeded it all the same, terrified that words might break
the spell and let reality flood in and destroy what she
was feeling. His eyes were hooded as they surveyed her
body, seeming to drink in every centimetre. Was she
imagining his gaze lingering longest on her belly? With
her notorious curves, she probably looked pregnant already. But now he was kissing her neck and her eyelids

were fluttering to a close so that it became all about sensation rather than thought and that was so much better.

Encouraged by the hand now sliding from breast to thigh, Molly flickered her fingertips over the taut dip of his belly, her touch as delicate as if she were making pastry. And didn't his groan thrill her and fill her with a sense of pride that *she*—inexperienced Molly Miller—could make a man like Salvio react this way? Emboldened by his response, she drifted her hand over his rocky thighs, feeling the hair-roughened flesh turn instantly to goosebumps, and something about that galvanised him into action, because suddenly he was on top of her. He was kissing her with a hunger which was almost *ferocious* and, oh, it felt good. Better than anything had a right to feel. She could feel the graze of his jaw and his lips felt hard on hers, though his tongue was sinuous as it slipped inside her mouth.

She gave a little cry as she twisted restlessly beneath him and he gave a low laugh which was tinged with mockery.

'How quickly my little innocent becomes greedy,' he murmured. 'How quickly she has learnt what it is she wants.'

His words sounded more like insults than observations but by then he was stroking her wet and urgent heat and Molly was writhing beneath his fingers. She moaned as the sensation built and built and she realised what was about to happen. He was going to make her have an orgasm with his... *finger*.

'Salvio,' she cried out in disbelief, but just as she went tumbling over the top he thrust deep inside her.

She gasped as he filled her completely—even bigger than she remembered—and he gave a loud moan in response. And so did she. It felt as if her world were imploding. As if a jet-black sky had suddenly been punctured by a million stars. As if the two of them were locked and mingled for all time. Molly clung to him as she felt him momentarily stiffen before thrusting out his own shuddering pleasure.

He stayed inside her for countless minutes and Molly revelled in that sticky closeness because, in a funny sort of way, it felt as intimate as the act of sex had done. Maybe even more so, because now neither of them were chasing the satisfaction which had somehow left her feeling empty and satisfied, all at the same time.

But eventually he withdrew from her and rolled to the other side of the bed. Molly was careful to hide her disappointment as he threw the duvet over them both, quickly covering her up, as if the sight of her naked body offended him. She licked her lips as she waited for him to speak, planning to take her lead from him. It was the habit of a lifetime—of allowing her employer to dictate the conversation—because, technically, Salvio was still her employer, wasn't he? And it seemed vital that she stay quiet for long enough to hear his thoughts. Because what was said between them now was going to determine the rest of her baby's life, wasn't it? His attitude towards her unplanned pregnancy was of vital importance if they wanted to have any kind of amicable future. Not that she was expecting much from him. Not now. She'd thought she could rely on kindness until she'd realised she didn't really know him at all. And now her heart began to pound with anxiety as she wondered whether she should have given herself so easily to him. Could she really hope for respect in the circumstances?

She found herself studying him from between her lashes as she met the hard glitter of his eyes.

'So now what?' he questioned slowly.

She took him literally, because wasn't it simpler all round if she remained practical and continued to do her job? 'I ought to go down and turn off all the lights—especially the tree lights.'

His face was incredulous. 'Excuse me?'

She pushed her hair away from her face and wriggled into a sitting-up position, though she was careful to keep the top of the duvet modestly covering her breasts. 'I haven't switched off the lights on the Christmas tree—and there's also the fire, which we've left unguarded,' she said. 'I can't possibly go to sleep until all that is in place.'

'The fireguard?' he echoed disbelievingly, looking momentarily bemused before nodding. 'Wait here,' he said, and climbed out of bed.

Quite honestly, Molly didn't feel as if she had the strength or inclination to go anywhere—especially not when an unclothed Salvio was walking towards the door, seemingly unaware of the fact that it was the middle of winter and the snow was thick on the ground outside. She gazed at him as if hypnotised—her eyes drinking in the pale globes of his buttocks, which contrasted so vividly with the burnished olive of his thighs. And then he turned round, frowning with faint concern as he surveyed her, as if he had suddenly remembered that she'd just announced her pregnancy and wasn't quite sure how to deal with her any more.

'Can I get you anything?'

She guessed he was being literal too and that it would have been pointless to have asked for a crystal ball to re-assure her about her baby's future. And pointless to have asked for some affirmation that he wasn't planning on deserting his unplanned child, even if he wanted nothing more to do with her. But unlike her brother, Molly had never been a fantasist. She cleared her throat and nodded. 'A drink of water would be nice.'

She waited for him to say something like, *I'll bring it to your room*, but he didn't. Which presumably meant it was okay to stay here.

Of *course* it was okay to stay here—they'd just had sex, hadn't they?

But it wasn't easy to shrug off a lifetime of being deferential and Molly even felt slightly guilty about rushing into the luxurious en-suite bathroom and avail-ing herself of the upmarket facilities. She splashed her face with water and smoothed down her mussed hair before returning to the bed and burrowing down be-neath the duvet.

And then he was back and Molly quickly averted her eyes because the front view of the naked Neapoli-tan was much more daunting than the back had been— particularly as he seemed to be getting aroused again.

Did he read something in her expression? Was that why he gave a savage kind of laugh as he handed her the glass of water? 'Don't worry,' he grated. 'I'll endeavour to keep my appetite in check while we discuss how we're going to handle this.'

The large gulp of water she'd been taking nearly choked her and Molly put the glass down on the bedside table with a hand which was trembling. 'There's nothing to handle,' she said shakily. 'I'm having this baby, no matter what you say.'

'You think I would want anything other than that?' he demanded savagely.

'I wasn't… I wasn't sure.'

Salvio climbed into bed, disappointed yet strangely relieved that her magnificent breasts weren't on show, meaning he'd be able to concentrate on what he needed to say and not on how much he would like to lose himself in her sweet tightness again. He pulled the cover over the inconvenient hardening of his groin. Was she really as innocent as she seemed? Physically, yes—he had discovered that for himself. But was she really so unschooled in the ways of the world that she didn't realise that she was now in possession of what so many women strived for?

A billionaire father for her baby.

A meal ticket for life.

And there wasn't a damned thing he could do about it. Fate had thrown him a curveball and he was just going to have to deal with it.

'Tell me about yourself,' he said suddenly.

She blinked. 'Me?'

The sigh he gave wasn't exaggerated. 'Look, Molly— I think you're in danger of overplaying the wide-eyed innocent, don't you? We've had sex on a number of occasions and you've just informed me you're pregnant. Ordinarily I wouldn't be interested in hearing about your past, but you'll probably agree that this is no ordinary situation.'

Molly's heart clenched as his cruel words rained down on her. Wouldn't another man at least have *pretended* to be interested in what had made her the person she was today? Gone through some kind of polite ritual of getting to know her. Maybe she should be grateful that he hadn't. He might be cruel, but at least he wasn't a hypocrite. He wasn't pretending to feel stuff about her and building up her hopes to smash them down again. At least she knew where she stood.

'I was born in a little cottage—'

'Please. Spare me the violins. Let's just cut to the chase, shall we?' he interrupted coolly. 'Parents?'

Molly shrugged. 'My father left my mother when she was diagnosed with multiple sclerosis,' she said flatly.

She saw a flare of something she didn't recognise in his black eyes.

'That must have been hard,' he said softly.

'It was,' she conceded. 'Less so for me than for my little brother, Robbie. He…well, he adored our mother. So did I, obviously—but I was busy keeping on top of everything so that social services were happy to let me run the home.'

'And then?' he prompted, when her words died away.

Molly swallowed. 'Mum died when Robbie was twelve, but they let us carry on living together. Just me and him. I fought like crazy not to have him taken into care and I succeeded.'

His dark brows knitted together. 'And what was that like?'

She thought she detected a note of sympathy in his voice, or was that simply wishful thinking? Of course it was. He was cruel and ruthless, she reminded herself. He was only asking her these questions because he felt he *needed* to—not because he *wanted* to. For a moment Molly was tempted to gloss over the facts. To tell him that Robbie had turned out fine. But what if he found out the truth and then accused her of lying? Wouldn't that make this already difficult situation even worse than it already was?

'Robbie went off the rails a bit,' she admitted. 'He did what a lot of troubled teenagers do. Got in with the wrong crowd. Got into trouble with the police. And then he started...'

Her voice tailed off again, knowing this was something she couldn't just consign to the past. Because the counsellor had told her that addictions never really went away. They just sat there, brooding and waiting for someone to feed them. And wasn't she scared stiff that they were being fed right now—that someone was busy dealing cards across a light-washed table in the centre of a darkened room somewhere in the Outback?

'What did he start, Molly?' prompted Salvio softly.

'Gambling.' She stared down at her short, sensible fingernails before glancing up again to meet the ebony gleam of his eyes. 'It started off with fruit machines and then he met someone in the arcade who said a bright boy like him would probably be good at cards. That he could win enough money to buy the kind of things he'd never had. And that's when it all started.'

'*It?*'

Molly shrugged. 'I think Robbie was still missing Mum. I know he'd been frustrated and unhappy that we'd been so poor while she was alive. Whatever it was, he started playing poker and he was good at it. At first. He started winning money but he spent it just as quickly. More quickly than it was coming in. And the trouble with cards is that the more you want to win—the worse you become. They say that your opponent can smell desperation and Robbie was as desperate as hell. He started getting into debt. Big debt. But the banks didn't want to know and so he borrowed from some pay-day lenders and they…they…'

'They came after him?' Salvio finished grimly.

Molly nodded. 'I managed to use most of my savings to pay them off, though there's still an outstanding debt which never seems to go down because the interest rates they charge are astronomical. I wanted Robbie to have a fresh start. To get away from all the bad influences in his life. So he went to Australia to get the whole gambling bug out of his system and promised to attend Gamblers Anonymous. That's why I was working for the Averys. They were hardly ever in the house so I got to live there rent-free. Plus they paid me a lot of money to look after all their valuable artefacts. They said their insurance was lower if they had someone living permanently on the premises.'

'And then I came along,' he mused softly.

Molly's head jerked back as something in his tone alerted her to danger. 'I'm sorry?'

His bare shoulders gleamed like gold in the soft light from the lamp. 'A young attractive woman like you must have found it incredibly limiting to be shut away in that huge house in the middle of nowhere working for people who only appeared intermittently,' he observed. 'It must have seemed like a gilded prison.'

'I was grateful for a roof over my head and the chance to save,' she said.

'And the opportunity to meet a rich man who might make a useful lover?'

Molly's mouth fell open. 'Are you out of your mind?'

'I don't think so, *mia bedda*,' he contradicted silkily. 'I base my opinions on experience. It's one of the drawbacks of being wealthy and single—that women come at you from all angles. You must have acknowledged that I was attracted to you, and I can't help wondering whether you saw me as an easy way out of your dilemma. Were the bitter tears you cried real, or manufactured, I wonder? Did you intend those sobs to stir my conscience?'

Molly sat up in bed, her skin icy with goosebumps, despite the duvet which covered most of her naked body. 'You think I *pretended to cry*? That I deliberately got myself pregnant to get you to pay off my brother's debts? That I would cold-bloodedly use my baby as a bargaining tool?'

'No, I'm not saying that. But I do think that fate has played right into your hardworking little hands,' he said slowly. 'Don't you?'

Her voice was shaking as she shook her head. 'No. No, I don't.' Pushing the duvet away, she swung her legs over the side of the bed, acutely conscious of her wobbly bottom as she bent down and started pulling on her discarded clothes with fingers which were trembling, telling herself she would manage. Somehow. Because she had always managed before, hadn't she? Fully dressed now, Molly turned round, steeling herself not to react to his muscular olive body outlined so starkly against the snowy white bedding. 'There's nothing more to be said, is there?'

He gave a bitter laugh. 'Oh, I think there's plenty which needs to be said, but not tonight, not when emotions are running high. I need to think first before I come to any decision.'

Molly was tempted to tell him that maybe he should have done that before he had taken her to bed and then come out with a stream of unreasonable accusations, but what was the point in inflaming an already inflamed situation? And she couldn't really blame him for the sex, could she? Not when she had been complicit every step of the way. Not when she had desperately wanted him to touch her.

And the awful thing was that she still did.

Tilting her chin upwards and adopting the most dignified stance possible—which wasn't easy in the circumstances—she walked out of Salvio's bedroom without another word.

CHAPTER SEVEN

A COLD BLUE light filtered into the tiny bedroom, startling Molly from the bewildering landscape of unsettled sleep—one haunted by Salvio and the memory of his hard, thrusting body. Disorientated, she sat up in bed, wondering if she'd dreamt it all. Until the delicious aching at her breasts and soft throb between her legs reminded her that it had happened. Her heart began to race. It had actually happened. At the end of an evening's service she had informed her employer she was pregnant with his baby.

And had then been carried up the staircase and willingly had sex with him, despite all the things he'd accused her of.

Did he really believe it was his wealth which had attracted her to him, when she would have found him irresistible if he'd been covered in mud and sweat from working the fields?

Slowly, she got out of bed. She didn't know what Salvio wanted. All she knew was what *she* wanted. Her hand crept down to cover the soft flesh of her belly. She wanted this baby.

And nothing Salvio did or said was going to change her mind.

She showered and washed her hair—pulling on clean jeans and a jumper the colour of a winter sky before going downstairs, to be greeted by the aroma of coffee. In the kitchen she found Salvio pouring himself an inky cupful, and although he looked up as she walked in, his face registered no emotion. He merely gestured to the pot.

'Want some?'

She shook her head. 'No, thanks. I'll make myself some tea.' She was certain herbal tea was better for babies than super-strong coffee, but mainly she welcomed the opportunity of being able to busy herself with the kettle. Anything rather than having to confront the distracting vision of Salvio in faded jeans and a sweater as black as his hair. She could feel him watching her and she had to try very hard not to appear clumsy—no mean feat when that piercing gaze was trained on her like a bird of prey. But when she couldn't dunk her peppermint teabag a moment longer, she was forced to turn around and face him, glad he was now silhouetted against the window and his features were mostly in shadow.

'So,' he said, without preamble. 'We need to work out what we're going to do about the astonishing piece of news you dropped into my lap last night. Any ideas, Molly?'

Molly had thought about this a lot during those long hours when sleep had eluded her. *Be practical*, she urged herself. *Take the emotion out of it and think facts.*

She cleared her throat. 'Obviously finding a job is paramount,' she said cautiously. 'A live-in job, of course.'

'A live-in job,' he repeated slowly. 'And when the baby is born, what then?'

Molly hoped her shrug conveyed more confidence than she actually felt. 'Lots of people don't mind their staff having a baby around the place. Well, maybe not lots of people,' she amended when she heard his faintly incredulous snort and acknowledged that he might have a point. 'But houses which already have children tend to be more accommodating. Who knows? I might even switch my role from housekeeper to nanny.'

'And that's what you want, is it?'

Molly suppressed the frustration which had flared up inside her. Of course it wasn't. But she couldn't really tell him that none of this was what she *wanted*— not without betraying the child she carried. She hadn't planned to get pregnant, but she would make the best of it. Just as she hadn't planned for the father of her child to be a cold-hearted billionaire who right now felt so distant that he might as well have been on another planet, rather than standing on the other side of the kitchen. She wanted what most women wanted when they found themselves in this situation—a stable life and a man who adored them. 'Life is all about adaptation,' she said stolidly when, to her surprise, he nodded, walking away from the window and putting his coffee cup down on the table before pulling out a chair.

'I agree,' he said. 'Here. Sit down. We need to talk about this properly.'

She shook her head. 'I can't sit down.'

'Why not?'

'Because I still have to clear up the house, after the party.'

'Leave it.'

'I can't leave it, it's what you're paying me—'

'I said leave it, Molly,' he snapped. 'I can easily get people in to do that for me later. Just sit down, will you?'

Molly opened her mouth to refuse. To tell him that the walls felt as if they were closing in on her and his presence was making her jittery. But what else could she do? Flounce out into the snow, two days before Christmas Day—with nowhere to go and a child in her belly? Ignoring the chair he was holding out for her, she chose one at the opposite end of the table and sank down onto it, her mouth unsmiling as she looked at him questioningly.

'I've given a lot of thought to what's happened,' he said, without preamble.

Join the club. 'And did you come to any conclusions?'

Salvio's eyes narrowed as she stared at him suspiciously. She wasn't behaving as he had expected her to behave. Although what did he know? He'd never had to face something like this before and never with someone like her. After her departure last night, he'd thought she might try to creep back into his bed—maybe even whisper how sorry she was for flouncing out like that—before turning her lips to his for another hungry kiss. He was used to the inconsistency of women—and in truth he would have welcomed a reconnection with those amazing curves. Another bout of amazing sex might have given him a brief and welcome respite from his concerns about the future.

She hadn't done that, of course, and so he had braced himself for sulks or tears or reproachful looks when he bumped into her this morning. But no. Not that either. Sitting there in a soft sweater which matched her grey eyes, with her hair loose and shining around her shoulders, she looked the picture of health—despite the shadows beneath her eyes, which suggested her night had been as troubled as his.

And the crazy thing was that this morning he hadn't woken up feeling all the things he was expecting to feel. There had been residual shock, yes, but the thought of a baby hadn't filled him with horror. He might even have acknowledged the faint flicker of warmth in his heart as a tenuous glimmer of pleasure, if he hadn't been such a confirmed cynic.

'Every problem has a solution if you come at it from enough angles,' he said carefully. 'And I have a proposition to put to you.'

She creased her brow. 'You do?'

There was a pause. 'I don't want you finding a job as a housekeeper, or looking after someone else's children.'

'Why not?'

Salvio tensed, sensing the beginning of a negotiation. Was she testing out how much money he was prepared to give her? 'Isn't it obvious? Because you're pregnant with my baby.' His voice deepened. 'And although this is a child I never intended to have, I'm prepared to accept the consequences of my actions.'

'How…how cold-blooded you make it sound,' she breathed.

'Do you want me to candy-coat it for you, Molly?' he demanded. 'To tell you that this was what I always secretly dreamed would happen to me? Or would you prefer the truth?'

'I'm a realist, Salvio,' she answered. 'I've only ever wanted the truth.'

'Then here it is, in all its unvarnished glory. Tomorrow, I'm flying home to Naples for the holidays.'

'I know. Your assistant told me when she hired me.'

'I return every year,' he continued slowly. 'To two loving parents who wonder where they went so wrong with their only child.'

She blinked at him in confusion. 'I don't…understand.'

'Who wonder why their successful, handsome son who has achieved so much,' he continued, as if she hadn't spoken, 'has failed to bring home a woman who will one day provide them with the grandchildren they yearn for.' He gave a sudden bitter laugh. 'When, hey, what do you know? Suddenly I have found such a woman and already she is with child! What a gift it will be for them to meet you, Molly.'

She stared at him, confusion darkening her grey eyes. '*Meet* them? You're not suggesting—'

'Like I said last night—it's time to lose all that wide-eyed innocence. I think you know exactly what I'm suggesting,' he drawled. 'We buy you a big diamond ring and I take you home to Naples as my fiancée.'

'You mean...' She blinked. 'You mean you want to marry me?'

'Let's put it another way. I don't particularly want to marry anyone, the difference is that I'm *prepared* to marry you,' he amended.

'Because of the baby?'

'Because of the baby,' he agreed. 'But not just that. Most women are demanding and manipulative but, interestingly enough, you are none of those things. Not only are you extremely beddable—I find you exceptionally...*agreeable*.' His lips curved into a reflective smile. 'And at least you know your place.'

Molly stared at him, wanting to tell him to stop making her sound like the UK representative for the international society of doormats. Until she realised that once again Salvio was speaking the truth. She *did* know her place. She always had done. When you worked as a servant in other people's houses, that was what tended to happen.

'So what's in it for me?' she asked, thinking she ought to say *something*.

He looked at her in surprise. 'It isn't very difficult to work out. You get financial security and I get a ready-made family. I can pay off your brother's debt in one swoop, on the understanding that this is the only time I bankroll him. And if I were you, I would wipe the horror from your face, Molly. It really isn't a good look for a woman who's on the brink of getting engaged.' His voice dipped into one of silky admonishment. 'And it isn't as if you have a lot of choices, do you?'

Molly felt the sudden shiver of vulnerability rippling

down her spine. He didn't have to put it quite so brutally, did he? She swallowed. Or maybe he did. It was yet another cruel observation but it was true. She *didn't* have a lot of choices. She knew there was nothing romantic about having to struggle. She'd done all that making-the-best-of-a-bad-situation stuff—seeing how many meals you could get out of a bag of black-eyed beans and buying her clothes in thrift stores. She knew how hard poverty could be.

And this was her baby.

Her defenceless little *baby*.

She was aware of her hand touching her belly and aware of Salvio's gaze following the movement before he lifted his black eyes to hers. She searched their dark gleam in vain for some kind of emotion, and tried to ignore the painful stab in her heart when she met nothing but a cold, unblinking acceptance in their ebony depths. Of course he wasn't going to feel the same way as she did about their child. Why *wouldn't* he look sombre? Having his life inextricably linked to that of a humble little housekeeper was surely nothing for the Neapolitan billionaire to celebrate.

'Very well. Since—as you have already pointed out—I have very little alternative... I agree,' she said, and then, because subservience was as much a part of her life as breathing and because deep down she *was* grateful to him for his grudging generosity, she added a small smile. 'Thank you.'

Salvio felt his gut clench, knowing he didn't deserve her thanks. Or that shy look which made him want to cradle her in his arms. He knew he could have asked her to marry him in a more romantic way. He could have dropped onto one knee and told her he couldn't imagine life without her. But why get her used to an attitude he could never sustain and raise expectations which could never be met? The only way he could make this work was if he was straight with her, and that meant not making emotional promises he could never fulfil.

But he knew one sure way to please her—the universal way to every woman's heart. 'Go and get your stuff together, *nicuzza*,' he said softly. 'We're going shopping.'

Molly stepped out onto the icy Bond Street pavement feeling dazed but warm. Definitely warm. Who would have ever thought a coat could *be* so warm? Wonderingly she brushed her fingertips over the camel cashmere, which teamed so well with the knee-length boots and the matching brown leather gloves which were as soft as a second skin. She caught sight of her reflection in one of the huge windows of the upmarket department store and stared at it, startled—wondering if that glossy confection of a woman was really her.

'*Sì*, you look good,' Salvio murmured from beside her.

She looked up into his ruggedly handsome face. 'Do I?'

'Good enough to eat,' he affirmed, his black eyes glittering out an unspoken message and Molly could do nothing about the shiver which rippled down her spine and had nothing to do with the icy temperature.

After a slow drive through the snow to London, he

had brought her to one of the capital's most famous streets, studded with the kind of shops which were guarded by burly security men with inscrutable expressions. But the faces of the assistants inside were far more open and Molly knew she hadn't imagined the faint incredulity which greeted her appearance, as women fluttered around Salvio like wasps on a spill of jam.

He asked for—and got—a terrifyingly sleek stylist, who was assigned the daunting task of dressing her. Endless piles of clothing and lingerie were produced—some of which were instantly dismissed by an impatient wave of Salvio's hand and some of which were met with a slow smile of anticipation.

'It seems a silly amount of money to spend since whatever I buy isn't going to fit me for very long,' she hissed in a fierce undertone after nearly fainting when she caught sight of one of the price tags.

He seemed amused by her attempt to make economies. 'Then we'll just have to buy you some more, won't we? Don't worry about the cost, Molly. You will soon be the wife of a very wealthy man.'

It was hard to imagine, thought Molly as a featherlight chiffon dress floated down over her head, covering an embroidered bra whose matching panties were nothing more than a flimsy scrap of silk. As she appeared from behind the velvet curtain of the changing room to meet Salvio's assessing gaze, she began to wonder if he'd done this whole transformation thing before. And she wondered whether she should show a little pride and refuse all the gifts he was offering.

But then she thought about the reality. Salvio probably came from an extremely wealthy family who might not take kindly to someone from her kind of background. Wouldn't she feel even more out of place if she turned up looking like a poor relation in her cheap clothes and worn boots? Which was why she submitted to the purchase of sweaters and jeans, jackets and day dresses—and the most beautiful shoes she had ever seen. Gorgeous patent stilettos in three different colours, which somehow had the ability to add precious inches to her height and make her walk in a different and more feminine way.

And when they were all done and the glossy bags had been placed in the limousine which had been slowly tailing them, Salvio guided her past yet another security guard and into a jewellery shop where inside it was all light and dazzle. Locked glass cases contained the biggest diamonds Molly had ever seen—some the colour of straw, some which resembled pink champagne, and some even finer than Lady Avery's vast collection of family jewels.

'So what's your ideal ring? What did you used to dream about when you were a little girl?' asked Salvio softly, his fingers caressing the small of her back as an elegant saleswoman approached them. 'Whatever takes your fancy, it's yours.'

Did he have to put it quite like that? Molly wondered, moving away to avoid the distraction of his touch. The only thing she used to dream about when she was a little girl was making sure there was a hot meal on the table, and wondering if she'd managed to get all Mum's pills from the pharmacy. Yet Salvio was making her sound like someone whose gaze was bound to be riveted by the biggest and brightest ring in the shop.

She could feel her cheeks growing hot, because suddenly this felt like the charade it really was. As if they were going through all the motions of getting engaged, but with none of the joy or happiness which most couples would have experienced at such a time. And while Salvio's handsome face was undeniably sensual, his jet-dark eyes were as cold as any of the jewels on display. Molly lifted her gaze from the display cabinet as a quiet air of certainty ran through her. 'I don't want anything which looks like an engagement ring,' she said.

Hiding her surprise, the assistant produced a ring to just that specification—a stunning design of three thin platinum bands, each containing three asymmetrically placed diamonds which glittered and sparkled in the sharp December sunlight. 'The diamonds are supposed to resemble raindrops,' the young woman said gently.

Or tears, thought Molly suddenly. They looked exactly like tears.

From Bond Street they were whisked to Salvio's home in a fashionable area of London. Molly had heard of Clerkenwell but had never actually been there—just as she'd never been in such a gleaming, modern penthouse apartment before. She wandered from room to room. Everything was shiny and clean, but it was stark—as if nobody really lived there. It was as if some designer had been allowed to keep all décor to a minimum, but its sleek emptiness wasn't her main worry—which was that it was no place for a baby.

What was left of the day rushed past in a whirl of organisation but for once it wasn't Molly doing the organising, since Salvio seemed to have fleets of people at his disposal. People to organise cars and planes. To book hotels and arrange the last-minute purchase of gifts. They ate an early supper, which was delivered and served by staff from a nearby award-winning restaurant who even provided candles and a fragrant floral centrepiece.

'You don't have a chef, or a housekeeper?' Molly asked, as she sat down at the glass dining table and tried not to think about how dangerous a piece of furniture like this might be for a young child.

'I prefer to keep resident staff to a minimum. It optimises my privacy,' Salvio explained coolly, as two delicate soufflés were placed in front of them. 'I hope you're hungry?'

'Very,' she said, shaking out her napkin and trying not to dwell on what he'd just said about privacy—because he was about to have it shattered in the most spectacular way. 'Have you lived here for very long?' she questioned.

'I've had the apartment for about five years.'

'And you're here a lot?'

'No, not really. I have other homes all round the world. This is just my base whenever I'm in London.' He gazed at her thoughtfully. 'Why do you ask?'

She shrugged. 'It's very tidy.'

He laughed. 'I thought, given your occupation, that tidiness might meet with your approval.'

And oddly enough, that hurt. It was yet another reminder of just how far out of her comfort zone she was. A reminder of how he really saw her. She would never be his equal, she thought, as a powerful wave of fatigue washed over her.

'Actually, I'm pretty tired,' she said. 'It's a been a long day and the baby…'

The baby.

Salvio pushed away his wine glass. They hadn't mentioned it all afternoon but the word no longer hit him like a shock. He was slowly getting used to the idea that she was pregnant, even if he wasn't exactly jumping for joy about it. And Molly Miller was proving easier company than he had expected. Undemanding and optimistic. There was something about her quiet presence which made him feel almost *peaceful*. He stared at her washed-out face and felt an unexpected wave of remorse wash over him. Why hadn't he noticed how tired she might be?

'You need to go to bed,' he said resolutely, pushing back his chair.

He saw her throat constrict.

'Where…where am I sleeping?'

'We're supposed to be an engaged couple, Molly,' he said, almost gently. 'Where do you think you'll be sleeping?'

'I wasn't…sure.'

He'd assumed she would be sharing his bed, because why wouldn't he? But something about her pallor and trepidation made him reconsider—for his own sake as well as for hers. Wouldn't a night apart re-establish his habitual detachment—especially since it was obvious neither of them had slept well last night?

He rose to his feet. 'There's no need to sound so fearful, Molly,' he said. 'I'll show you the spare room. You'll have plenty of peace in there.'

He saw the sudden look of uncertainty which crossed her features and then she nodded her head, the way he'd seen her do before.

'That sounds like a good idea,' she said, with what sounded like obedience, and once again he was reminded of the fact that she was, essentially, a servant.

CHAPTER EIGHT

BATHED IN THE bright December sunshine which flooded in through the giant windows of their Neapolitan hotel suite, Molly turned to Salvio, who was just changing out of the jeans and leather jacket he'd worn for the trip over, into something a little more formal.

'We still haven't discussed—' Molly hesitated '—what we're going to tell your parents.'

Pausing in the act of straightening his tie, Salvio turned to look at his fiancée. She looked…incredible, he thought. With her shiny hair scooped on top of her head and her curvy shape encased in a dress the colour of spring leaves, there was no trace of that shy and frumpy housekeeper now. They'd just arrived in his home city— his jet descending through the mountains surrounding the mighty Mount Vesuvius, with all its unleashed power and terrible history. It was an iconic view which took away the breath of the most experienced traveller and he had found himself watching Molly for her reaction. But, oblivious to the beauty which surrounded them, she had seemed lost in thought. Even when the car had whisked them to this luxury hotel overlooking the Castel dell'Ovo and a lavish suite which even *he* could not fault, she seemed barely to register the opulence of their penthouse accommodation.

He wondered if she'd noticed the sideways stares he'd been receiving from the moment they'd stepped off the plane. The double takes and the *'Is it him?'* looks which were as familiar to him as breathing, whenever he returned to his native town. Yet Molly had been impervious to them all.

'We tell them the truth,' he said eventually, giving some thought to her question. 'That you're pregnant and we're getting married as soon as possible.'

She winced a little. 'Do you think we need to be quite so...?'

His gaze bored into her. 'So what, Molly?'

She licked her lips and, mesmerised by the resulting gleam which emphasised their soft beauty, Salvio momentarily cursed himself for not admitting her to his bed last night. Had he really imagined such an action might make him more detached and rational, when he'd been obsessing about her all night long?

'Brutal,' she concluded, pursing her lips together as if it wasn't a word she particularly wanted to use.

'Brutal?'

She shrugged and began walking across the room, pausing only to peer into the elevated stone hot tub which stood at the far end of the enormous suite—an extravagant touch eclipsed only by the tall decorated Christmas tree which was framed in one of the tall windows.

Eventually she came to a halt and perched on an orange velvet chair to look at him. 'You told me you're known as someone who is a commitment-phobe. Someone who doesn't want to get married,' she said.

Salvio gave his tie a final tug. That wasn't the whole story, but why burden her with stuff she didn't need to know? 'What of it?'

'So this sudden marriage is going to come as a bolt out of the blue to your parents, isn't it?'

'And?' he questioned coolly. 'Your point is?'

She studied her left hand warily, as if she couldn't quite get used to the diamond knuckle-duster she was wearing. 'I'd prefer not to say anything about my pregnancy—at least, not yet. It's still very early days. I just thought it might be nice if we could at least *allow* them to think it might be about more than just the unwanted fallout of a…a…'

Her words tailed away and Salvio wondered if, in her innocence, she simply didn't know all the expressions—some of them crude—she could have used to describe what had happened between them that first night. 'A hook-up?' he put in helpfully, before adopting a more caustic tone. 'Are you saying you want to pretend to my parents that this is some great kind of love affair?'

'Of course not.' She flushed before lifting a reproachful grey gaze to his. 'I don't think you're that good an actor, are you, Salvio?'

He inclined his head as if to concede the point. 'Or that good a liar?'

'That's another way of putting it, I suppose.'

He acknowledged her crestfallen expression. 'I don't want to raise your hopes, Molly—or theirs. It's just who I am. And the bottom line is I just don't do emotion. That's all.'

'That's…that's quite a lot,' she observed. 'Do you think…?' She seemed to choose her words very carefully. 'Do you think you were born that way?'

'I think circumstances made me that way,' he said flatly.

'What kind of circumstances?'

Salvio frowned. This was deeper than he wanted to go because he was a man with a natural aversion to the in-depth character analysis which was currently in vogue. But what had he imagined would happen—that he could take an innocent young girl as his wife and present to her the same impenetrable exterior which had made scores of women despair at his coldness in the past? He walked over to the drinks cabinet, ignoring the expensive bottles of wine on display, pouring instead two crystal glasses of mineral water before walking across the room to hand her one. 'You don't know much about me, do you, Molly?'

She shook her head as she sipped her drink. 'Practically nothing. How would I? We haven't exactly sat down and had long conversations since we met, have we?'

He almost smiled. 'You weren't tempted to go and look me up online?'

Molly didn't answer immediately as she met the scrutiny of his piercing black gaze. Of course she'd been *tempted*. Someone like Salvio was high profile enough to have left a significant footprint on the Internet, which she could have accessed at the touch of a computer key, and naturally she was curious about him. But she'd felt as if their lives were unequal enough already. The billionaire tycoon and the humble housekeeper. If she discovered stuff about him, would she then have to feign ignorance in the unlikely event that he wanted to confide in her? If she heard anything about him, she wanted to hear it *from* him—not through the judgemental prism of someone else's point of view.

'I didn't want to seem as if I was spying on you.'

'Very commendable.'

'But it would be useful to know,' she continued doggedly. 'Otherwise your parents might think we're nothing but strangers.'

'And is that what concerns you, Molly?' His black gaze continued to bore into her. 'What other people think?'

Molly bit back her instinctive response to his disdainful question. If she'd been bothered about things like that then she would never have got through a childhood like hers. From an early age she'd learnt there were more important things to worry about than whether you had holes in your shoes or your coat needed darning. She'd learnt that good health—the one thing money couldn't buy—was the only thing worth having. 'I believe it's best to be respectful of other people's feelings and that your parents might be confused and possibly upset if they realise we don't really know one another. But the main reason I need to know about you is because I'm having your baby.' She saw the increased darkening of his eyes—as if she had reminded him of something he would rather forget. But he couldn't forget it, and neither could she. 'I don't know anything about your childhood,' she finished simply. 'Nothing at all.'

He appeared to consider her words before expelling a slow breath of air. 'Very well. First and foremost you must understand that I am a Neapolitan to the very core of my being.' His voice became fierce, and proud. 'And that I have a great passion for this beautiful city of mine.'

So why don't you live here? Molly thought suddenly. *Why do you only ever visit at Christmas?* But she said nothing, just absorbed his words the way she'd absorbed other people's words all her working life.

'I grew up in the Rione Sanità, a very beautiful area, which is rich with history.' There was a pause. 'But it is also one of the poorest places in the city.'

'You?' she echoed disbelievingly, unable to hold back her shocked reaction. 'Poor?'

He smiled cynically as he flicked a disparaging finger towards his sleek suit jacket. 'You think I was born wearing fine clothes like these, Molly? Or that my belly never knew hunger?'

Yes, that was exactly what she'd thought, mainly because Salvio De Gennaro wore his wealth supremely well. He acted as if he'd never known anything other than handmade shoes and silk shirts, and people to drive his cars and planes for him. 'You've come a long way,' she said slowly. 'What happened?'

'What happened was that I had a talent,' he told her simply. 'And that talent was football. The moment my foot touched a ball, I felt as if I had found what I was

born to do. I used to play every moment I could. There
was nowhere suitable close to my home so I found a
derelict yard to use. I marked a spot on the wall and I
used to hit that same spot over and over again. Word
got out and people used to come and watch me. They
used to challenge me to see how long I could keep the
ball in the air and sometimes I used to take their bets
because many of them thought they could put a ball
past me. But I could always score, even if there were
two people against me in goal. And then one day the
scouts turned up and overnight my whole life changed.'

'What happened?' she prompted as his words faded
away.

Salvio stared out of the window, drinking in the sapphire beauty of the bay. Would it sound boastful to tell
her he'd been called the greatest footballer of his gen-
eration? Or that the superstar lifestyle had arrived far
more quickly than expected? 'I trained every hour that
God sent, determined to fulfil all that early promise,
and very quickly I was signed by one of the country's
most prestigious clubs where I scored a record number
of goals. I knew success, and fame, and for a while it
was a crazy life. Everywhere I went, people would stop
me and want to talk about the game and I don't remember the last time I was made to pay for a pizza.'

'But…something went wrong?' she observed. 'I
mean, badly wrong?'

He narrowed his eyes. Was her blithe comment
about knowing nothing of his past just another of the
lies which slipped so easily from women's lips? 'What
makes you ask that?'

She hesitated. 'I'm not sure. Maybe the note of finality in your voice. The look of…'

'Of what, Molly?' he demanded. 'And please don't just give me the polite answer you think I ought to hear.'

She met his eyes, surprised at his perception because she had been about to do exactly that. 'Bitterness, I guess,' she said. 'Or maybe disappointment.'

He wanted to deny her accusations—if that was what they were—but he couldn't. And suddenly he found himself resenting her astuteness and that gentle look of understanding which had softened her face. He'd agreed to tell her the basics—not for her to start peeling back the layers so that she could get a closer look at his damned soul. So why did he continue with his story, as if now he'd lifted the lid on it, he found it impossible to put it back?

'I'll tell you what happened,' he said roughly, becoming aware of the heavy beat of his pulse at his temple. 'My life was a fairy tale. It wasn't just the success, or the money—and the chance to do good stuff with all that money—it was the fact that I loved playing football. It was the only thing I ever wanted to do. And then one day I was brought down by an ugly tackle and tore my cruciate ligament. Badly.' His mouth twisted. 'And that was the end of the fairy tale. I never played again.'

Silence followed his stark statement and then she spoke in that soft voice. 'Oh, Salvio, that must have—'

'Please. Spare me the platitudes,' he ground out, hardening his heart to the distress which had made her eyes grow as dark as storm clouds—because he didn't need her sympathy. He didn't need anything from anyone. He'd learnt what a mistake *that* could be. 'The injury I could have learned to live with. After all, every professional sportsman or woman has to accept that one day their career will end—even if that happens sooner than they wanted. What made it worse was the discovery that my manager had been systematically working his way through my fortune before leaving town.' There was a pause. 'Suddenly, everything I thought I had was gone. No job. No money. My fall from grace was...spectacular.'

'So what did you do?' she whispered.

Salvio shrugged. He had raged for several days and thought seriously about going after his manager and pinning him to the nearest wall until he had agreed to pay the money back. Until he'd realised that revenge was time-consuming and ultimately damaging. That he didn't want to spend his life in pursuit of his broken dreams and to dwell on the glories of his past, like some sad loser. And then had come the final blow. The final, bitter straw which had made him feel a despair he had vowed never to repeat. Resolutely, he pushed the memory away. 'I sold all my cars and the fancy apartment I'd bought in Rome,' he said. 'And gave most of the proceeds to my parents. Then I took what was left and bought a plane ticket to the US.'

'That's a long way from Naples,' she observed slowly. 'Why there?'

'Because it was a big enough place to lose myself in and to start again. I didn't want to be defined by a career which had been cut short and I was young and strong and prepared to work hard.' He'd worked to the exclusion of pretty much everything else in order to get the break he'd needed and, when it had come, he had grabbed at it with both hands. Perceptive enough to recognise that people were starting to move downtown and that run-down areas of the city were potential goldmines, he had started buying up derelict properties and then renovating them. On his Christmas trip back to Naples that first year, he had brought his mother a fancy coat from Bloomingdales. These days he could give her the entire store—and frequently tried—but no amount of material success could ever fill the emptiness in his heart.

He stared at Molly, amazed at how much he had told her. More than he'd ever admitted to anyone, even to Lauren. His gaze raked over her and he thought how different she looked from the first time he'd seen her, eating cake in the kitchen, her ripe body looking as if it was about to burst out of her uniform. Her green dress exuded all the class and sophistication which was an inevitable by-product of wearing designer clothes which had been chosen by an expert. Yet it was the softness of her eyes he noticed most—and the dewy perfection of her creamy skin. She still radiated the same wholesome sex appeal which had drawn him to her in the first place and he wondered why he was wasting time talking like this. What would he be doing with any other woman he was sharing a bedroom with—let alone the one who was wearing his ring?

He felt the erratic hammer of his pulse as he glanced down at his watch. 'I don't want to talk about the past any more.'

'Okay,' she said cautiously. 'Then we won't.'

'And we don't have to be at my folks' place for a while,' he said unevenly. 'Do you want a tour of the city?'

'Is that what you'd like to do?' she questioned, with the compliance which was such an essential part of her nature.

'No. That's the last thing I want to do right now. I can think of a much better way to pass the next couple of hours. Can't you?'

Molly thoughts were teeming as she met his dark gaze. So much of what he'd told her hadn't been what she was expecting, yet now she knew the facts they didn't really come as a surprise. The first time she'd seen him she'd noticed the power-packed body of a natural sportsman and the faint limp which he had all but managed to disguise. The single physical flaw in a man who was looking at her now with a question in his eyes.

She was still a relative novice at sex, but already she could recognise the desire which was making his face grow tense. She knew what he wanted. What *she* wanted too. Because she hadn't really enjoyed their night apart, last night. And even though the bed had been amazingly comfortable, she kept thinking about Salvio lying next door. Wondering why he hadn't tried a bit harder to sleep with her. Wondering if he'd gone off her and didn't fancy her any more. And—desire aside—wasn't the truth that she felt *safe* in his arms—even if that feeling passed as quickly as a summer storm? She stared into his molten black eyes and, for once, said exactly what was in her heart.

'Yes, I can think of a few things I'd like to do,' she agreed shyly. 'As long as they involve us being horizontal.'

She was unprepared for the curve of his smile as he walked towards her or for the way he lifted her hand to his, kissing each finger in turn before leading her over to the huge bed which overlooked the famous bay. She was eager to feel his naked skin against hers but this time there was no urgency as he began to undress her. This time his fingers were leisurely as they unclipped her bra and her swollen breasts came spilling out, his moan appreciative as he caught one taut nipple between his teeth. Molly squirmed beneath the teasing flick of his tongue but her frustration didn't seem to have any effect on his lazy pace. And didn't her heart pound with joy when he bent his head to drop a series of tender kisses on her belly as if he was silently acknowledging the tiny life which grew inside her?

'S-Salvio?' she stumbled tentatively as she felt the brush of his lips against her navel.

'It's going to be okay,' he said, his voice growing husky.

What was he talking about—their future, or meeting his parents? Or both?

But suddenly Molly was beyond caring as his movements became more urgent.

She cried out when he entered her and clung to him fiercely as he made each hard thrust. It felt so deep— he seemed to be filling her body completely, as if he couldn't get enough of her. And it felt different, more *intimate* than it had ever been before. Was that because he'd trusted her enough to tell her things she suspected he usually kept locked away—or was this sudden closeness all in her imagination? But the pleasure she was experiencing wasn't imaginary. Her senses felt exquisitely raw and heightened so that when her orgasm came, Molly felt as if rocked by a giant and powerful wave—her satisfaction only intensified by the moan he gave as he spilled his seed inside her. Afterwards she felt as if she were floating on a cloud. His breath was warm and comforting against her neck and she missed his presence when he withdrew from her and rolled to the other side of the mattress.

'That was just…perfect,' she said dreamily, the words out of her mouth before she could prevent them.

But Salvio didn't answer and, although the sound of his breathing was strong and steady, Molly wasn't sure whether or not he was asleep. Was he just lying there ignoring her? she wondered, with a sudden streak of paranoia. Lying there and *pretending*?

But she decided it was pointless to get freaked out by his sudden detachment, even if she'd had the energy to do so. Nestling herself down into the big mound of feathery pillows, Molly gave a little sigh and fell asleep.

CHAPTER NINE

PERHAPS INEVITABLY, THEY slept for longer than they'd intended and Molly woke with a start, looking round in mild confusion as she tried to get her bearings. Maybe they'd been catching up on too many restless nights, or maybe the amazing sex they'd just enjoyed had taken it out of them. Either way, the Neapolitan sky outside their hotel suite was ebony-dark and sprinkled with stars and when she glanced at her watch, she saw to her horror that it was almost seven—and they were due at Salvio's parents for Christmas Eve dinner in just over an hour.

'Wake up,' she urged, giving her sleeping fiancé's shoulder a rough shake. 'Or we're going to be late!'

Hurrying into the bathroom, she had the fastest shower on record before addressing the thorny issue of what to wear when meeting Salvio's parents for the first time. She still wasn't used to having quite so many clothes at her disposal and was more than a little dazzled by the choice. After much consideration, she opted for a soft knee-length skirt worn with a winter-white sweater and long black boots. Taking a deep breath, she did a little pirouette.

'Do you think your mother will approve of what I'm wearing?' she asked anxiously.

Salvio's black gaze roved over her in leisurely appraisal, before he gave a nod of approval. 'Most certainly,' he affirmed. 'You look demure and decent.'

Molly's fixed smile didn't waver as they stepped into the penthouse elevator, but really…*demure* and *decent* didn't exactly set the world on fire, did they?

They reached the lobby and as the doorman sprang forward to welcome them, Molly became aware of the buzz of interest their appearance was creating. Or rather, Salvio's appearance. She could see older men staring at him wistfully while women of all ages seemed intent on devouring him with hungry eyes. Yet despite the glamour of the female guests who were milling around the lobby, Molly felt a sudden shy pride as he took her arm and began guiding her towards the waiting car. Because *she* was the one he'd just been making love to, wasn't she? And *she* was the one who was carrying his child.

The luxury car was soon swallowed up in heavy traffic and before long they drew up outside an elegant house not too far from their hotel. Molly's nerves— which had been growing during the journey—were quickly dissolved when they were met by a tiny middle-aged woman dressed in Christmas red, her eyes dark and smiling as she opened the door to them. She hugged Molly fiercely before drawing back to look at her properly.

'At last! I have a daughter!' she exclaimed, in fluent though heavily accented English, before turning to her son and rising up on tiptoe to kiss him on each cheek, a faint note of reproof in her voice. 'And what I would like to know is why you are staying in a hotel tonight instead of here at home with your parents, Salvatore De Gennaro?'

'Because you would have insisted on us having separate rooms and this is the twenty-first century, in case you hadn't noticed,' answered her son drily. 'But don't worry, Mamma. We will be back again tomorrow.'

Slightly mollified, Rosa De Gennaro ushered them towards a beautiful high-ceilinged sitting room, where her husband was waiting and Molly stepped forward to greet him. Tall and silver-haired, Paolo De Gennaro had handsomely-rugged features which echoed those of his son and Molly got a poignant glimpse of what Salvio might look like when he was sixty. *Will I still know him when he's sixty?* she wondered, unprepared for the dark fear which shafted through her and the sudden shifting sense of uncertainty. But she shelved the useless thought and concentrated on getting to know the older couple whose joy at their son's engagement was evident. As Rosa examined her glittering ring with murmurs of delight, Molly felt a flash of guilt. What if they knew the truth? That the only reason she was here on Christmas Eve, presenting this false front of togetherness with their son, was because one reckless night had ended up with an unplanned baby.

But guilt was a futile emotion and she tried to make the best of things, the way she always did. The house seemed full of light and festivity—with the incomparable air of expectation which always defined the night before Christmas, no matter how much you tried to pretend it didn't. A beautiful tree, laden with gifts, was glittering in one of the windows and she could detect delicious smells of cooking from elsewhere in the house.

It was a long time since she'd been at the centre of a family and Molly found herself wondering what Robbie was doing tonight. She'd tried to ring him earlier that day but he hadn't picked up. *Please don't let him be gambling*, she prayed silently. *Let him have realised that there's more to life than debt and uncertainty and chasing impossible dreams.* Staring down at the nativity set which stood on a small table next to the tree, she focussed on the helpless infant in the tiny crib and tried to imagine what her own baby would look like. Would he or she resemble Salvio, with those dark stern features and a mouth which rarely smiled, but which when it did was like no other smile she'd ever seen?

She remembered the way he'd kissed her belly just before they'd made love and felt a stir of hope in her heart. He'd certainly never done *that* before—and surely that response hadn't been faked? Because the fleeting tenderness she thought she'd detected had meant just as much as the sexual excitement which had followed. And wasn't tenderness a good place to start building their relationship?

Refusing champagne and sipping from a glass of fruit juice, Molly was laughing as she examined a photo of a fourteen-year-old Salvio holding aloft a shining silver trophy, when she felt a brief pain, low in her belly. Did she flinch? Was that why Salvio's mother guided her towards a high-backed brocade chair and touched her gently on her shoulder?

'*Per piacere.* Sit down, Molly. You must be tired after your travels—but soon we will eat. You are hungry, I hope?'

Obediently, Molly took the chair she'd been offered, wondering why people were always telling her to sit down. Did she look permanently tired? Probably. Actually, she *was* a bit tired. She thought about the reason for her fatigue and her heart gave a little skip as she smiled at Salvio's mother.

'Very hungry,' she said.

'Here in Southern Italy we are proud of our culinary traditions,' Rosa continued before directing a smile at her son. 'For they represent the important times that families spend together.'

Soon they were tucking into a feast of unbelievable proportions. Molly had never *seen* a meal so big, as dish followed dish. There was spaghetti with clams and then fried shellfish, before an eel-like fish was placed in the centre of the elegant dining table with something of a flourish.

'*Capitone!*' announced Rosa. 'You know this fish, Molly? No? It is a Neapolitan tradition to eat it on Christmas Eve. In the old days, my mother used to buy it from the market while it was still alive, and then keep it in the bath until it was time to cook it. Do you remember the year it escaped, Salvio—and hid under your bed? And you were the only one brave enough to catch it?'

As his parents laughed Molly sneaked a glance at Salvio and tried to imagine the billionaire tycoon as a little boy, capturing an elusive fish which had slithered underneath a bed. Just as she tried to imagine him cradling an infant in those powerful arms, but that was too big a stretch of the imagination. At times he was so cool and distant—it was only in bed that he seemed to let his guard down and show any real feeling. She stared at the small piece of *capitone* left on her plate, wondering how it was going to work when she had his baby. She'd already established that his London penthouse wasn't particularly child-friendly—but where else would they live? He'd mentioned other houses in different countries but none of them had sounded like home, with the possible exception of his Cotswolds manor house.

They finished the meal with hard little biscuits called *rococo* and afterwards Molly insisted on helping her hostess clear the table. Efficiently, she dealt with the left-over food and dishes in a way which was second nature to her, washing the crystal glasses by hand and carefully placing them on the draining board to dry, while asking her hostess questions about life in Naples. She was just taking off the apron she'd borrowed when she noticed Rosa standing in the doorway of the kitchen watching her, a soft smile on her face.

'Thank you, Molly.'

'It was my pleasure, Signora De Gennaro. Thank you for a delicious meal. You have a wonderful home and you've been very welcoming.'

'Prego.' Rosa gave a small nod of satisfaction. 'I have been waiting many years for a daughter-in-law and I think you will be very good for my son.'

Molly's heart pounded as she hung the apron on a

hook beside the door, hoping Rosa didn't want to hear the romantic story of how she and her son had first met. Because there wasn't one. She suspected the truth would shock this kindly woman but Molly couldn't bear to tell her any lies. *So concentrate on the things you* can *say*, she told herself fiercely. *On all the things you wish would happen.*

'Oh, I hope I will be,' she said, her voice a little unsteady as she realised she meant every word. 'I want to be the best wife I can.'

Rosa nodded, her dark eyes intense and watchful. 'You are not like his other girlfriends,' she said slowly.

Was that a good thing or a bad thing? Molly wondered. 'Aren't I?'

'Not at all.' Rosa hesitated. 'Though he only ever brought one other to meet us.'

Molly stilled, telling herself it would be foolish to ask any more questions. But she hadn't factored in curiosity—and curiosity was a dangerous thing. Wasn't it the key which turned the lock in an invisible door—exposing you to things you might be better not knowing? And the crazy thing was even though she *knew* that, it didn't stop her from prying. 'Oh?' she questioned. Just one little word but that was all it took.

'She was no good for him,' said Rosa darkly, after a brief pause. '*Sì*, she was very beautiful but she cared only for his fame. She would never have helped with the dishes like this. She wanted to spend her Christmases in New York, or Monaco.' She touched her fingertips to the small golden cross at her neck. 'I give thanks that he never married her.'

Married her? Molly's heart constricted. Had Salvio been engaged to someone else? The man who had told her he didn't 'do' emotion? The nebulous twist of pain in her stomach which she'd felt earlier now returned with all the ferocity of a hot spear, which Molly bore behind the sunniest smile in her repertoire. But she was relieved when Salvio phoned his driver to take them back to the hotel, and leaned back weakly against the car seat, closing her eyes and willing the pain to leave her.

'Are you okay?' questioned Salvio beside her.

No, I'm not okay. I discovered tonight that you were going to marry someone else and you didn't tell me. That even though I'm carrying your baby you don't trust me enough to confide in me.

But she couldn't face a scene in the car, so she stuck to the positive. 'I'm fine!' she said brightly, still with that rictus smile in place. 'Your parents are lovely,' she added in a rush.

'Yes,' he said, and smiled. 'They liked you.'

But Molly thought he seemed lost in thought as he stared out at the festive lights of his city. Was he thinking about his other fiancée and comparing the two women? She found herself wondering why they had broken up and wondered if she would summon up the courage to ask him.

But the cramps in her stomach were getting worse. Cramps which felt horribly familiar, but which she tried to dismiss as stress. The stress of meeting his parents for the first time, or maybe the stress of discovering that she wasn't the only woman he'd asked to marry. She found herself breathing a sigh of relief when they arrived back in their penthouse suite and she unbuttoned her coat.

'Would you mind if I checked on my emails?' Salvio said as he removed the coat from her shoulders. 'I just want to see if something has come in from Los Angeles, before everything shuts down for the holidays.'

'No, of course I don't mind,' she said weakly, aware that he was already disappearing towards his computer.

She slipped into the bathroom and locked the door behind her, when she felt a warm rush between her legs and the sudden unexpected sight of blood made Molly freeze. She began to tremble.

It couldn't be.

Couldn't be.

But it was. Of course it was. On a deeper level she'd known all evening that this was about to happen, but the reality was harsher than she ever could have imagined. Her fingers clutched the cold rim of the bathtub as her vision shifted in and out of focus. She found herself wishing she were alone so that she could have given into the inexplicable tears which were welling up in her eyes. But she wasn't alone. She dashed the tears away with the tips of her fingers and tried to compose herself. Out in that fancy hotel room on the night before Christmas was her fiancé…except that the reason he'd slid these diamonds on her finger no longer existed. He would be free now, she thought—as a silent scream of protest welled up inside her.

She found her wash-bag, praying she might find what she needed—but there was no gratitude in her heart when she did, only the dull certainty of what she needed to say to Salvio. But she was loath to go out and face him. To utter the words he would probably be relieved to hear. She didn't think she could face his joy—not when she was experiencing such strange and bitter heartache.

Straightening up, she stared into the mirror, registering the pallor of her face, knowing that she couldn't tell him now. Not tonight. Not when the bells of Naples were peeling out their triumphant Christmas chorus about the impending birth of a baby.

CHAPTER TEN

'So when...?' There was a pause. 'When exactly were you going to tell me, *bedda mia*?'

The words left Salvio's lips like icy bullets but he knew immediately that his aim had been accurate. He could tell by the way Molly froze as she came out of the bathroom, the white towelling robe swathing her curvy body like a soft suit of armour.

'Tell you what?' she questioned.

Maybe if she'd come straight out and admitted it, he might have gone more easily on her but instead he felt the slow seep of anger in his veins as her guileless expression indicated nothing but a lie. A damned lie. His mouth hardened. 'That you aren't pregnant.'

She didn't deny it. She just stood in front of him, the colour leeching from her face so that her milky skin looked almost transparent. 'How did you...?' He saw the sudden flash of fear in her eyes. 'How did you know?'

Her confirmation only stoked the darkness which was building inside him. 'You think I am devoid of all my senses?' he demanded. 'That I wouldn't wonder why you turned away from me last night, then spent hours clinging to the other side of the mattress…pretending to be *asleep*?' he finished with contempt.

'So it's because we didn't have sex,' she summarised dully.

'No, not just because of that, nor even because of the way you disappeared into the bathroom when we got back from my parents' house and refused to look me in the eye,' he iced back. 'I'm not stupid, Molly. Don't you realise that a man can tell when a woman is menstruating? That she looks different. Smells different.'

'How could I ever be expected to match your encyclopaedic knowledge of women?' she questioned bitterly. 'When you're the first man I've ever slept with.'

Salvio felt the pounding of a pulse at his temple. Was she using her innocence as a shield with which to defend herself? To deflect him from a far more disturbing possibility, but one he couldn't seem to shake off no matter how hard he tried. 'Or maybe you were never even pregnant in the first place,' he accused silkily.

She reacted by swaying and sinking down onto a nearby sofa, as if his accusation had taken away her ability to stand. 'You think *that*?' she breathed, her fingers spreading out over her throat as if she was in danger of choking.

'Why shouldn't I think that?' he demanded. 'I've never actually seen any proof, have I? Is that why you didn't want to tell my parents about the baby—not because it was "too early" but because there *was* no baby?'

'You really believe—' she shook her damp hair in disbelief '—that I would lie to you about something as important as that?'

'How should I know what you'd do if you were desperate enough? We both know you were having trouble paying off your brother's debt and that marriage to me would mean the debt would be wiped out overnight.' His gaze bored into her. 'And I was careful that night, Molly. You know I was.'

She was still staring at him as if he were the devil incarnate. 'You're saying that I…made it up? That the whole pregnancy was nothing but an *invention*?'

'Why not? It's not unheard of.' He shrugged. 'It happens less often these days but I understand in the past it was quite a common device, used by women keen to get a wedding ring on their finger.' His mouth hardened. 'Usually involving a wealthy man.'

Her body tensed and Salvio saw the change in her. Saw the moment when her habitual compliance became rebellion. When outrage filled her soft features with an unfamiliar rage which she was directing solely at him. Her eyes flashing pewter sparks, she sprang to her feet, damp hair flying around her shoulders.

'I *was* pregnant,' she flared, her hands gesturing wildly through the empty air. 'One hundred per cent pregnant. I did two tests, one after the other—and if you don't believe me, then that's your problem! And yes, I was waiting until this morning to tell you, because last night I just couldn't face having the kind of discussion we're having now. So if keeping the news to myself for less than twelve hours is harbouring some dark secret, then yes—I'm guilty of that. But I'm not the only one with secrets, am I, Salvio?'

He heard the allegation in her voice as he met her

furious gaze full on and braced himself for what was coming next.

'When were you going to let me know you'd been engaged before?' she continued, her voice still shaking with rage. 'Or weren't you going to bother?'

His eyes narrowed. 'My mother told you?'

'Of course your mother told me—how else would I know?'

'What did she say?'

'Enough.' Her voice wobbled. 'I know the woman you were going to marry was rich and I'm not. I know she was beautiful and I'm not.'

Something about the weariness in her tone made Salvio feel a sharp pang of guilt. He stared at her shadowed eyes. At the milky skin now tinged with the dull flush of fury. At the still-drying shiny hair and the voluptuous curves which had lured him like a siren's call into her arms. And he felt an unexpected wave of contrition wash over him.

'You *are* beautiful,' he stressed.

'Please. Don't,' she said, holding up her hand to silence him. 'Don't make things even worse by telling me lies!'

Her dignified response surprised him. Had he been expecting gratitude for his throwaway compliment about her looks? Was he, in his own way, as guilty as Lady Avery had been of underestimating her? Of treating her like an object, rather than a person—as someone born to serve rather than to participate? Did he think he could behave exactly as he liked towards her and she would just take it?

'You *are* beautiful,' he affirmed, as repentance flowed through him. 'And yes, I was engaged before. I didn't tell you because...'

'Because it's too painful for you to remember, I suppose?'

The pulse at Salvio's temple now flickered. In a way, yes, very painful—though not in the way he suspected she meant. It was more about the betrayal he'd suffered than anything else because, like all Neapolitans, he had an instinctive loathing of treachery. It had come as a shock to realise that Lauren hadn't loved him—only what he represented. He gave a bitter smile. Perhaps he should have had a little more empathy for Molly since he too had been treated like an object in his time. 'It happened a long time ago,' he said slowly. 'And there seemed no reason to rake it up.'

She looked at him in exasperation. 'Don't you know anything about women? On second thought, don't answer that since we've already proved beyond any reasonable doubt that what you don't know about women probably isn't worth knowing. Except maybe you don't know just how far you can push them before they finally snap.' She tugged the towelling belt of her white robe a little tighter. 'Who was she, Salvio?'

Salvio scowled. Did he really have to tell her? Rake up the bitterness all over again? He expelled air from his flared nostrils, recognising from the unusually fierce expression on Molly's face that he had to tell her. 'Her name was Lauren Meyer,' he said reluctantly. 'I met her at an official function on a pre-season tour of America and brought her back here with me to Naples.'

'And she was blonde, I suppose?'

'Yes, she was blonde,' he said, ignoring her sarcastic tone. 'What else do you want to know, Molly? That she was an heiress and that she loved fame and fortune, in that order?'

'Did she?'

'She did. She met me when I had everything.' He gave a short laugh. 'And dumped me the moment I lost it all.'

'So, what…happened?' she said, into the silence which followed.

Salvio's lips tightened, because Lauren had been the catalyst. The reason he had kissed goodbye to emotion and battened up his heart. During his career there had been plenty of women who had lusted after his body and his bank account—but he'd made the mistake of thinking that Lauren was different.

His gaze flicked over to the dark sweep of the bay before returning to the grey watchfulness in Molly's eyes and suddenly he was finding it easy to talk about something he never talked about. 'After the accident, she came to visit me. Every day she sat by my bedside, always in a different outfit, looking picture-perfect. Always ready to smile and pose for the photographers who were camped outside the hospital. She was there when the physiotherapists worked on my leg and she was there when the doctor told me I'd never play professional football again. I'll never forget the look on her face.' His laugh was harsh. 'When I was discharged, she didn't come to meet me, but I thought I knew the reason why. I went home expecting a surprise party because she loved parties, and that's when I discovered she'd flown back to the States and was seeing some all-American boy her parents wanted her to marry all along. And that was that. I never saw her again.'

There was a pause while she seemed to take it all in.

'Oh, Salvio, that's awful,' she said. 'It must have felt like a kick in the teeth when you'd lost everything else.'

'I didn't tell you because I wanted your pity, Molly. I told you because you wanted to know. So now you do.'

'And, did you…did you love her?'

He felt a twist of anger. Why did women always do this? Why did they reduce everything down to those three little words and place so much store by them? He knew what she wanted him to say and that he was going to have to disappoint her. Because he couldn't rewrite the past, could he? He was damned if he was going to tell her something just because it was what he suspected she wanted to hear. And how could he possibly dismiss lies as contemptible if he started using them himself? 'Yes, I loved her,' he said, at last.

Molly hid her pain behind the kind of look she might have presented to Lady Avery if she'd just been asked to produce an extra batch of scones before teatime, and not for the first time she was grateful for all the training she'd had as a servant. Grateful for the mask-like calm she was able to project while she tried to come to terms with her new situation. Because in less than twelve hours she'd lost everything, too. Not just her baby but her hopes for the future. Hope of being a good wife and mother. Hope that a baby might help Salvio loosen up and become more human. And now it was all gone—whipped away like a rug being pulled from beneath her feet. There was no illusion left for her to cling to. No rosy dreams. Just a man who had once loved another woman and didn't love her. A man who had accused her of lying about her baby.

A baby which was now no more.

She wanted to bury her face in her hands and sob out her heartbreak but somehow she resisted the compelling urge. Instead she chose her words as carefully as a resigning politician. 'I don't want to upset your parents but obviously I can't face going for lunch today. I mean, there's no point now, is there? I don't think I'm capable of pretending everything's the same as it was—especially on Christmas Day. I think your mother might see right through me and there's no way I want to deceive her. So maybe it's best if I just disappear and leave you to say whatever you think is best.' She swallowed. 'Perhaps you could arrange for your plane to take me back to England as soon as possible?'

Salvio stared at her, unprepared for the powerful feeling which arrowed through his gut. Was it *disappointment*? Yet that seemed much too bland a description. Disappointment was what you felt if there was no snow on the slopes during a skiing holiday, or if it rained on your Mediterranean break.

He furrowed his brow. After Lauren he'd never wanted marriage. He'd never wanted a baby either but, having been presented with a *fait accompli*, had done what he considered to be the right thing by Molly. And of *course* it had affected him, because, although his heart might be unfeeling, he was discovering he wasn't made of stone. Hadn't he allowed himself the brief fantasy of imagining himself with a son? A son he could teach to kick a ball around and to perfect the *elastico* move for which he'd been so famous?

Only now Molly wanted to leave him. Her womb was empty and her spirit deflated by his cruel accusations and she was still staring at him as if he were some kind of monster. Maybe he deserved that because hadn't she only ever been kind and giving? Rare attributes which only a fool would squander—and he was that fool.

'No. Don't go,' he said suddenly.

She screwed up her eyes. 'You mean you won't let me use your plane?'

'My plane is at your disposal any time you want it,' he said impatiently. 'That's not what I mean.' His mouth hardened. 'I don't want you to go, Molly.'

'Well, I've got to go. I can't hang around pretending nothing's happened, just because you don't want to lose face with your parents.'

'It has nothing to do with losing face,' he argued. 'It has more to do with wanting to make amends for all the accusations I threw at you. About realising that maybe—somehow—we could make this work.'

'Make *what* work?'

'This relationship.'

She shook her head. 'We don't have a relationship, Salvio.'

'But we could.'

She narrowed her eyes. 'You're not making any sense.'

'Aren't I?' He lowered his voice. 'I get the feeling you weren't too unhappy about having my baby.'

She stared down at her feet and as he followed the direction of her gaze, he noticed her toenails were unvarnished. It occurred to him that he'd never been intimate with a woman whose life hadn't been governed by beauty regimes and his eyes narrowed in sudden comprehension. Was that shallow of him? She looked up again and he could see the pride and dignity written all over her face and he felt the twist of something he didn't recognise deep inside him.

'If this is a soul-baring exercise then it seems only fair I should bear mine. And I couldn't help the way I felt about being pregnant,' she admitted. 'I knew it wasn't an ideal situation and should never have happened but, no, I wasn't unhappy about having your baby, Salvio. It would have been...'

'Would have been what?' he prompted as her words tailed off.

Somebody to love, Molly wanted to say—but even in this new spirit of honesty, she knew that was a declaration too far. Because that sounded needy and vulnerable and she was through with being vulnerable. She wished Salvio would stop asking her all this stuff, especially when it was so out of character. Why didn't he just let her fly back to England and let her get on with the rest of her life and begin the complicated process of getting over him, instead of directing that soft look of compassion at her which was making her feel most...peculiar? She struggled to remove some of the emotion from her words.

'It would have been a role which I would have happily taken on and done to the best of my ability,' she said. 'And I'm not going to deny that on one level I'm deeply disappointed, but I'll… I'll get over it.'

Her words faded into silence. One of those silences which seemed to last for an eternity when you just knew that everything hinged on what was said next, but Salvio's words were the very last Molly was expecting.

'Unless we try again, of course,' he said.

'What are you talking about?' she breathed.

'What if I told you that fatherhood was something which I had also grown to accept? Which I would have happily taken on, despite my initial reservations? What if I told you that I was disappointed, too? *Am* disappointed,' he amended. 'That I've realised I *do* want a child.'

'Then I suggest you do something about it,' she said, her words brittle as rock candy and she wondered if he had any idea how much it hurt to say them. Or how hard it was to stem the tide of tears which was pricking at her eyes. Tears not just for the little life which was no more, but for the man who had created that life. Because that was the crazy thing. That she was going to miss Salvio De Gennaro. How was it that in such a short while he seemed to have become as integral to her life as her own heartbeat? 'Find a woman. Get married. Start a family. That's the way it usually works.'

'That's exactly what I intend to do. Only I don't need to find a woman. Why would I, when there's one standing in front of me?'

'You don't mean that.'

'Don't tell me what I mean, Molly. I mean every word and I'm asking you to be my wife.'

Molly blinked in confusion. He was asking her to *marry* him—despite the fact she was no longer carrying his baby? She thought about the first time she'd ever seen him and how completely blown away she'd been. But this time she was no longer staring at him as if he were some demigod who had just tumbled from the stars. The scales had fallen from her eyes and now she saw him for what he was. A flawed individual— just like her. He had introduced her to amazing sex and fancy clothes. They'd made love on a giant bed overlooking the Bay of Naples and he had kissed her belly when a tiny child had been growing there. She had met his parents and they had liked her—treating her as if she were already part of the family. And somehow the culmination of all those experiences had changed her. She was no longer the same humble person who would accept whatever was thrown at her. The things which had happened had allowed her to remove the shackles which had always defined her. She no longer felt like a servant, but a woman. A real woman.

Yet even as that realisation filled her with a rush of liberation, she was at pains to understand why Salvio was making his extraordinary proposition. He was off the hook now. He was free again. Surely he should be celebrating her imminent departure from his life instead of trying to postpone it?

'Why do you want to marry me?' she demanded.

His gaze raked over her but this time it was not his usual sensual appraisal—more an impartial assessment of her worth. 'I like your softness and kindness,' he said slowly. 'Your approach to life and your work ethic. I think you will make a good mother.'

'And that's all?' she found herself asking.

He narrowed his eyes. 'Surely that is enough?'

She wasn't certain. If you wrote down all those things they would make a flattering list but the glaring omission was love. But Salvio had loved once before and his heart had been broken and damaged as a result. Could she accept his inability to love her as a condition of their marriage, and could they make it work in spite of that?

Behind him, Naples was framed like a picture-postcard as he began to walk towards her and for once his limp seemed more pronounced than usual. And although the thrust of his thighs was stark evidence enough of his powerful sensuality, it was that tiny glimpse of frailty which plucked at her heartstrings.

'I wanted this baby,' he said simply.

Her heart pounded—not wanting to be affected by that powerful declaration. But of course she *was* affected—for it was the most human she had ever seen him. 'You had a funny way of showing it.'

He lifted his shoulders as if to concede the point. 'I'm not going to deny that at first I felt trapped. Who wouldn't in that kind of situation? But once I'd got my head around it, my feelings began to change.'

Molly felt the lurch of hope. Could she believe him? Did she dare to? She remembered the way he'd kissed her belly yesterday—and how loving she'd felt towards him as a result. And that was dangerous. When she stopped to think about it, everything about this situation was dangerous. 'So this time you're not asking me to marry you because you have to?' she continued doggedly. 'You're saying you actually *want* to?'

'Yes.' His shadowed jaw tightened. 'I do. For old-fashioned reasons rather than the unrealistic expectations of romantic love. I want a family, Molly. I didn't realise how much until the possibility was taken away from me. I want someone to leave my fortune to—because otherwise what's the point of making all this money? Someone to take my name and my genes forward. Someone who will be my future.'

Molly's heart clenched as she listened to his heartfelt words. She thought of his pain when he'd lost his career and fortune in quick succession. She thought about the woman who had betrayed him at the worst possible time. The woman he had loved. No wonder he had built a wall around his heart and vowed never to let anyone touch that heart again. She drank in the hardness of his beautiful face. Could she dismantle that wall, little by little, and would he allow her close enough to try? She knew it was a gamble—and, despite all the stern lectures she'd given her little brother, a gamble she intended to take, because by now she couldn't imagine a life without him.

But if she was to be his wife then she must learn to be his equal. There had been times in the past when she'd told Salvio what she thought he wanted to hear because that was all part of her training as a servant. But it wasn't going to be like that from now on. From now on they were going to operate on a level playing field.

'Yes, I will be your wife,' she said, in a low and un-emotional voice.

He laughed, softly. 'You drive me crazy, Molly Miller,' he said. 'Do you realise that?'

The look she gave him was genuine. 'I don't know how.'

'I think,' he observed drily, 'that's the whole point. Now come here.'

He was pulling her into his arms and for a moment Molly felt uncertain, because she had her period and surely… But the touch of his fingertips against her cheek was comforting rather than seeking and the warmth of his arms consoling rather than sexual.

'I'm sorry about the baby,' he whispered against her hair, so softly that she might have imagined it.

It was the first time he had ever held her without wanting sex and Molly pressed her eyelids tightly shut, her face resting against his silky shoulder, terrified to move or to speak because she was afraid she might cry.

CHAPTER ELEVEN

THEY WERE MARRIED in Naples in a beautiful church not far from the home of Salvio's parents. The ancient building was packed with people Molly barely knew—friends of the family, she guessed, and high-powered friends of Salvio's who had flown in from all around the world. Most of them she'd met the previous evening during a lavish pre-wedding dinner, but their names had flown in one ear and out of the other, no matter how hard she'd tried to remember them. Her mind had been too full of niggling concerns to concentrate on anything very much, but her main anxiety had been about Robbie.

Because Salvio had quietly arranged for her brother to fly from Australia to Naples as a pre-wedding surprise and Molly's heart had contracted with joy as Robbie had strolled into the restaurant where everyone was eating, flashing his careless smile, which had made many of the younger women swoon.

She had jumped to her feet to hug him, touched by Salvio's unexpected thoughtfulness, as she'd run her gaze over her brother in candid assessment. From the outside Robbie looked good—better than he'd looked in a long time. He was tanned and fit, his golden curls longer than she remembered, and his clothes were surprisingly well chosen. But she'd seen his faintly avaricious expression as he'd taken in the giant ring on her finger and the expensive venue of the sea-view wedding reception.

'Well, what do you know? You did good, sis. Real good,' he'd said slowly, a gleam entering his grey eyes. 'Salvio De Gennaro is *minted*.'

She'd found herself wanting to protest that she wasn't marrying Salvio for his money but Robbie probably wouldn't have believed her, since his teenage years had been dedicated to the pursuit of instant wealth. She'd wondered if his reluctance to maintain eye contact meant that his gambling addiction had returned. And had then wondered if she was simply transferring her own fears onto her brother.

But she wasn't going to be afraid because she was walking into this with her eyes open. She'd made the decision to be Salvio's wife because deep down she wanted to, and she was going to give the marriage everything she could. Who said that such a strangely conceived union couldn't work? She was used to fighting against the odds, wasn't she?

Holding herself tall, she had walked slowly down the aisle wearing the dress which had been created especially for her by one of London's top wedding-dress designers. The whole couture process had been a bit of an ordeal, mainly because a pale, shiny fabric wasn't terribly forgiving when you were overendowed with curves, but Molly had known Salvio wanted her to look like a traditional bride. And in her heart she had wanted that, too.

'Your breasts are very…generous.' The dressmaker had grunted. 'We're going to have to use a minimising bra, I think.'

Molly had opened her mouth to agree until she'd remembered what she'd vowed on the day of Salvio's proposal. That she was going to be true to herself and behave like his equal because the strain of doing otherwise would quickly wear her down. And if she tried to be someone she wasn't, then surely this whole crazy set-up would be doomed.

'I think Salvio likes my breasts the way they are,' she'd offered shyly and the dressmaker had taken the pins out of her mouth, and smiled.

The look on his face when she reached the altar seemed to endorse Molly's theory—and when they left the church as man and wife, the strangest thing happened. Outside, a sea of people wearing pale blue and white ribbons were cheering and clapping and Molly looked up at Salvio in confusion as their joyful shouts filled the air.

'Some of the supporters of my old football club,' he explained, looking slightly taken aback himself. 'Come to wish me *in bocca al lupo.*'

'Good luck?' she hazarded, blinking as a battery of mobile-phone cameras flashed in her face.

'*Esattamente.* Your Italian lessons are clearly paying dividends,' he murmured into her ear, his mouth brushing against one pearl-indented lobe.

Just that brief touch was enough to make her breasts

spring into delicious life beneath the delicate material of her wedding dress and Salvio's perceptive smile made Molly blush. Lifting up her bouquet of roses to disguise the evidence of physical desire, she thought how perfectly attuned he was to her body and its needs. Their sexual compatibility had been there from the start— now all she needed to concentrate on was getting pregnant.

After the wedding they flew to their honeymoon destination of Barbados, where they were shown to a large, private villa in the vast grounds of a luxury hotel. It was the closest thing to paradise that Molly could imagine and as soon as they arrived, Salvio went for a swim while she insisted on unpacking her clothes—because she didn't quite trust anyone else to do it so neatly. *Old habits die hard*, she thought ruefully.

Knotting a sarong around her waist, she went outside where her brand-new husband was lying on a sun lounger the size of a double bed, wearing a battered straw hat angled over his eyes and nothing else. A lump rose in her throat as she watched him lying in the bright sunshine—completely at ease with his bare body which was gleaming with droplets of water drying in the sun. For a moment she couldn't actually believe she was here, with him. His wife. She swallowed. Even her title took some getting used to. Signora Molly De Gennaro.

He turned to look at her, his gaze lazy as it ran a slow and comprehensive journey from her head to the tips of her toes.

'How are you feeling?' he questioned solicitously.

Trying not to be distracted by the very obvious stirring at his groin, she nodded. 'Fine, thank you,' she said politely. 'That sleep I had on the plane was wonderful.'

'Then stop standing there looking so uncertain.' Pushing aside a tumble of cushions, he patted the space beside him on the giant sunbed. 'Come over here.'

It occurred to Molly that if she wasn't careful she would end up taking orders from him just like before, but it was probably going to take a little time to acclimatise herself to this new life. To feel as if she had the right to enjoy these lavish surroundings, instead of constantly looking around feeling as if she ought to be cleaning them.

Aware of the sensual glitter of his eyes, she walked across the patio and sank down next to him. Straight ahead glimmered a sea of transparent turquoise, edged with sand so fine it looked like caster sugar. To her left was their own private swimming pool and any time they wanted anything—*anything at all*, as they had been assured on their arrival—all they had to do was to ring one of the bells which were littered around the place and some obliging servant would appear.

She stuck out her feet in front of her, still getting used to toenails which were glinting a fetching shade of coral in the bright sunshine.

'You've had a pedicure,' Salvio observed.

She blinked and looked up. 'Fancy you noticing something like that.'

'You'd be amazed what I notice about you, Molly,' he murmured. 'Is that the first one you've ever had?'

'I'm afraid it is.' She lifted her chin a little defensively. 'I suppose that shocks you?'

'Not really, no. And anyway—' he smiled '—I like being shocked by you.'

His hand was now on her leg and she felt his finger-tips travelling slowly over her thigh. Little by little they inched upwards and her mouth grew increasingly dry as they approached the skimpy triangle of her bikini bottoms. She swallowed as his hand came to a tanta-lising halt just before they reached the red and white gingham. 'Salvio,' she breathed.

'*Sì*, Molly?' he murmured.

'We're outside. Anyone can see us.'

'But the whole point of having a *private* villa,' he emphasised, 'is that we *can't* be seen. Haven't you ever wondered what it might be like to make love in the open air?'

She hesitated. 'Maybe,' she said cautiously.

'So why don't we do it?'

'What, now?'

'Right now.'

She swallowed. 'If you're *sure* we really can't be seen.'

'I may be adventurous,' he drawled, 'but I draw the line at rampant voyeurism.'

'Go on, then,' she whispered encouragingly.

Salvio smiled as he trailed his lips down over Mol-ly's generous cleavage which smelt faintly of coconut oil and was already warm from the sun. Through her bikini top a pert nipple sprang into life against his lips and he thought how utterly entrancing she could be with that potent combination of shyness and eagerness, de-spite her lack of experience. 'You are for my eyes only,' he added gravely, hearing her sharp intake of breath as he began to undo the sarong which was knotted around her hips. 'Except you are wearing far too much for me to be able to see you properly.'

The sarong discarded, his finger crept beneath her bikini bottoms to find her most treasured spot, where she was slick and wet. Always wet, he thought achingly. Her enjoyment of sex was so delightfully fervent that it made him instantly hard. He expelled a shuddering breath of air as she responded to his caress by reaching down to touch him intimately, and he moaned his soft pleasure. He liked the way she encircled him within those dextrous fingers and the way she slid them up and down to lightly stroke the pulsing and erect flesh. He liked the way she teased him as he had taught her to tease him and to make him wait, until he felt like her captive slave. But today his hunger would not be tempered and he could not wait, his desire for her off the scale. He had let her sleep on the plane because she had looked exhausted after the wedding, but now his appetite knew no bounds. The bikini was discarded to join the sarong as he wriggled his fingers between her legs. She jerked distractedly as he found her tight bud, her nails digging into his bare shoulders as he increased his rhythmical stroke.

'You like that,' he observed, with a satisfied purr.

'Don't...don't stop, will you?' she gasped.

He gave a low laugh. 'I have no intention of stopping, *bedda mia*. I couldn't stop, even if I wanted to.' But suddenly he no longer wanted to pleasure her with his finger and, positioning himself over her, he parted her thighs and drove into her. He groaned as she matched each urgent thrust with the accommodating jerk of her hips. He revelled in the feel of her, the taste of her and the smell of her. Was it because there was no need for a condom that sex with Molly felt even more incredible than it had done before? Or because he was the one who had taught her everything? She'd never taken a man into her mouth before him, nor sucked him until he was empty and gasping. Just as she'd never had anyone's head between her thighs other than his. He closed his eyes as excitement built at a speed which almost outpaced him. Was he really so primitive that he got some kind of thrill from having bareback sex with his onetime virgin? He drove into her again. Maybe he was.

She began to come, her moans of pleasure spiralling up from the back of her throat and hovering on the edge of a scream, so that he clamped his mouth over hers in an urgent kiss. He felt the rush of her breath in his mouth and the helpless judder of her body clenching around him—and his own response was like a powerful wave which crashed over him and pulled him under. With a groan, he ejaculated, one hand splayed underneath her bottom while the other tangled in her silken hair. Beneath the Barbadian sun he felt the exquisite pulsing of his body as passion seeped away.

For a while he just lay on top of her, dazed and contented, his head cushioned on her shoulder as he dipped in and out of sleep. But eventually he stirred, his fingertips tilting her jaw, enjoying the beatific smile which curved her lips as she opened her eyes to look at him.

'So. We have a choice,' he said slowly. 'We can get

dressed again and ring for drinks, or I can go inside and fix us something and you can stay exactly as you are, which would be my preference.'

She hesitated for a moment. 'I wouldn't mind you waiting on me for a change,' she said. 'Unless you're going to do that helpless man thing of making a mess of it because it's *domestic*, so that you'll never have to do it again.'

His mouth twitched into a smile as he rose from the lounger. 'Is that what men do?'

'In my experience—well, only my working experience, of course. Every time.'

'Not this one.' He picked up the battered straw hat which had fallen off, jamming it down so that the shadow of the brim darkened his face. 'I don't like to fail at anything, Molly.'

She watched him go. Was it that which had hurt the hardest when his life had imploded around him—the fact that he would be perceived as a failure? Had that been at the root of his reluctance to return to Naples very often? Yet he had picked himself up and started all over again. He had made a success of his life in every way, except for one. Just before they'd boarded his private jet to fly here, he'd told her how delighted his parents were that he had chosen her as his bride and she found herself thinking how skewed life could be sometimes. His mother hadn't liked Lauren Meyer, but Salvio had loved her. He'd told her that himself. And if this marriage was to continue, she must resign herself to the fact that she would only ever be second-best.

But that had been her life, hadn't it? It wasn't as

if she wasn't used to it. When you worked in other people's houses you had to put yourself second, because you were only there to help their lives function smoothly. You had to be both efficient yet invisible, because people didn't really see *you*—only the service you provided.

Did Salvio see *her*? she wondered. Or was she simply a vessel to bear his child? The woman he had transformed with his vast fortune, so that she could lie in a Barbadian paradise, looking out over an azure sea as if she'd been born to this life?

The chink of ice made her glance towards the entrance to their villa, where Salvio was standing holding two tall, frosted glasses. As he began to walk towards her she wondered how a man could look so utterly at ease, completely naked save for his sunhat.

Handing her a glass, he joined her on the lounger and for a while they sipped their drinks in silence.

'Salvio,' she said eventually, watching the ice melt in the fruity cocktail.

He turned his face towards her. 'Mmm…?'

'What am I actually going to *do*? I mean, once we get back to England and you go back to work.'

He swirled the ice around in his glass, his fingers dark against the sunlit condensation. 'Weren't we planning to have a baby?'

'Yes, we were. Are,' she corrected. 'But that might not happen straight away, might it? And I can't just sit around all the time just…*waiting*.'

There was a pause. 'You want me to find you something to do?' He studied her carefully. 'There's a charitable arm belonging to my company. Do you think you'd like to get involved in that?'

She hesitated, genuine surprise tearing through her at the realisation he must think her good enough to be a part of his organisation. But it wasn't his validation which pleased her as much as the thought that this would make her a more integral part of his life—and wasn't that what marriage was all about? 'I'd like that very much.' She smiled, but his next words killed her pleasure stone dead.

'You know your brother tapped me for a loan at the wedding?'

The glass she was holding almost slipped from her suddenly nerveless fingers and quickly Molly put it down, her cheeks flaming. *'What?'*

'He said he had an idea for a new business venture and asked if I'd like to invest in it.'

'You didn't say yes?'

'You think I'm in the habit of throwing money away? I asked him how much he had already raised, and how—but he seemed reluctant to answer.' Beneath the shadowed brim of his hat, she saw that his eyes were now as hard and as cold as jet. 'Did you know about this, Molly?'

It hurt that he should ask but, when she thought about it afterwards, why *wouldn't* he ask? Salvio had been a target for women during his playing days and had fallen for someone who saw him as nothing but a trophy husband. He made no secret of not trusting women—so why should he feel any differently about her?

'Of course I didn't know he was going to ask you,'

she said in a low voice. 'And if he'd sought my opinion I would have told him not to even think about it.'

He nodded as he stared out at the bright blue horizon and the subject was closed. But Molly's determination not to let his silky accusation ruin the rest of the day only went so far, and suddenly she was aware of the aching disappointment which made the sunny day feel as if it had been darkened by a cloud.

CHAPTER TWELVE

'So HOW LONG will you be away?' Amid the croissant-crumbed debris of their early-morning breakfast, Molly glanced across the glass dining table at Salvio, who was reading one of the Italian newspapers he had couriered to his London apartment each morning.

'Only a few days,' he said, lifting his dark head to look at her. 'I'm just flying into Los Angeles for back-to-back meetings and then out again.'

'It seems an awfully long way to go,' she observed, taking a final sip of the inky black coffee she'd learned to love and which she now drank in preference to cappuccino. 'For such a short visit.'

'It is. So why don't you come with me?' His eyes gleamed as he put the newspaper down. 'We could add on a few extra days and take the highway to San Francisco. Turn it into a holiday. You've never been to the US, have you?'

She'd never actually been further than the Isle of Wight and that had been years ago. Highly tempted, Molly considered the idea, until she remembered her own responsibilities. 'I can't. I have a lunch with the charity later.'

'You could always cancel it.'

'I can't just *cancel* it, Salvio, or it won't look like I'm committed. Like I'm only playing at being on the board just because I'm your wife.'

A smile played around the edges of his lips as he got up and moved towards her, his dark eyes glittering with an expression she knew so well. 'Which means you'll just have to be patient and wait for me to get back, *mia sposa*, even though it means you'll be without me for four whole nights. In fact, just thinking about it makes me want to kiss you.'

A kiss quickly turned into Molly being carried into their bedroom with a demonstration of that effortless mastery which still dazzled her, no matter how many times it happened. She loved the way he impatiently removed the clothes he'd only just put on and the way he explored her body as if he had just stumbled across a newly discovered treasure. She loved the warm skin-to-skin contact with this man as they tumbled hungrily onto the bed. She loved him, she suddenly realised, as he plunged deep inside her. She just couldn't help herself.

She was still feeling faintly dizzy with pleasure when Salvio returned from the shower wearing the lazy smile of the satisfied predator, and she watched him as he began to dress. 'You are insatiable,' she observed.

'And don't you just hate it?' he mocked, picking up his tie and walking over to the mirror to knot it.

She hardly ever noticed his almost imperceptible limp but she noticed it today—and something about the contrast of frailty and strength which existed in his

powerful body stirred a memory in her which she had
unwittingly stored away.

'Salvio?'

He stared at her reflected image in the glass. 'Mmm…?'

She hesitated. 'You remember our wedding day?'

'I'm hardly likely to forget it, am I?' he questioned
drily. 'And even if I had, it wouldn't be a diplomatic
thing to admit after a mere three months of marriage.
What about it?'

'Well.' His response didn't sound very promising
but Molly forced herself to continue. 'I was wondering
whether your charitable organisation ought to include
some kind of football sponsorship, which I notice it
doesn't do at the moment.'

'Some kind of football sponsorship?' he repeated
slowly.

'Yes. You know—you could offer a financial scheme
for a promising young player from a poor background.'
Again, she hesitated. 'To help the type of boy you once
were,' she finished, on a rush.

There was a pause while he finished knotting his tie
and when he spoke, his voice was cool. 'But I don't have
anything to do with football any more, Molly. You know
that. I walked away from that life many years ago.'

'Yes, I know you did. But things have moved on now.
You saw all those people wearing your old club's colours who came to wish you luck on your wedding day.
They…they love you, Salvio. You're a legend to them
and I just thought it would be…nice…' Her words faded
away. 'To give something back.'

'Oh, did you?' Moving away from the mirror, Salvio

swept his gaze over his wife, who looked all pink-cheeked and tousled as she lay amid the rumpled mess they'd just made of the bed. A muscle began to work in his cheek. He'd thought that, given her previous occupation, she would have been a rather more compliant partner than she was turning out to be. He'd thought it a generous gesture to give her a seat on the board of his charity and had expected her to be grateful to him for that. But he'd imagined her turning up regularly at meetings and sitting there quietly—not to suddenly start dishing out advice. Surely she, more than anyone, must have realised it was inappropriate as well as unwanted? 'I really don't think it's your place to start advising me on how I spend my money, Molly,' he drawled.

She went very still. 'Not *my place*?' she echoed, the colour leeching from her face and her dark lashes blinking in disbelief. 'Why not? Do you think the one-time servant should remain mute and just go along with what she's been told, rather than ever showing any initiative of her own? Are you making out like there's still all those inequalities between us, despite the fact that I now wear your ring?'

'There's no need to overreact,' he said coolly, even though that was exactly what he *did* think. 'And I really don't want an argument when I'm just about to fly to the States. We'll talk about it when I get back.' He dipped his head towards her with a smile she always found irresistible. 'Now kiss me.'

Knowing it would be childish to turn her face away, Molly attempted a close approximation of a fond kiss, but inside she was seething as the door of the apartment slammed shut behind her departing husband. She felt as if the pink cloud she'd been floating on since the day they'd wed had suddenly turned black. Was it because, behind all the outward appearances of a relatively blissful new marriage, nothing much had changed? Despite him giving her a seat on the board of his charity, it seemed she wasn't allowed to have any ideas of her own. She might be wearing his shiny gold wedding band but at that precise moment she felt exactly like the servant she'd always been. And there was another pressure, too. One she hadn't dared to acknowledge— not even to herself, let alone to Salvio.

Gloomily, she got out of bed and went to stare out of the window, where there was no sign of new life. They were already into April but spring seemed to have been put on hold by the harsh weather. Even the daffodils in the planters on Salvio's roof terrace had been squashed by the unseasonable dump of snow which had ground the city to a halt for the last few days.

No sign of life in her either.

Her hands floating down to her belly, she prayed that this month she might get the news she was longing for, even though the low ache inside her hinted at an alternative scenario. She linked her manicured fingers together, dreading another month of unspoken disappointment. Of cheerfully convincing herself it would happen eventually. Of wondering how long she could continue walking this precarious tightrope of a marriage which had only taken place because her wealthy husband wanted an heir. Because what if she *couldn't* conceive? She'd been pregnant once, yes, but there was no guarantee it would happen again. Life didn't provide guarantees like that, did it?

Forcing herself to get on with the day, she showered and dressed—slithering into a dress she wouldn't have dared to wear a few months ago, even if she could have afforded to. But her body shape had changed since living with Salvio—and not just because she'd checked out the basement gym in this luxury apartment block and discovered she liked it. She ate proper regular meals now because her Neapolitan husband's love of good food meant that he wasn't a great fan of snacks, and as a consequence she was in the best shape of her adult life.

She took a cab to her charity lunch, which was being held in the ballroom of one of the capital's smartest hotels and was today awarding acts of bravery involving animals as well as humans. She particularly enjoyed hearing about the kitten who had been rescued from the top of a chimney pot by a nineteen-year-old university drop-out who had previously been terrified of heights. She chatted to him afterwards and he told her that he'd decided he was going to train as a vet, and Molly felt a warm glow of pleasure as she listened to his story.

She was just chopping vegetables for a stir-fry when Salvio rang from Los Angeles, telling her he missed her and, although she wanted to believe him, she found herself wondering if he was just reading from a script. It was easy to say those sorts of things when he was thousands of miles away, when the reality was that he'd made her feel she'd stepped out of line this morning just because she'd dared express an opinion of her own.

Well, maybe it was time to stop drifting around in a

half-world of pretence and longing. She would sit him down when he returned from his trip and they would talk honestly because, even though the truth could hurt, it was better to know where you stood. And even though her stupid heart was screaming out its objections she couldn't keep putting it off. She would ask him if he really wanted to continue with the marriage and maybe it was better to confront that now, before there *was* a baby.

But then something happened. Something which changed everything.

It started with an email from her brother which arrived on the day Salvio was due to return from America. Robbie was notoriously unreliable at keeping in touch and she hadn't heard from him since the wedding, even though she'd sent several lovely photos of him dancing with one of Salvio's distant cousins at the reception. She hadn't even mentioned the loan he'd asked her husband for—deciding it was an issue best settled between him and Salvio.

So her smile was one of pleasure when she saw new mail from Robbie Miller, which had pinged into her inbox overnight, with the subject line: Have you seen this?

'This' turned out to be an attachment of an article taken from a newspaper website. An American newspaper, as it happened. And there, in sharp Technicolor detail, was a photograph of her husband, sitting outside some flower-decked restaurant with a beautiful blonde, the sapphire glitter of a sunlit sea in the background.

Her fingers clawed at the mouse as she scrolled down the page but somehow Molly knew who Salvio's companion was before she'd read a single word. Was it the woman's poise which forewarned her, or simply the way she leaned towards Salvio's handsome profile with the kind of intimacy which was hard-won? Her heart clenched with pain as she scanned the accompanying prose.

Heartthrob property tycoon Salvio De Gennaro was pictured enjoying the sea air in Malibu today.

Newly wed to former maid Molly Miller, in a lavish ceremony which took place in the groom's native Naples, the Italian billionaire still found time to catch up with ex-fiancée Lauren Meyer.

With the ink barely dry on her divorce papers, perhaps heiress Lauren was advising Salvio on some of the pitfalls of marriage.

Either that, or the Californian wine was just too good to resist...

Hands shaking, Molly stared at the screen, closing her eyes in a futile bid to quell the crippling spear of jealousy which lanced through her like a hot blade, but it was still there when she opened them again, her gaze caught by the glitter of the diamonds at her finger. The diamonds she had once compared to tears, rather than rain. But there were real tears now. Big ones which were splashing onto her trembling fingers. Pushing her chair away from the desk, her vision was blurred as blindly she stumbled into the bedroom. She rubbed her fists into her eyes but the stupid tears just kept on flowing, even though deep down she knew she had no right to feel sorrow. Because it wasn't as if theirs was a *real* relationship, was it? She had no right to be jealous of a husband who had never loved her, did she? Not really. It had only ever been a marriage of convenience—providing each of them with what they wanted.

Or rather, what she'd *thought* she'd wanted... Security and passion with a man she'd begun to care for and, ultimately, a family of her own. Only now the truth hit her with a savage blow as she forced herself to acknowledge what it was she *really* wanted. Not the fancy penthouse or the different homes dotted all around the globe. Not the platinum credit card with its obscene spending limit.

She wanted Salvio's love, she realised—and that was just a wish too far. He didn't do love—at least, not with her. But he *had* loved Lauren. And try as she might, she just couldn't put a positive spin on his reunion with his ex-fiancée in that sunny and glamorous Malibu setting. For the first time in her life she was right out of optimistic options.

There were no tears left to cry as she walked across the bedroom, but she was filled with a strange new sense of calm as she opened up the wardrobe and took out her battered old suitcase, knowing what she intended to do.

She would do the brave thing.

The right thing.

The only thing.

'Molly?' Salvio frowned as he walked into an apartment which instinct told him was empty. Yet he'd texted her to tell her he was on his way home and he'd assumed she would be waiting with that soft smile which always greeted him when he arrived home from work. 'Molly?' he called again, even though the word echoed redundantly through the quiet apartment.

He found the note quickly, as he had obviously been intended to. One of those brief notes which managed to say so little and yet so much, in just a few stark words. And sitting on top of it was her diamond ring.

Salvio.
I've seen the newspaper article about you and Lauren and I want to do the best thing, so I'm staying in a hotel until I can get a job sorted out.
I'll send you my address when I have one, so you can instruct your lawyers.
*It's been an amazing experience, so thank you for everything. And...*in bocca al lupo.

Crushing the note in an angry fist, he strode over to the computer and saw the article immediately, reading it with a growing sense of disbelief before cursing long and loud into the empty air. Why hadn't any of his staff alerted him to this? Because his assistant had been instructed to treat gossip columns with the contempt they deserved, by ignoring them. He stared at the photo, thinking that whoever said the camera didn't lie must have been delusional. Because it did. Big-time.

He saw Lauren's finely etched profile and the angled bones of her shoulder blades. Her long blonde hair was waving gently in the breeze and she was leaning forward with an earnest expression on her face. It must have been taken just before his response had made her delicate features crumple and her blue eyes darken with disbelief.

Pulling the phone from his pocket, he found Molly's number and hit the call button, unsurprised when it went straight to voicemail over and over again, and his mouth hardened. Did she think she could just walk out on him, leaving nothing but that banal little note?

Scrolling down, he found another number he used only very infrequently. His voice lowered as he began to speak in rapid Neapolitan dialect, biting out a series of terse demands before finally cutting the connection.

CHAPTER THIRTEEN

MOLLY STARED AT the richly embossed walls of the fancy hotel and the dark red lilies which were massed in a silver vase. She'd chosen the five-star Vinoly because she'd heard Salvio mention it, but as from tomorrow she would start searching for somewhere cheaper to stay. No way was she going to try to cling to the high-life she'd enjoyed during her brief tenure as his wife, because that life was over and she needed to get used to it.

The phone rang but she didn't need to look down to see who was calling. Salvio. Again. After yet another brief internal tussle she chose to ignore it, just like she'd avoided reading the texts he'd been sending. Because what was the point in hearing anything he had to say? What if his smooth weasel words tempted her back into his arms and the guarantee of heartbreak? She didn't want to hear excuses or half-truths. She wanted to preserve her sanity, even if her heart had to break in the process.

But first she needed to start looking for a job. A live-in job she could practically do with her eyes closed. She would sign up with an agency in the morning and tell them she wanted a fresh start. Somewhere she'd never been before—like Scotland, or Wales. Somewhere new so she could be completely anonymous while licking her wounds and trying to forget that for one brief shining moment she'd been the wife of a man who...

She bit her lip.

A man she'd fallen in love with, despite all her best efforts to remain immune to him.

But Salvio hadn't wanted her love. Only Lauren's. She swallowed. Was the beautiful heiress willing to give Salvio a second chance? Was that the reason behind their secret liaison when they'd been making eyes at one another in the Californian sunshine?

She didn't feel hungry but she hadn't eaten anything since breakfast and she always used to tell Robbie that your brain couldn't function properly unless you kept it nourished. Ordering a cheese omelette from room service, she thought about her brother. She hadn't replied to his email, mainly because she couldn't think of anything to say. Not yet, anyway. She wondered if he'd acted out of the goodness of his heart. If sending the proof of Salvio's clandestine meeting was a brotherly intervention to protect her from potential hurt. Or had Robbie been motivated by spite—because his wealthy new brother-in-law had refused to give him the loan he'd wanted?

She paced the room, unable to settle. Unable to shift the dark features of her husband from her mind and wondering whether she would ever be able to forget this interlude. Or to—

Her thoughts were interrupted by a loud rap on the door.

'Who is it?' Molly called out sharply.

'Room service!'

She opened the door to the woman's voice, her heart crashing against her ribcage when she saw Salvio standing there, holding a tray dominated by a silver dome. In the distance was the retreating view of a hotel employee, who'd obviously been rewarded for allowing this bizarre role-reversal to take place. Which was exactly what it felt like. Salvio in a subservient role holding a tray, and her opening the door of some swanky hotel room. Except he didn't stay subservient for very long.

'Step aside, Molly,' he clipped out.

'You can't come in.'

'Just try stopping me.'

She didn't dare. She'd never seen him look so determined as he stormed into her room. There was a clatter as he slammed the tray down and Molly shuddered to think what damage he must have inflicted on her cheese omelette. Not that she wanted it any more. How could she possibly have eaten anything when she could barely breathe?

He turned round and she was taken aback by the fury which was darkening his imposing features into an unrecognisable mask. 'Well, Molly?' he snarled.

'Well, what?' she retorted. 'How did you find me?'

'You booked this room with our joint credit card.'

'And?'

'And therefore you were traceable. I had one of my contacts look into it for me.'

She screwed up her brow. 'Isn't that…illegal?'

He shrugged. 'When a man wishes to find his errant wife then surely he will use whatever means are available to him.'

'Well, you've wasted your time because there's nothing to say!'

'I disagree. There's plenty to say, and we're having this out right now.'

And suddenly Molly knew she couldn't let him take over and dominate this situation by the sheer force of his indomitable character. Yes, he was powerful, rich and successful, but she was his wife. His *equal*, despite the inequality of their assets. That was what she'd vowed to be when she had agreed to marry him, but somewhere along the way her resolve had slipped. Was that because the more she'd started to care for him, the harder she had found it to assert herself?

Well, not any more. She needed to make it plain that, although she might not have anything of material value, she valued *herself*. And she would not allow Salvio De Gennaro to make a fool of her, or for her heart to be slowly broken by a man who was incapable of emotion.

'I saw the article from the American newspaper.'

'I know you did. Your brother sent it to you.'

'Did you find *that* out illegally, too?' she scorned.

'No, Molly. You left your computer open.'

'Well, if you'd looked a little harder you'd have seen that I also did a room search for the Vinoly hotel,' she said triumphantly. 'Which wouldn't have involved getting someone to snoop on me!'

Unexpectedly, he sighed and a sudden weariness

touched the corners of his dark eyes as he looked at her. 'What do you think I did in Los Angeles, Molly?' he questioned tiredly. 'Do you think I had sex with Lauren?'

A spear of pain shot through her. 'Did you?'

He winced as he raked his fingers back through his jet-dark hair. 'No, I did not. She heard I was in town and got in touch with me and I agreed to meet her for lunch.'

'Why?'

'Why?' He gave an odd smile. 'I thought it made sense to put away the past for good.'

'Only I suppose she'd suddenly realised the stupid mistake she'd made in letting you go?' accused Molly sarcastically.

He shrugged. 'Something like that. She is recently divorced. She asked for another chance.'

'And you said?'

There was silence for a moment and Molly actually thought that her heartbeat had grown audible—until she realised that the silver clock was thumping out the hour.

'I said I was in love with my wife,' he said simply. 'Only I'd been too stupid to show her how much.'

She shook her head, not believing him. Not believing he would ever admit to love *or* stupidity. 'I don't believe you,' she whispered.

'I know you don't and maybe I deserve that.' He hesitated, like someone who was learning the words of a new language. 'I know that at times I've been cold and difficult.'

'It isn't that, Salvio! It's the fact that you're completely backtracking on everything you said. You told me you didn't *do* love. Not any more. Remember? That you'd loved Lauren and after you broke up, you'd closed off your heart. And if that *was* true—if you really *did* love her like you claim—then how come it has all just died? Is love only a temporary thing, Salvio—which changes like the moon?'

Deeply admiring of her logic at such an intense moment, Salvio took a deep breath. He felt as if he were on a platform in front of a thousand people, about to make the most important speech of his life. And he was. But not to a thousand people. To one. To Molly. The only one who really mattered.

And his whole future hinged on it.

'I thought I loved Lauren because that's how I felt at the time,' he said, in a low voice. 'And surely it is a kind of treachery to deny the feelings we once had? That would be like trying to rewrite history.' There was a pause. 'But I see now it wasn't real love—it was a complex mixture of other stuff which I was too immature to understand.'

'What kind of stuff?' she questioned, as his voice tailed off.

'It was more to do with a young man who wanted to conquer the elusive,' he admitted. 'A man who for a while became someone he wasn't. Someone blinded by an ideal, rather than a real person—and Lauren *was* that ideal. And then I met you, Molly. The most real person in the world. You charmed me. Disarmed me. You crept beneath my defences before I even realised what was happening. You made me feel good—you still do—and not just in the obvious way. It's like I'm the best version of myself whenever you're around. Like I can achieve anything—even if my instinct is to fight against it every inch of the way, because there's a part of me which doesn't really believe that I deserve to be this happy.'

'Salvio—'

'No. Please. Let me finish,' he said and his voice was shaking now. 'You need to understand that all this is true, because there is no way I would say it if it wasn't.' His black eyes raked over her. '*Do* you believe me, Molly? That I would walk to the ends of the earth for you and further, if that's what you wanted? And that I love you in a way I've never loved before?'

Molly stared into the molten darkness of his eyes, but she didn't have to give it a lot of thought, because she did believe him. She could read it in the tender curve of his lips, even if he hadn't uttered those quietly fervent words which had rung so true. But if they were shining a spotlight on their relationship then they couldn't allow any more shadows to lurk in unexplored corners, and she needed the courage to confront what was still troubling her.

'But what about the baby?' she whispered.

'What baby?' he said gently. 'Are you trying to tell me you're pregnant?'

'I don't know. I don't think so. But that's the whole point. What if…?' She swallowed. 'What if, for some reason, I can't give you the child you long for?'

'Then we will go to the best doctors to find out why, or we will adopt. It's not a deal-breaker, Molly. Not even a deal-maker. Not any more. I want you. *You.* That's all.'

That's all? Molly blinked as for the first time she re-alised that Salvio De Gennaro was truly captivated by her. Her! A flush of pleasure heated her skin and maybe someone else in her position might have briefly revelled in her newly discovered power. But this wasn't about power. It was about love and equality. About consideration and respect. About loyalty and truth.

It was about them.

She smiled, the happiness swelling up in her heart making it feel as if it were about to burst open. 'I believe you,' she said softly. 'And I love you. So much. I think I've always loved you, Salvio De Gennaro, and I know I always will.'

'Then you'd better come here and kiss me,' he said, in a voice which sounded pretty close to breaking. 'And convince me that this is for real.'

EPILOGUE

SALVIO STARED AT the lights as he lay back contentedly. Rainbow-coloured lights which jostled for space among all the glittering baubles which hung from the Christmas tree. Behind the tree glittered the Bay of Naples and, inside the main reception room of their newly purchased home, he lay naked next to his beautiful Molly on a vast velvet sofa which had been chosen for precisely this kind of activity.

'Happy?' he murmured, one hand idly teasing her bare nipple while his lips lazily caressed the soft silk of her hair.

'Happy?' She nuzzled into his neck. 'So happy I can't even put it into words.'

'Well, try.'

Molly traced her finger over the loud rhythm of her husband's heart. Next door their ten-month-old son Marco lay sleeping—getting as much rest as possible in preparation for the excitement of his first Christmas. And this year, everyone was coming to *them*. Salvio's parents would be arriving later for the traditional Eve of Christmas feast. And so would Robbie, who was currently meeting the parents of Salvio's cousin, who he had recently started dating. Molly prayed he wouldn't let anyone down—most of all himself—but she was hopeful that her brother had finally sorted himself out. Much of it was down to Salvio and the well-intentioned but stern advice he had delivered. He'd told Robbie he would support him through college, but only if he kicked his gambling habit for good.

And he seemed to have done just that. Molly had never seen her brother looking so bright-eyed or *hopeful*. It was as if a heavy burden had been lifted from his strong, young shoulders. Was it the presence of a powerful male role model which had been the making of him?

In the very early days of her pregnancy, she'd persuaded Salvio that his London penthouse apartment was no place for a baby and he had surprised her by agreeing. So they'd moved into his sprawling Cotswold manor house where she had fun envisaging Marco and his siblings playing in those vast and beautiful gardens. Salvio had also bought this sea-view home in Naples where they tried to spend as much time as possible.

She sighed against the warmth of his skin. 'You make me so happy,' she whispered. 'I never thought I could feel this way.'

He stroked his fingers through her hair. 'It's because I love you, Molly. You're so easy to love.'

'And so are you. At least, you are *now*,' she added darkly.

He laughed. 'Was I such a terrible man before?'

'Terrible,' she agreed, mock-seriously. 'But terribly sexy too.'

'Are you angling for more sex, Signora De Gennaro?'

'There isn't time, darling. I've got to oversee last-minute preparations for tonight's dinner because there's a lot of pressure when you're cooking for your in-laws for the first time.' She frowned. 'And I'm worried I'm going to ruin the *capitone*.'

His fingertips tiptoed over her belly. 'You're not going anywhere until you tell me you love me.'

'I love you. I love you more than I ever thought possible. I love that you're a brilliant father and husband and brother-in-law and son. I love the fact that you've opened a football academy here in Naples and are giving a chance to poor boys with a dream in their hearts. How's that? Is that enough?'

'Curiously, it leaves me wanting more,' he growled. 'But then you always do.'

'More of wh-what?' she questioned unsteadily, as his hand moved towards her quivering thigh.

'More of this.' He smiled as he found her wet heat and stroked, enjoying her soft moan of pleasure.

'But, Salvio, there isn't time,' she said, her eyes growing smoky as he continued his feather-light teasing. 'What about the *capitone*?'

And then Salvio said something which, as a good Neapolitan, he had never imagined himself saying— but in the circumstances, perhaps was understandable. He pulled her on top of him and touched her parted lips with his own. 'Stuff the *capitone*,' he growled.

* * * * *

REVENGE
AT THE ALTAR

LOUISE FULLER

To the Nell, for holding my hand on the plane
and not cutting your hair!

All my love.

CHAPTER ONE

As THE WHEELS OF her private jet hit the runway Margot Duvernay looked up from her laptop and gazed pensively out of the window, her fingers twisting at the 'Team Bride' wristband on her arm.

As CEO of the legendary House of Duvernay champagne business, she worked hard. The last five years had been particularly challenging, both emotionally and financially—so much so that, incredibly, Gisele's bachelorette week in Monte Carlo was the first time off she'd had in months.

But her father Emile's unexpected message had abruptly cut short her stay.

Walking purposefully across the T tarmac, she climbed into the waiting air-conditioned limousine and pulled out her phone. She replayed his message, frowning at the giggling and the Bossa Nova music she could hear in the background. If only she had picked it up sooner, she thought regretfully, her soft brown eyes creasing. Emile was just so unreliable, and so easily distracted...

But on the plus side he had definitely mentioned *selling* his shares, and that was a first.

Leaning back against the seat, she watched as the beautiful mansard-roofed headquarters of her family's two-hundred-and-fifty-year-old business came into view, feeling a familiar mix of pride and responsibility. She loved everything about the building—the cool, quiet interior, the sense of history in the wood-panelled boardroom and the symmetry of the façade. To her, it was more than just bricks and plaster. It was a legacy—and also a burden.

Just like the position of CEO.

Margot breathed out slowly.

Growing up, she had never imagined being in charge of Duvernay—never once wanted the power or the responsibility. By nature, she loathed being in the spotlight, and after graduating she'd been happy to head up the company's newly created environmental department.

However, her older brother Yves's tragic death on the ski slopes of Verbier had left her with no alternative but to take over the family business. Of course, Emile would have liked the status of running a global brand. But even if he hadn't been cold-shouldered by his in-laws, he preferred topping up his tan to analyzing market trends. Her brother Louis might have been taller than her, but at just sixteen he had been far too young to step up, and her grandfather had been too old, too devastated by grief. It had been hard enough for him to deal with his daughter's accidental drug overdose, but the shock of losing his grandson too had caused a series of strokes from which he had still not fully recovered.

And so it had been left to Margot to do what she had always done—pick up the pieces—and that was why she was hurrying back to Epernay this morning.

Inside the brightly lit foyer, the reassuring familiarity of everything calmed her slightly, but as she stepped into the lift her phone began to vibrate in her hand and she felt her composure wobble. Glancing down at the screen, she drew in a quick, shaky breath and her heart began to pound with a mixture of hope and relief.

Thank goodness! Finally it was her father.

'Emile. I was just about to call you—'

'Really? I thought you might be sulking.'

Gritting her teeth, Margot felt a spasm of irritation. Honestly, her father was so exasperating, and so monumentally thoughtless sometimes. When he hadn't returned her messages she had started to panic, to worry that maybe he'd changed his mind. Clearly, though, he'd just been playing hard to get.

But now she could hear the elation in his voice and suddenly she didn't care about his stupid games. What mattered was that she knew he'd been telling the truth. Finally he was ready to sell the shares.

Her heart began to beat faster.

The timing couldn't be better.

Not only would it mean that the business would be whole again in time for her brother Louis's wedding, it would also give her grandfather a much-needed boost. Since his last stroke he hadn't been himself, but this would be the perfect tonic. For this wedding was more than just a romantic ceremony—it was about continuing the family name and ensuring the future of Duvernay.

She felt her chest tighten. And, of course, for her, buying back her father's shares would have an additional and thankfully undisclosed benefit of sending a strong message to the bank.

'Oh, Papa.' Her father was such a child, but today of all days she was prepared to indulge him, and so, despite her annoyance, she spoke placatingly. 'You know I've been trying to get hold of you. I must have rung you at least a dozen times.'

She felt a rush of excitement as she played back her father's rambling message inside her head. He'd mentioned something about flying up to Reims, but that had been hours ago. She glanced at her watch. Surely he must be here by now?

Her mouth was suddenly almost too dry to get words out. 'Where are you staying? I can come to you, or I can send a car to pick you up.'

Her pulse accelerated. She couldn't believe it. Finally it was happening. The moment she'd been waiting for almost her whole life.

Buying back the 'lost' shares, as her grandfather referred to them, was a goal that had preoccupied her since she'd taken over the reins of the business. In doing so, she would not only make Duvernay whole again, she would also bring closure to the whole sorry complex mess of her parents' marriage and the repercussions that had followed her mother's tragic death.

She felt her pulse tremble.

Her father and her grandparents had always had a fraught relationship. Emile might look like a film star, but to them he was just a horse trainer—eloping with their nineteen-year-old daughter had not endeared him to her straitlaced and image-conscious family. His decision to live off Colette's trust fund had merely deepened the rift.

But after her death, it had been his refusal to turn over her shares to his children that had turned a difficult relationship into a bitter stand-off.

Emile had always claimed it was an act of self-preservation. Her grandparents had seen it as an act of spite. Either way, the facts were undeniable. Her father had threatened to take her and her brothers to Switzerland if he wasn't allowed to hold on to the shares, and her grandfather had agreed to his demands on two conditions: that he give up custody of his children to his in-laws and that they keep their mother's name.

Margot shivered. Once she had thought that grief might

bring the two sides of her family closer. In fact the reverse had happened. There was still such bad blood between Emile and his in-laws that even now they both took every opportunity to point-score.

But maybe now that might finally change.

The thought made her heart leap upwards. It would just be so wonderful to put all of this behind them before Louis's wedding. Her first task, though, was to pin Emile down…

'Papa?' she repeated, trying to sound casual. 'Just tell me where you'd like to meet.'

'That's why I'm calling—'

His voice had changed. He sounded a little uneasy—defiant, almost—and briefly she wondered why. But before she had a chance to give it any more thought he started talking again.

'I did try, so you can't blame me— Not now, *chérie*, put it over there. I waited as long as I could…'

Hearing a soft but unmistakably feminine murmur, Margot frowned. Even now her father couldn't manage to give her his full and undivided attention. Her mouth thinned. No doubt he was already celebrating the upcoming sale of his shares with his current batch of hangers-on.

And then her heartbeat froze, and she felt her fingers tighten involuntarily around the phone as his words bumped into one another inside her head like dodgems at the funfair. 'Blame you for what?'

'I waited as long as I could, *poussin*, but it was such a good offer—'

His use of her childhood nickname as much as his wheedling tone sent a ripple of alarm over her skin. Her father only ever called her *poussin*—little chick—when he wanted something or when he wanted to be forgiven.

'What offer?' she said slowly.

The lift doors opened and she stepped out into the glass-ceilinged atrium. Straight ahead, she noticed her PA hovering nervously in front of her office door, and her heart gave a sickening thump.

'What have you done, Papa?'

'I've done what I should have done a long time ago.' The wheedling tone had shifted, become defensive. 'So I hope you're not going to make a fuss, Margot. I mean, it's what you've been telling me to do for years—sell my shares. And now I have. And I have to say I got a damn good price for them too.'

It was as if a bomb had exploded inside her head. Blood was roaring in her ears and the floor seemed to ripple beneath her feet.

'You said that if you were going to sell your shares you'd come to me first.' Margot felt panic, hot and slippery, run down her spine.

'And I did.' There was a burst of laughter in the background and she felt her father's attention shift and divert away from her. 'But you didn't pick up.'

'I couldn't. I was having a massage.' She let out a breath. 'Look, Papa, we can sort this out. Just don't sign anything, okay? Just stay where you are and I will come to you.'

'It's too late now. I signed the paperwork first thing this morning. And I *mean* first thing. He got me out of bed,' he grumbled. 'Anyway, there's no point in getting out of shape with me—just talk to *him*. He should be there by now.'

'Who—?' she began, but even without the tell-tale clink of ice against glass she could tell her father was no longer listening.

She heard the click of his lighter, then the slow expulsion of smoke. 'Apparently that's why it all had to be done so early. He wanted to get up to Epernay…take a look around headquarters.'

Margot gazed dazedly across the honey-coloured parquet floor. No wonder her staff were looking so confused. Clearly the newest Duvernay shareholder was already on site. But who was he—and what had he told them?

Her pulse stuttered in time with her footsteps. There were already enough rumours circulating around the company as it was—and what would the bank think if they heard that Emile had suddenly decided to sell his shares?

Silently she cursed herself for not picking up her messages—and her father for being so utterly, irredeemably selfish.

'It'll be fine,' Emile was saying briskly.

Now that the worst was over he was clearly itching to be gone.

'You're so rational and practical, *poussin*.'

She could almost see him shuddering even at the concept of such qualities.

'Just talk to him. Maybe you can persuade him to sell them back to you.'

He was desperate to be off. If Margot had been the sort to scream or hurl abuse she would have unleashed the tide of invective churning in her throat. But she wasn't. A lifetime of watching the soap opera that had been her parents' marriage had cured her of any desire for a scene. For a moment, though, she considered telling Emile in the most *ir*rational, *im*practical terms exactly what she thought of him.

Only, really, what was the point? Her father's 'me first' morality was precisely why he'd kept the shares in the first place.

'Although somehow I doubt it…'

Her father exhaled again, and she pictured him stubbing out his cigarette with the same careless force with which he had upended her dreams of taking back control of Duvernay.

'He seemed absolutely set on having them. But, truthfully, I think I might have done you a favour. I mean, he *is* the man of the moment, right?'

The man of the moment.

Margot blinked. Her brain was whirling, her thoughts flying in a hundred directions. She had read that headline. Not the article, for that would have been too painful. But, walking through the centre of Paris last month, she had found it impossible to tear her gaze away from the newsstands. Or more particularly the head-and-shoulders shot that had accompanied the article, and those eyes—one blue, one green—staring down the Champs-Élysées as if he owned it.

'Man of the moment?'

Her voice sounded blurred, shapeless—like a candle flame that had burnt the whole wick and was floundering in wax.

'Yeah—Max Montigny. They say he can turn water into wine, so I guess he'll give those stuffy vignerons a run for their money— Yeah, I'll be right there.'

Margot tried to speak, but her breath was thick and tangled in her throat. 'Papa—' she began, but it was too late. He was talking over her.

'Look, call me later—well, maybe not later, but whenever. I love you, but I have to go—'

The phone went dead.

But not as dead as she felt.

Max Montigny.

It had been almost ten years since she'd last seen him. Ten years of trying to pretend their relationship, his lies, her heartbreak, that none of it had happened. And she'd done a pretty good job, she thought dully.

Of course it had helped that only Yves had ever known the full story. To everyone else Max had been at first a trusted employee, and later a favoured friend of the family.

To her, though, he had been a fantasy made flesh. With smooth dark hair, a profile so pure it looked as though it had been cut with a knife, and a lean, muscular body that hummed with energy, he had been like a dark star that seemed to tug at all her five senses whenever she was within his orbit.

Only as far as he was concerned Margot had been invisible. No, maybe not invisible. He *had* noticed her, but only in the same jokey way that her own brother had—smiling at her off-handedly as he joined the family for dinner, or casually offering to drive her into town when it was raining.

And then one day, instead of looking through her, he had stared at her so intently she had forgotten to breathe, forgotten to look away.

Remembering that moment, the impossibility of not holding his gaze, her cheeks felt suddenly as though they were on fire.

She had been captivated by him, enthralled and enchanted. She would have followed him blindly into darkness, and in a way she had—for she had gone into his arms and to his bed, given herself to him willingly, eagerly.

From then on he had been everything to her. Her man of the moment. Her man for ever.

Until the day he'd broken her heart and walked out of her life without so much as a flicker of remorse in those haunting eyes.

Afterwards, the pain had been unbearable. Feigning illness, she'd stayed in bed for days, curled up small and still beneath her duvet, chest aching with anguish, throat tight with tears she hadn't allowed herself to weep for fear that her grandfather would notice.

But now was not the time for tears either and, swallowing the hard shard of misery in her throat, Margot greeted her PA with what she hoped was a reasonable approximation of her usual composure.

'Good morning, Simone.'

'Good morning, *madame*.' Simone hesitated. Colour was creeping over her cheekbones and she seemed flustered. 'I'm sorry, I didn't know you were coming in today. But he—Mr Montigny, I mean—he said you were expecting him.'

Smiling, Margot nodded. So it was true. Just for a moment she had hoped—wanted to believe that she had somehow misunderstood Emile. But this was confirmation. Max was here.

'I hope that's okay…?'

Her PA's voice trailed off and Margot felt her own cheekbones start to ache with the effort of smiling. Poor Simone! Her normally poised PA looked flushed and jumpy. But then no doubt she'd been a recent recipient of the famous but sadly superficial Montigny charm.

'Yes, it's fine, Simone. And it's my fault—I should have called ahead. Is he in my office?'

She felt a stab of anger. Max had only been back in her life for a matter of minutes and already she was lying for him.

Simone shook her head, her confusion giving way to obvious relief. 'No, he said that he would like to see the boardroom. I didn't think it would be a problem…'

Margot kept smiling but she felt a sudden savage urge to cry, to rage against the injustice and cruelty of it all. If only she could be like any other normal young woman, like Gisele and her friends, drinking cocktails and flirting with waiters.

But crying and raging was not the Duvernay way—or at least, not in public—and instead she merely nodded again. 'It's not. In fact, I'll go and give him the full guided tour myself.'

Straight out the door and out of my life, she thought savagely.

Turning, she walked towards the boardroom, her eyes fixed on the polished brass door handle. If only she could just keep on walking. Only what would be the point? Max Montigny wasn't here by chance. Nor was he just going to give up and disappear. Like it or not, the only way she was going to turn him back into being nothing more than a painful memory was by confronting him.

And, lifting her chin, she turned the door handle and stepped into the boardroom.

She saw him immediately, and although she had expected to feel *something*, nothing could have prepared her for the rush of despair and regret that swept over her.

It was nearly ten years since he had walked out of her life. Ten years was a long time, and everyone said that time was a great healer. But if that was true why, then, was her body trembling? And why did her heart feel like a lead weight?

Surely he shouldn't matter to her any more? But, seeing him again, she felt the same reaction she had that first time, aged just nineteen. That he couldn't be real. That no actual living man could be so unutterably beautiful. It wasn't possible or fair.

He was facing away from her, slumped in one of the leather armchairs that were arranged around the long oval table, his long legs sprawled negligently in front of him, seemingly admiring the view from the window.

Her heart was racing, but her legs and arms seemed to have stopped working. Gazing at the back of his head, at the smooth dark hair that she had so loved to caress, she thought she might throw up.

How could this be happening? she thought dully. But that was the wrong question. What she needed to ask—*and answer*—was how could she *stop* it happening? How could she get him out of her boardroom and out of her life?

Letting out a breath, she closed the door and watched, mesmerised, as slowly he swung round in the chair to face her. She stared at him in silence. This was the man who had not only broken her heart, but shattered her pride and her romantic ideals. Once she had loved him. And afterwards she had hated him.

Only clearly her feelings weren't that simple—or maybe she had just forgotten how effortlessly Max could throw her off balance. For although heat was rising up inside her, she knew that it wasn't the arid heat of loathing but something that felt a lot like desire.

Her mouth was suddenly dry, and her heart was beating so fast and so loud that it sounded like a drumroll— as though Max was the winner in some game show. She breathed in sharply. But what was his prize?

Gazing into his eyes—those incredible heterochromatic eyes—she saw herself reflected in the blue and green, no longer nineteen, but still dazzled and dazed.

All those years ago he had been model-handsome, turning heads as easily as he now turned grapes into wine and wine into profit. His straight, patrician jaw and high cheekbones had hinted at a breathtaking adult beauty to come, and that promise had been more than met. A shiver ran through her body. Met, and enhanced by a dark grey suit that seemed purposely designed to draw her gaze to the spectacular body that she knew lay beneath.

Her breath caught in her chest and, petrified that the expression on her face might reveal her thoughts, she pushed aside the unsettling image of a naked Max and forced herself to meet his gaze.

He smiled, and the line of his mouth arrowed through her skin.

'Margot…it's been a long time.'

As he spoke she felt a tingling shock. His voice hadn't changed, and that wasn't fair, for—like his eyes—it was utterly distinctive, and made even the dullest of words sound like spring water. It was just so soft, sexy…

And utterly untrustworthy, she reminded herself irritably. Having been on the receiving end of it, she knew from first-hand experience that the softness was like spun sugar—a clever trick designed to seduce, and to gift-wrap the parcel of lies that came out of his mouth.

'Not long enough,' she said coolly.

Ignoring the heat snaking over her skin, she stalked to the opposite end of the room and dropped her bag on the table. 'Why don't you give it another decade—or two, even?'

He seemed unmoved by her rudeness—or maybe, judging by the slight up-curve to his mouth, a little amused. 'I'm sorry you feel like that. Given the change in our relationship—'

'We don't *have* a relationship,' she snapped.

They never had. It was one of the facts that she'd forced herself to accept over the years—that, no matter how physically close they'd been, Max was a cipher to her. In love, and blindsided by how beautiful, how alive he'd made her feel in bed, she hadn't noticed that there had been none of the prerequisites for a happy, healthy relationship—honesty, openness, trust…

The truth was that she'd never really known him at all.

He, though, had clearly found *her* embarrassingly easy to read. Unsurprisingly! She'd been that most clichéd of adolescents: a clueless teenager infatuated with her brother's best friend. And, of course, her family was not just famous but *in*famous.

Even now, the thought of her being so transparently smitten made her cringe.

'We don't have a relationship,' she repeated. 'And a signature on a piece of paper isn't about to change that.'

His gaze held hers, and a mocking smile tugged at his mouth as he rotated the chair back and forth.

'Really?' He spoke mildly, as though they were discussing the possibility of rain. 'Why don't we call my lawyer? Or yours? See if they agree with that statement.'

Her head snapped up. It was a bonus that Max hadn't spoken to Pierre yet, but the very fact that he was hinting at the possibility of doing so made her throat tighten.

'That won't be necessary. This matter is between you and me.'

'But I thought you said we didn't have any relationship?'

She glared at him, hearing and hating the goading note in his voice.

'We don't. And we won't. I meant that this matter is private, and I intend to keep it that way.'

Max stared coldly across the table. Did she *really* think that he was going to let that happen? That she was in control of this situation.

Nearly a decade ago he had been, if not happy, then willing to keep their relationship under wraps. She had told him she needed time. That she needed to find the right moment to tell her family the truth. And he had let her beauty and her desirability blind him to the real truth—that he was a secret she would never be willing to share.

But he wasn't about to let history repeat itself.

'Are you sure about that? I mean, you know what they say about good intentions, Margot,' he said softly. 'Do you really want to head down that particular road?'

There was a taut, quivering silence, and Margot felt her face drain of colour, felt her body, her heart, shrinking away from his threat.

There's no need! she wanted to shout into his handsome face. *You've already cast me out of heaven and into a hell of your making.*

But she wasn't going to give him the satisfaction of knowing how raw her wounds still were and how much he had mattered to her.

She returned his gaze coldly. 'Are you threatening me?'

Watching the flush of colour spread over her collarbone, Max tilted his head backwards, savouring her fury. He had never seen her angry before—in fact he'd never seen her express any strong emotion.

At least not outside the bedroom.

His pulse twitched and a memory stole into his head of that first time in his room—how the directness of her gaze had held him captive as she had pressed her body against his, her fingers cutting into his back, her breath warm against his mouth.

Margot might have been serious and serene on the surface, but the first time he had kissed her properly had been a revelation. She'd been so passionate and unfettered. In fact, it had been not so much a revelation as a revolution—all heat and hunger and urgency.

Suddenly he was vibrating with a hunger of his own, and he felt heat break out on his skin. Slowly, he slid his hands over the armrests of the chair to stop himself from reaching out and pulling her against him. The muscles in his jaw tensed and he gritted his teeth.

'Only the weak and the incompetent resort to threats.

I'm merely making conversation.' He looked straight into her flushed face. 'You remember conversation, don't you, Margot? It's the thing you used to interrupt by dragging me to bed.'

Margot stared at him, her body pulsing with equal parts longing and loathing. If only she could throw his words back in his face. But it was true. Her desire for him had been frantic and inexorable.

She lifted her chin. So what if it had? Enjoying sex wasn't a crime. And it certainly wasn't sneaky or dishonest—like, say, deliberately setting out to seduce someone for their money.

Eyes narrowing, she yanked out one of the chairs with uncharacteristic roughness and sat down on it. Pulling her bag closer, she reached inside.

Max watched in silence as she pulled out a fountain pen and a leather-bound case. Ignoring him, she flipped it open and began writing with swift, sure strokes. Then, laying the pen down, she tore the paper she'd been writing on free and pushed it across the table towards him.

It was a cheque.

A cheque!

His breathing jerked and his jaw felt suddenly as though it was hewn from basalt. He didn't move, didn't even lower his gaze, just kept his eyes locked on her face as with effort he held on to the fast-fraying threads of his temper.

'What's that?' he asked softly.

Her mouth thinned. 'I don't know how your mind works, Max, and I don't want to, but I know why you're here. It's the same reason you were here ten years ago. *Money.*' Margot gestured towards the cheque. 'So why don't you just take it and go?'

He was watching her thoughtfully, his expression somewhere between incredulous and mocking. But there was a tension in him that hadn't been there before.

'That's amazing,' he said finally. 'I didn't know people actually did this kind of thing in real life. I thought it was just in films—'

'If only this was a film,' she said coldly. 'Then I could just leave you on the cutting room floor.'

Max gazed across the room, anger shrinking his focus so that all he could see was the small rectangular piece of paper lying on the tabletop. Of course it would come down to money. That was all their relationship had ever been about. Or, more precisely, his complete and utter lack of it.

Margot was a Duvernay, and Duvernays didn't marry poor outsiders. His breath seemed to harden in his lungs. Not even when they had claimed them as family, welcomed them into their home and their lives.

Briefly he let the pain and anger of his memories seep through his veins. Officially he might have been just on the payroll, but for nearly three years he had been treated like a member of the clan—and, stupid idiot that he was, he had actually come to believe in the fiction that although blood made you related, it was loyalty that made you family.

Later, when his perception hadn't been blunted by desire and emotion, it had been easy to see that any invitation into the inner sanctum had been on their terms, and it had never extended to marrying the daughter of the house.

Only by then he had lost his job, his home and his pride. He had been left penniless and powerless.

But times had changed. Leaning back, he smiled coldly. 'It's not enough.'

Margot clenched her jaw, her brown eyes glowing with anger like peat on a fire. 'Oh, believe me, it is.'

Even if she had written a row of zeros it would be more

than he deserved. He had already cost her enough—no, too much—in pain and regret.

'So take it and go.'

He shifted in his seat, and she felt another stab of anger that he should be able to do this to her. That after everything he'd already taken he could just swan back into her life, into her boardroom, and demand more.

Controlling her emotions, she closed her chequebook with exaggerated care and looked up at him. 'Why are you here, Max?'

He shrugged. 'Isn't that obvious? I'm a shareholder and a director now, so I thought we should talk.'

'You could have just telephoned,' she snapped.

'What?' His mouth curved up at one corner. 'And miss all the fun.' He let his eyes home in on the pulse beating at the base of her throat. 'Besides, I wanted to choose my office.'

She watched almost hypnotised as he gestured lazily around the room. 'Pick out a desk…wallpaper maybe…'

Folding her arms to stop her hands shaking, she glowered at him. The shock of everything—her father's phone message, Max buying the shares, his sudden and unwelcome reappearance in her life—was suddenly too much to endure a moment longer.

'Just stop it, okay? *Stop it*. This is insane. You can't seriously expect to work here. Or want to.'

He raised an eyebrow. 'Is there a problem?'

She looked at him in disbelief. 'Yes, of course there's a problem. You and me…our history—'

Breaking off, she fought to control the sudden jab of pain at the memory of just how cruelly one-sided that history had been.

'I don't care how many shares you buy, you are not stepping foot in this boardroom again. So how much is it?' She forced a business-like tone into her voice. 'How much do you want?'

She waited for his reply but it didn't come. And then, as the silence seemed to stretch beyond all normal limits, she felt her spine stiffen with horror as slowly he shook his head.

'I don't want and I certainly don't need your money.'

Watching the doubt and confusion in her eyes, he felt suddenly immensely satisfied. Buying the shares had been an act of insanity on so many levels, but now, having Margot in front of him, knowing that his mere presence had dragged her here, it all felt worth it.

Colour was spreading slowly over her cheeks.

'Take the cheque or don't—I don't care.' She lifted her chin. 'But either way this conversation is over. And now I suggest you leave before I have you removed—'

'That's not going to happen.' His voice sounded normal—pleasant, even—but she felt a shiver of apprehension, for there was a strand of steel running through every syllable that matched the combative glint in his eyes.

'I'm not just the hired help now, baby. I'm CEO of a global wine business. More importantly, as of today, I'm a bona fide director of this company.'

He paused, and she felt as if the air was being sucked out of the room as he let his gaze linger on her face. Pulse racing, she realised that only a very foolish woman would underestimate a man like Max Montigny.

'*Your* company.'

He lounged back, and suddenly her heart was thumping against her ribs.

'Although that may be about to change.'

'What do you mean?' Her voice was like a whisper. She cleared her throat. 'What are you talking about?'

He shrugged. 'Right now you might live in the big chateau, have a private jet and a chauffeur-driven limousine, but I've seen your accounts.'

She frowned, started to object, but he simply smiled and she fell silent, for there was something knowing in the gaze that was making her skin start to prickle with fear and apprehension.

'Your father showed them to me. And they make pretty bleak reading. Desperate, in fact. Oh, it all looks good on the outside, but you're haemorrhaging money.'

Margot could feel the colour draining from her face. His words were detonating inside her head like grenades. Suddenly she was deaf, dazed, reeling blindly through the dust and rubble of the mess she had sought so hard to contain, struggling to breathe.

'That's not true,' she said hoarsely. Her lungs felt as though they were being squeezed in a vice. 'We've just had a difficult few months—

'More like five years.' He stared at her for a long moment, his gaze impassive. 'You asked me why I'm here. Well, that's it. That's why. Your family is about to be ruined and I want to be here to see it.'

He stared at her steadily, his eyes straight and unblinking, and Margot stared back at him, stilled, almost mesmerised by his words. 'What are you talking about?'

'I'm talking about retribution. You and your family ruined my life, and now I get to watch your world implode.'

Margot shook her head. Stiffening her shoulders, she forced herself to look him in the eye. 'No, you seduced me, and then you asked me to marry you just so you could get your hands on my money.'

For a moment he didn't reply, then he shrugged, and it was that offhand gesture—the casual dismissal of the way he'd broken her heart—that told her more clearly than any words that he was being serious.

Watching the light fade from Margot's eyes, Max told himself he didn't care. She deserved everything that was coming. They all did.

'And I paid for that. You and your family made sure I lost everything. I couldn't even get a reference. No vineyard would touch me.'

Remembering the shock and helplessness he'd felt in the hours and days following Margot's rejection, he bit down hard, using the pain of the past to block out her pale, stunned face.

'Now it's your turn.'

He leaned back against the leather upholstery, his eyes never leaving hers.

'I only bought shares in your company to get a ringside seat.'

CHAPTER TWO

MARGOT SAT FROZEN, mute with shock, her heart lurching inside her chest like a ship at sea in a storm.

'How dare you?' Blood was drumming in her ears, and her body vibrated with anger and disbelief. 'How dare you stand here in my boardroom and—?'

'Easily.'

She watched in mute horror as Max stood up and, raising his arms above his head, stretched his shoulders and neck. His apparent serenity only exacerbated the anxiety that was hammering against her ribcage.

'And I'll find it easier still to stand in your office and watch the administrators repossess that beautiful custom-made Parnian desk of yours.'

He was walking towards her now, and suddenly her breath was coming thick and fast.

'That won't happen.' She stood up hastily, her gaze locking on his, trying to ignore both the intense maleness of his lean, muscular body and the way her pulse was jumping like a stranded fish in response to it.

'Oh, it will.'

He stopped in front of her, his eyes—those beautiful hypnotic eyes—pinning her to the floor even as her head spun faster.

'Your business is in a mess, baby—a bloated, unstable, debt-ridden mess. House of Duvernay?' His eyes narrowed. 'More like house of straw!'

'And you're the wolf, are you? Come to huff and puff?' she sneered, her gaze colliding with his.

It was the wrong thing to say—not least because there was more than a hint of the wolf about his intense, hostile focus and the restrained power of body. For a moment, she held her breath. But then he smiled—only it felt more as if he was baring his teeth.

'I won't need to.' He studied her face. 'I won't need to do anything except sit back and watch while everything you love and care about slips through your fingers.'

The air was vibrating between them. 'You're a monster,' she whispered, inching backwards. 'A cold-blooded barbarian. What kind of man would say something like that?'

He shrugged, his expression somewhere between a challenge and a taunt. 'The kind that believes in karma.'

Margot was struggling to speak. She wanted to deny his claims. Prove him wrong. But the trouble was that she knew that he was right.

The business *was* a mess.

Her brother Yves might have resented his glamorous parents, but he had been more like Colette and Emile than he'd cared to admit, and five years after his death she was still trying to clear up the consequences of his impulsive and imprudent management style. Only nothing she did seemed to work.

Her heart began to beat faster. How could it? She didn't have her great-grandfather's vision, or her grandfather's ruthless determination and drive. Nor was she full of Yves's flamboyant self-assurance. In fact, if anything, the opposite was true. She'd found the responsibility of ensuring that the family legacy stayed intact increasingly overwhelming and as her self-doubts grew the profits continued to shrink. Finally—reluctantly—she'd decided to put up the chateau as security.

Her pulse began to beat faster.

Even just thinking about it made her feel physically sick. Not only had the chateau belonged to her family for sixteen generations, in less than two months it was supposed to be the setting for her brother Louis's wedding.

It had been a last-ditch attempt to reassure the bank. Only it hadn't worked. Max was right. The business was failing.

She shivered.

Or rather *she* had failed, and soon the whole world would know the truth that she had so desperately tried to hide.

Watching her in silence, Max breathed out slowly.

He'd waited nearly ten years for this. Ten long years of working so hard that he would often fall asleep eating his evening meal. Unlike Margot, he'd had to start at the bottom. His jaw tightened. His job at Duvernay should have opened doors to him throughout the industry but, thanks to her family, that ladder had become a snake with a venomous bite.

After being more or less banished from France, it had taken him years to claw back his reputation. Years spent working punishingly long hours at vineyards in Hungary, and studying at night school until finally he had got a break and a job on an estate in California.

But every backbreaking second had been worth it for this, and although the shares had been expensive he would have paid double for this moment of reckoning.

His chest tightened. Finally he'd proved the Duvernays wrong!

He was their equal—for he was here, in their precious

boardroom, not as some low-paid employee but as a share-holder.

He wanted to savour it. But although Margot looked suitably stunned—crushed, in fact, by his words—strangely, he was finding it not nearly as satisfying as he'd imagined he would.

Confused, and unprepared for this unexpected development, he stared at her in silence. And then immediately wished he hadn't, for with the light behind her, the delicate fabric of her white dress was almost transparent, and the silhouetted outline of her figure was clearly visible. It was almost as if she was naked.

A beat of desire pulsed through his veins.

Not that he needed a reminder. Margot's body was imprinted in his brain. He could picture her now, as he'd seen her so many times in those snatched afternoons spent in the tiny bedroom of his estate cottage. Lying in his arms, the curve of her belly and breasts gleaming in the shafts of fading sunlight, a pulse beating frantically at the base of her throat. Each time, he'd felt as though he was dreaming. He'd been completely in her thrall—overwhelmed not just by desire but by an emotion he had, until meeting her, always dismissed as at best illusory and at worst treacherous.

At first he'd tried to deny his feelings, had avoided her, and then, when avoiding her had become untenable, had been offhand almost to the point of being brusque, willing her to brand him rude and unapproachable if it meant hanging on to some small remnant of self-control.

But it had been so hard, for his body had been on fire, his brain in turmoil, all five senses on permanent high alert. He'd wanted her so badly, and for a time he'd believed that she wanted him in the same way. Insistently. Relentlessly.

Unconditionally.

And so he'd proposed—wanting, needing to make permanent that passion, that sense of belonging to someone, and of her belonging to him. He'd had no words for how he'd felt. It had defied description. All he had known was that he had a place in her life, her world. He had believed that unquestioningly. Only of course he'd been wrong.

Margot had wanted him, but her desire had been rooted in the transitory and finite nature of an affair—and more specifically in the illicit thrill of 'dating' her older brother's employee.

He felt anger spark inside him, and his eyes cut across the room to the line of portraits of Duvernays past and present.

Of course proposing to her had been his second mistake. His first had been to believe that his rapport with Yves was real, that it meant something. He had been lured not so much by the family's wealth and glamour, but by their sense of *contra mundum*, and the chance to be admitted into their world had been irresistibly potent to someone with his past.

With hindsight, though, he could see that his presence had always been subject to the grace and favour of the Duvernay family. They might have tolerated him, but he had never really belonged—just as Margot had never really belonged to *him*.

He felt his heart start to beat faster.

As a suitor, he'd always known that he was an underdog, a wild card—but, stupid and naive fool that he'd been, he'd actually respected her for seeing beyond his bank account and his background. Admired her for choosing him, for taking that risk. Now, though, he knew that the risk had been all his.

His hands trembled and he felt a rush of irritation at his naivety. No wonder he wasn't really *feeling* this moment.

He might have created a business to rival theirs, but what had haunted him—and what still rankled and had made every relationship since Margot a short-lived and deliberately one-sided affair—was the fact that, just like his mother, he hadn't been good enough to marry.

The Duvernays might have welcomed him into their home, but ultimately they had never considered him worthy of permanently joining their inner circle. Not even Margot. *Especially not Margot.*

His head was suddenly pounding.

For nearly a decade he'd told himself that watching the House of Duvernay implode would be enough. Enough to erase the sting of humiliation and the pain of being so summarily cast out and ostracised. Only now, here, standing in this boardroom, it was clear to him that there was another, more satisfying revenge to be had: namely, seizing control of the business from Margot.

It was the only possible way to exorcise this lingering hold she had on him. To punish her as she deserved to be punished. For she had wronged him the most. Her betrayal was the most personal and the deepest.

His pulse twitched as for the first time he noticed the band on her wrist, his brain swiftly and efficiently deciphering the cursive writing. He felt warmth spread across his skin. And it just so happened that he knew the perfect way to make his revenge exquisitely and fittingly personal.

Exhilaration hit him like a shot of pure alcohol and, resting his gaze on her profile, he steadied himself. 'I know how you must be feeling...'

Her head jerked towards him, her long pale blonde hair catching the light as it flicked sideways.

'I doubt that.' Dark brown eyes wide with anger and outrage locked on to his. 'Having feelings would make you human, and you clearly don't have an ounce of humanity.'

Staring at the pulse beating in the base of her throat, Max gritted his teeth. He had plenty of feelings for Margot, unfortunately most of them seemed to be occurring somewhere in the region of his groin.

Fighting off the frustration that was circling like a caged dog inside his head, Max took a step towards her. 'I *do* know. You might not have thought I had much to lose, but thanks to your brother I lost the little I had,' he said coolly.

Margot blinked. At the mention of her brother's name anger surged up inside her like a hot spring. 'Yves was protecting me.'

'Yes, by destroying me.'

She reeled back from the controlled fury in his voice. 'That wasn't his intention.'

'You think?'

She glared at him, not knowing what she hated more: the coolness in his eyes or the mockery distorting his beautiful mouth. 'Yes, I do. He just did what any brother would do. I wouldn't expect you to understand that. I wouldn't expect you to understand feelings like loyalty and lo—

She broke off, appalled at what she had so nearly spoken out loud—not just the fact that she had loved him but loved him rapturously, with her body, heart and soul. Only her love had been unreciprocated—humiliatingly unilateral. Worse, it had blinded her to what he was really thinking.

A sudden sharp spasm of pain twisted her stomach, and the words he'd spoken to her so long ago suddenly echoed inside her head.

'It was all about the money. You and me. That's why I proposed. I just wanted your money.'

She felt his clear-eyed gaze probing her face, and more than anything she wanted to raise her hands and shield her eyes, conceal the emotions that were rising up inside her. But she wasn't about to give him the satisfaction of knowing how badly he'd hurt her. Or that the pain of his betrayal felt as fresh today as it had ten years ago.

Ignoring the thudding of her heart, she glared at him. 'Just because you don't care about anything but money—'

'You mean the money that you don't currently have?' he said softly. 'Remind me, Margot. What is Duvernay's net to EBITDA ratio these days?'

Their eyes clashed, and she flinched inwardly at the anger and resentment taking shape in the no-man's land between them.

Forcing herself to stand her ground, she wrapped her fingers around her elbows. 'Why do you care? Or do you just want to gloat about that too?'

His face was still, but his eyes were glittering in a way that made the air thump out of her lungs. For a moment they stared at one another in silence, and then finally he shrugged. 'I wasn't gloating,' he said simply.

The mildness of his tone caught her off guard, for it was so at odds with the adversarial tension swirling around the room and inside her chest.

'I just like to be in full command of the facts. That's how I run my business.'

His eyes were fixed on hers, calm, appraising, unnerving, and she felt her breathing jerk, saw the muted colours of the walls slamming into focus.

'Well, luckily for me, whatever you might like to believe, Duvernay isn't your business,' she said, lifting her chin and returning his gaze, her brown eyes sparking with resentment.

How dare he do this? Saunter back into her life with his newly acquired shares and his careless gaze, unlocking the past and upending the present.

For a second there was total silence, and then his mouth

curved slowly upwards. Despite herself, she felt her pulse flutter, for his smile was still so difficult to resist, and even though she wanted to deny its power she could feel a trembling heat starting to creep over her skin.

And he hadn't even touched her, she thought, her heart lurching against her ribcage.

'Well, *luckily for you*—' he paused, his eyes resting calmly on her face '—that could all be about to change.'

Abruptly his smile was forgotten, and she stared up at him in confusion, her skin tingling, mouth drying with fear and anticipation, trying and failing to make sense of his casual statement.

'All you need to do is say yes.'

His words hung in the air between them and she felt panic spread through her. Suddenly she was having to work hard to breathe. Her pulse gave a leap of warning. Something was happening—something undefined but important.

'Yes to what?' She was aiming for the same tone of neutral formality, but instead her voice sounded oddly hollow and strained.

Max held her gaze. He wanted to see her reaction. To watch the moment of impact. 'To marrying me.'

Margot gazed at him, rooted to the spot, her stomach clenching with shock. She knew her face had drained of colour, but she was too busy trying to quiet the chaos inside her head to care.

'Marry you!' Shaking her head, she gave a small, disbelieving laugh. 'You're crazy. Why would I want to marry *you*?'

'Is that a no?'

His face was closed, expressionless, but she could feel the anger rippling beneath his skin. Only she didn't care. Right now all she wanted to do was hurt him in the same way that he'd hurt her—was still hurting her. Or maybe not in the *same* way, for that would mean Max had a heart, and she knew from bitter, personal experience that wasn't the case.

But she could certainly puncture the beating core of Max Montigny—his masculine pride.

'A no? Of course not.' She glared at him, her own rage shocking her. 'Who could possibly resist a man like you, Max? I mean, it's every woman's dream to marry a lying, scheming hustler!'

Sarcasm did not come naturally to her any more than anger did, but coming so soon after her father's betrayal and the shock of seeing Max again his proposal was just too cruel, too painful.

Once, marrying Max had been her dream. When he and Yves had turned up for supper one evening she had looked up from her plate and just like that she had fallen in love. Actually, not fallen—it had been more like plummeting…like a star falling to earth.

His presence in her life had felt miraculous. The thrill of seeing him, talking to him, had been a new kind of bliss—both pleasure and pain—for he had been so smart and sexy, bewitchingly beautiful and impossibly laid back, and yet so unattainable. She had been desperate, hopeful, smitten—and then, unbelievably, it had happened.

Only she had never suspected why. Stupid, naive and crazily in love for the first time, she had never imagined the truth until that terrible afternoon when Yves had discovered them.

'Feeling better? Or do you want to start throwing punches as well as insults?'

Max's voice was as cold and toxic as nerve gas. Lifting her head, she cleared her throat, straightening her back, feeling the zip of her dress tingling against her spine.

'Sorry,' she said, without a hint of remorse. 'But I just can't imagine under what circumstances you think I'd ever, *ever*, even consider marrying *you*.'

His gaze didn't flicker. 'How about circumstances in which I agree to save your business?'

She stared at him, the sheer unexpectedness of his words making the edges of her vision watery. 'Save my business…?' she repeated slowly.

He nodded. 'If you agree to become my wife.' He paused, studying her face. 'It's up to you, of course.'

He was speaking with a mock courtesy that made her want to hurl her bag at his head.

'I can just leave. The choice is yours.'

Her skin was prickling and her heart was beating so loudly that it was getting in the way of her thoughts. 'That's not a choice,' she said hoarsely. 'That's blackmail.'

For what felt like a lifetime he stared at her thoughtfully, and then finally he gave a casual shrug.

'Yes, I suppose it is. But on some levels all business is blackmail.' His face was impassive, his eyes steady on hers. 'And that's what this is, Margot. It's just business.'

The truth, of course, was that he wanted to prove her and her family wrong. To demonstrate irrefutably that he *was* good enough to marry her. That his name was equal to hers. But his instincts warned him against revealing the truth, for surely it would show weakness to admit that their low opinion—*her* low opinion—still tormented him?

Besides, there was no need to reveal anything. Not when he already had a ready-made reason at his fingertips. Widening his stance, he focused his attention on the woman in front of him.

'Unlike yourself, I'm not in the habit of throwing good money after bad, and your father's shares are useless to me if Duvernay goes bankrupt.'

She took a breath, bracing herself as though for a blow. 'What has that got to do with marrying me?' she asked stiffly.

Tuning out the apprehension in her voice, he let her words echo around the room. 'Isn't it obvious? I'll marry you, and in return you'll give me your shares. That will make me the majority stakeholder in Duvernay and allow me to run the business as I see fit.' His mouth curled into a goading smile. 'By that I mean profitably.'

Her eyes narrowed. 'You're so arrogant.' Seething inwardly, Margot watched him gaze dismissively around the boardroom.

'It shouldn't be too hard. Frankly, I could turn this company around in a heartbeat.'

She gave a short, mirthless laugh. 'Wouldn't that require you to have a *heart*, though, Max?' she said sweetly.

He smiled. 'Oh, I have a heart, Margot—and more importantly, unlike your brother, I also have a head for business.'

Her brown eyes narrowed. 'I don't want to know what you think about my brother any more than I want your money,' she spat.

He gazed down at her, unperturbed by her outburst. 'No, I'm sure you don't,' he conceded.

His eyes gleamed, the centres darkening so that suddenly it felt as though she was being dragged bodily into his pupils.

'But whether you want my money or not is largely irrelevant. The fact is, you need it.'

'I don't—' she began.

He waved her words away as though they were some kind of irritating insect. 'You do. And, frankly, the sooner the better. I'll give you free rein with the wedding arrangements...' he was watching her lazily, as though her consent was a foregone conclusion '…although I draw the line at wearing any kind of patterned waistcoat. So marry me, give me control over our destinies, and I'll make all your problems go away.'

'I doubt that. From where I'm standing, *you* are the biggest problem. You're conceited and selfish and utterly lacking in sensitivity.'

His smile widened. 'Presumably that's why I now own a quarter share of your business?'

Stifling an impulse to slap his smug, handsome face, Margot fixed her gaze on the gardens outside. How long was he going to carry on with this game? For surely that was all this talk of marriage was to him. A game designed to humiliate her further.

So stop playing it, then, she told herself irritably. *You're the CEO of a global business, not some dopey nineteen-year-old student.*

With a strength that surprised her, she turned and met his gaze head-on. 'I'm not going to give you my shares, Max,' she said flatly. 'And I'm definitely not going to marry you.'

His expression didn't change, but somehow she found that less reassuring rather than more, and moments later she realised why. She might have thought she was simply stating the obvious, but Max clearly thought she was calling his bluff.

'Is that right?'

She glared at him, her skin prickling with resentment—not just at his arrogance but at the beat of desire pulsing through her veins, and the knowledge that only Max had ever done this to her. Got under her skin and made her feel so off-balance. And the fact that he could still make her feel this way, that he still had this power over her, threatened her as much as his words.

She took a step back. 'Yes, it is,' she said quickly. 'You

and I were a mistake I'm not planning on repeating. We're certainly not marriage material.'

'Why not? I'm a man...you're a woman. There are no obstacles preventing us from tying the knot.'

Jamming her hands into the pockets of her dress, she looked up at him, disbelief giving way to exasperation, then fury. 'Aside from mutual loathing, you mean?'

Glancing around the boardroom, he shook his head slowly. 'You see? This is why your business is struggling, baby. You're just too resistant to change, to new ideas.'

Her eyes narrowed. 'Oh, I'm sorry. I didn't realise blackmail was so on-trend!'

He laughed, and before she could stop herself—before she even knew she was doing it—she was laughing too. How could she not when his mouth curled up so temptingly at the corners, wiping the mockery from his face so that he looked heartbreakingly like his younger self?

And, fool that she was, she felt her pulse lose speed, felt a sudden overwhelming urge to reach out and touch the curve of his lips, to feel again the hard, masculine pressure of his body against hers.

Heat burned in her cheeks and she breathed in sharply. Her reaction had been instinctive, involuntary, but she was already regretting it. How could she *laugh* with him after everything he'd done to her? And how could she let herself feel anything other than hatred and contempt for this man who was backing her into a corner, demanding something that was impossible for her to give?

She felt his gaze on the side of her face.

'What was that you were saying about mutual loathing?' he asked.

The mocking note was back, and she looked up defiantly, her whole body stiffening into fight mode. 'Just because you can make me laugh *once*, it doesn't mean anything.'

Dragging her gaze away from the indecently lush mouth, she stared past him.

Except that it did.

She winced inwardly. It was all there in her voice—everything that she didn't want him to hear or to know about how she was feeling—and that was why this conversation had to stop now.

'You might have a head for business, Max, but you have zero understanding of human nature. If—*if*—we were to get married, we wouldn't just be talking in the boardroom.' She felt a sudden prickle of ice run down her spine. 'We'd have to live together. Share a home.'

Share a bed, she thought silently, her face suddenly hot as his eyes narrowed on hers and something moved across the irises that made her breathing quicken.

Cheeks burning, she began speaking again. 'Share our lives. And how are we going to do that? We can't even be in the same room together without—'

But she never finished her sentence. Instead she made the mistake of looking up at him, and instantly the words stalled in her throat.

She felt her body tense, almost painfully, and then her legs started to shake just as they had the first time she had ever seen him. Dressed in faded jeans, a T-shirt that hugged the muscles of his arms, and wearing dark glasses, he had looked like a cocktail of one part glamour to two parts cool. And then he'd taken his glasses off, and it had been like a thunderclap bursting inside her head.

Over time she had, of course, grown used to how he looked. But at least once a day it had caught her off guard, and now apparently nothing had changed. The seemingly random arrangement of mouth, nose, cheekbones still had the same power to rob her of even basic impulses, such as breathing and speaking.

'Without what?'

Her stomach tightened with awareness. The air felt suddenly charged with a different kind of tension, and his voice had grown softer. Too soft.

She could feel it slipping over her skin like a caress, so warm and tempting and—

Deceptive! Had she really learned nothing from what happened between them?

Ignoring his eyes, she crossed her arms in front of her body, shielding herself from the pull of the past. 'It doesn't matter.'

'Oh, but it does. You see, I need an answer,' he said, and the smoothness of his voice in no way diluted his uncompromising statement.

'Well, tough!' Her eyes widened. 'You can't seriously expect me to give you one here and now?'

For a moment he didn't reply, just continued to stare at her thoughtfully, as though he was working out something inside his head.

'Actually, I can—and I am.'

Her pulse shifted up a gear as he glanced at the surprisingly understated watch on his wrist.

'Deals have deadlines, and this one runs out when I walk back out through that door.'

She took a breath, fear drumming through her chest. 'But that's not fair. I need time—'

'And *I* need an answer.'

The commanding note in his voice whipped at her senses so that suddenly her head was buzzing and the glare of the sunlight hurt her eyes.

'And, to be fair, you have had ten years.'

Margot blinked. 'You can't compare what happened

then with this.' She felt suddenly sick. Surely he didn't think that this 'proposal' somehow picked up where they'd left off?

'This is nothing like before,' she said shakily.

'I agree. This is far better.'

She gaped at him speechlessly, uncertain of how to interpret his words, and then suddenly she shook her head, her eyes snapping upwards. 'Better! What are you talking about?'

Her voice was too loud. So loud that someone in the corridor would be able to hear her. But for the first time in her life she didn't care what other people might think.

'How is this better? How could this ever be better?'

'It's simpler. More transparent.' His gaze dropped to her throat, then lowered to the V of her dress. 'What you see is what you get. And, despite all your talk of mutual loathing, I think we can agree that we both like what we see.'

Margot felt something dislodge inside her. His closeness was making her unravel. She wanted to disagree. To throw his remark back in his face. Only she didn't trust herself to speak—not just to form the words inside her head but to say them out loud.

Her pulse hiccupped with panic, and his gaze cut to hers. Surely though he couldn't sense the way he made her feel?

But of course he could—he always had. And, as though reading her mind, he reached out and gently stroked her long blonde hair, his touch pulling her not just closer, but back to a past that she had never quite relinquished.

'I can't give you time, Margot, but I can give you a reason to marry me.'

His gaze rested on her face, his eyes drawing her in, and she felt her nerves quiver helplessly in response to the message in the darkening irises.

'You have given me a reason, Max,' she said shakily. 'It's called blackmail.'

There was a moment of silence, and then his gaze shifted from her eyes, dropping and pressing onto her mouth. Suddenly her skin felt too hot and too tight, and she had a slip-sliding sense of *déjà-vu* as he took another step closer, the intensity of his eyes tangling her breathing.

'Actually, I have a better reason.'

For perhaps a fraction of a second her brain was screaming at her to turn, to move, to run. And then his lips closed on hers and heat surged through her body as his arm curved around her waist. Her hands rose instinctively, palms pressing into the rigid muscles of his chest—but not to push him away. Instead her fingers curled into the front of his shirt and she was pulling him closer, even as his hand curled around her wrist.

The touch of his mouth, his hands, his body, was so familiar, so intoxicating, that she would have had to be inhuman not to respond. He was warm and solid and real—more real than anything else in the room, in the world.

It was impossible to deny, and he was impossible to re-sist…like drowning. The pain and the misery of the last ten years was fading into a pleasure that she had never expected to feel again, a pleasure she had only ever felt in Max's arms.

Something stirred in her head and she felt a kick of resistance.

Only it was all a lie, a cold-blooded seduction. He hadn't felt anything. Not then, and definitely not now.

And just like that the spell was broken. Heart still racing, she jerked her mouth free and pushed him away.

Resurfacing into the cool, sedate daylight of the board-room, she felt heat burning her face. Only now it was the heat of humiliation. How had she let that happen? Why had she given herself to this man? A man who felt nothing for her and used her feelings as a weapon against herself.

Oh, he *wanted* her—but certainly not because he was powerless to do otherwise...

Skin burning, she took a step back and pressed her hand against her mouth, trying to blot out the imprint of his lips, wishing there was a way she could erase him as quickly and permanently from her life and her memory.

But the truth was that even when she'd had every reason to do so she hadn't managed to wipe Max from her mind. And now she actually had a reason for him to be in her life.

Her pulse fluttered and she felt a momentary swirling panic rise up inside her chest like storm water. And then just as swiftly it drained away. This was not a time for feelings to get in the way of facts. And the facts were bleak.

The business was not just failing, it was heading for bankruptcy. And it wasn't just Duvernay the business that was facing ruin. If—no, *when* the business collapsed, her family would be thrown into the spotlight, humbled and humiliated. Worse, they would be homeless.

She didn't want to marry Max, but without his money her life and that of her family—the life they all took for granted—would not just be difficult, it would cease to exist. And how would she—how would *they*?—cope living like ordinary people?

Her heart contracted. They wouldn't. And she couldn't expect them to do so.

Briefly, she felt the weight of her responsibilities. For if this was to work then once again she would have to put her family before herself. To lie and keep secrets. But what choice did she have?

Right now, Max was her only option. Without him all would be lost.

Heat burned in her cheeks. But wasn't there just a tiny part of herself that was relieved to have Max there, going into battle alongside her? And, really, was marriage such a big sacrifice to make for the sake of your family and a two hundred year legacy?

She stilled her breathing, like a diver preparing to jump, and then, before she could change her mind, she said quickly, 'Okay, I'll marry you. But it has to look and feel real, like a traditional wedding. We'll need to talk about it properly.'

As an attempt to reassert her power it was pretty meaningless. She was in no position to demand anything—she knew it, and he knew it too—and yet she also knew instinctively that she couldn't allow herself to be a push-over.

She'd half expected him to rise to her challenge. Only he didn't. Instead he merely nodded, as though she'd asked him to email her an invoice rather than discuss the conditions of their marriage of convenience.

'Of course. I'll be in touch.'

And with that he turned, and suddenly she was alone.

She stared after him, her heart beating out of time, her limbs shaking with relief and a strange kind of excitement.

Finally he was gone—but of course she would see him again soon. Only that wasn't the reason why her heart was fluttering to the ground like a wounded bird. It was because the next time she saw him it would be as his fiancée.

CHAPTER THREE

STRIDING BACK INTO his Parisian hotel suite an hour later, Max tossed his phone carelessly onto one of the large velvet-covered sofas in the main living area.

He didn't know whether to feel elated or stunned.

Or just plain furious!

He should be on his way to Longchamp. He was due there to present a trophy to the winner of the big race, and normally he loved going to the races—whatever happened at the bookies, fast horses and beautiful woman were a winning combination.

But after leaving the Duvernay headquarters he'd got his PA to cancel. He'd had no choice. Margot had not only got under his skin, she was resonating inside his head. Her every word, every gesture, was running on a continuous loop like a live news feed from which it was impossible to turn away.

But why? He'd got what he wanted, hadn't he?

His mouth thinned. It should have all been so straightforward. A part of him had been planning some sort of revenge against the Duvernays for nearly a decade, painstakingly working towards the moment when finally he would prove to Margot, her brother, her whole damn family that they had been wrong about him.

And everything had been on schedule—right up until

the moment she'd walked into the boardroom. His mind scrolled back to when he'd turned around and seen her in that dress—a dress that despite its couture credentials had somehow managed to conjure up memories of carefree summers, feel-good songs playing on car radios and the smell of hot bare skin.

Margot's hot bare skin.

He blinked. No wonder he'd been driven to act like that. Proposing marriage and then kissing her. His brain had been like bubble gum.

Frowning, he slid his hand under his tie and tugged it loose, before pulling it over his head and tossing it in the same direction as his phone. He felt tired, and the tension in his neck was making his back ache.

Infuriated by the devastating impact Margot had wrought on his mood and on his body, he slowly scanned the exquisite room, as though the opulent *fin de siècle* furnishings and huge gold-framed mirrors might offer up some kind of antidote. When that failed, he turned and stalked across the gleaming wood floor to the open French windows, stepping outside onto the roof terrace that adjoined his suite.

Directly opposite, the Eiffel Tower rose above the Paris skyline. Normally he found the sight of the city's most iconic monument inspirational for, like him, it too had initially struggled to be accepted before finally finding national and global fame.

Now, though, as he looked across at the familiar iron structure, it seemed oddly insubstantial.

His jaw tightened. A bit like the 'logic' that had driven his most recent actions.

He felt a rush of irritation, his shoulders tensing so that a spasm of pain nipped his spine. For 'logic' read 'libido'.

Barely registering the incredible three-hundred-and-sixty-degree views of the city, he gripped the balustrade, breathing out slowly as for maybe the hundredth time he ran through the morning's events, trying to disentangle the motives behind his behaviour.

Buying Emile's shares had been a luxury—overpriced and self-indulgent. Buying them, though, had served a purpose, for it had taken him to the Duvernay boardroom and a showdown with Margot.

A showdown that should have ended there.

And it would have ended there if he hadn't asked her to marry him.

Tilting his head back, he closed his eyes. At the time, marrying her and taking possession of her shares had seemed like a perfectly reasonable next step. The best and the only way to satisfy the hunger for revenge that had driven him back to France after nearly a decade.

Now, though, he could see that, whatever chain of events he had triggered in that boardroom, the truth was that his actions had been driven not just by a desire to possess Duvernay, but by a desire to possess Margot herself.

It had been if not a moment of madness then an act of impulse—an instinctive urge both to let go and move on from the past and at the same time continue that tantalising *pas-de-deux* with the only woman who had left an imprint on his soul. A woman who had burned him so badly that he had spent the intervening years running from the hurt, afraid to slow down and face his feelings, afraid to feel full-stop.

But for some reason, as he'd come face to face with her in that picture-lined room, he had decided not only to stop running but to re-stake his claim.

To what? he mocked. *Certainly not her heart.*

She might have accused him of being cold-blooded, but Margot's heart lay buried beneath a layer of permafrost.

Opening his eyes, he gazed irritably across the skyline. None of this would have happened if he'd just stuck to the plan—only he'd had to go and let things get personal.

But of course he had. Because it was personal. Deeply and guttingly personal.

Margot had mattered to him like no other woman ever had. But then, she'd been like no other woman he'd ever known—and it hadn't just been about the sex. Before he'd met her he'd been so messed up—hungry for respect and respectability and yet resentful that he had to keep on earning it, asking for it, pushing for it.

She had been his serenity. His salvation.

His mouth thinned. Or so he'd believed until that evening when she'd tossed his proposal back in his face like a glass of wine. Ever since then he'd been carrying his pain and resentment like a dark storm cloud.

A storm cloud that had burst with a clap of thunder in that boardroom today.

But was it really that surprising? He might have bought the shares and engineered the meeting, but seeing her again had still been a shock.

Before she'd arrived he'd told himself she wasn't going to be as beautiful as he remembered, or as desirable. That kind of loveliness didn't last. But he'd been wrong—actually, more like deluded!

His body had responded to hers with a swiftness and an intensity that he'd never experienced around any woman except her. And as for her looks—

Well, he'd been wrong about that too.

Aged nineteen, she had possessed a beauty that had already been straining at the leash. With a pure clean-cut profile, pensive light brown eyes and almost ludicrously long legs, she'd been a mesmerising mix of coltish hesitation and a seriousness not common in one so young.

Today, though, she would not have looked out of place sashaying down the catwalk at Paris Fashion Week—or, better still, circling the paddock at Longchamp with all the other thoroughbreds. For she had outgrown or maybe grown into her long limbs, and there was no trace of that youthful hesitation. Only the soft half-pout and simply styled long, pale blonde hair still hinted at the girl he'd proposed to all those years ago.

He felt his pulse dart. Or it would have done if that girl had ever been real. But he knew now that she had only ever existed inside his head.

So who, then, was he marrying? And, perhaps more importantly, why was he prepared to go ahead with such an impulsive and ill-thought-out decision?

Breathing out slowly, his mind took him back to that first and last summer they'd spent together. A summer of love—secret, snatched love.

Margot had told him she needed to find the right moment to tell her family and, smitten with feelings that were powerful and compelling in their unfamiliarity, it had been an easy decision for him to go along with her wishes.

Cocooned together in the bedroom of the cottage that had come with his job, nothing had ever felt so good, so right—not even the first time he'd stepped foot in a vineyard.

It had been so new to him…so precious. He'd thought going public would end his bubble of happiness instantly. There would be no more just the two of them. Everything would change irrevocably.

His mouth curved downwards. Of course he hadn't anticipated quite how catastrophic that change would be—although maybe he'd always suspected the truth. That her secrecy and hesitation stemmed not from a desire to prolong the perfect private bliss of their affair, but from a belief that he was only good enough for sex, and that one day she would discard him like pomace—the unusable skins, pulp, seeds and stems from the wine grapes.

He was suddenly working to breathe.

This time, though, it would be different. This time there would be no sneaking around, no secrecy, no hiding him away.

If it had just been about recouping his money then, yes, he would have sat back and waited for her business to fail before stepping forward to scoop up the spoils. But why wait? Marrying her would have the same outcome, only it would be immediate—and it would be much more pleasurable.

Not only would he be in the driving seat at Duvernay, but Margot Duvernay—heiress and aristocrat of the wine world—would be his wife. His lawfully and very *publicly* wedded wife.

Gazing down at the city, he smiled happily, back no longer aching, suddenly immensely gratified with how the morning had played out.

Switching off the shower, Margot smoothed the water away from her face and silently breathed in the scented steam.

The camellia and jasmine body wash had promised to soothe her body and mind, but judging by the way her heart was still racing it clearly wasn't powerful enough to soothe away the aftershocks caused by the morning's events.

To be fair, though, she couldn't really blame the shower gel. Short of industrial quantities of alcohol. or maybe concussion, she wasn't sure that *anything* could counteract a close encounter with Max Montigny.

Chewing her lip, she wrapped a towel around her damp

body, grateful for the comforting warmth and softness of its embrace.

Had anyone else bought her father's shares it would have been an awkward but bearable meeting, with a discussion followed perhaps by coffee. But instead it had been more like a gladiatorial battle, and there had been only one proposal on the agenda—Max's.

A proposal she had accepted.

Her pulse accelerated, and the saliva dried in her mouth as panic and fear at what she'd consented to do spiralled up inside her like a swarm of bees.

However, panicking wasn't going to change the facts—and they were simple. Not only had she agreed to transfer her shares to Max, she had also agreed to become his wife.

After he'd left she had briefly considered calling her lawyer. Only what would have been the point? She knew without even bothering to check that the contract he'd signed with Emile would be watertight.

Besides, right now, taking Max's money was the only way she could save her business *and* her family. And if that meant giving him her shares and marrying him, then that was what she would do.

She felt her stomach lurch, and some of her bravado began to ooze away. That was easy to say, but she couldn't pretend even to herself that the reality was going to be anything but challenging.

Glancing down at her wrist, she shivered. She could still feel his handprint on her skin, could remember the way their bodies had fitted together as they'd kissed, and the helpless, sightless oblivion of her passion.

Her hands fluttered involuntarily in her lap. Closing her eyes, she clutched the towel more tightly.

Her response to him wasn't that surprising, she thought defensively. And, given their history, surely she could forgive herself? The physical attraction between them had always been so overpowering and relentless that kiss had been inevitable. But, while her craving for Max might be understandable, even forgivable, giving in to it would only complicate things.

For the sake of her sanity and her pride it was clear that this deal would only work if she kept her feelings out of it. Viewed that way, she might just be able to believe that their marriage was simply another business transaction— a civilised, functional, mutually beneficial agreement between two consenting adults.

She felt her breath clog in her throat. All she needed to do now was believe her own sales pitch.

Opening her eyes, she stared slowly around her bedroom.

If only she had somebody she could confide in. It wasn't that she didn't have friends. She did. But friends were for fun—for nights out and playing tennis, going shopping. Telling them the truth about her life was just not an option. After so many years of keeping so much of the Duvernay drama under wraps, what would she say? Where would she start?

Nor could she share her fears and anxieties with her family, for they relied on her to be strong and steady and solicitous.

If only there was someone she could trust with her burden.

Her mouth twisted. *Like a husband.*

But, although her feelings for Max might be complicated and confusing, she knew with absolute certainty that she didn't trust him. Or at least that she only trusted him to hurt her.

Her pulse twitched and she felt a sudden urgency to move, to escape the loop of her thoughts. Stalking into the dressing room, she snatched a pair of faded blue jeans, a V-neck T-shirt and a pale grey ballet-style wrap.

If only she could just disappear. Get into her car and keep driving. Leave France, Europe—or better still become an astronaut...

She tugged the wrap around her waist and knotted it savagely. And do what?

She might escape Max, and the mess-in-waiting that was her business, but she would never escape her feelings. Even if she was floating hundreds of miles above the earth in a space station she would still be worrying about her family and trying to manage the chaos they produced.

That was what she did. What she'd always done since childhood, during the many evenings and weekends when her parents' volatile relationship had spilled over into a merry-go-round of accusations and denials.

When finally one of them—usually Colette—had stormed off in tears, it had been down to Margot to act as a go-between. And then, after they had inevitably retreated to the bedroom, it had been down to her to make up some story for the maids about how that vase had got broken, or why her father's clothes were scattered over the lawn. Yves, of course, was long gone, hiding out at a friend's house, and Louis had been a baby.

For a moment she stared silently at her reflection in the full-length mirror, seeing not herself but the dutiful little girl who had always done the right thing. Sorting out her parents' messes even if that had meant lying and keeping secrets.

And now she would be lying and keeping secrets for the rest of her life.

It would be easy simply to blame Max. *Marry me, or watch your business fail and your family end up homeless* was hardly much of a choice. But it wasn't that simple.

No one had made her go into the boardroom and face him. She could have got back into the lift, and sent in the lawyers. But some part of her had *wanted* to see him— and not just see him, she thought, her cheeks flaming as she remembered that kiss.

And Max hadn't come simply to gloat, or to pick out an office. He could have scheduled the meeting some- where public, like a restaurant, but he had wanted to be alone with her too.

Looking down, she saw that her hands were shaking again. Theoretically, she knew that she should loathe him. But clearly her body hadn't received the memo about how it was supposed to behave when she met the man who had crushed her dreams and broken her heart.

It might make no sense, and even just thinking it made her feel helpless and angry, but although she might have to lie to everyone else she wasn't going to lie to herself. And the truth was that in spite of everything that had hap- pened between them, and the fact that they no longer liked or trusted or respected one another, they still wanted each other with an intensity and desperation that overrode all logic and history.

Tipping her head back, she let out a long, slow breath. Perhaps, though, it was just the shock of seeing him again, she thought hopefully. Maybe when she saw him next time she would be immune to his charms.

She sighed. It didn't seem likely, but at least she wouldn't have long to find out.

The thought of seeing him again was making her heart pound so loudly that it took her some seconds to register that her phone was ringing.

She felt her muscles tense, her body pulling up sharply, like a horse refusing to jump a fence, and suddenly the air was humming around her.

Was it Max?

Instantly her heart gave a great leap, and as she walked swiftly back into her bedroom she gazed nervously down at the phone, oscillating from side to side on the polished surface of her dressing table.

But it was just Louis, calling from his week-long bachelor party in Marrakech.

Her heartbeat started to slow and she stared down at the screen, unnerved by the sharp sting of disappointment she felt at reading her brother's name. Usually she loved talking to her younger brother.

Louis had been too young to really register his parents' turbulent marriage so, unlike his older siblings, he had no memories of the past to colour his present. Instead he had inherited his parents' best qualities. Handsome and charming, like his father, he also had his mother's spontaneity. He was loved by everyone, and in return for this universal gift of love he wanted everyone around him to be happy. Particularly Margot.

The thought drove her back a step.

It was starting already. The lies and the secrecy. Only she wasn't ready. She wasn't ready to lie to Louis yet, she thought, panic blooming in her throat as her brain finally registered the tiny camera icon on the screen. And definitely not to his face.

But she was going to have to. For how could she suddenly just announce that she was going to marry a man she had never so much as mentioned before?

Louis would be stunned, devastated and hurt. Just picturing the lines of his face made her heart contract painfully and she felt a flicker of despair. Would it never end? Would she ever be free to just live?

Her pulse accelerated.

She could almost picture Max's handsome face. Could hear his soft, goading voice daring her to make a choice.

Her hand hovered over the phone and then, cursing softly, she took a quick, sharp breath and picked it up, swiping her fingers across the screen.

'Louis! How lovely to hear from you!'

Her breath ached in her chest as she smiled down at her brother's face.

'How's Marrakech?'

'It's amazing. I feel like I'm on a movie set.'

She smiled. His face was so unguarded, so flushed with happiness, and she felt some of the tension inside of her loosen.

'Well, I got the photos you sent and it looks beautiful,' she said truthfully. 'Are you having fun?'

'Of course. You know, I can't believe you haven't been out here.'

Louis sounded genuinely confused, and Margot experienced the sensation that she often did when speaking to her brother—a kind of shock that she was related to such a normal, well-balanced person. To him, Marrakech was just a beautiful, glamorous destination. The perfect backdrop for a week of hedonism. The fact that his family owned a former palace in the old city was just a bonus and a happy coincidence.

To her, though, the Palais du Bergé would always be the place where her parents had fled after their many rows— only Louis didn't need to know that.

And that was the other reason she'd agreed to marry Max. Louis needed protecting from the truth, and Max's money and her silence would make sure that continued to happen.

When the time was right she would give him an ex-purgated version of the last few days. But right now she was just grateful for the chance to think about something other than Max's life-changing reappearance in her life.

She cleared her throat. 'Oh, you know—I've just never really got round to it. Too busy at work. But let's not talk about that now. Tell me what you've been up to.'

'I'm not ringing to talk about me, Margot.'

Louis looked and sounded so uncharacteristically stern that she found herself smiling. 'So who *do* you want to talk about?'

'I want to talk about you, and why you're in France when you're supposed to be in Monaco. Is this your way of telling me that you still don't approve of me getting married?'

Margot grimaced, guilt digging her beneath the ribs. With all the drama with Max, she had completely forgotten about Gisele and Monte Carlo.

'No, of course not,' she said quickly. 'And I never didn't approve. I was just worried—you're both so young.'

She had been worried at first, but although both Gisele and Louis were impulsive and indulged, they lacked the self-absorption and wilfulness of her parents—and, more importantly, their relationship was not simply based on sex.

'So why did you leave?'

The petulance in her brother's voice was fading, but he was still frowning.

'Oh, Louis, I'm sorry. I really did want to stay, only something came up—'

'Something or *someone*?'

She froze, his words slamming into one another inside her head. Her body reacted instinctively, like a hare spooked by the shadow of a hawk, stilling and shrinking inwards as her legs gave way beneath her and she slid noiselessly onto the bed.

Damn Max! Had he spoken to Louis? Had he spoken to her grandfather as well? And, if so, what had he said to them?

'So? Are you going to tell me what he wanted or not?'

Louis's voice was impatient now, but she hardly registered the shift, so great was her misery at the way all the parts of her life that she'd worked so hard to keep separate were now suddenly and violently converging.

'Yes, of course.' The smile on her face was starting to hurt, and it was an effort to force herself to speak. 'I just didn't want to bother you while you were away. I thought it would just be easier if I handled it—him—on my own.'

She heard her brother sigh. 'He knows how to pick his moments, doesn't he? I mean, he makes no effort to have any sort of relationship with me, and then when I'm not even in the country he just randomly leaves me a message.'

Margot blinked in confusion. 'What message?'

Louis frowned. 'Exactly! *What* message? It was just him drinking and talking rubbish. Except for the part when he said that he didn't really want to talk to me. That he was just trying to get hold of you and he couldn't.' There was a moment's silence. 'So what was it then? What was so incredibly urgent that the great Emile Lehmann actually deigned to call *me*?'

For a moment she couldn't speak. Her whole body felt weak, buffeted by a fast, wild, rushing relief, and she badly wanted to laugh. Only suddenly it felt horribly close to wanting to cry—for what if she'd actually blurted everything out?

Tightening her grip around the phone, she took a breath and said as casually as she could manage, 'He just wanted to talk about a business venture.'

'You mean he wanted money? Seriously, Margot. Did he know where you were, or what you were doing there?'

He shook his head, exasperation in his voice. 'No, of course not. I mean, why would he know anything about my life? I'm only his son.'

She bit her lip, for now there was more than exasperation, there was pain too.

After she and her brothers had gone to live with her grandparents, Yves had refused to see Emile any more. He had always distanced himself from their parents' behaviour, so maybe he'd thought distancing himself from a father he considered weak and embarrassing was the next logical step.

Her grandparents had seemed to think so too, and had done nothing to dissuade him. Nor had they encouraged Louis to stay in contact with his father. In fact it had been Margot alone who had kept in touch with Emile.

She breathed out softly. She knew her father should have done more. But her grandparents had made it so difficult for him that inevitably he'd given up. It was all so stupid and senseless—but that didn't mean that Louis wasn't hurt by the fact that their father only ever talked to her.

'It wasn't just business,' she said quickly. 'He wanted to get you and Gisele a wedding present.'

The lie was so swift and slick that for a moment she almost believed it herself. And, of course, by the time the wedding happened she would have chosen a gift, coaxed Emile into sending it, and then it wouldn't be a lie any more.

'I think he felt awkward.'

She felt suddenly tired. How had she become this person? Not only was she able to lie to her own brother without flinching, she already knew the arguments she would use against herself later to rationalise her behaviour.

'He said that?' Louis looked at her uncertainly, but he

sounded somewhat appeased. 'I'm surprised he even re-membered I'm getting married.' He paused. 'But why did that mean you had to leave Monte Carlo?'

She didn't blink. Instead she stared across her bedroom at the Renoir lithograph of a young woman that had been a gift from her grandfather for her twenty-first birthday. It had always been one or her favourite pictures, and now she found the girl's calm expression particularly comforting.

'There was a problem at work,' she said quickly. 'Me coming back had nothing to do with Emile. It was just a coincidence.' She hesitated. 'Did Gisele mind?'

'A little. But she didn't actually think you would go at all, so—'

'I wanted to go,' she protested. 'And I would have stayed. I was having fun.'

'Liar!' Louis burst out laughing. 'You hate themed par-ties.'

She started to laugh too, and for a moment it was just the two of them, and life was simple and sunny again. 'True, but I'm only human—and there's something strangely ir-resistible about a lace body stocking and fingerless gloves.'

She'd wanted to hear her brother laugh again, and lis-tening to his whoop of delight she felt a rush of pure, un-complicated love for him.

'Please tell me there are photos.'

She smiled. 'Maybe! But what happens on bachelorette week stays on bachelorette week.'

'So, did you sort it out?'

The shift in topic caught her off guard, and it took a moment for her to understand the question. Without even meaning to do so Louis had introduced Max into the con-versation, and just like that she was back in the boardroom, her body just inches from his, the pull between them like a living, pulsing force of nature…

Quickly pushing the image aside, she cleared her throat.
'Yes—it's all sorted.'

Her heart began to pound. *Was it?* Did agreeing to
marry a man you loathed simply to save your family from
public humiliation count as sorted?

Yes, she thought fiercely. It did. It might not be the future she'd pictured, but it would be far better than any she
could produce without Max's investment.

'My sister the big-shot boss.'

Louis sounded gleeful. He had no interest in the business, but his admiration of Margot was partisan and un-
questioning, and she felt another rush of love for him.

'You are *so* going to give this new *terroiriste* a run for
his money. Have you met him yet?'

Margot frowned. The term wasn't new to her. There
was a growing movement among wine-growers around
the world that wines should be a unique expression of soil
and climate—not a result of artificial intervention from
chemical pesticides and fertilisers. She had been trying
for years to push Duvernay to become more biodynamic,
but change had been slower than she would have liked, because change required money that she simply didn't have.

Her pulse twitched, and she realised that her thought
process was inching dangerously back towards Max and
that conversation in the boardroom. With another effort
of will she dragged her mind back to Louis's impatient,
handsome face.

'Have I met who? What are you talking about?'

'You know—this Max Montigny. Guillaume had a chat
with him at the country club and he told him that he's looking to move into the region. Apparently he's already got
his eye on one of the big champagne estates.'

For a moment Margot couldn't speak. The shock of
hearing Louis say Max's name out loud was just so deep

and sudden. Only not as much of a shock as learning that Max's intentions were a matter for public discussion. Somehow that made everything feel a little sharper, more in focus. More urgent.

She pressed a fingertip against the side of her head, pushing down on the pain that had begun pulsing there. 'What did Guillaume think?'

Guillaume was Gisele's father, a genial industrialist who had made a fortune in telecommunications and was now looking to move into politics.

'What? About Montigny? Oh, he liked him—but he said he couldn't figure him out. That he looked like a film star but sounded like a banker. Until he started talking about wine. And then he sounded like a revolutionary.' Louis paused, as though he couldn't figure Max out either. 'But I don't think you need to worry about him, Comtesse du Duvernay.'

She smiled automatically. It was a childhood nickname. Yves and Louis had used to call her that whenever they'd thought she was being too bossy. Only now it felt like a cruel joke—an empty title for a woman who had traded herself like a chattel, marrying not for love but money.

'Is that right?' she said quickly, forcing a lightness into her voice that she didn't feel.

Louis grinned, the tiny screen barely diminishing the infectious power of his smile. 'Damn right, it is. If anyone can handle him it'll be you.'

After she'd hung up Margot blow dried her hair, and applied her make-up with careful precision. Glancing in the mirror, she felt her stomach clench. She might be CEO of one of the biggest champagne producers in the world, but this was her real skill. Presenting an image of serenity and control to the world while inside chaos reigned.

With an effort, she tried to arrange her thoughts to

match her outward composure, but Louis's words kept stubbornly weaving through her head like the subtitles to a movie she didn't want to watch.

Film star. Banker. Revolutionary.

Blackmailer.

She gritted her teeth. It sounded like a warped child's nursery rhyme, but in fact it was just another reminder of how little she knew Max. And, despite her brother's faith in her, of how ill-prepared she was to manage him.

Her throat tightened. But then she wasn't just *managing* Max, was she? She was marrying him.

CHAPTER FOUR

'WOULD YOU LIKE sparkling or still water?'

Glancing up from the bread roll she had spent far too long buttering, Margot smiled politely at the waiter. 'Still, please.'

She glanced across the table to where Max was discussing the wine with the hotel's sommelier. They were having lunch in his hotel suite. He had texted her an hour earlier, telling her what time to arrive, and although she was irritated by the no doubt deliberate short notice she was grateful not to have to prolong the agony, and relieved that he'd suggested lunch and not dinner.

Although now she was here she couldn't help feeling on edge, for being summoned to his rooms had made her feel like some kind of concubine.

Carefully, she laid her knife across her side plate. He had also—and this time she had no doubt that he'd done it deliberately—omitted to tell her where he was staying.

Of course he hadn't been hard to find. Judging by the amount of column inches given over to his presence in Paris, Max Montigny's whereabouts were not just a key piece of information to her, but a matter of fascination to most of the French public.

Her heartbeat twitched.

His casual, arrogant assumption that she'd have no

choice but to track him down made her want to reach over
and slap his beautiful face. But what did it matter, really?
In the wider scheme of things it was just another hoop for
her to jump through—a nudge to remind her that he was
in charge. Not that she really needed the balance of power
in their relationship to be pointed out. Every humbling
second of yesterday's meeting was seared onto her brain.

But, although it been painful and humiliating to have
to accept his proposal, of the many emotions she was feeling the one that was overriding all others was not anger,
nor even misery, but oddly relief. Since Max had offered
to marry her and turn her business around, for the first
time in the longest time some of the crushing burden of
responsibility she'd been carrying around seemed to have
lifted from her shoulders.

Finally there would be somebody by her side. Somebody who would have her back. She shivered. If still felt
strange, though, putting her life and her family's future
into the hands of Max Montigny.

Her mouth felt suddenly dry.

If only the secrecy and lies surrounding their arrangement had felt equally unfamiliar. But they hadn't. Instead
everything—the half-truths she had told her grandfather
about where she was going, her decision to drive herself
and thus not include her chauffeur in the deception—had
all conspired to make time contort.

And the unsettling sensation of past and present blurring hadn't gone away when, having kept her waiting
for ten minutes, Max had finally strolled into the room,
dressed casually in jeans and a grey T-shirt.

His lateness had been as deliberate as his failure to tell
her where they were meeting, and she had found it just as
provoking, but that wasn't the reason her heart had begun
beating faster.

Watching him move towards her, with a languid purpose that had made her stomach tighten painfully, she had been forced to face the truth. That her body's response to him in the boardroom had been no one-off. And that, even while she loathed him, his beauty could still reduce the world around her to mere scenery.

'Good.'

Max's voice cut into her confused thoughts and, looking up, she felt her eyes bump into his. Instantly, she felt a rush of nerves, as though she was about to tackle the Cresta Run instead of merely eat lunch.

'Thanks, Jean-Luc.' His gaze never leaving her face, he dismissed the sommelier with a nod of his dark head. 'I hope you don't mind but I thought it would be easier if I selected the wine.' The corners of his mouth twitched. 'Save any arguments.'

'Of course,' she said tightly, her heart banging against her chest. 'What did you choose?'

'A Clement-Dury Montrachet to start, and then a Domaine-Corton Pinot Noir to follow.'

'I like them both,' she said truthfully. 'Especially the Montrachet. It has such a good finish.'

Max grinned suddenly, and the unguarded excitement in his eyes caught her off-balance.

'It does, doesn't it? I like the balance of flavours—and that citrus really resonates.' He picked up the wine menu and flicked through it idly. 'They've got a great list here… really strong on small producers.' His face grew mocking. 'Although, rather embarrassingly for them, the management turned me down when I was starting out.'

Margot looked at him blankly, caught off guard by his remark, for—just like the rest of his life—Max's dizzyingly rapid rise to success was a mystery to her.

'It must have been hard for you,' she said cautiously. 'It's amazing…what you've done.'

He shrugged. 'I worked hard, and it helped that we got some outstanding reviews in the wine press.'

She nodded, but she hardly took in his words. She was too distracted by the speed with which their relationship was moving. Yesterday they had been hurling the verbal equivalent of thunderbolts at one another, and yet here there were today, talking almost normally, just like any other couple having lunch.

Tearing off a piece of her roll, she slid it into her mouth and forced herself to chew. And that was what she'd wanted, wasn't it? A civilised arrangement, free from unsettling feelings and even more unsettling actions.

Her skin grew warm as once again she remembered that kiss in the boardroom, remembered pleasures buried but not forgotten, the glowing imprint of his lips and fingers on her skin…

The sommelier returned at that moment and, heart pounding, she waited for him to pour the wine into their glasses. When finally they were alone again she said crisply, 'Is that why you chose this place?' She made herself look across at him. 'Or was it the allure of the black door?'

She was referring to the famous hidden entrance to the building, which allowed the hotel's A-list clientele and their overnight guests to come and go without having to face the intruding lenses of the paparazzi.

His mouth curled upwards. 'The former, I'm afraid. Sadly, I don't have anything or anyone to hide from the press.' He made a show of hesitating, his eyes glittering with amusement. 'Oh, I'm sorry. Was that the Duvernay way of telling me that you're planning on staying over?'

She glared at him, torn between fury at his arrogance and despair at the lurch of heat his words produced.

Picking up another piece of bread, she mashed butter into it savagely. 'If you seriously believe that, then you must have an awfully vivid imagination.'

He stared at her across the table. His expression was still pleasant and interested, but there was a definite tension in the air.

'I don't need an imagination to remember what it's like between us, Margot.'

Her body felt suddenly soft and boneless. She knew he was talking about what had happened in the boardroom, but she deliberately chose to misinterpret him.

'I'll have to take your word on that,' she said stiffly. 'What happened between us was such a long time ago and so brief I can barely remember it.'

'Really?'

The word slid over her skin like a caress, and he gave her a smile that made the edges of her vision start to blur. Breathing in unsteadily, she curled her fingers into her palms, feeling her skin tighten with shame at how easily she had succumbed to the pull of the past. At how even here, now, her body was responding to his with a hunger and a lack of judgement that was both undeniable and humiliating.

As though reading her thoughts, he leaned forward, his eyes resting on her face, watching the colour spread slowly over her cheeks.

'Then your memory must be *awfully* poor, indeed. Or just in need of refreshing, perhaps.'

For a second they both stared at one another, and then he picked up his wine glass. '*À ta santé.*'

The meal was perfect. The hotel's chef was renowned, and clearly he was determined to impress. Ratte potatoes topped with a mousseline of smoked haddock and Sologne caviar was followed by turbot with wild pink garlic in a brown butter zabaglione. There was an array of seasonal regional French cheeses, and to finish an iced coffee parfait with a lemongrass-infused chocolate sorbet.

Laying down her cutlery, Margot felt sudden panic squeeze her chest. Throughout lunch the constant presence of the staff had prevented any long, awkward silences, and she had been able to smile and chat quite naturally. But now the meal was coming to an end, and as the waiters quietly left the room, she felt her pulse start to accelerate.

Being alone with Max had been difficult enough when she'd been shocked and angry. Now, though, the shock had faded, and her anger was at best intermittent—like Morse Code.

Unfortunately, what hadn't faded was her susceptibility to his beauty and sexuality. Her shoulders stiffened. But even if she couldn't control her body's response to him, she certainly didn't have to act on it.

Yes, she might have agreed to become his wife, but there was a huge difference between what was legal and what was *real*. Their wedding might be legal, but it would be purely for show. No ceremony, lawful or otherwise, could stop Max being the man who was blackmailing her into marriage—in other words, her enemy.

Remembering again that near-miss kiss in the boardroom, she shivered. Except what kind of enemies kissed?

Picking up her glass, she took a sip of wine. She wasn't going to think about that now. All she wanted to do at this moment was get through this meal, discuss the terms of their agreement and then leave.

Her mouth twisted. That, at least, was different from the past.

Back then she and Max had been desperate to be alone.

To have privacy to talk, to touch, to laugh, to listen. But there had always been people around them—estate workers, guests staying at the chateau, and of course her family. Back then it had been like a kind of torture to have to remember that they were 'just friends', and that she couldn't touch him as she did in private.

Quashing the memory of just how much she had liked to touch him in private, she looked up and found Max watching her appraisingly, the blue and green of his gaze so level and steady that her heart began banging inside her throat.

Hoping that her face revealed nothing of her thoughts, and eager to be away from his scrutiny, she said stiffly, 'Shall we take coffee in the lounge?'

To her relief, he nodded, but as she walked into the large, opulent sitting room she swore silently. It was bad enough there were no armchairs, but the curtains had been drawn against the piercing afternoon sun, and there was something about the shadowy room and the sleek black velvet sofas that made her stomach flip over—some hint of a private salon, of soft breathing and damp skin...

Summoning up what she hoped was a casual smile, she sat down. Seconds later she felt him drop down beside her, as she'd known he would, and then his weight tipped her slightly sideways, and she felt her pulse stumble as his leg brushed against hers.

Instantly the hairs on her arms stood up, and it took every ounce of willpower she had not to lean into the heat and hardness of his thigh and press her body against his.

Shaken by the close contact, shocked by the explicitness of her thoughts, she turned and stared quickly across the room to the gap between the curtains.

Outside the window Paris was all pink blossom and golden sunlight. It was the most perfectly romantic of backdrops and her heart began to beat faster, for it seemed so glaringly at odds with what she and Max were agreeing to do.

'Coffee?'

She blinked, then nodded, but in truth her mind was already slipping away—back to the memory of another sunlit afternoon and another cup of coffee.

It had been a moment of rare impulsiveness. Knowing it was Max's day off, she had gone to his cottage alone. She had felt bold and reckless—in short, nothing like her normal self. But when Max had finally opened the door, shirtless, his eyes neither green nor blue but somewhere in between, her bravado had fled, her body stilling, her mind blank with panic. Because that was as far as she'd got inside her head.

Everything else had been just a fantasy.

And maybe it would have stayed a fantasy—only, incredibly, Max had asked her in and made her a cup of coffee. A cup of coffee that had sat and gone cold while her fantasy became real. Or so she'd thought at the time.

She cleared her throat. 'Just black. Thank you.'

'When did you drop the sugar?'

Drop the sugar? She stared at him blankly. Was that some kind of code or slang?

He raised an eyebrow. 'You used to take sugar.'

It was not quite a question, and his voice sounded softer, almost teasing, as though the nod to their shared past had softened his mood.

But it wasn't fair of Max to change the tone from *sotto* to *scherzando* without warning. Nor was it fair of him to smile like that, she thought helplessly, her eyes drawn inexorably to the slight fullness of his lower lip. It wasn't fair of him to remind her of the past she'd worked so hard to forget. A past that hadn't even been real.

She cleared her throat.

'Yes, I did.' She nodded. 'But I stopped putting it in my coffee a few years ago. In fact, we barely eat any sugar at home any more—extra sugar, I mean.'

Max stared at her in silence, his face showing none of the emotion that was tearing through his chest.

Watching her talk, he had forgotten just for the briefest of moments why she was there. Forgotten why 'it'—the two of them—had ended all those years ago. Instead, he could only think of the reasons it had started.

Her smile. Her laughter. Her brain. He'd loved that she was smart—not just book-smart, although she had always been that but perceptive in a way that had suggested she was far older than nineteen.

And her body.

Useless to lie. He was a man, and what normal heterosexual man wouldn't respond to that arrangement of contours and curves and clefts. His heart thumped against the roof of his mouth and an answering pulse of desire started to beat in his groin.

Ignoring the heat breaking out on his skin, he forced himself to speak. 'Any particular reason?'

Margot shrugged. She hadn't expected him to pursue the topic, and suddenly she was grappling with how much to give away. Her grandfather's poor health was not common knowledge, but to give no answer would be just as revealing.

'My grandfather had a stroke about six months ago,' she said flatly. 'Modifying his diet was something the doctors suggested we do afterwards.' She took a deep breath. 'But I'm sure you didn't invite me here to talk about my grandfather's diet.'

Glancing down at her diamond-set wristwatch, she lifted her chin.

'And I know you must be as busy as I am. So perhaps we should start discussing the terms of our arrangement?'

Max felt himself tense. If he'd needed a reminder as to why their relationship had always been a non-starter it was there in those sentences, he thought on a rush of fury and resentment. For even now, when she was here *only* at his bidding, she still couldn't stop herself drawing a line in the sand, pointedly shutting him out of anything that trespassed on Duvernay matters and bringing the conversation back to business.

Briefly he considered telling her that the deal was off. That if she wanted money that badly there was a bank two doors down from the hotel and another one on the next street. But then he felt his pulse slow.

Looked at differently, Margot had done him a favour, reminding him of what mattered to her: her business and her bloodline. Both of which had been off-limits to a nobody like Max—until now.

He let his gaze drift slowly over her face. 'From memory, it was less of an invitation and more or an instruction,' he said softly. 'Or do you still think you have some say in what's happening here?'

Her eyes flared and he felt a beat of satisfaction, watching her struggle to stay calm.

'Fine! You told me to come,' she retorted, a note of frustration sharpening her voice, 'and I'm here. So, are we going to discuss our marriage or not?'

He lounged back, the shadow of stubble on his jawline co-ordinating perfectly with the velvet nap of the sofa. 'We are,' he said finally, his eyes never leaving her face, 'but first I want to give you this.'

Reaching into his jacket, he pulled out a small, square box.

His mouth curled into a mocking smile. 'Don't get too

excited. It's from necessity, not any sort of romantic impulse on my part. You'll need to wear it. In public, at least.'

Flipping open the lid, he dropped the box carelessly into her open hand.

There was a short, spiralling silence.

Gazing down, Margot felt her stomach clamp tight, like a vacuum sealing inside her. The ring was beautiful. A huge yellow diamond flanked by two smaller white diamonds. And yet for some reason she couldn't seem to take it in. Instead she could feel herself being dragged back in time, to the moment when Max had stood in front of her, a pear-cut sapphire set in a band of gold in his outstretched hand.

It had been the most exciting moment in her life.

And the most terrible.

The picture was frozen inside her head. Max, his face expressionless, herself, silent and rigid with shock. And then Yves strolling in, his easy smile twisting, his mood turning from sweet to sour in the blink of an eye, shouting accusations and threats, teeth bared like a cornered dog.

Her brother's anger had been shocking, awful, brutal. But not as brutal as Max's admission that none of it had been real. That he'd only ever wanted her for her money.

'It's beautiful.' She knew her voice sounded stilted, fake, but it was all she could manage.

Max studied her face. It was his own fault. For years he'd wanted to believe that he'd been wrong. That she had really wanted to be his wife, and that given the opportunity—

He gritted his teeth. But of course he'd been right the first time. Yves's intervention had merely brought things to a head. Showing not a flicker of emotion, he said quietly, 'I'm glad you like it.'

Margot looked up. Something in his voice elbowed

aside the promise she'd made not to ask about his personal life. She couldn't help the sudden swirling riptide of curiosity from rising up inside her, for of course she was curious.

And so, in spite of her intention to stay silent, she found herself saying, 'It's lucky neither of us had other commitments.'

She held her breath, waiting for an answer, a sharp needle of jealousy stabbing beneath her heart.

Max felt something heavy dragging down inside of him. If only he could reach across and shake that fixed, polite smile from her mouth. Or maybe it was himself he wanted to shake—anything to shift the dark, leaden ache in his chest.

Watching her, he felt his breath tangle into knots. Luck had nothing to do with it. After Margot he'd had relationships—no-strings, sexually satisfying affairs that had helped ease the sting of her rejection. But work had been his real commitment, for there he had been able to harness his anger and resentment, and that had driven the ambition that had taken him back to France and to that meeting with Emile.

Clearing his throat, he bit down on the anger rising inside him. 'Don't you mean lucrative?' he said coolly.

Her head jerked up, and the stunned, helpless expression on her face made something claw at him inside. But he told himself he didn't care, and pretending he'd noticed nothing, he smiled casually.

'I've picked out wedding rings for both of us, so all you need to do is speak to your family,' he continued relentlessly. 'Tell them that you'll be away for a couple of days. Oh, and you'll need a dress.'

'Away where? And why do I need a dress?' She frowned suspiciously.

He raised an eyebrow. 'To get married in, of course. We leave for the Seychelles tomorrow.'

She gazed at him in wordless disbelief, a flutter of fear skittering down her spine. 'Tomorrow?'

His eyes were cool and mocking. 'What?' he asked softly, and she could hear the taunting note in his voice. 'Did you think I was going to wait another ten years?'

Her head was suddenly aching and her vison was going watery at the edges. She opened her mouth, then closed it again. Her brain seemed to have stopped functioning. 'This is a joke, right? I mean, you can't expect me to marry you *tomorrow*.'

'I don't. The paperwork won't be ready in time.' The upward curve of his mouth was like a fish hook through her heart. 'I do, however, expect you to marry me in three days.'

For a moment she could only stare at him in stunned silence. And then finally she shook her head, her blonde hair flicking from side to side like a lioness's tail. 'I don't care about what you expect,' she snapped, her eyes clashing with his. 'That isn't going to happen.'

Over the last twenty-four hours she had, if not fully adjusted to her fate, at least accepted the benefits of marrying Max. But as far as she was concerned telling her family was a long way off. She'd anticipated an engagement period of several months, during which time she would have got her grandfather and Louis used to the idea of Max as her boyfriend, then her fiancé. Now, though, the option of gently breaking her future plans to them was not just under threat, it was in pieces.

She shivered. Her stomach felt as though it was filling with ice.

For most people a wedding in an exotic location with few legalities and a minimal waiting time would probably sound spontaneous and romantic. To her, though, it sounded like an exact duplicate of her parents' hasty elopement.

But she couldn't explain that to Max. Not without revealing more about herself than she was willing to share with a man who was not only blackmailing her into marriage, but was incapable of even the most basic human empathy.

She gazed at him stonily. 'Surely you can understand that? I mean, what exactly am I supposed to tell my family? I can't just roll up and announce that I'm getting married.'

He shrugged. 'Come, come, Margot. You're a Duvernay. You can do what you like. Besides, you've had a lot of practice in lying. I imagine you'll think of something.'

The rush of fury was intoxicating. Suddenly she was on her toes like a boxer, fingers twitching, clenching and unclenching. 'You unspeakable pig—'

He cut across her, his voice razor-edged and cold as steel. 'Spare me the outrage. You lied to your family for months about our relationship last time. Now you only have to do it for three days.'

'Wasn't it lucky that I did?' she snarled. 'At least they were spared *your* lies and deceit.'

There was a charged silence. He didn't reply, just continued to sit there, his face taut, his eyes impassive. And then, just as she was about to demand a response, he abruptly stood up and with careless, unhurried ease, walked to the door and yanked it open. Stepping aside, he stared coolly back across the room, his jawline and cheekbones suddenly in shadow.

'Let me make this simple for you, Margot. Either you agree to marry me in three days or you walk through this door now and take your chances with the bank.'

His tone was pleasant, but there was no mistaking the ultimatum in his voice.

Margot gazed at him in silence, her heart skidding sideways like car on black ice. Surely he was calling her bluff. He had to be. And yet she couldn't bring herself to find out, for if she got up and walked towards the door it was just possible that she would lose everything.

She had no weapons to bring to the fight, and escalating things would only make that fact obvious to Max. All she could do was back down with as much dignity as she could manage.

'Since you put it so charmingly,' she said stiffly, ignoring the heartbeat that was telegraphing frantically inside her chest, 'I'll do it.' She lifted her chin, her brown eyes locking on to his face, staring him down. 'But on one condition.'

'Condition?'

She heard the hint of surprise in his voice, and felt a fleeting quiver of satisfaction. 'Yes, damn you.' Matching his level, assessing gaze with what she hoped was one of her own, she gave a humourless laugh. 'What did you think? That I'd just bow down to your threats and intimidation?'

Max let his eyes drift over her face, seeing both the pulse quivering at the base of her throat—that beautiful, graceful throat—and the discs of colour spreading over her cheeks. No, he hadn't thought that, and in a way he hadn't wanted it either. He would never want that from this woman who had been like a living flame in his arms.

Casually he pushed the door shut and walked across the room, stopping in front of her. 'Name it,' he demanded.

'As soon as we're married I want to tell my grandfather and brother in person—before details are released to the press.'

The marriage would be a shock to both of them, but she knew that they would accept and understand it better if she told them herself.

Max stared down at her, trying to ignore the heady scent of her perfume. It was a shock. Not her demand—which was almost laughably inconsequential—but the intensity of his relief that she hadn't got up and stormed through the door. Irrational though it sounded, it didn't matter that the marriage hadn't happened. She already felt like his wife. And, having got so far, he wasn't about to lose her now.

Letting her win this particular battle was unimportant in the scheme of things. It certainly didn't mean that he was about to give her power over anything else—like his feelings, for example. Besides, he had other, more effective ways to remind her that he was in charge.

He raised his shoulders dismissively. 'Okay. I'm happy for you to do that.' His eyes locked on to hers. 'Just as I'm sure *you're* happy to sign the prenuptial agreement I sent over.'

Turning, he picked a laminated folder up from the table behind the sofa and held it out to her.

'I take it you've read it?'

Margot nodded. Her heart began to thump against her chest.

He had emailed it over last night, and she'd gone over it twice. It contained no surprises. But it still jarred, though—stung, actually—the fact that ten years ago she had taken him at his word, whereas now he was demanding that she make no claim on his estate.

Her lips tightened. 'Yes, I've read it. There don't seem to be any problems.'

Aside from the small, incontrovertible fact that she was bartering herself to a man she had once loved without restraint, and with a hope she now found inconceivable.

Suddenly she just wanted to sign the damned thing and be gone. To be anywhere that Max wasn't.

She reached into her bag, but he was too fast for her.

'Here—use mine.'

He was holding out a black and gold fountain pen. It was identical to the one her grandfather used, and just for a moment she thought she might be sick. But, swallowing the metallic taste in her mouth, she took the pen from his fingers with what she hoped was an expression of pure indifference and, flipping through the document to the last page, carelessly scrawled her signature next to his, doing the same again seconds later on the other copy.

Misery snaked over her skin, but she wasn't about to let Max know how much she was hurting. He might hold all the cards, but there was some small satisfaction to be had from not acknowledging that fact—particularly to him.

Only suddenly that wasn't enough. Suddenly she didn't just want to hide her pain, she wanted to hurt him as he had hurt her. Laying the pen carefully on top of the paper, she looked up and deliberately fixed her gaze on his maddeningly handsome face.

'One last thing. Just so we're clear, this marriage is a business arrangement. Sex—' she punched the word towards him '—is not and is never going to be part of the deal. Whatever physical relationship we had, it happened a long time ago.'

A mocking smile tugged at his mouth. 'I wouldn't call twenty-four hours a long time.'

Mortified, she felt the air thump out of her lungs. How she regretted that kiss—or if not the kiss then the treacherous weakness of the body that had allowed it to happen.

'That was just curiosity,' she said quickly, trying to sound as if she meant it, as though only a fraction of her mind was on him.

'I just wanted a taste—you know, an *amuse bouche*. See if the menu was still worth sampling.' She was aware that her cheeks were flushed, that her voice was shaking ever so slightly, but she forced herself to hold his gaze. 'Only I guess I've grown up a lot. Had a bit more experience…tried different flavours. I know some couples go for that "sex with the ex" thing, but I'm going to pass on it.'

She could hardly believe the words that were coming out of her mouth. It felt unreal, talking that way, and to Max in particular, but she knew that she had his attention. For a moment she held her breath, waiting for his reaction, already anticipating his fury. But his face didn't change, and when finally he spoke his voice was as expressionless as his unblinking eyes.

'Of course you are—and now, unfortunately, I have another meeting scheduled. I hope you enjoyed your lunch…'

Gazing up at him, it took a moment for his words to sink in, and then, as they did, she realised with a rush of embarrassment that he was waiting politely and patiently for her to leave.

Back in her car, it took several minutes of deep breathing before her hands stopped shaking and she could start the engine. Pulling out into the late-afternoon traffic, she could feel questions pawing at her brain like a pack of dogs with a bone. Why had he acted like that? Why hadn't he thrown her remark back in her face?

Leaning back against the smooth leather seat, she rested her arm against the doorframe, and gnawed distractedly at her thumbnail.

Even at the most basic level her words would have been insulting to any man. But to Max it had been personal. So why had he deliberately chosen not to respond?

She pressed her thumb against the corner of her mouth.

It was probably just another attempt to belittle her. Or maybe he was trying to mess with her head so that she'd end up with all these unanswerable questions swamping her brain. Or—

An icy shiver slipped down her spine, and she groaned softly.

Or maybe he just hadn't believed her.

And, really, why would he? When she didn't even believe herself?

Remembering the moment when he'd pressed his mouth to hers—the all-encompassing heat of that kiss and the way her body had surrendered to his—she felt heat flare low in her pelvis...

The blast of a horn burst into her thoughts, and she watched dully as a taxi surged past her, the driver gesticulating and shouting abuse into the warm, sticky air.

Her arms felt like jelly, and with an effort she indicated left, out of the city.

She was such a fool! Instead of puncturing his pride, her stupid denial had merely drawn attention to the terrible, humiliating truth. That she still wanted him with an intensity that was beyond her conscious control. But, terrible though it was to have betrayed herself like that, what was far worse was the private but equally devastating realisation that she couldn't imagine a time when that humiliating fact would ever change.

CHAPTER FIVE

RESTING HER HANDS against the edge of the balcony adjoining her hotel bedroom, Margot gazed out across the Indian Ocean, her brown eyes narrowing against the glare of morning sunlight, the thin silk of her robe lifting in the warm breeze coming off the water.

In just over five hours she would be Mrs Max Montigny—even just thinking that sentence made her feel dizzy. Or maybe that was the adrenaline. Her muscles clamped tighter. Either way, everything had all happened with such surreal speed that none of it felt real, and the sense of unreality was only being exacerbated by her idyllic surroundings.

Her gaze drifted back inland. The view from her hotel room was pure fantasy. A castaway island of palm-tree-framed beaches fusing with a dreamy turquoise sea. But there was a wildness to its beauty too, so that it was easy to feel you were the first person ever to leave your meandering footprints in the powdery white sands.

Raising a hand to block out the sun, she squinted down the beach. Perhaps not quite the first person. A figure was moving effortlessly across the dunes, covering the distance with impressive speed.

Wearing a black vest and shorts, his tanned skin gleaming like polished wood in the sunlight, Max was returning from his morning run. He moved with a focus and steadiness that in turn steadied *her*, so that some of her tension ebbed away.

Even from a distance, and with the sun in her eyes, his body looked just as spectacular as she remembered it—lean and sculptured and powerful. Her eyes lingered greedily on the striped bands of his taut, abdominal muscles before dropping to where the V of his obliques met the sagittal line of fine dark hair in the centre of his stomach.

He was so perfect, so tempting. An intoxicating blend of strength and beauty that made her feel weak with desire. Her mouth twisted. Not that she'd given in to temptation again. But being around Max again was not just unsettling physically, it was messing with her head too—dredging up memories, making her question the life she was living, the choices she'd made.

Over the last few years boyfriends had come and gone, but none had lasted, and that was completely understandable. Running the House of Duvernay was most definitely not a nine-to-five job, so her personal life had by necessity taken a back seat to her professional one, and she'd been grateful it had, for she hadn't been ready or willing to get too involved, to get hurt again, to *feel*.

Or rather she'd been scared not of feeling something but of never feeling *as much* for anyone as she'd felt for Max.

She bit her lip. Even now she could remember it—the stunned realisation, part-fear, part-euphoria that he had chosen *her*, wanted *her*.

Her stomach clenched. No, not her. Her money.

Breathing out, she gazed at the moving figure.

If only she could go back to that time—back to when she'd believed that he wanted her for herself. Her heart gave a twitch of irritation. And do what? Let her stupid, treacherous body betray her again?

She glanced back at Max, her eyes tracking his progress. The sun was already high overhead, but he seemed immune to the heat of its rays. He was running—no, make that sprinting—effortlessly across the sand, as though he was training for some elite military unit.

And then, as though he'd crossed an imaginary finishing line, he pulled up sharply, his legs slowing to a jog, then to a walk as he glanced down at his watch.

Her pulse was racing as hard as if she too had just run the length of the beach, and then her breath stalled in her throat as she watched him reach into the pocket of his shorts and pull out his phone.

She felt her eyes narrow. Surely today of all days he might have stopped working. But it was pointless getting angry about it. After all, it wasn't as though this marriage was anything other than a business arrangement for either of them.

Although, thanks to Max's extensive and careful preparations, nobody except the two of them would ever know that it wasn't real. Not only had he organised the paperwork and arranged the venue, he had sorted out the food, the flowers, and flown out a team of stylists to oversee everything on site. And everything was spot-on.

All she'd had to think about was the dress...

A light breeze lifted her hair in front of her face and, pushing it aside, she felt her pulse dip. Given that she was only marrying Max to save her business, it really shouldn't matter what she wore. But, to her surprise, her wedding gown still felt like more than just a dress to her.

Staring up at the cloudless sky, she let the sun warm her face. Back in Paris, feeling harried by the pace of his arrangements, she had considered choosing an off-the-peg dress from one of the big department stores. It had been a childish impulse, really—another meaningless attempt to prove how little she cared about him and their phony wedding.

But in the end she hadn't been able to bring herself to do it. And it hadn't just been because of the risk that somebody might spot her browsing the rails and leak it to the media.

Lowering her head, she drew in a deep breath. She was a Duvernay, and in her family's history weddings were not just celebrations but life-impacting events, defined not just by who you married but what you wore.

Her grandmother's dress had been spectacular. A fairy tale confection with metres of tulle and millions of hand-sewn pearls. It had taken fifty seamstresses nearly three months to create.

In contrast, her mother had recycled the simple knee-length tulle-skirted dress that she'd worn for her eighteenth birthday party.

Each had known instinctively what she wanted to wear to marry the man she had chosen to be her husband. Only where did that leave her? She was marrying a man she didn't love, out of necessity. What exactly was the dress code for a marriage of convenience?

Despite the heat of the sun, Margot shivered.

It didn't help that she was being forced to do something she'd actually dreamed of doing. Ten years ago she had been happily imagining a wedding day in the future. Only Max had been more than just her groom—he'd been the air she breathed, the gravitational pull of her world.

For a second she braced herself against the pain, fingers tightening against the balustrade. But that had been then. In the present, this wedding wasn't about Max. Just like the rest of her life, it was about creating an illusion.

She needed her grandfather to accept her sudden decision to get married. Actually, she wanted him to be happy about it. Only with the speed and secrecy of the arrangements so closely mirroring his daughter's elopement, she knew that the only way to make that happen was by staging the perfect wedding.

And, no matter how little time there had been, Max Montigny's wife would *never* wear a department store dress. Her gown, just like her ring, would have to look the part. As her groom undoubtedly would.

Max was still talking on his phone, his handsome face relaxed and unguarded, and something about his expression made her heart contract—for she could still remember just how heavenly it had felt to be the object of that gaze.

Her fingers trembled against the smooth wood as she wondered what it would feel like if today was actually real, and instead of her money or her business, Max actually wanted her.

It was not the first time that thought had crossed her mind. In fact, it had been popping into her head with maddening regularity ever since she'd watched him walk out of her boardroom that first day. But thinking it could ever happen would require an almost childlike level of imagination, and she was done with building castles in the air. The only castle she cared about now was her family home.

She needed to focus on the facts—which were that Max might be in control of her business, but she was in control of everything else. And that included how she chose to respond to him. All she had to do was stay cool and detached and civil and their marriage would hopefully be civilised too.

Glancing down at Max's sweat-slicked skin, she licked her lips. That might be easier in theory than in practice. Although Max wasn't quite the barbarian she'd accused him of being, he was still the least civilised person she'd ever met, seemingly untroubled by blackmail and extortion.

However, even from the short amount of time they'd spent discussing his plans for Duvernay, she had to admit that he'd actually been modest when he'd said he had a head for business. He was smart, quick and creative—and, although he had an innate authority that reminded her of her grandfather, he was also surprisingly willing to listen to his staff. And even more surprisingly to her.

She had expected to be swept aside, but instead, at his suggestion, they would be working together as co-CEOs, his argument being that having 'two in the box' was better than one.

If only their marriage could be as equable and as close, she thought wistfully.

At that moment, almost as if he could hear her thoughts, Max turned and stared fixedly across the beach towards her balcony.

Her pulse jumped. Hot-cheeked, horrified that she had been discovered in such a blatant act of voyeurism, she turned her face away from the magnetic pull of his gaze and inched back into her room.

Her skin was prickling. *Oh, how was she going to do this?* She couldn't even face him at a distance and from the safety of her hotel room. How was she going to stand opposite him and repeat vows neither of them believed to be true?

If only there was another way…

But there wasn't.

Duvernay's problems were not going to just disappear, and that was why she was here and why she was going to go through with this marriage.

A knock on the door broke into her thoughts and, grateful for the interruption, she tightened her wrap. The time for thinking was over. Now she needed to get ready for her wedding.

Three hours later she was standing nervously in front of the mirror, gazing at her reflection. The transformation was complete.

'You look beautiful.'

Her eyes darted gratefully to Camille Feuillet, friend and premier couturier from her favourite fashion house, who had flown out from Paris late last night. She had known the older woman ever since she was a gauche teenager, struggling with shyness and a famous mother. Camille had helped her find a style, and she was the one person she'd trusted to design a dress for her wedding day.

'It's lovely,' she said slowly. 'Camille, you are so clever. I never dreamed that it would look like this—that I could look like this.'

She had expected to feel different, but this was like alchemy. The dress was exquisite—and romantic. Camille had insisted on finishing the final details herself, hand-embroidering Margot and Max's initials into the beautiful, intricate floral lace veil.

Margot felt suddenly shy. Thanks to the woman standing beside her she would not only be able to convince her family and the world's media that she was marrying the love of her life, she would be able to do so feeling good about herself—just like a real bride.

'Thank you, Camille,' she said softly.

'You are so welcome.' Camille smiled, and then her face creased and she brushed a hand against her eyes. 'I promised myself I wouldn't cry but I can't help it. You just look so lovely.'

'More like lucky!' Despite the ache in her chest, the smile she gave the other woman was genuine. Camille had made her a wedding dress of heart-stopping beauty. It wasn't her fault the wedding itself was a sham of what it might have been.

'You've given me so much help and inspiration. I couldn't have done it without you, so thank you. And thank you for coming all this way. I know how busy you are—'

'It was my pleasure.' Camille hesitated, and then, glancing over at Margot, she giggled. 'Besides, I think this might be the one time your extremely cool fiancé actually gets a little hot under the collar, and I wouldn't want to miss that for anything.'

Margot nodded. Her smile didn't falter, but she felt her pulse quiver. No doubt most grooms *did* get emotional, seeing their bride, but then most grooms hadn't blackmailed their bride down the aisle. And Max didn't *do* emotion—or at least not the romantic, helpless kind of emotion that Camille was talking about.

Instead, he was fine-tuned for winning.

Remembering the dark, calculating glitter in his eyes when he'd kissed her in the boardroom, she knew that his desire was as cold and controlled as his heart. Whatever Max was feeling and thinking right now, she would lay odds that it had more to do with his business than his forthcoming nuptials.

'Are you ready?'

Camille's voice broke into her thoughts and, steadying her breathing, she turned and nodded. Then, pinching the edges of the veil between her fingers, she lowered it carefully over her face and walked slowly towards the door and her future.

On the other side of the hotel, his dark suit a contrast to the bleached boards of the chapel, Max Montigny stared down at his phone, his fingers hovering over the keyboard.

He was standing slightly apart from the priest, and the two elderly estate workers who had been carefully chosen by his security team to act as witnesses for the wed-

ding were waiting patiently behind him, but he was barely
aware of them, or of his surroundings.

Not the sun that had drained the colour out of the sky,
or the tiny open-sided chapel that was smothered in white
frangipani flowers. All his concentration was fixed on
his phone.

He read the message on the screen, deleted a few words,
retyped them and then finally deleted them all.

Switching the phone to 'silent', he dropped it in his
pocket. It had taken him nearly ten years to get to this
point, and he wasn't about to tempt fate with an unneces-
sary and premature text. Soon enough Margot would be
wearing his ring, and then the whole world would be able
to see that Max Montigny was the equal of the Duvernays.

He breathed in sharply. The thought of Margot finally
becoming Mrs Montigny was dizzying. Bracing his shoulders, he gazed at the ocean. If only he could steady his
breathing… But it was impossible to do so, for every time
he inhaled, the warm, fragrant air reminded him of the
perfume Margot wore.

It was driving him crazy. Not just the fact that the scent
of her seemed to be following him everywhere, but the
way it conjured up the memory of her brown-eyed challenge in his hotel room.

'I just wanted a taste…you know, an amuse bouche. *See
if the menu was still worth sampling. I know some couples
go for that "sex with the ex" thing, but I'm going to pass.'*

He'd known she was lying, but somehow that only made
her claim more maddening—and frustrating.

Ignoring the pulse beating in his groin, he straightened
his cuffs and turned towards the priest and the witnesses,
nodding in acknowledgement. From years of keeping his
own counsel he knew that the expression on his face gave
nothing away—not even a hint as to the thoughts twisting

through his head—and the thought calmed him. Revealing emotion—*feeling* emotion—was an act of self-destruction, a handing over of power to the person most equipped to hurt you the most.

And that was particularly true of the woman he was about to marry.

He let out a slow, unsteady breath. What amazed him was that he'd actually got this far. Back in France when Margot had given in to his demands, he had been too busy struggling with the various emotions produced by seeing her again to register the full consequences of his proposal.

It had been an act of impulse and pride—for, much as he'd moved on with his life, a part of him had never forgotten or forgiven her for throwing his proposal back in his face, just as he himself had been thrown off the Duvernay estate.

Now, though, impulse would become legal fact—a contract only dissolvable by law. In less than an hour Margot would be his wife, and that thought blew his mind. Or it would have done if he hadn't chosen that particular moment to look up.

His heart gave a lurch and his fingers tightened involuntarily as he watched Margot step tentatively into the chapel, her wary brown gaze resting on his face as she approached him.

Behind him, he heard someone—the priest, probably—clear his throat. There was a flurry of activity and he knew that he should turn round, that he needed to turn round in order for the ceremony to start. But he couldn't look away. His eyes were beyond his control, following her hungrily, pulled by some inexorable force, like twin tides dragged by the luminous pale loveliness of a new moon.

He felt his heart slam against his ribcage, his eyes taking in every detail as she took another step towards him—

and then stopped. A hush like a held breath had fallen over the chapel, and even the ocean's waves seemed to be silent, as though their ceaseless motion had been stilled by the presence of such flawless beauty.

She looked exquisite. Beneath the veil her long blonde hair was scooped into some kind of low bun, her bare shoulders were gleaming in the sunlight, and her dress...

His gaze travelled over the delicate lace of her bodice to the gently flaring skirt. He had expected her to look lovely—what bride didn't? But Margot was more than just beautiful. She had always been more than just beautiful. She was a mystery that he'd obsessively wanted to solve, that had always been just beyond his reach.

Until now.

And so, ignoring tradition, he walked towards her and held out his hand.

The service was short and to the point. Speaking the vows, and listening to Margot repeat the familiar promises of love and loyalty in her soft, unwavering voice, he couldn't actually believe that it was happening. And yet here he was, sliding the band of diamonds set in gold onto her finger, and she was pushing a plain gold band onto his.

Lifting her veil, he watched the pupils of her eyes widen in the shade of the chapel. The certificate they would sign in a moment would be tangible evidence that finally he had proved her and her family wrong. That was why he was here, and he should be feeling relief, satisfaction, triumph... And yet he felt tense, almost restless, as though there was something more...something more important than retribution only he wasn't sure what it was.

His gaze shifted, slid upwards to her eyes, and he took a deep breath, confounded by the conflict he saw there. It reminded him of that first winter he and his mother had moved to Paris, struggling with the sudden loss of their old life and with feelings he hadn't understood.

He'd felt so young and helpless, so lost and alone, so stripped of all defences, and the thought that Margot should be feeling like that now resonated inside him, so that suddenly his stomach was churning, his breath jamming in his throat.

His hand twitched and he almost reached out, as any human would, instinctively wanting to comfort her. But to have done so would have been clumsy—inappropriate, somehow.

Quickly, he reminded himself that the only way this marriage would work would be to keep memories and emotions out of it. She had agreed to become his wife and he didn't owe her any gentleness. He could simply have sat back and watched her business collapse, but instead he had given her and her family a way out from financial ruin and public humiliation.

It might not be the marriage she wanted, to the man she wanted, but as far as he was concerned she had got more than she deserved.

'Margot and Max, you have expressed your love to one another through the commitment and promises you have made, and celebrated your union with the giving and receiving of rings.' The priest smiled.

It was just words, Margot told herself nervously.

But, hearing the priest talk about love and commitment, she felt her heart start to pound. Glancing down at her hand, Margot stared at the diamond band nestling against her engagement ring. It was breathtakingly beautiful. Elegant. Timeless. And it wasn't just the ring. Everything—the sun-soaked setting, the lush, fragrant flowers, the smiling priest, even Max himself—was so perfect it was impossible to resist.

Her pulse gave a leap like a startled deer.

Especially Max.

He was close enough that she could differentiate between the heat of his body and the warmth of the spice-warm air.

Dry-mouthed, she stared at him, her eyes fluttering helplessly over the man standing beside her, her gaze drawn to his face. Not because he was now her husband, but because he was and would always be her magnetic north, and the pull between them was beyond any kind of rational thought.

Particularly when he looked so devastating.

The dark fabric of his suit fitted him like a second skin, and the pure, brilliant whiteness of his shirt perfectly off-set his compelling eyes and *café crème* colouring. In the shade of the chapel his features looked as though they might have been cast from bronze.

He was the perfect groom in every way, and just for a moment she couldn't help herself. All the promises she'd made to herself earlier that morning were overridden, and she let herself imagine what it would be like if this was a marriage of love and Max simply wanted *her*.

That thought was still uppermost in her mind as the priest looked across and, smiling again at both of them, said quietly, 'You are no longer simply partners and best friends. Today you have chosen to be joined in marriage. Therefore, it is my pleasure to pronounce you husband and wife. Max, you may now kiss your bride!'

Max felt a jolt pass through his body. So that was it. It was over—finished. Done.

Or maybe it was just beginning.

His breath seemed to tear his throat as he looked into Margot's eyes. Something was happening in them. They held an expression half-startled, half-spellbound.

And then he realised why.

He wasn't sure of how or when it had happened but he was holding her, his arm curving around her back so that she was pressed against his body.

He stared down at her, a flutter of heat sidewinding over his skin. Her lips were the same colour as rose petals, her mouth a curving pink bow that he knew tasted as good as it looked. Kissing her was part of the ceremony. But after what she'd said to him in his hotel it felt more like a dare. A chance to raise the stakes. A challenge he could not walk away from.

He wanted to prove her wrong—to show her and everyone watching that she couldn't resist him. And, lowering his head, he let his mouth brush against hers. It was more of a graze than a kiss, fleeting and feather-light. But even as he lifted his head he felt his stomach flip. She stared up at him in silence, her gaze finding something, needing something...

And, looking down into her wide, unguarded brown eyes, he felt a rush of possessive desire as swift and unstoppable as white water rapids.

Finally, she was his wife.

His.

Pulling her soft body closer, her slid a finger under her chin and tipped her head up. His heart was pounding and the air was tightening around them as he studied her face. And then he was kissing her hungrily, one hand wrapping around her waist, the other pushing through her hair, anchoring her against him.

Margot felt the ground tip beneath her feet.

Grabbing at his jacket, she clutched at the smooth fabric

as his tongue parted her lips. And then she was falling…
falling back in time…her body responding unquestioningly, willingly, to the power and heat of his mouth.

Around her the world was spinning faster and faster,
like a ride at the funfair. She felt giddy and clumsy and
boneless. All she could do was cling on tight to the one
solid object she could find. And, leaning into Max's hard,
muscular body, she closed her eyes.

And suddenly there was only Max. His mouth, his
hands, the warm density of his chest. She wanted him,
and she had no conscious thought or physical wish to hold
back, to do anything but open her body to his.

But even as the taste of him filled her mouth she felt
his body tense, and then he was breaking the kiss, and instead of his pulse beating through her veins like a metro-
nome she could hear the tranquil sound of nearby waves
washing onto the beach.

Dazedly she looked up at him, pressing her hand against
his chest to steady herself. But only for a second.

She felt her body stiffen, and a damp stickiness began
creeping over her skin. Only it had nothing to do with the
balmy subtropical heat and everything to do with the cool,
appraising look in his eyes.

Her limbs felt as if they were made of wood.

Had she learnt nothing from the past?

Ten years ago Max had used other such kisses to seduce
her, to fool her into believing his lies. This time, though,
he didn't need to fool her. It was the priest and the witnesses he needed to convince, so that they would see what
he wanted them to see. Not an act of coercion or revenge,
but two people declaring their love for one another.

And clearly it had worked.

She felt her stomach plunge as the priest stepped forward, his gentle face creased in a smile of wonder and ap-

proval. 'You have kissed many times, I'm sure. But today your kiss means so much more. It has sealed your marriage. Today, your kiss is a promise.'

Max looked over at her, his eyes glinting as they swept over the flush that she knew was colouring her cheekbones.

'Yes, it is,' he said slowly. 'One I fully intend to keep.'

They were signing the register. Margot felt as though she was sleepwalking. Posing above the heavy leather-bound book, pen in hand, she smiled for the photographer, trying her hardest to look like the radiant bride that her grandfather and brother would be expecting to see.

There was confetti, champagne and congratulations. By the time they were walking back to the hotel Margot's mouth was aching with the effort of smiling and she felt exhausted, but also relieved, for now that it was done there was no more need to agonise over whether she was doing the right thing.

She was Margot Montigny now. And she knew that her grandfather and Louis would accept her marriage. For the first time since Emile had dropped his bombshell the burden she was carrying felt lighter. Now all she wanted to do was get back to France and break the news to her family.

Stomach swooping downwards, she stepped unthinkingly into the waiting limousine. And then, as the doors closed and the sleek black car began to move forward, she felt a sharp dart of apprehension.

Frowning, she turned to Max. 'Where are we going? I thought we were eating at the hotel.'

His handsome face looked relaxed, and the colour of his eyes was indistinguishable in the cool, shaded interior of the car. 'It's a surprise,' he said softly.

Her heart thumped clumsily against her ribs. 'I don't like surprises.'

His eyes rested on her face, and something about the steady calmness of his gaze unnerved her more than his words.

'Is that right? I thought all women liked surprises.'

She glared at him. 'Flattering though it is to be compared to every other female on the planet, I would rather just stick to the plan. The plan we agreed on.'

Something flared in his eyes. 'We just got married. Can't I be just a little bit romantic?'

Ignoring the prickle of heat in her cheeks, Margot stared at him. 'Not in my experience—no. Besides, we both know this isn't about romance, so stop pretending it is and take me back to the hotel.'

His gaze was steady on her face. 'That's not going to happen.'

She shook her head. 'Oh, yes, it is. You said we would eat and then fly home.'

'I did, didn't I?'

He shifted in his seat, and something in the casual way he leaned back against the leather made a fog of panic swirl up inside of her.

'So what's changed?' She glowered at him.

He shrugged, but his eyes on hers were curiously intent. '*You* have, baby. Before you were just a woman—now you're my wife.'

Her heart contracted. 'I know I'm your wife,' she said mutinously. 'But I don't see why that means we can't eat at the hotel. Or not eat at all.' She held his gaze. 'I'd be happy to fly home now.'

'And miss our honeymoon?' he said softly. 'What would people think? And I know how much you care about what people think, Margot.'

The blood drained from her face. Something cold and clammy was inching down her spine. 'No, that's not what we agreed, Max.' Her voice was a whisper now. 'You can't do that—'

'And yet I am.' His gaze swept over her face. 'Don't worry. It's no trouble. You see, I have a house here. Just along the coast. And that's where we're going to spend the next two weeks. Just the two of us. What could be more romantic than that?'

CHAPTER SIX

THE DRIVE TO the house passed quickly and silently.

For Margot, silence was the only possible option. Pressed into the corner of the car, she was just too angry to speak. But inside her head angry accusations were whirling around like a flock of seabirds.

How dared he do this?

How dared he unilaterally change their plans? Ignore everything that they'd agreed, trample over her feelings and wishes?

She'd agreed to marry him on one condition—that she could speak to her family before rumours of their wedding became public knowledge. It was the only condition she'd set, and even though she was doing everything he'd asked he still hadn't managed to do that one thing for her.

Her jaw clenched painfully. How could she be so gullible? All that rubbish about being happy to tell her grandfather in person, letting her believe that they were going to fly back to France, when all the time he'd just been pretending so that he could do what he'd said he'd wanted to do right at the start—watch her family suffer.

She glared at him, her cheeks flushing with colour. He was selfish, thoughtless and utterly untrustworthy.

Her fingers curled into the fabric of her dress. All her life it had been the same, the people who were supposed to love her had just done what they wanted, put their needs above hers, and then expected her to put up with it.

No, not just put up with it, she thought savagely. They actually expected her to smile in public while in private they turned her world upside down.

But then selflessness was not part of her family's DNA. Or apparently her new husband's.

Beside her, Max stretched out his legs—a man without a care in the world. A man who was apparently either oblivious to or unconcerned by her silence.

She clenched her teeth. It wasn't that she'd expected him to be thoughtful. Given that he was blackmailing her into marrying him that would have been insane. But surely the whole point of this stupid arranged marriage was that there were rules…boundaries. They'd made an agreement and now Max had broken it.

Her hands tightened in her lap. It wasn't the unfairness of his actions that was so upsetting. Nor did she really care about ego. This was about her grandfather and her brother, and how they would feel when they woke up tomorrow and discovered that she'd sneaked off behind their backs to get married.

Her heart contracted. There was no way she could get in touch with her grandfather. She couldn't risk waking him with news like that—not when his health was so precarious. And while she *could* try ringing Louis… really, what would be the point? It was the last night of his holiday. He was probably out celebrating and having fun with his friends. If she spoke to him now it would ruin everything.

Her heart gave an angry thump.

If Max had done what he'd agreed they'd do, and they had flown back to France, she would have been able to make things right.

She'd had it all planned. They would go straight to the
chateau and Max would wait downstairs while she took
breakfast up to her grandfather. His favourite breakfast:
café au lait and eggs benedict—a legacy of his time in
America—but using a slice of *tartine* instead of muffins.
Then she would sit on the chair beside his bed and take
as long as was necessary to reassure him that she hadn't
turned into her mother.

It wouldn't be easy, but she knew that she would make
him understand. And once he was dressed and composed
they would go downstairs together, and everything would
be fine.

She swallowed. Now, though, Max had made that moment impossible. Now her grandfather would wake to the
news headlines that his beloved and utterly reliable grand-
daughter had been lying to his face and had eloped.

He would be heartbroken. And there was no doubt in
her mind that, whatever he'd just told her about wanting
to surprise her, that had been Max's intention all along.

*'I know how much you care about what people think,
Margot.'*

Her skin felt hot, her cheeks burning with humiliation
that she should have been so stupid as to trust him. Stiff,
angry words were bubbling in her throat and she turned
towards him, her eyes seeking his in the cool darkness of
the limo's interior.

But before she could open her mouth to unleash her
fury she felt the car start to slow and realised that they
had arrived at Max's house.

She watched him step out into the sunshine, and then
somehow she was taking his hand. There was a small
round of applause and, glancing up, she saw that they
were not alone. A group of people—presumably Max's
staff—all wearing white polo shirts and cream-coloured

shorts were standing in two lines on either side of the stairway leading up to the house, their friendly faces beaming down at her.

But it was not their smiles or even the brightness of the sun that made her blink. It was the building behind them.

Her heart bumped against her ribs. Theoretically, she knew the extent of Max's wealth. But, gazing up at the beautiful white modernist villa, she finally understood just how hard he must have worked, and despite the fury simmering inside her she couldn't stop herself from admiring the way he had managed to create this life for himself.

Was it really so surprising, though? Even when she'd first met him it had been clear that Max was no average employee. It hadn't been just his good looks that had made him stand out from everybody else. He'd been bright, focused, creative and exceptionally determined.

Her mouth twisted.

No doubt the same ruthless determination that had made him such a successful businessman made it equally easy for him to disrespect her wishes. She needed to remember that the next time she felt like admiring him.

Inside the villa the decor was modern, almost austere, and only a subtle change in flooring from bleached wood to the palest pink marble signalled the transition between inside and out. But even if the change had been signposted with flashing neon lights she would barely have noticed the difference, for her attention was fixed on the terrace where, beside the bluest pool she had ever seen, a beautiful glass table was set for two beneath a gleaming white sail-like canopy.

Gazing past the table to the ocean beyond, Margot swallowed. She had forgotten all about eating, and she was simmering with so much suppressed rage that she'd completely lost her appetite anyway. But this was her 'wedding breakfast', and of course to accompany the meal there would be—

'Champagne, darling?'

Max stepped forward, his eyes resting on her face, the irises so startlingly blue and green that she had a sudden vivid flashback to the first time they'd met, and how it hadn't felt real. Not just the dual colours of his gaze, but the fact that he was *there*, in her kitchen, this extraordinary, arrestingly beautiful man, talking and laughing and smiling...

Her spine stiffened. And now he was smiling at her again. Only not as a dangerously handsome stranger, but as her dangerously handsome, *self-serving* husband.

'I chose it especially,' he said softly. Leaning forward, he twisted the bottle towards her so that she could see the label. 'It's the Duvernay Grand Cru from the year we first met.'

Her lips curved into a stiff smile as she took the brimming glass. 'How considerate of you,' she said tightly.

There was a pulsing silence, and then he gently tapped his glass against hers.

'You see—it's almost like your family are already here, giving us their blessing.' His mocking gaze flickered over her face. 'And, really, what better way could there be to mark the start of *our* married life than a glass of champagne from *our* estate?'

She stared past him. 'Oh, I can think of one or two scenarios.'

He laughed. 'Why do I get the feeling that all of them involve me being in some kind of mortal peril?'

Shaking his head, he lounged back against his seat.

'I meant what I said in the chapel, Margot. As of now, you're my wife. For better, for worse...for richer, for poorer.' He gave a slow smile. 'Or, given our particular agreement, maybe that should be for poorer, for richer.'

For a moment she considered throwing the contents of her glass in his face, but just then one of his staff stepped forward with a selection of canapés, and instead she took a mouthful of champagne.

It was a good year, she thought dispassionately. An almost perfect balance of citrus and cream, with a just a hint of raspberry.

Her muscles tightened. Her grandfather had always said that a great champagne was like a love potion, but it would have to be a remarkable vintage indeed for her to forget that their marriage was a business merger in everything but name. And that Max was a total snake in the grass.

Through a combination of polite, if a little stilted, conversation and carefully timed smiles, she managed to get through the meal. Then the still smiling staff started to melt away, and finally they were alone.

Instantly she pushed her untouched cup of coffee away, her fingers twitching against the table-top.

Max stared at her with a mixture of mockery and resignation. 'The monsoon season is over for this year,' he said softly, lowering his gaze so that his eyes were suddenly in shadow. 'And yet I sense a storm is brewing.'

'Damn right it is.' Instantly her bottled-up resentment rose to the surface, like the bubbles in her family's legendary champagne. 'If you think I'm staying here for two weeks with you, acting out some pantomime of a honeymoon, then you must be insane. We had a deal. I have kept my side of that deal, and I expect you to keep yours. So, unless you have a reason for changing our plans other than sheer bloody-mindedness, I suggest you get hold of your pilot and tell him that we will be leaving for France tonight.'

'Or what? Are you going to swim home?'

She glared at him. 'If it means getting away from you, then, yes.'

He didn't reply—just stared at her so intently and for so long that she wanted to scream. And then finally, in a gesture that seemed designed solely to aggravate her, he shrugged carelessly.

Margot glanced at him helplessly. She felt as though she would burst with rage. Was that the sum total of his response? Was that seriously supposed to be some kind of answer?

'What does that mean?' she snapped. She could hear her overstretched nerves vibrating in her voice, but she didn't care any more. 'You're not in some *nouvelle vague* film, Max. This is real life. My life. And I am your wife—legally, at least—so could you at least do me the courtesy of actually saying something?'

Raising an eyebrow, seemingly unperturbed by either her words or her tone, he gazed at her impassively. 'Okay—it means that any deal we made most certainly did *not* include you flouncing off to the airport to catch the first flight home after we'd exchanged our wedding vows.'

His expression didn't shift, but she felt a sudden rise in tension as she mimicked his tone. 'Well, *any deal we made* also didn't include you and me building sandcastles for two weeks.' She glared at him. 'I mean, what exactly do you think we're going to spend our honeymoon doing?'

There was a tiny quivering pause, just long enough for her to realise the full, horrifying idiocy of what she'd said, and then the air seemed to ripple around her as her words continued to echo into the sudden silence.

What she had been trying to say was that as theirs wasn't a regular kind of marriage, their honeymoon was

hardly going to be all moonlight walks and long afternoons in bed.

Only it hadn't sounded the way she'd intended. In fact
it couldn't have sounded any worse.

Her throat felt suddenly scratchy and dry as, leaning
forward, he gave her an infuriating smile.

'Oh, I expect we could probably think of something to
pass the time…'

She wanted to deny it. But the trouble was, he was
right—and, no matter how much she wanted it to be otherwise, it didn't change the fact that her body still ached
for the wordless, exquisite satisfaction that he alone had
given her.

Rigid with mortification, her cheeks flooded with colour, she glanced past him, cursing herself, cursing him,
and cursing her father for putting her in this impossible
position.

If only she could just flick a switch so that she could
stop feeling like this. If only it was just thinking. If only
she could just separate her body from her brain. But as her
mind filled with images of her and Max moving in blurred
slow motion she felt her breath quicken.

Suddenly her heart was pounding, and she could almost
taste the adrenalin. She felt like a gladiator, waiting outside the arena, poised and ready for combat. Only this time
it was herself she was fighting. Her desire for Max was
dangerous and, as she knew from experience, the kind of
passion they shared came at a price. It trampled over your
pride, crushed your dreams and cleaved your heart in two.

Ignoring the clamouring demands of her body, she
lifted her chin. 'I know we could. But that doesn't mean
that we should.' She swallowed, struggling to find the
words that would stop her feeling, stop her needing. 'So

if that's why you broke our agreement then I'm sorry to disappoint you, but unlike you I have principles.'

His eyes glittered and, sensing the anger unfurling beneath his apparently calm demeanour, she felt her stomach clench. But he had no right to feel angry. He hadn't been bullied and manipulated. He hadn't been made to perform like a puppet on a string.

She took a breath, desperate to divert the conversation to less dangerous territory. 'Besides, in case you've forgotten, you're supposed to be saving my business—and you can't do that if we're both here cavorting about on a beach!'

Her heartbeat scampered. Even now that Max was co-running Duvernay she still felt horribly responsible. She had already been worried about taking more time off work so soon after going to Monte Carlo, but she had been expecting to be gone for just a few days, not two weeks.

His lazy gaze didn't shift from her face, but the air felt suddenly fat with tension.

'Luckily for you, I can multitask,' he said coolly.

Max stared at her. He was good at multitasking, but right now he was struggling to hold on to his temper at the same time as trying to justify why just one kiss had overridden his meticulous and completely non-negotiable plan to return to France immediately after the wedding.

His temper wasn't improved by Margot insisting on talking about Duvernay. She was acting as if he was just some troubleshooter she'd hired to fix her damned business instead of her husband. And she had accused him of being unromantic!

He gritted his teeth. Maybe they should have gone home. Everything had been in place. His private jet had been waiting on the runway and he had personally signed off on a carefully worded statement to the press about his sudden marriage to Margot Duvernay. All that there had been left to do was make a phone call—a call he had been wanting and waiting to make for so long—and then finally he would have been able to flaunt his new wife to the world.

Only as he'd brought his mouth down on hers and she'd leaned into him everything had changed.

Holding her body, feeling her frantic, unguarded response, he had been engulfed by a raw and ferocious need that had blotted out all logical thought. There and then he'd decided that the rest of the world could wait. Finally Margot was his wife. She was his, and—for the foreseeable future, at least—he was not going to share her with anyone.

But he was not about to admit that out loud, and certainly not to Margot—particularly when all she seemed bothered about was her wretched business.

'I don't leave things to chance,' he said. 'I have people reporting back to me and everything's running smoothly.' He lounged back in his chair, letting his long legs sprawl out in front of him. 'Why are you making this into such a big deal? You wanted traditional, and a honeymoon is a wedding tradition. I'm just ticking all the boxes,' he lied.

Margot looked at him resentfully. It was true that she had wanted to keep the wedding as traditional as possible, but only for the benefit of her grandfather and Louis. And she had never so much as hinted at having a honeymoon.

A honeymoon!

Her brain stumbled, tripping on a thought of just exactly how she and Max might spend their honeymoon. Sunlit hours passing into darkness, hands splaying against warm, damp skin, bodies shuddering, surrendering to one bone-dissolving climax after another—

Her heart was pounding.

'Then I suggest you untick them,' she said curtly.

His gaze didn't so much as flicker. 'I must say I'm a

little surprised—I wasn't expecting wedding day nerves,' he said lazily. 'And there was I, thinking you were only marrying me for my money.'

She gave a humourless laugh. 'You're deluded.'

'And you're overreacting,' he said coolly.

'Overreacting?' She shook her head in disbelief. 'If you don't understand why I need to get back then you must be even more insensitive and self-serving than I thought.'

Her brown eyes narrowed.

'Perhaps you were raised by wolves. Or maybe you don't have any family,' she snarled. 'Or maybe, like every other unfortunate soul who crosses your path, they prefer to keep well clear of you. Frankly, I don't much care.'

Watching his features grow harder, she felt a quiver of unease. But so what if she'd offended him? If someone basically lied, and then lied again, why should she be nice about it?

She took a deep breath. 'But I do care about my family. You knew I wanted to tell to my grandfather in person. You knew it, and yet you completely ignored my wishes.'

He let his gaze rest on her accusing face. '*Your life. Your wishes.* You seem to be forgetting that this isn't just about you. It's about us. But then you never really got the hang of *us*, did you, Margot?'

Margot stared at him unsteadily, the air thumping out of her lungs. How was this her fault? He wasn't the one who'd been tricked and manipulated, lied to and misled.

Her body was quivering with anger and frustration. Was this how it was going to be? Every conversation filled with pitfalls and traps, like a game of snakes and ladders where a stray move or two could send them tumbling back into the past.

Suddenly her eyes felt hot, and she blinked frantically. She was not going to cry. She was not going to let him know that he could hurt her. But she also wasn't going to sit here and listen to his stupid, self-righteous accusations—not after everything he'd said and done to her.

'That's because there was no *us*, Max.' Her breathing jerked, for even as she said the words, a part of her was hoping he would deny them. But of course he didn't. He just continued to stare at her, his face expressionless, his eyes still and steady.

She cleared her throat. 'There was me, and there was you. We were different people. We wanted different things then, and we want different things now. Nothing's changed.'

His eyes lifted to hers. 'Except that now you're my wife,' he said slowly.

Mesmerised by the possessive note in his voice, she was suddenly holding her breath. And then almost immediately she felt a chill come over her body. Was she really that shallow? Surely this conversation encapsulated everything that had been wrong between them, and explained why their relationship could never be what it should. Sex acting as a substitute for tenderness and sensitivity? Aged nineteen, she hadn't really understood the difference, or maybe she'd thought it would be enough.

But now she did—and it wasn't.

'So what if I am?' she said, finally finding her voice. 'You've made it clear that I don't matter to you. You don't respect me or my feelings, or care about my opinions. And you sure as hell don't understand relationships. Or is this *really* what you think marriage is supposed to be like?'

She broke off, hating the emotion in her voice. Suddenly she couldn't bear it any more. There was no point in talking to him. Standing up, she took hold of her wedding ring and tugged it loose from her finger.

'Here—you can have this back. You see, it doesn't matter how many rings you give me, Max, or even how many bits of paper I sign, I will never truly belong to you.'

She tossed the ring onto the table and then, clutching the fabric of her skirt, she turned and walked stiffly towards the villa.

Somehow she found her way to her—their—bedroom. It was decorated in the same style as the rest of the house, all pale wood and neutral-coloured walls. Cool, contemporary, masculine.

Except the bed.

She gazed in stunned, wordless disbelief at the beautiful four-poster bed, a lump building in her throat. On the other side of the room the doors to the deck had been left open, and the canopy of muslin above the bed was quivering in the warm tropical breeze. Beneath the canopy, the white sheets and pillows were strewn with the palest pink and white petals. It was ludicrously, perfectly romantic.

Her pulse was suddenly racing, and warmth stole over her skin as, dazedly, she stepped closer to the bed. Reaching down, she let her fingers drift over the crisp white sheets. Kicking off her shoes, she felt her heart contract. Everything was such a mess.

Ten years ago this would have been everything she wanted, and she wished with an intensity that was painful that she could just forget the past and—

And what? What exactly was she supposed to do and feel now?

There were hundreds, maybe thousands of books and blogs outlining wedding etiquette, and probably even more devoted to achieving a happy marriage. But what were the rules for Max and Margot? The first time she had loved him unconditionally and he had wanted her money. Now he wanted her business and she needed his financial support.

She felt suddenly close to tears again.

Being married to Max was just so much more complex than she'd imagined it would be. In her head, she'd pictured something like her grandparents' marriage—traditional, formal. They had married young, not for love but for dynastic reasons. But despite that unpromising start they had grown to care for one another, and there had always been respect and trust. How were she and Max ever going to get to that stage?

Her body tensed, and she sensed that she was no longer alone. Somebody had come into the bedroom, and without turning she knew it was Max. She didn't have to see him. The connection between them was so intense she recognised him simply by the prickling heat creeping over her skin, and the way the compass point inside her began to quiver.

She couldn't help herself. Turning, she felt her body still as she watched him walk slowly towards her.

Don't come any closer, she thought, her breath catching in her throat.

'Why not?' he said softly, and her pulse began to race as she realised that without meaning to do so she must have spoken out loud.

'There's no reason for you to do so,' she said, flattening the emotion out of her voice. 'You've got the marriage licence and the share certificates, so you have everything you want.'

He stopped in front of her, and for one endless moment they stared at each other, wide-eyed, their bodies barely inches apart.

'Not quite everything.'

Jolted by the roughness in his voice, she tried to answer. But before she had a chance even to think about what words to use, let alone form them into a sentence, he took another step closer.

She tried to move, to put some distance between them, but her body was rooted to the floor. The air felt suddenly heavy and tangled, as though the monsoon he'd mentioned earlier was about to break inside the room. Heat was chasing over her cheeks and throat, and then her stomach flipped over as he reached out and, taking her hand, gently slid the wedding ring back on her finger.

'I came to tell you that you do matter. And I do respect you.'

She stared at him. He looked tense, serious, not at all like the teasing, self-possessed man who had dominated her life for the last few days.

'And I do care about your feelings and opinions.'

He paused, and she realised that his hand was still holding hers. It was lucky that he was, for she felt suddenly strangely unsubstantial, as though at any moment she might simply float away.

'Although, given how I've behaved, I can completely see why you would think the opposite.'

Margot stared at him, confused. There was strain in his voice—not anger...uncertainty, maybe—and although he hadn't actually said he was sorry, his words had sounded almost like an apology. Whatever she had expected Max to say, it hadn't been that, and she wasn't sure how to reply.

But the part of her brain that was still functioning prodded her to respond, and so she said the first word that came into her head. 'Okay.'

His eyes bored into hers and she felt her legs wobble, for there was no mockery or hostility in the blue and green of his irises, and no anger in her heart. With a mixture of panic and yearning, she realised that without the restraining presence of their mutual animosity he was too close, that his mouth—that beautiful, temptingly kissable mouth—was dangerously close, and that she was starting to feel dizzy.

Dizzy with…

His hand slid around her waist, and even as her fingers curled into her palms she felt the floor tilt beneath her feet. Every ounce of reason and self-preservation she possessed was telling her to move, to push him away. This—*them*—was a bad idea. She needed to stop it from going any further. Stop it while she still could.

Lifting her hand, she pressed her fists against his chest, meaning to push him away. But somehow her fingers weren't responding. Instead they seemed to be uncurling and sliding over his shoulders, and she couldn't seem to stop herself from gazing at his mouth.

She was giving out all the wrong signals, and yet they felt right—more than right. They felt inevitable and necessary.

'Okay…?' His brows drew together, the muscles in his face tightening with concentration. 'Okay, and now you want me to leave? Or okay, you want me to stay?' he asked hoarsely.

Somewhere inside the wreckage of her brain, it occurred to her that his breathing was as uneven as hers. There was a long, simmering silence. She inhaled shakily. Her body was throbbing with a desperate yearning to feel his soft mouth on hers, to give in to the teasing pleasure of his tongue—only she knew that to tell him that would be foolhardy and self-destructive.

She knew she should lie to him. But she was so sick of lying. Everything else about their relationship might just be for show, but this—this need they felt for each other—was real so why fight it?

'Margot…'

She was suddenly too scared to meet his eyes, scared that he would see the indecision and the longing in her face.

But, lifting a hand, he cupped her chin and forced her to look at him, and the dark, blazing intensity of his gaze made her breath catch.

'I want you,' he said hoarsely and, lowering his mouth, he brushed his lips momentarily against hers. 'I've wanted you ever since you walked into that boardroom. I want you so badly I can't think straight. I don't even know who I am any more. All I know is that my body burns for you...'

He hesitated, and she could sense that he was steadying himself, that he would stop if she asked him to.

'But you need to tell me what *you* want.'

She stared at him dazedly, her blood humming, an ache of desire spreading out inside her like an oil spill, and then finally she slid her fingers up into his hair and whispered, 'I want you too.'

Lifting her chin with his thumb, he stared down into her eyes for so long that she thought she would fly apart with wanting him, and then slowly he lowered his head and kissed her.

She could hardly breathe. Gently, he parted her lips, pushing his tongue into her open mouth, tasting her, his breath mingling with hers as his fingers slid over the lace of her bodice.

Her skin was growing warm, and an ache that felt both hollow and yet so heavy was spreading out inside her. His fingers were moving ceaselessly, brushing against her breasts, slipping around her waist, and then lower to the curve of her buttocks. She moaned against his mouth and instantly felt his body respond. His fingers grew more urgent, and suddenly he was pulling at the buttons down the back of her dress, and as each button came loose she felt something inside her open up too.

'Max…' she whispered, and her own fingers dropped to the waistband of his trousers and began to tug at the fabric, pressing against the hard outline of his erection.

Max breathed out unsteadily. As his fingers slipped beneath the bodice of her dress he felt his groin harden. Her skin felt impossibly smooth and, lifting his mouth from hers, he buried his lips against her neck, seeking out that pulse at the base of her throat. He felt her stir against him, blindly seeking more, and suddenly he wanted more too. More of that skin, more of her mouth, and more of that pulsing heat that he could feel beneath her dress.

Breaking free, he took a step back and yanked at the collar of his shirt. Ignoring her hands, he tugged it over his head and then, his eyes holding hers, he reached forward and released her shoulders, watching dry-mouthed as the dress slid slowly to the floor.

Underneath she was naked except for a pair of rose-coloured panties tied at the sides with ribbons. Gazing at her naked breasts, he felt his skin catch fire. She was so beautiful—more beautiful than he'd remembered—and, stepping towards her, he tugged her body against his, feeling her nipples harden as they brushed against his bare chest. Lowering his head, he sucked first one and then the other into his mouth, almost blacking out as he felt her squirm beneath his tongue. And then she was pulling at the buckle of his belt, her hands clumsy, her breath suddenly uneven as she freed him from his clothes.

'Margot, Margot—slow down,' he begged. 'Just wait.'

But she wasn't listening, or maybe she was ignoring him. Suddenly he didn't care. Pulling her against him, he lifted her and not quite steadily lowered her onto the bed. Leaning forward, he yanked the ribbons of her panties free, and then she was clutching at his shoulders, pulling him closer, guiding him inside her.

Margot gasped. Looping her arm around his neck, she gripped him tighter, her hips rising, her body opening to meet his thrusts, her hands digging into the muscles of his back. She was shaking with eagerness and relief, for there had never been anyone like him and she knew there never would be. With him, there was no need to think. Everything was pure instinct, and each knew exactly what the other wanted and needed.

As the heat building inside her fanned out like a solar flare she was arching upwards, her thighs splaying, her body gripping him inside and out, until she could hold back no more and she shuddered beneath him. She felt his hands tighten in her hair, his body tense, and then, his breath quickening, he buried his face against her shoulder and, crying out her name, thrust inside her.

CHAPTER SEVEN

It was nearly ten o'clock. Already the quivering sun was high in the sky, and soon the pale sand would be too hot to stand on in bare feet.

Glancing down, Max frowned. As a child, he'd been to the seaside twice—once with his mother and Paul, and once with his school. But it was a long time since he'd walked barefoot anywhere, except between his bathroom and his bedroom or to and from his pool. In fact, it might even be the first time he'd ever been on a beach without shoes as an adult.

But, unusual as that was, walking barefoot couldn't really compete with some of his other more recent and less rational 'firsts'.

Staring out across the bay, to where a couple of seabirds were bobbing peacefully on the water, he ticked them off inside his head.

Obviously getting married to a woman he didn't love or trust took pole position. But a close second was buying those shares from her father. He'd never paid over the odds for anything and, looking back on it, there had been absolutely no need for him to do so. Although Emile had been maddeningly evasive and capricious, his demand had been modest in comparison to what he'd ended up offering for the shares.

Which brought him to another first—paying for a woman.

Beneath his dark glasses, his eyes narrowed. He didn't like the way it sounded but, despite what he'd said to Margot, and told himself about why he'd married her, that was in essence what he'd done.

And then, of course, last night had been the first time he'd ever chased a woman—or at least followed one.

Watching Margot turn and walk away, he had been too angry to move, his head simmering with barely contained frustration that within the space of a heartbeat she had thrown their honeymoon *and* her ring back in his face. And what had she meant by him not understanding relationships?

He gritted his teeth. He understood relationships perfectly. He should too: he'd had the ultimate learning experience, watching his mother put her life on hold, waiting, hoping—and for what?

For nothing, that was what.

He took a calming breath. No, Margot was wrong. He *did* understand relationships. It was simple, really. If you didn't ask you didn't get.

A wave broke, spilling water over his feet, and he realised that in the time he'd been walking down the beach the tide had begun to turn.

He glanced down at his wrist automatically and frowned. He'd left his watch on the bedside table.

And left Margot sleeping in his bed.

He felt his muscles tighten, heat lapping over his skin like the tide on the beach. In bed, their quarrel had been forgotten, their bodies blurring in a passionate embrace that had shaken him not just physically but emotionally— for he never had felt that close, that committed before. But of course he'd never been married before.

Margot might be sleeping now, but she hadn't slept much last night. Neither of them had. His lips curved upwards. In fact, her curiosity had almost killed them both. But as the dawn had crept into their room he had woken out of habit, and then...

Then he'd had two choices. Stay and wait for Margot to wake too, and carry on where they left off. Or get up and go.

A movement out in the bay caught his eye, and he saw that the two seabirds were squabbling over something—food...territory, maybe. Whatever it was, their battle was really not that different from his fight with Margot yesterday—every relationship was just a power struggle.

His mouth twisted. But his argument with Margot had been nothing in comparison to the conflict raging inside him when he'd woken this morning.

Stay or leave?

It had been a simple enough choice. Only for some reason he had never struggled so much to make a decision.

His pulse jumped in his throat and he felt an instant answering pulse in his groin. Obviously his body had been urging him to stay. Waking to find her legs tangled between his and her long, silken hair spilling over his chest had felt good—more than good. It had been intoxicating. And as he'd breathed in the scent of her he'd had to force himself back from an edge of almost primal, driving desire.

He stared not quite steadily down the beach, remembering how it had felt to run his urgent hands over her warm skin and feel the sweetness of her tight body gripping his. Watching her beautiful pink lips part and then melt into a half-pout of surrender, he'd lost control. She had been so responsive, so hot.

Even now the memory of the fierce directness of her

gaze as he'd moved inside her was turning him inside out. Everything—all the bitterness, the lies, the anger, all of it—had ceased to exist. There had been only Margot, and finally she had been his.

So why had he got up and left?

He drew in a deep breath. He'd thought he had it all figured out. Buy the shares—prove the Duvernays wrong. Marry Margot—prove her wrong. Sleep with Margot—prove her wrong again. Feel better.

His muscles tensed. Only it had been he who had been wrong—times four.

He should have felt sated and complete, and physically he did. Only he hadn't been able to shift a sense that something was missing, or maybe off-key.

He still felt like that now, and that irritated him, for he had no reason to feel that way. Margot was his wife and yesterday, and again and again this morning, she had become his lover, clinging to him, pulling him deep inside her body with a desperation that had matched his own.

Breathing out unsteadily, he wondered why that thought should make his chest tighten?

But it was obvious, really, he thought with relief a moment later.

Even before he'd made his first million, few women— if any—had been out of his reach, and his reputation for playing hard to get was completely justified.

Only ever since he'd walked into the House of Duvernay headquarters his self-control seemed to have gone AWOL.

Yesterday he had been like a starving man, satisfying his hunger. His need to take Margot had been shocking in its urgency, and it had understandably caught him by surprise for he was used to being the one in charge both in business and emotionally. But today, he couldn't pretend that it would be anything other than reckless to show her how much power she had over him.

And that was why he'd had to get up and leave this morning—to demonstrate some of that famed self-control.

So now they were all square. He'd proved his point. Why then was he still here, watching the wildlife and the waves? After all, this was his honeymoon.

Honeymoon—the word and all that it implied ping-ponged inside his head and, feeling his body harden, he turned towards the villa. And then he stopped. Glancing down at the outline of his erection, he breathed out slowly. Perhaps it might be a good idea to wait just a little longer…maybe cool off first. A quick swim would be the perfect way to damp down his libido and dull his senses before seeing Margot again, and it wouldn't hurt to keep her waiting and wanting more.

Without giving himself a chance to change his mind, he tugged his shirt over his head, tossed it onto the sand and began wading purposefully into the water.

Margot woke to sunlight and the sound of waves. It took her perhaps half a second before she realised that she was alone, and that the Max-sized space in the bed beside her was empty.

Rolling over, she touched the pillow. It still had the imprint of his head, and she could smell his aftershave and the scent of his skin, and for some reason she found herself smiling.

It was stupid, really, to feel so happy—probably it was asking for trouble—and yet…

She breathed out slowly.

And yet the strain of the last few days seemed to have lifted from her shoulders. She felt not just spent, but serene, for now she was free to touch Max, and to taste him, to wrap her legs around his quickening body without guilt or shame.

Now that it had happened, she could admit that it had always been just a question of when, not if. But when exactly had it started?

Maybe in the car, when Max had thrown that curveball at her. She had been so angry and hurt. But then, at the villa, his 'apology'—or at least his honesty following so quickly on the back of their row—had caught her off guard.

Her pulse twitched. Or maybe it had started before that. In the boardroom. Or perhaps when she'd walked past that newsstand in Paris and read his name.

Her name too now!

Max had left his watch on the bedside table and, glancing over at it, she frowned. It was almost midday and she wondered where he was.

Her pulse jitterbugged.

She couldn't remember falling asleep, but she could remember the way he'd curved his hand around her waist, anchoring her to him. Could remember too the way that same hand had cradled her head as his powerful body had thrust into hers.

She had never felt so wanted, so desired—and, okay, it had been just sex, but it had been *real*. Nobody could fake that kind of passion, that kind of tenderness.

And didn't that somehow change things a little between them? Perhaps they could be honest with one another on one level at least.

'You're awake.'

She blinked and, rolling over, she lifted her head and gazed up at him. Max was standing motionless on the deck outside the bedroom, wearing nothing but a pair of faded black shorts, an unbuttoned denim shirt and a pair of dark glasses. Droplets of water clung to the tanned muscular skin of his chest and legs, and his sea-drenched dark hair was moulded to the beautiful bones of his skull.

He looked cool and relaxed and impossibly sexy—like a photo shoot for a modern-day pirate—and as his eyes locked on to hers she felt something tug beneath her skin just as she remembered that she was naked. Her cheeks began to tingle and she felt suddenly shy—which was stupid, really. It wasn't as though he hadn't seen all of her already. And not just seen, she reminded herself, her heart jumping at the memory of how his hands had moved over that same naked skin he was staring at now.

As though reading her mind, he smiled slowly, the edges of his mouth curling up in a way that made her skin instantly grow warmer. Cheeks burning now, she tried to match his smile with a casual one of her own. But it was difficult to act naturally when all she could think about was what else that mouth could and was probably about to do.

Swallowing hard, she sat up and said quickly, 'I didn't hear you get up. I would have come with you.'

His gaze hovered over her flushed face, and then dropped to the tiny pulse beating at the base of her throat.

'That's okay. You needed to sleep.'

Tugging off his dark glasses, he stepped inside the room and walked slowly across the smooth wooden floor. He stopped beside the bed, and her pulse jumped in her throat as inch by inch his eyes drifted over her bare skin, slowly tracing the contours of her body.

Looking up at him, she felt as if she was floating—and then her heart began beating against her ribcage as, dropping his sunglasses on the bedside table, he leaned forward and kissed her gently on the mouth. She arched her back, her lips parting, and she felt her insides start to melt as he deepened the kiss.

'Sweet…' he murmured against her mouth, and then he was kissing her again, such tender, slow kisses, as though they had the whole of their lives before them.

Which they did, she thought dazedly a moment later, as his hand cupped her breast, his thumb teased the nipple and she felt her body shudder in response.

In an instant he had stolen her thoughts, her identity, even her breath, so that suddenly she was panting. 'Max, please…'

She reached up, blindly seeking more contact, expecting him to move, wanting him to touch her. But he didn't move closer. Instead he ran his hand over her breast and up to her shoulder and then released her.

She stared up at him, her hands balling into fists, her body so hot and tight and tense she thought it would explode.

'I thought—' she began, but her words dried up as he turned and, picking up his watch, frowned down at it.

'Baby, I need a shower and some breakfast. And besides…' His gaze burned into hers and she felt her pulse leap. 'Surely I more than satisfied your curiosity yesterday and this morning.'

Watching him unzip his shorts and push them down over his muscular thighs, Margot felt her stomach flip over. But not from desire this time. His words echoed ominously in her head, and suddenly she knew what he was getting at. It was that stupid, *stupid* remark she'd made in his hotel room, and clearly he'd been waiting for just the right moment to throw it back in her face.

She felt hot and dizzy, anger mingling with shame that she had actually thought Max had wanted her with the same desperate urgency with which she'd wanted him, when all the time it had just been about proving a point.

It might have felt real, but then Max was good at that, she thought savagely—good at making her believe what she wanted to believe. And she'd even given him some help, by listening to that tiny part of her mind that had wanted to be wrong about him, wanted to believe in the fantasy of their explosive sexual chemistry.

A rush of misery and helplessness broke over her, like one of the waves splashing against the shore outside their room. It was the same old story—a story that had started when she was a child, trying to defuse the tension between her parents, and then her father and her grandparents. She was so used to seeking out the good and ignoring the bad that it was almost second nature now for her to spin straw into gold.

Only she wasn't a child any more, and nor was she a spectator. This was her marriage. Her life. And she wasn't just going to stand by with a smile on her face while he played power games.

Her dress—her beautiful wedding dress—lay where Max had pulled it from her frantic body and, sliding out of bed, she picked it up and draped it over one of the cream-coloured armchairs that sat on either side of the doors to the deck.

Stalking into the dressing room, she yanked a pale blue embroidered sundress off the shelf. She pulled it over her head and, without even bothering to look at her reflection or brush her hair, she pushed her feet into some flip-flops and strode onto the deck.

Outside, the beach felt gloriously open and empty. Kicking off her shoes, she walked down to where the lightest imaginable surf was trickling over the sand like champagne foam.

Her mouth thinned. Actually, *not* champagne. She was sick of champagne. Sick of the whole wine-making world and everyone in it. Particularly Max.

She grimaced. Even just thinking about him and his stupid, mammoth ego made her head pound as though she'd drunk a magnum of Grand Cru.

She had thought that having sex with him would be the one true part of their marriage. Only now it seemed that it had been just as superficial and sham as the rest of their relationship—and not just in the present. The memory of what they'd once shared now felt unbearably tainted too.

And she only had herself to blame. She'd known what he was like. Or she should have. After all, what kind of a man blackmailed a woman into marriage?

Her stomach clenched. Sex might have made it feel more intimate and personal, but the truth was that this had never been anything other than a business arrangement—a merger of money and power and status. Anything else was just nonsense, concocted inside her head.

The sound of music and laughter broke into her thoughts and, glancing out to sea, she spotted a cruiser dipping through the water. On the gleaming white deck a group of men and women were dancing, their heads tipped back to the sun, swimsuit-clad bodies radiating heat and happiness.

She stared at them enviously. They seemed so at ease, so uninhibited, and in their loose-limbed freedom they reminded her of Louis and Gisele and their friends. She watched for a moment, lost in her own thoughts, and then, just as she was about to carry on walking, one of the men must have noticed her, for suddenly he was waving, and then they were all waving and calling to her.

It was impossible to hear what they were saying, but their excitement and enthusiasm was infectious, and without even realising that she was doing it she began waving back at them.

'What the hell do you think you're doing?'

A hand gripped her arm and her body was pulled round sharply. Max was standing beside her, wearing a pair of swim-shorts. Her first thought was that he had changed clothes. Her second was that he was incandescent with fury.

She shook his hand off, her own simmering anger rising swiftly to boiling point. 'I would have thought that was obvious. It's called *waving*—'

'Don't give me that.' He interrupted her. 'It's our honeymoon, and you're standing out here on your own, waving at strangers. What if that had been a boat full of photographers?'

She glared at him. 'It wasn't. And even if it was, what I do or don't do—including waving at strangers on boats—is none of your business. Now, if you're done with throwing your weight around, I'm going to go for a walk.'

Staring down into her defiant face, Max felt his body tense with frustration. It was a feeling that was becoming increasingly familiar since Margot had re-entered his life.

Earlier, returning to the villa from the beach, he had felt the barriers he had so arrogantly created inside his head all but disintegrate as he'd caught sight of her glorious body, spread out so invitingly on the rumpled sheets. Thankfully he had succeeded in hanging on to his self-control by a thread, helped by what must surely have been the coldest shower he'd ever had.

But when he'd walked back into the bedroom his hard-won composure had instantly evaporated as he'd realised that Margot had simply upped and left without so much as a word. His mood hadn't improved as he'd stalked stiffly through the villa. Not wanting to alert his staff to the fact that his wife appeared to have vanished, he'd been forced to pretend that he'd mislaid his phone.

He gritted his teeth. And now, when finally he'd tracked her down, not only was she completely unrepentant, she was clearly looking for a fight.

His eyes narrowed and, by holding his breath, he managed to hang on to his temper. 'Actually I'm far from done. You're my wife now, and if you're expecting our marriage to be civilised—'

'Civilised!' Her gaze clashed with his. 'You don't know the meaning of the word. Do you seriously think it's civilised to just take what you want and move on when you're done—?' She broke off as he started to shake his head.

'So that's what this is about? It was just a shower, Margot.'

The dishonesty of his remark made her breathing jerk in her throat. 'Don't do that, Max. Don't treat me like I'm stupid. It was not *just* a shower. It was you making a point. And I will not let you treat me like some toy you can pick up and play with and then forget about.'

He frowned. 'Are you insane? How could I forget about you? I've just spent the last thirty-five minutes looking for you.'

Her heart was trying to get out of her chest. 'Well, you wasted your time. You might be my husband legally, but our marriage is just a business agreement. It only exists when we're on show, in public—as you just proved to me.'

Max took a step towards her. A thread of fury was soaring up through his body like mercury in a thermometer. He felt breathless with anger and frustration.

'Better that than only existing in the bedroom,' he snarled, unable to hide his emotions any longer.

'What is *that* supposed to mean?' she snapped.

The air around them felt suddenly thick and dark and volatile, like a cloud of bees about to swarm.

'You know exactly what it means. It's the reason you didn't want to marry me all those years ago.'

She glared at him. 'I didn't want to marry you because you only wanted my money. Or have you forgotten telling me that was why you proposed?'

His gaze didn't flicker. 'That was after you'd already let your brother do your dirty work. But the least you could do now is have the guts to tell it like it was.'

'And what was it like, Max?'

His face hardened. 'I was good enough for sex, just not for marriage.'

There was a short, sharp pause. Margot was staring at him as though he'd suddenly started speaking in a foreign language, but he wasn't sure if it was what he'd said or the harshness with which he'd said it that had silenced her.

Margot stared at him in confusion. Her heart was thumping hard against her chest. She was shocked by his words. More shocked still by the fact that he obviously believed them.

Her mouth twisted. Or, more likely, wanted to believe them.

'That's not true—that wasn't how it was! It *wasn't*,' she repeated, as he began shaking his head dismissively.

'Really? Then why were you so worried about keeping us a secret? Oh, sorry, I forgot—' his mouth curled upwards into a sneer '—you were waiting for "the right time" to tell everyone.'

Anger flared inside her. How dared he be so self-righteous? 'Yes, I was. But what was your excuse?' she snapped. 'Because it wasn't just me who wanted to keep our relationship quiet, was it?'

Max breathed out silently. For a moment he thought about telling her the truth. That going public would have meant sharing her with her family, breaking the spell of that summer. And then he came to his senses.

'Nice try. But next to you I'm an amateur when it comes to keeping quiet.'

'What are you talking about?' she said hoarsely.

'I'm talking about when I asked you to marry me before. I gave you a ring. Do you remember what you did? What you said?' His voice was steady, but a muscle was pulsing in his cheek. 'No? Then let me remind you. You did nothing, said nothing. You basically acted like I'd embarrassed you.' His eyes burned into her. 'No, actually, like I'd embarrassed myself.'

She shivered. That wasn't how she remembered it. In her head it had been a moment of shock, drowned out almost immediately by Yves's arrival. Her brother had been white-lipped with rage at what he'd clearly thought was personal betrayal by a man he'd liked and trusted. He'd been angrier, though, with himself, for not protecting her, and so he'd been cruel and unfair. She should have stopped him, only…

'I wasn't embarrassed,' she said slowly. 'I was in shock.'

His mouth thinned. 'Why?' he demanded. 'We'd talked about getting married—'

'Yes, in the *future*.' She stared at him, her pulse stop-starting like a stalled car. 'But not right then. I was nineteen, Max. I was still at university. No, hear me out.' She held up her hands as he started to interrupt. 'You have to understand. I had no idea you were going to ask me. It wasn't in my head. I wasn't ready. I was young and…' She hesitated.

They were heading into dangerous territory, and the

thought of confronting what lay ahead made her want to crawl into a darkened room and roll up in a ball. But, looking up at the tense, set expression on his face, she knew that retreating was not an option.

She drew in a breath. 'And I was scared.'

Max stared at her in silence. She was telling the truth. He could hear it in her voice, feel it stinging his skin.

'Why would you be scared?' He'd sounded harsher than he'd intended and she looked over at him. Hearing her breathe out unsteadily, he felt his stomach clench, for he could see that she was still scared now. 'You were scared of *me*?' The thought horrified him so much that he actually couldn't speak any more.

'Of *you*?' She shook her head, eyes widening with horror. 'No, of course not. I was scared of making a mistake, of doing what—'

As she looked up into his eyes he saw her face stiffen, as though she was doing some complicated arithmetic in her head, and then she bit her lip.

'Oh, what's the point? You wouldn't understand.'

For a moment he thought about his own past, and his own private fears. And then he stopped thinking.

Reaching out, he took her hands. 'I might,' he said gently.

He felt her body go rigid, and for a moment he thought she was going to pull away from him, but finally she sighed.

'Okay… This is going to sound crazy, and you probably won't believe me, but when you proposed I wasn't even thinking about us or the ring you'd given me. I was thinking about my mother's engagement ring.'

Hearing the taut note in her voice, Max frowned. It did sound crazy, but for some reason he still believed her.

'I know you probably don't have much interest in celebrity gossip, but you might have heard about my parents?'

He nodded. He could remember his mother following the story in the newspapers, only he'd been too young to care. 'Just the basics. They eloped, and later on your mum accidentally overdosed.' He spoke gently, wanting to ease the impact of his words.

Her face stilled. 'They eloped when she was nineteen. It was a massive scandal. Everyone was looking for them. They ended up hiding in Marrakech, in the house where Louis is staying.'

She smiled bleakly, and he felt something heavy settle on his shoulders at the flash of hurt.

'They were so young and so beautiful, and everyone thought it was incredibly romantic. But it devastated my grandparents, and the reality wasn't romantic at all.'

He felt her fingers tighten around his, and her smile faded.

'They might have looked like the perfect couple from the outside, but honestly, though, their whole relationship started and ended with sex. It wasn't happy or healthy—just compulsive…like an addiction.'

She looked up at him defiantly, only somehow her expression seemed to accentuate her vulnerability.

'And that's what you thought we'd be like?' he asked.

Margot blinked, the directness of his question momentarily silencing her. 'I didn't think anything,' she said finally. 'I just panicked.'

For a moment she considered telling him the *whole* truth. That she'd loved him, and that he was still the only man she'd ever loved. But she'd laid enough of herself bare. Telling the truth now wouldn't alter the facts. Max hadn't loved her then, and he didn't love her now.

Looking back to that devastating moment when his

world had imploded, Max felt his chest tighten painfully as for the first time he contemplated a different version of events. And a new and unsettling realisation that he might not only have misjudged Margot all those years ago, but completely overreacted.

'Why didn't you tell me about your parents before?'

She shrugged, and the resignation in that simple gesture made his breath catch in his throat.

Looking down at her feet, she began digging her bare toes into the sand. 'I suppose I didn't know if I could trust you.'

He frowned. 'Is that why you kept us a secret?'

She didn't answer for a moment, and then slowly she shook her head. 'Maybe at first. But not later. Then I wanted it to be just you and me. I love my family, but they can be so demanding.'

'You mean your father?'

Margot stared at him. For a moment she'd actually forgotten that Max had met Emile. She gave him a weak smile. 'I hear you woke him up.'

Max grimaced. 'I paid for those shares in ways you'll never know.'

He was attempting a joke, trying to lighten the mood, but she couldn't shift the memory of his accusation.

She bit her lip. 'You were wrong, Max. I was never ashamed of you. I just knew that if I told my family they would complicate things. It's what they do.'

He stared down at her, his eyes glittering strangely. 'And what do *you* do?'

'Me? I'm a fixer-upper.'

That was an understatement. She seemed to have spent most of life problem-solving for her family, and with a tiny wrench of doubt she wondered what would happen if she just stopped. Was that why they loved her? For what she could do for them, not who she was.

Swallowing the lump of misery in her throat, and fearing she had given too much away, she shrugged. 'I make it all look perfect—which with my family is practically a full-time job. They might look flawless from the outside, but my father is living proof that appearances can be deceptive.'

Max hesitated. For a moment he stared at her in silence, as though working something out in his head, and then, taking a step closer, he pulled her into his arms.

'True,' he said slowly. 'But sometimes things are what they appear to be. Like the chemistry between us. That's real. You can't fake it, or pretend it doesn't exist.' Gently he reached up and stroked her hair. 'You were right about this morning. I was trying to prove a point. Only unfortunately I've just ended up proving what an idiot I am.'

He stared down at her, trying to make sense of everything that was going on inside his head. Coming down to the beach, his anger had been hot and righteous, but now her honesty, and the courage it had taken for her to be so honest, made him feel angry with himself. Margot was not the person he had thought she was. She was not selfish or self-absorbed. On the contrary, she seemed to have spent most of her life sacrificing herself to the demands of her family.

Breathing out softly, he slid his hand under her chin and tilted her face upwards. 'Why do you think I changed my mind about going back to France?'

Margot stared at his face in silence, not understanding why he was asking her that question now, and wondering where the conversation was heading.

His grip tightened. 'Because I want you as much as you want me, Margot. More than I've ever wanted any woman. I didn't want a honeymoon just because of what people might say if we didn't have one.' He smiled faintly. 'I think you know me well enough to believe that I can hold my own in the world.'

She nodded mutely, her heart hammering in her chest as his smile twisted.

'But clearly I haven't given you reason enough to believe that changing my mind was not an act of complete thoughtlessness. So let me make it clear now. Changing our plans wasn't supposed to upset you or your family. But I know now that it did, and I'm sorry. For not talking to you about it first. And for being a jerk this morning.'

Lifting her hand to his mouth, he kissed it lightly.

'I know I haven't covered myself in glory these last few days, but I'm not a monster.' He stared down into her eyes. 'It's not too late to fly back. If that's what you want, then tell me and I'll make it happen.'

Margot bit her lip. It was an olive branch, or maybe an attempt at reparation…

'You'd do that? For me?'

His fingers closed more firmly around hers. 'Of course. You're my wife. I'm not in the habit of making empty promises. I made vows, and I meant them.'

She wondered what he meant by empty promises, but something in his expression warned her that now was not the time to ask him.

It's not too late to fly back. I made vows, and I meant them.

Gazing up at him, his words echoing inside her head, Margot was torn. Part of her wanted to make things right with her grandfather. But Max had apologised, and he'd admitted that he wanted her. That the attraction between them was special. For a moment she was in a daze, but as she caught sight of her wedding ring she made up her mind.

'I want to stay. But I'd like us to talk to my grandfather and Louis.'

His expression didn't change, but he wrapped his arms around her, pulled her closer, and she felt his heart beating unsteadily.

'Then that's what I want too,' he said softly.

CHAPTER EIGHT

ROLLING ONTO HER FRONT, Margot closed her eyes and let the book she'd been failing to read slip from her fingers.

After a night in Max's arms she was feeling drowsy and sybaritic, so she had decided to spend an hour by the pool. The sun felt wonderful on her bare skin, and she was feeling wonderful too, the tranquillity of her mind complementing the languor of her body.

It wasn't just the heat that was making her feel so relaxed. Today felt almost like a new beginning, for finally she had told her family about her marriage.

She had spoken first to her grandfather and then to Louis, and even now she couldn't quite believe how well it had gone. It had been so much easier than she'd expected—mainly thanks to Max.

He had been with her the whole time, literally holding her hand. Remembering his quiet but easy self-assurance, she felt her pulse jump. She doubted there were many people who had the charisma and confidence to manage a man of her grandfather's status and gravitas. But, hearing Max talk, she had known that nobody would question the validity of their marriage. He had seemed utterly unfazed, and his certainty had been irresistible.

But then everything about Max was irresistible. His

looks, his resoluteness and his power were an aphrodisiac that made her ache to feel his hands on her body again.

Pushing aside an image of what those hands could do, she wondered how and when he'd learned to behave with such poise. He might be her husband, but his background was still as much of a mystery to her as it had been nearly ten years ago.

Stretching her arms out, she shifted against the cushion of the sun lounger and thought back to their argument on the beach, and the confession that had spilled out of her afterwards. Their anger had been so intense it had felt like a storm cloud breaking. Only somehow, out of her fury and his, they had come to a better understanding.

Her skin began to prickle. Or rather *he* now understood *her*, for the sharing of information had been entirely on her side.

She hadn't meant to confide in him about her parents' relationship, but between the endless blue of the ocean and the relentless blue and green of his gaze there had been nowhere to hide.

And, even though she had never put it into words before, it had been easy to tell him the truth—maybe because he had listened to her in a way that no one else had ever done. Her staff hung on her every word at work, and her family were always asking for advice, but Max had really *listened* to her, as if she mattered to him. And it had been his concentration and persistence which had finally broken down the barriers she'd built to stop the prying gaze of the world.

Remembering his remark about empty promises, she wondered what he'd meant. She would have liked to ask him, only his manner had not exactly encouraged further discussion. And it had been no different in the past. If ever she had tried to ask him about himself he had simply batted her questions away and changed the subject.

Aged nineteen, she'd thought it didn't matter that she hardly knew anything about him. In truth, she'd been too in love, and too astonished that he was no longer treating her just as Yves's younger sister but as a woman, to do anything but bask in his attention.

There had been other reasons, too, why she had purposely not cross-examined him. As someone who valued her own privacy, she was sympathetic to other people's reticence, and so she'd been if not happy then understanding of his silence.

But now…?

She sighed. They might have reached a kind of truce, but no matter how much she would have liked to peek into the complexities of Max's mind she wasn't feeling nearly brave enough to question him about his background or his private life.

Or, worse, his feelings.

And maybe she didn't need to, for when her body was pressed against his, and she could feel his heart beating in time to hers, she felt as if she knew everything there was to know about him.

She felt a pang of remorse as she remembered how she'd accused him of being insensitive and self-serving.

He wasn't. She knew that now. He was capable of compassion and, unlike a lot of people with money and power, capable and willing to apologise.

Realising how much he had upset her, he had offered to return to France, and even though she had agreed to stay at the villa she knew that he had meant what he'd said. And, although she had wanted to tell her family in person, she didn't regret her decision. On the contrary, right now she could think of nowhere she'd rather be—so much so that she was struggling to remember why she had ever thought that having a honeymoon was such a bad idea.

She felt a warm, tingling feeling in the pit of her stomach. After they'd called her grandfather Max had led her back to the bedroom and stripped both of them naked, his mouth urgently seeking hers, kissing her so deeply that she was breathless and dizzy. And, curling her legs around him, her hands shaking with eagerness as they'd spread over the muscles of his back, she had guided him inside her restless, aching body.

Lifting her head, she turned her face away from the sun. But it wasn't just about the sex. Max was great company too. He was well-read, and interested in what she'd read—they had talked about everything from tax reform to the rise in popularity of Peruvian food. And he made her laugh—*really* laugh—in a way she had almost forgotten she could.

It was easy to see why her teenage self had fallen under his spell. And here in the sunshine, far away from the relentless, unforgiving demands of real life, it would be as easy to feel the same way about him now.

Her stomach clenched. Easy, but terrifying at the same time.

For despite knowing that she was letting herself get swept away by the romantic setting and the new openness between them, the truth was that a part of her had always wanted to believe in him—to reimagine their history with a happy ending.

And, even though it was stupid and pointless and crazy, even dangerous to think that way, with every hour that passed she just couldn't seem to stop herself wanting to believe that their intimacy and mutual hunger for one another was more than just physical attraction.

A pair of warm hands slid over her back and her pulse darted forward like a startled fish.

'Hey, sleepyhead.'

Max nuzzled her neck, and she felt heat rush to the spot where his lips were caressing her bare skin. Tipping her head back slightly, she let her cheek graze his, breathing in the mix of coffee and cologne and some undefined but potent essence of maleness that made her heat rush through her body.

Rolling over onto her back, she opened her eyes and gazed up at him, wondering if she would ever get used to how gorgeous he was. Stomach flipping, she reached out and curled her hands around his biceps, her thumbs pressing into the hard muscles.

'I'm not sleeping, I'm worshipping the sun,' she protested, a beat of blood starting to drum inside her head. 'Why don't you join me?'

Gently cupping her face in his hand, he lowered his mouth, brushing his lips against hers. 'I'd much rather worship you,' he whispered.

He raised his head, and the intent in his beautiful eyes made her body feel suddenly boneless.

'But, as I'm very devout, and it may take me some time, I think we should go somewhere a little more comfortable,' he said softly. And, pulling her to her feet, he led her back to their bedroom.

They made slow, passionate love all morning, stopping only for Max to crawl out of bed and bring back some lunch, which they ate with their fingers.

Later, they walked along the shoreline, happy just to hold hands and pick up shells and pieces of driftwood, until finally it became too hot and they retreated to the villa and to bed again.

'Are you okay?'

Margot glanced up at Max. She was lying in his arms, her body damp and feverish, still trying to catch her breath. 'I am—are you?'

His eyes were dark and lazy as they rested on her face.

'Yes, but...' He paused, his hand caressing the curve of her hip in a way that made her body start to shake inside.

'But what?' she asked quickly, knowing that if she waited too long to reply her skin would grow warm and she would rapidly lose the power of both thought and speech.

He sounded casual, but in contrast his expression was tense, expectant. 'I need to make a phone call.'

What? Now? Can't someone else do it?

Her disappointment was instant, and clearly it must have showed on her face for, grimacing, he shook his head and answered her unspoken questions. 'I can't delegate this one, but it won't take long.' His gleaming eyes drifted hungrily over her naked body. 'I promise.'

Kissing her lightly on the lips, he slid out of bed and tugged on a pair of linen trousers.

Staring at him, she frowned. 'Where are you going?'

'I'm going to use the study. I have to,' he said as she started to protest. 'There's no way I can concentrate with you here like—'

His words faltered as she leaned back against the pillow and moistened her lips. 'Like what?' she asked innocently.

He groaned. 'Margot, please don't make this any harder than it already is,' he said hoarsely.

Tilting her head to one side, she smiled. 'Make *what* harder, Max?'

'Very funny.'

His eyes narrowed, and the slow, hot glance he gave her made her heart ping-pong inside her chest. 'Do not leave this bed. I'll be ten minutes, tops, and then you and I are going to...'

She held his gaze, and there was a moment of pure, pulsing silence.

And then, his jaw tightening, he swore forcefully. 'Ten minutes,' he said softly, and before she had a chance to reply he turned and walked swiftly out of the room.

Watching him leave, Margot rolled over and pulled his pillow against her stomach, wanting to capture the last traces of warmth from his body.

It was silly, really, given that it was only lust, but the fact that he clearly wanted her so badly made her feel ludicrously happy, even though the space in the room where he'd been made her feel empty inside.

It was annoying that work had intruded, but in a way she was pleased that he was so committed to making good on his promise to turn her business around. He'd made at least one call a day since they'd arrived at the villa, usually while she was in the pool or taking a shower. But they were always short, and afterwards he was doubly attentive.

Clutching the pillow tighter, she wrapped the still-warm sheet around her naked body and, listening to the calming rhythm of the sea, imagined his return...

She must have dozed off. Waking, and aware of a shift in the light, she reached over to the bedside table and picked up her phone. Glancing at the screen, she frowned. Max had said ten minutes, but he'd been gone more like twenty-five.

She bit her lip, uncertain of whether to stay in bed or go and find him. Reluctant to move, she fell back against the pillow. He would probably be back soon, she told herself.

But after another five minutes she couldn't bear it any longer. Sliding out of bed, she picked up the shirt that he'd discarded the night before and pulled it over her head.

As usual, aside from the sound of the surf, the villa was
still and quiet. The staff were not just discreet, they were
virtually invisible—since that first day, she had only seen
Aurelie, the housekeeper, once.

In the hallway, she headed towards the study, but as
she reached the half-open door she hesitated as she heard
Max's voice. If he'd been talking to a member of his staff
then she would have walked right in, and had he sounded
angry she would probably have sneaked away. But he
wasn't angry, and he definitely wasn't talking to his PA
or his accountants or his lawyer.

Her pulse stumbled.

She couldn't hear exactly what he was saying, but there
was a warmth and ease to his voice—a tenderness that
made her hands start to shake. It was the kind of shared
tenderness that only two people in a long and close relationship would have, and she knew instinctively that he
was talking to a woman.

And not just any woman—a woman he loved very
much.

For a moment she couldn't move. Her legs seemed to
have turned to ice. And then, breathing out unsteadily, she
took hold of the handle and slowly pushed the door open.

Max had his back to her. He was gazing out of the window, his phone pressed against the side of his head, and
suddenly the blood was roaring in her ears—for this was
almost exactly how she'd found him in the boardroom.
Only then he'd been sitting down, wearing a suit, and
now he was standing bare-chested, shifting restlessly, the
hard, primed muscles of his beautiful athlete's body rippling as he talked.

'Look, I have to go now.'

The gentleness in his voice made her feel hollowed out
with misery.

'I know. I wish you were here with me too. But I'll speak to you tomorrow, I promise.'

He rang off, and she watched his fingers curl around the phone, her pulse staggering, her chest so tight she thought it would burst. And then he turned and saw her. And, however bad she had felt moments before, she knew that nothing in her life would ever hurt as much as seeing his face and the truth in his eyes.

'How long?' she whispered. Her throat was so constricted that it hurt to speak, but the pain was nothing to the pain in her chest. 'How long?' she repeated, more loudly this time. 'How long have you been seeing her?'

He stared at her blank-eyed. 'I think you must be a little confused—' he began.

But she cut across him, for there was no way she could listen to any more of his lies.

'No, actually, I think I was a *lot* confused. So confused, in fact, that I'd actually started to believe that you wanted to make this work.' Her mouth curved with contempt. 'What was it you said? *"I'm not in the habit of making empty promises."'* Clenching her teeth, fighting the desolation and despair clogging her throat, she shook her head. 'I'm such an idiot. I really thought you were talking about me, when all the time you were talking about your mistress!'

'Mistress!'

His face hardened, and before she had a chance to register the flash of white-hot anger in his eyes he had crossed the room in three strides.

'You clearly are confused if you think I'd ever make any woman my mistress.'

'Don't lie to me, Max,' she exploded, his denial lighting the fuse of her shock and anger. 'I heard you. I heard you talking to her—'

'No, you didn't, Margot.' His mouth twisted, and she could see the muscles in his arms and chest straining. 'You heard me talking to my mother.'

There was a dull, heavy silence. She stared at him, almost floating with shock, her anger swept aside by his words. Up until that moment she'd never heard him refer to any kind of relative, even in passing. In fact, she'd thought that maybe he didn't actually have any family, and that was why it had been easy for him to be so blasé and dismissive about hers.

'Your mother?'

'Yes. My mother.'

There was a different tone to his voice now—a roughness that wrenched at something inside her, made her want to reach out to him. As if he sensed that, he turned abruptly and walked towards the window.

Staring after him, Margot swallowed. His back was towards her, and she could see the effort with which he was holding himself still, holding in the emotion which had split his voice.

'Max—' She took a step forward and then stopped, her pulse skipping a beat. She knew his anger—knew that it could be ice-cold or like a fire beneath his skin. But this was different. If it was anger, then it was a desperate and stricken kind that she had never seen before.

His shoulders tensed, and his breathing was ragged. 'Just go, Margot.'

He couldn't bear to look at her, to have to see what she was feeling.

'No. I'm not going anywhere.'

She spoke softly, as if she was unsure as to how or even if he would respond, but even without seeing her face he could sense that she meant what she was saying.

Turning slowly, he stared at her in silence.

Mistress.

How could one word cause so much pain? But was it that surprising, given that it embodied both his mother's crushed hopes and his own sense of helplessness? A helplessness he couldn't let Margot see.

Only there was no way out, for she was standing just inside the room, her body blocking the doorway.

'This is not your problem,' he said flatly.

Shaking her head, she took a step closer. 'Yes, it is. You see, I made promises too.'

'Yes—under duress.'

He had made her do it so that he could right an alleged wrong. Or that was what he'd told himself. But marrying Margot had never really been about getting his money's worth for her father's shares, or punishing her for not wanting him ten years ago. The truth was both simple and more complex. Only he'd never discussed his mother with anyone—never so much as hinted at the turmoil of his past—and he didn't know what to say or even how to start now.

Brown eyes flaring, she held his gaze. 'That's not true. I had choices, and I walked into that chapel willingly.'

She hesitated, and before he had a chance to react she had taken two quick steps forward and taken his hand.

'And I'm here willingly too.' She hesitated again. 'Are you okay?'

He could hear that she was worried about him, see by the slight tremble of her mouth that she cared, and that in itself made his head spin. But it was her touch, gentle but firm, that convinced him to tell her the truth. For she was standing in front of him not as some bargaining chip or sacrifice but as an equal. And as for telling a difficult truth—hadn't she done that herself, yesterday?

He nodded. 'She worries about me if I don't ring when

I say I'm going to ring. That's why I couldn't stay with you earlier.'

Margot nodded. He was keeping his promises. Her head was filled with a blur of questions and conjecture but, glancing up at him, she knew there was only one question she needed to ask right now.

'Is everything all right?'

His face tightened. 'She misses me. But I've talked to her and she's okay now.'

Margot nodded. More than anything she wanted to stay on the island with Max but, remembering his reaction when she'd got upset about her grandfather, she didn't hesitate. 'Do you need to go back?'

He shook his head slowly. 'She has people with her. They're good—not just professional, but kind. She trusts them.'

A pulse was throbbing in the side of her head. 'Is your dad not around?'

She gazed at him uncertainly. Even as she had spoken she'd wondered why she didn't already know the answer to such a basic question. And why it felt as if his answer would be the key to unlocking this complex, compelling man who had dominated her life since she was a teenager.

Slowly he shook his head again. 'He's never been around. The relationship was over before she even found out she was pregnant. She told him, but—' Catching sight of her face, he shrugged. 'It's fine. You can't miss what you don't know.'

Thinking about her own childhood, and how much she'd longed for her life to be simple and stable, Margot wasn't sure if she agreed with him. But she was too scared to say so for fear of disturbing the thread of his thoughts and derailing this uncharacteristic openness on his part.

'I suppose not. But it must have been hard for her by herself.'

She felt his fingers tense, and then tighten around hers.

'She managed okay.' His eyes were intent on her face. 'And she wasn't always by herself. When I was about eleven she met this guy called Paul. She was working as a receptionist at a law firm, and he was one of the clients.'

'What was he like?'

He turned towards her, the hazy sunlight floating into the room making his eyes glitter like gemstones.

'I was eleven. I don't think I knew what he was like.' He gave her a crooked smile. 'He ran a logistics company. But as far as I was concerned he had three cars—two of them convertibles—and he supported the same football team as me, so I thought he was cool.'

His face softened.

'And he made my mum happy. She always used to worry so much about money, and work, and me, but after she met Paul she seemed to relax. I guess it was good for her to have someone around she could rely on.'

Margot nodded. She knew exactly how Max's mother must have felt. The relief of not being alone, of not always having to be the person in charge.

'We moved into a new house, and Paul more or less moved in with us. He was away on business a lot, but it didn't matter. By then I'd worked out that he wasn't that interested in me. But that didn't matter either, because he took us on holiday and he bought me new football boots.'

He paused.

'Only it was different for my mum. I knew she really wanted to marry him. I asked him about it once, but he said it was too soon and that he needed to get his business established. He gave her a necklace instead of a ring, and then I went to boarding school and I suppose I just forgot about it.'

Something in his voice pulled her chest tight, but she made herself say lightly, 'Did you like school?'

He shrugged. 'It was fine. I was good at most things, and I was in the football and rugby squads, so I was always training or playing matches. I didn't really have time to get homesick.'

She felt it again—this time in her throat. A tightening, almost a nervousness, and then her heart began to beat a little faster. 'But you did go home?'

His shoulders were so rigid now it looked as though they would snap. 'Only Saturday afternoons, after the match. Except this one time.'

The muscles in his arms shifted and tensed.

'Why? What happened?' Holding her breath, she waited for him to answer.

'I'd been away at school about a year. It was the end of November and the school boiler broke. We got sent home, only some of us decided not to go home. We went into Paris instead. And that's when I saw him.'

She saw that Max was staring out of the window, except a moment later she realised he was actually staring at their reflection.

'We were walking past a restaurant and he was inside, sitting at a table with this woman and three children—a boy and two girls. And that's when I realised. It wasn't that he didn't want to marry my mum. He couldn't. Because he was already married.'

Margot felt her stomach coil in on itself.

'That's awful. Did you tell her?'

For a moment he didn't reply, and the silence seemed to stretch out of the room and across the ocean to the blurred line of the horizon.

'I didn't have to,' he said finally. 'She already knew. She'd known for years and she'd just been waiting and hoping.' He shook his head. 'I got mad—*really* mad with her. I told her she had to have it out with Paul and give him an ultimatum.' He smiled tightly. 'You know how I love an ultimatum.'

He was attempting to make a joke, but the weariness in his voice made the breath catch in her throat.

'And then what happened?'

'She confronted him. And he told her that even if he hadn't already been married, she wasn't "wife material". That women like her were only good for sex.'

She groped for something to say but she couldn't speak. In part she was stunned by the brutality of Paul's remarks, but what had left her speechless was the fragment of memory rising to the surface of her thoughts. Max's accusation on the beach that he had been *"good enough for sex, just not for marriage"*.

At the time she'd thought he was just throwing out insults. Now, though, she saw that his choice of words had been deliberate. And now she knew why. Ten years ago, when she had been too stunned to speak in his defence, he had thought—understandably—that history was repeating itself, that she was judging him as Paul had judged his mother.

Her heart contracted and she felt a sudden overwhelming urge to cry—for she could see now that her silence had been as cruel as Paul's words. Not only had she hurt him, she had reinforced his deep-rooted fear that he wasn't good enough. No wonder he had wanted her father's shares so badly. He had wanted to prove himself—prove her wrong.

Max breathed out unsteadily. He had never talked so much, or so openly. He felt drained but, looking at Margot's face, he could see only concern, and that gave him the strength to continue.

'I don't think he liked being made to feel like the bad guy, so that was it. He broke up with her. Stopped paying the rent and my school fees. My mum had a kind of break-down. She couldn't leave the house, let alone work. She still can't. That's why she didn't come to the wedding. She couldn't have—not even if it had been in France.' He threw her a small, stiff smile. 'In the end, we got this apartment in Saint-Denis. You might have heard of it?'

She nodded and, looking past her, he gritted his teeth. Of course she'd heard of it. The tenth *arrondissement* was notorious for its sprawling concrete estates and for having a higher than average crime rate.

Even now he could still remember moving into the apartment, with its broken windows and graffiti-covered door. In no time at all his mother had retreated into herself, and he had begun truanting and dabbling in petty crime.

He gave a humourless laugh. 'It was a difficult time. Moving house, changing school, and then my mum being so crushed. I started getting into trouble at school—if I even went. Smoking, stealing, fighting... And then I sur-passed myself and broke into Paul's office.'

Watching her face, he gave a sardonic smile.

'Don't worry! You're not married to a criminal. Weirdly, Paul came down and talked to the police and they let me off. And then he got me a job, helping out at his friend's vineyard. The first day I helped graft a vine and I was hooked. Five years later I ended up working for Yves, and the rest you know.'

He stopped abruptly. After the closeness of his con-fession the sudden silence was such a shock that all she wanted to do was to fill the void, so she said the first thing that came into her head. 'Why do you think Paul helped you?'

He frowned. 'I think he felt guilty about what he'd said to my mother, and how he'd treated her, and maybe even me too.'

Eyes narrowing, she nodded slowly. 'So he should.'

The indignation in her voice made him smile properly. 'And there I was, thinking you'd be all for putting me in handcuffs.'

Their gazes locked and a pulse of heat began to beat over her skin. 'Thinking or hoping?' she asked softly.

He breathed in sharply and she reached out for him and suddenly he was pulling her closer and burying his face into her hair. 'I'm sorry,' he murmured.

'For what? I was the one making stupid assumptions and even stupider accusations. And if you're talking about our marriage,' she added fiercely, 'then I meant what I said earlier. I walked into that chapel willingly. And I'd walk into it again now.'

As she spoke her heart gave a jolt, and she felt something inside her splitting apart and, with a mixture of fear and relief, she realised that for her their relationship was way more than physical. That at some unspecified point she had opened her heart to him.

For a moment she came dizzyingly close to telling him that she still loved him—more so even than she had before. And not just willingly, but unconditionally. But, glancing up at his set face, she knew that this was not about her and her feelings.

He stared down at her, his face still strained. 'That doesn't mean I'm not sorry for putting you in an impossible situation.' He hesitated. 'And that isn't the only reason I'm sorry.' Lifting his head, he looked down at her. 'When I met you, I was still a mess.'

She gave him a small, swift smile. 'You looked pretty good to me.'

His mouth curled upwards. 'On the outside, maybe. But everything had been so difficult for so long. When we got together I didn't want to be like my mum—just sitting around, waiting and wishing. I wanted to be in control.'

He frowned. It was the first time he'd ever articulated those thoughts to himself, let alone out loud, but for some reason—maybe the firmness of her arms around his waist, or the softness in her eyes—he wanted her to know them.

'Deep down, I think I knew it was too soon, and that you weren't ready, but I just wanted things to be definite between us—that's why I proposed. Only then Yves turned up, and he was so appalled and so opposed to even the idea of it—'

'He was shocked,' Margot said quickly. 'He felt the same way I did about our parents' marriage. I promise you, it would have been the same with any man.'

He frowned. 'I want to believe you, and maybe I can now. But he made me feel stupid and small, and you didn't say anything. I was angry and upset. So I told you that I'd only wanted you for your money. But I didn't. It was a lie. I just wanted to hurt you.'

Margot stared at him, misery swelling in her chest, seeing that moment as though from his perspective. Of course he'd been hurt. Yves had been brutal, and in her silence she had only condoned his brutality.

It was all such a mess.

They had both assumed the worst of each other. But by trying not to repeat the mistakes of the past they had succeeded in ruining their future together.

She bit her lip. 'I should have stopped Yves. If I'd said something—'

He looked down at her hand in his, and for a moment

she thought he was going to release his grip. But instead he lifted her fingers, tilting her rings up to the light.

'It wouldn't have made any difference. He was too angry and upset. We all were. And it doesn't matter any more, anyway. It might have taken us a long time to get here, but everything's worked out fine.'

His eyes on hers were soft, and she felt warmth spread over her skin.

'You're my wife, and we're together now. That's all that matters.'

She was breathless from his nearness. It was all she could do to stay standing as he cupped her face in his hands and kissed her. Her heart wanted to burst, for she couldn't ignore the facts. She might want Max to love her but he didn't. Not then and not now.

But as his fingers slid under her shirt all conscious thought was swept away. One hand splayed out over the skin of her back, the other tugged at her buttons until her shirt fell open and she felt cool air wash over her stomach and breasts. Her nipples tightened and, moaning softly, she reached out and touched his chest.

Breathing in sharply, he pulled her against him...

CHAPTER NINE

HER HEART WAS beating hard and fast. Her hands slid up through his dark hair and she moved backwards clumsily, his arm guiding her. Or was she pulling him? And then he was lifting her onto the desk, sweeping papers aside and lowering her to the gleaming wood.

For a moment he watched her, his eyes dark and glittering with desire, and then, breathing shallowly, he leaned over and kissed his way down her neck to her breast, rolling his tongue around first one rosy-tipped nipple then the other.

Arching upwards, she gasped, and then she collapsed back against the desk as he dropped to his knees and took her with his mouth.

Panting, she shifted against him, raising her hips, her body already starting to tremble, wanting more. And then her fingers tightened in his hair and she pulled him up. Her hands fumbled with the button on his trousers and suddenly she was pulling him free, her fingers closing around him in a fist.

He grunted, catching her hand with his. He pushed it away and, raising her up, thrust inside her, flattening her body with his.

'Look at me,' he muttered.

Wrapping her legs around his hips, she gazed up at

him as he pushed harder and deeper, the blaze in his eyes matching the burning heat between her thighs. Suddenly she was grasping his head in her hands, her muscles clenching as he surged into her again and again, and then, tensing, she cried out, her body joining his in a shuddering climax.

Feeling him bury his face in her throat, Margot closed her eyes and breathed out shakily. She couldn't move, certainly couldn't speak. And she didn't want to. All she wanted to do was lie there in his arms for ever, breathing in the air that he breathed.

She felt him shift above her and, feeling his gaze, she opened her eyes. He was gazing down at her, his face flushed, his breathing unsteady.

'Are you okay? I didn't hurt you, did I?'

She shook her head. 'This desk is actually more comfortable than it looks.'

Lifting her hand, she traced her finger along his jawline and over the shadow of stubble on his chin.

Frowning, he gently withdrew and pulled her upright, supporting her with his arm. 'I kept thinking we should go the bedroom, but I was desperate.'

She smiled. 'I don't know whether to be offended that you were clear-headed enough to think anything at all, or flattered that you were so desperate.'

Stroking her blonde hair away from her face, his gaze held hers. He smiled. '"Clear-headed" might be pushing it.' He kissed her lightly on the lips then, dipping his mouth to her throat, brushed the sensitive skin of her collarbone and the slope of her breast. 'I don't know what happens when I'm with you but it's got very little to do with thinking. Just wanting. And feeling.'

Her heart gave a lurch, but she knew that the feelings

he was talking about were physical, not emotional, and sexual desire was nothing like love.

Blocking the ache in her chest, and keeping the smile on her face, she said lightly, 'Me too.'

Breathing out, Max pulled her closer. Tipping her head back, he kissed her deeply, and as her nipples brushed against his chest he felt her stir restlessly against him. Instantly his body began to throb in response.

Moaning softly, she broke the kiss, and pressed a hand to the middle of his chest. 'Max…'

'Yes, Margot?' he said hoarsely.

'Do you think we could make it to the bedroom this time?'

He nodded slowly, his eyes on her mouth, and then, grabbing her wrist, he tugged her towards the door.

Later they swam in the pool and lay in the sun.

'Is this okay for you?' Margot glanced over at him, frowning slightly. *She* didn't actually want to go anywhere or do anything, but then she was in love. All she wanted to do was spend every minute of every hour with Max, savouring every moment, absorbing every detail.

But she wasn't ready to reveal her true feelings to him yet—in fact she wasn't sure that she would ever be ready. It had been hard enough to explore her own. Having to face up to the fact that Max couldn't and wouldn't ever share those feelings was not worth spoiling this new intimacy between them for. And besides, right now his body inside and beneath and on top of hers was enough.

She cleared her throat. 'I mean, we haven't actually left the villa once, and we've only got another five days. Is there nothing you'd rather do?'

His eyes rested intently on hers, and she shook her head, her mouth curving into a smile.

'You have a one-track mind.'

'It's not one-track,' he said lazily, reaching over to caress her hipbone in a way that made heat rush though her. 'It's just one destination.'

She reached for his hand, intending to still it, knowing that if she didn't she'd be begging him to take off her clothes—take *her*, full stop, out on the terrace. But his fingers curled around her wrist and he pulled her towards him, so that her stomach was pressing against the hot, toned muscles of his abdomen.

For a moment she stared at him, dry-mouthed. She loved what they shared, loved the press of his mouth on hers, the touch of hand and the weight of his body. Only, feeling as she did, she knew she should be careful. Wrapped in his arms, it was temptingly, dangerously easy for her to start fantasising about true love and happy endings, for that was when they were at their most intimate. But every time she thought about taking a step back she only had to look at him and she was struggling to breathe.

The trouble was that her hunger for him far outweighed her willpower, and each time she gave in to that hunger it got harder and harder not to tell him how she felt.

'What is it?'

He was staring at her, studying her closely so that for one terrible moment she thought she must somehow have revealed her thoughts.

'Nothing.' She gave him a casual smile. 'It just seems a shame to come all this way and not even have a look around. It's so beautiful… I'm sure there must be something stunning to see.'

His eyes slid slowly over the three turquoise triangles tied around her body. 'That bikini is pretty stunning.'

She rolled her eyes. 'I was talking about sightseeing.'

He grinned. 'In that case, now you come to mention

it, there is something I'd like to take a closer look at. You have this tiny little scar, just below your—'

Reaching over, she punched him lightly on the arm and he broke off, laughing.

'You're impossible!' She was laughing too. 'People do other things on their honeymoon beside tearing each other's clothes off.'

'And is that what you want to do? Other things? Like sightseeing.'

Assuming that he was still teasing her, and about to respond in kind, she looked up, her mouth curving at the corners. But as their eyes met she felt her heart start to pound. Max was smiling, but his eyes were serious, expectant, as though her answer mattered. Her smile seemed suddenly out of place. Why was he asking? Did he think that she was bored? Or that she wanted to be somewhere else, *with* someone else?

Meeting his gaze, she shook her head. 'No, I'm happy being here with you, relaxing,' she said carefully. 'I just wasn't sure if that was what *you* wanted.'

'I don't care what we do as long as I'm with you.' Leaning forward, he tipped her face upwards and kissed her softly on the mouth. 'That's all I want—to be with you.'

Letting her lashes shield her eyes, she kissed him back, feeling a shot of pure, sweet happiness. Maybe it was cowardly not to tell him the truth, but kisses were so much simpler than feelings—and even more so when his feelings were so far removed from hers.

Lying back on the lounger, Max stretched out his legs, closing his eyes to the beat of the sun. Despite his easy words he felt a ripple of unease snake across his skin, only he wasn't entirely sure why.

These last few days had been hard. Arguing with Margot, seeing her so upset and then confessing his past to her had been painful. But it had been worth it, for now he had everything he'd ever wanted. He was the biggest shareholder in one of the oldest and most prestigious champagne businesses in the world and, more importantly, Margot was his wife.

His life was complete, and he should be enjoying that fact. He *wanted* to enjoy it, but he wasn't. Instead he felt restless and uneasy.

Watching Margot turn the pages of her book, a tiny frown of concentration creasing her forehead, he knew that the problem was his alone. She seemed utterly happy—happier, even, than that slightly serious young girl he'd known all those years ago.

He, on the other hand, felt anything but relaxed. It didn't help that since they'd walked up to the terrace together their earlier conversation had been playing more or less on repeat inside his head.

Talking about his mother, remembering how devastated she had been by Paul's hurtful remarks and his lack of commitment, had made his muscles tense and a familiar feeling of anger and helplessness push against his ribcage.

For years those memories and feelings had been like fish in a pond over winter—there, but not there, still and silent beneath the ice. Now, though, it was as if he had smashed the frozen surface, and he couldn't seem to stop thinking about his mother and Paul. Himself and Margot.

He hadn't been consciously trying to rewrite history, and yet for the first time he could see that in so many ways his past had been driving his actions—pushing him to seek the certainty and legitimacy that his mother had craved. How else had he managed to build a global business worth billions in less than ten years?

His chest rose and fell.

Why else would he have proposed to Margot after see-

ing her in secret for just two months? And why else had he
ignored logic and instinct and married her five days ago?

At the time, he'd justified his behaviour in any number
of ways. Only he didn't care any more about the money
he'd paid for the shares. Nor did he feel the need to take
her business and turn it around, for he knew now that she
hadn't judged him unworthy.

He breathed in sharply. Opening his eyes, he glanced
over at where Margot was sitting, her sleek limbs gleaming in the sunlight. Always, right from the beginning,
he'd seen their relationship from *his* point of view. It had
been his past that mattered, his pride, his feelings—his
motivation.

But this wasn't just about him.

'I had choices, and I walked into that chapel willingly.'

As her words replayed inside his head his thoughts
slowed in time to his heartbeat, and suddenly and acutely
he knew why he was feeling so uneasy.

Margot might be his wife, but the fact was there was
no way she would have chosen to marry him if he hadn't
forced the issue—forced her to choose between sacrificing herself or her family.

Really, what kind of a choice was that?

He had pushed her into this marriage, using the love
she felt for her grandfather and her brother to get his own
way. But now, having forced her to choose, where did that
leave him—*them*?

'I was thinking about what you said earlier about doing
other things.' Leaning forward, Max kissed Margot's bare
shoulder. 'And I thought we might go scuba diving this
morning. Danny can take us out in the boat, and we could
spend a couple of hours in the water.'

They were eating lunch on the terrace. A delicate salad

of lobster and asparagus, followed by tuna carpaccio and a lime tart.

Gazing up at him, Margot felt her skin grow warm, a pulse of love beating through her veins. 'I'd like that.'

She loved the serenity and the slow-motion way of life beneath the waves. There was something intensely peaceful about slipping beneath the surface of the water, and the deeper you went the easier it was to forget your landlocked worries.

And that was exactly what she needed to do—what she had decided to do. Today she would concentrate on the good and stop dwelling on what she couldn't change. Most couples would envy the sexual connection that she and Max shared, and although he didn't love her he had confided in her, and that surely meant that he needed her for something other than sex.

It wasn't perfect, but few marriages were. And look how far they had come in just a few days.

She felt his fingers curl around hers.

'And you're okay swimming with sharks?' he asked softly.

She held his gaze. 'Isn't that what I've been doing all week?'

He grimaced. 'Is that how you see me?'

She studied his face. So much had changed in such a short time. A week ago she might only have noticed the ruthless line of his jaw, or the carefully guarded expression in his eyes. Now, though, she knew he was no shark. She'd experienced his softer side first-hand—not just when he was making love but in how he'd opened up to her.

'No, I don't think you're a shark.' Her eyes creased. 'You're more of a clownfish.'

There was a beat of silence, and then she shrieked with

laughter as he grabbed her onto his lap and buried his face in the hollow of her neck.

She was still laughing when she heard a distant rumble. 'What was that?'

Turning, they both gazed towards the ocean. On the horizon, so far away it looked almost like smoke, a loose dark cloud was hovering above the sea. Down on the beach, the waves were slightly choppier and more uneven than usual.

'Must be a storm.' His arms tightened around her and he smiled down at her easily. 'Don't worry, it'll probably miss us. But even if it doesn't it won't last long at this time of year.' Picking up his cup, he took a gulp of coffee. 'I'll go talk to Danny. He tracks all the weather for miles, so he'll know if we can still go out and—'

He broke off as his mobile started to ring.

Glancing down at the screen, his face shifted, the smile fading. 'Sorry, it's my mother. I'd better take it.'

Before she had a chance to speak he was tipping her gently off his lap onto her chair and standing up and walking swiftly across the terrace to the pool, lifting the phone to his ear as he did so. Watching him, she felt oddly bereft, almost hurt by his leaving, for it felt as if he was rejecting her...

But it wasn't that, she told herself quickly. He just wasn't used to sharing that part of himself.

It was impossible to hear what he was saying, and she couldn't see the expression on his face. But over the last few days she had become increasingly sensitive to the tiniest shift in his manner and, staring at his broad back, she knew something was wrong. His shoulders were pressing against the flimsy fabric of his shirt as though he was holding himself back—or holding something in.

She chewed her lip. Should she stay sitting or should she go over to him? Or maybe she shouldn't even be there.

She was just contemplating this new, third option when she heard Max hang up. For a moment she waited for him to turn round, her heart bumping nervously against her ribs. But he didn't turn round. He just carried on standing there in silence, his head slightly bowed as though he was praying.

Suddenly she could bear it no longer. It was probably a bad idea. Almost certainly it was. Only she didn't know any other way to be, for she cared that he was hurting. And so, standing up, she walked towards him.

'Max—is everything okay?'

She breathed out softly. Around them the air was heavy and motionless, and the birds were suddenly unusually quiet, as though sensing the sudden shift in tension on the terrace.

He turned slowly. 'Not really, no,' he said at last.

She felt cold on the inside. Trying not to think the worst, she said quickly, 'Is something the matter with your mum?'

He nodded. 'She needs me to come home, so I'm going to have to go back to France.'

'To France?' Whatever answer she had been expecting, it wasn't that.

He stared at her impatiently. 'Yes—that's where she lives.'

'But why? What's happened?'

'It doesn't matter. You don't need to worry about it.'

His voice was curt, but it wasn't his voice that made a chill settle on her skin. Moments before he'd answered the phone his eyes had been soft and teasing. Now, though, they were hard and flat and distant. And just like that time reversed, so that suddenly he was back to being the same remote man who had confronted her in the boardroom.

'But I am worried,' she said simply. 'I can see you're upset—'

He looked over at her blankly, almost as though he wasn't quite sure who she was, and then, running a hand over his face, he sighed.

'She's got the press camped out on her doorstep. Somehow they've found out about us. There are hundreds of them, all waiting outside, trying to get photos and hassling the staff. I can't expect her to deal with that.'

'Of course not.' She moved swiftly to his side, her hand reaching for his. 'We can leave now.' She glanced down at her bikini. 'I'll just go and get changed—'

His fingers tightened on hers, but even if they had been standing on opposite sides of the pool she would have known that she'd said the wrong thing, for she felt his entire body tensing beside her.

'You don't have to do that,' he said curtly, and then, as though hearing the harshness in his own voice, he softened his refusal by lifting her hand to his mouth and kissing it. 'In fact, it's probably better if you don't. They want a story, and it will be far easier for me to give them one if I'm on my own. So just stay here. I will fix this, and then I'll fly back.'

'But—' Margot started to protest but it was too late. He had already let go of her hand and was walking purposefully towards the house.

She stared after him in silence, her body quivering with a mixture of confusion and frustration. Theoretically, she'd accepted that Max would never love her, but now, faced with concrete evidence of that fact, she felt angry and hurt.

She sort of understood why he didn't want her to go back with him. Max knew how to handle himself, and she certainly didn't enjoy dealing with the *paparazzi*. Nor did she want to meet his mother for the first time with a pack of howling press slavering outside for a photo. So perhaps it would be better if she stayed here.

But if that was true then why did she feel as though he was only telling her part of the story? And, more importantly, why was she still standing here when she should be asking him that question?

Striding into his dressing room, Max yanked down a shirt and pushed his arms into the sleeves. He grabbed a tie and knotted it round his neck, then pulled his jacket on. After so long in beachwear, he felt as if his clothes were as unfamiliar and unwieldy as a suit of armour. But he wasn't planning on wearing them for long, or staying in France for any more time than it took to get whatever legal decision he needed to protect his mother. However, he sure as hell wasn't going to make the trip in swim-shorts and flip-flops.

Or with Margot there.

Remembering the hurt expression on her face, he closed his eyes. He didn't want to leave her behind, but how could he take her with him? The press were relentless, and with a story like this they would be like the sharks he had jokingly mentioned over lunch. Hungry, ruthless and unstoppable.

Without her, he could handle them, and that was why he would be going back to France alone.

Gritting his teeth, he walked back into the bedroom and picked up his wallet and his watch. Frowning, he stared down at the face. If he left in the next hour he would be back sometime after—

'I want to come with you.'

He turned. Margot was standing in the doorway, not quite blocking it but with a stubborn set to her chin that suggested she might be about to do so.

He sighed. Had he really thought that she would just give up?

Holding her gaze, he shook his head. 'It's not a good idea. If we go together it will only turn into a feeding frenzy—and, frankly it's bad enough that they're hounding my mother. I don't need them turning on my wife as well.'

She stared at him mutinously. 'I disagree. If we both go back then we can give them what they want. The two of us together. Mr and Mrs Max Montigny.'

He glanced away from her. She was saying everything he'd ever wanted to hear, offering him the kind of support and loyalty that he had always craved, and yet...

Something shifted inside him—a tectonic convergence of conversations and memories—and he heard not just her words but the calm acceptance in the voice.

'I'm a fixer-upper. I make it all look perfect.'

His heart was beating fast and uneven, as though he'd been running. Maybe because he was running away from a truth that he didn't want to face—away from facts that he could never change, no matter how much he wanted to.

He took a deep breath, his gut tightening, finally acknowledging the real reason why he couldn't take her with him.

Margot had spent all her life fixing her family: managing her parents' marriage, her grandparents' expectations and the demands of her brothers, sacrificing her plans and her hopes and dreams time and time again.

And here, on this archipelago, he had made her sacrifice herself to him. But knowing that, was he really going to ask her to do it again?

He felt her eyes on his face, and then the touch of her hand on his arm.

'I thought you wanted to be with me,' she said softly. 'That's what you said.'

Watching his face grow still and remote, Margot felt a chill spread over her skin. He might have spoken the words, but clearly he hadn't meant them. Like so much of what Max said, it bore little relation to what was going in that handsome head of his.

'I do—' he began.

Her pulse jumped and she took a step closer. 'So prove it. Take me with you. I should be there. I want to be there. I know it's been difficult between us, but I am your wife.'

Wife.

Remembering the vows they had taken, he felt suddenly unsteady, and a chill started to roll out over his skin. He had promised to love and to cherish her.

But he had lied.

Ever since the moment he had walked into the boardroom at the House of Duvernay headquarters he had treated her with a ruthlessness that now sickened him. A ruthlessness that equalled—no, *surpassed* Paul's treatment of his mother, for he had exploited her misfortune to give, by proxy, his mother the happy ending she'd so wanted.

It was all such a mess.

He'd made Margot a pawn—bullying her, blackmailing her, rushing her into marrying him. Using her to solve the issues inside his head in the same way that Paul had used his mother for sex and to boost his ego. Using the real love Margot felt for her family to get his own way. He had hurt her and humbled her, deliberately and repeatedly, and she had risen above his treatment in ways he could hardly fathom and certainly didn't deserve.

Any more than he deserved her support now.

What she *did* deserve, though, was to have the freedom to choose. To be with the person she wanted. Not be saddled with a life sentence to a man she had been to all intents and purposes forced to marry.

Margot stared at him, her frustration shifting up a gear. 'You wanted this, Max. You wanted this marriage.

I thought you wanted—' Her insides turned over and abruptly she broke off, leaving the sentence unfinished.

He didn't want her.

She couldn't actually say the words out loud. Even thinking them was so painful that it hurt to breathe, but she knew she was right. The fact that he didn't want her to go with him told her everything she needed to know.

Had he trusted and valued her, then returning to France would have been the perfect opportunity for them to showcase their marriage in public. But he would rather go alone.

The thought ripped through her like a serrated knife.

Max stared down at her face. She had never looked more beautiful to him and he had never wanted her more. He felt a sudden warm rush of hope rising inside him. 'Okay, I'll take you with me,' he said slowly. 'But on one condition.'

He could feel the warmth fading, and in its place a chill spreading out as she looked up at him uncertainly.

'I want you to tell me the truth,' he said.

Outside the window he could see the darkening sky, feel the heaviness of the approaching storm, and yet it seemed feeble, even frivolous, compared to the tension swirling inside his chest.

'Okay.' She nodded, her brown eyes searching his face, her relief at his change of heart mingling with obvious apprehension at where the conversation was leading.

Holding her gaze, he cleared his throat. 'I want you to tell me why you agreed to marry me.'

Her face stilled, and she frowned. 'Well, because...'

She hesitated, and her eyes dropped as though she couldn't meet his gaze, and then he knew. He knew that it had all been worthless. He could never take Margot to meet his mother for she would know in an instant that it was a phony marriage. It would break her heart, and he could no more do that to her then continue to use guilt and financial threats to keep Margot as his wife.

Margot shivered. She wasn't sure what was happening, just knew that they were no longer simply talking about whether or not she should return with him to France.

She tried again. 'You know why.'

'But I want you to tell me in your own words,' he said softly.

Too softly, she thought a moment later, her throat drying as she looked up into his taut, set face. 'I needed the money—' she began, but he cut her off.

'So there was no other reason.'

Yes, there was—there were. So many reasons—too many—but she wasn't brave enough to start listing them now.

It took her a moment to realise that he wasn't asking a question, just stating a fact. For perhaps a minute he stared at her in silence, and then, just as she was about to protest, to tell him that it wasn't that simple, he lowered his mouth to hers and kissed her gently.

Her heart lurched with relief, her fingers curling around the muscles of his arm as he deepened the kiss, her longing for him stealing her words, her thoughts, even her fear.

Reaching up, she clasped his face. But as she tried to deepen the kiss she felt his hands on hers, and suddenly he was stepping away from her, breathing unsteadily.

'Don't follow me,' he said, and the finality in his voice cast a spell over her body, rooting her to the cold tiles.

She knew without asking that he didn't just mean out of the room. He meant to France, to wherever, and the shock knocked the air out of her lungs, so that before her stunned brain could even register what he was doing he had turned and walked swiftly out of the room.

CHAPTER TEN

IT TOOK THE first tiny clumps of raindrops slamming against the window to drag Margot's eyes away from the empty doorway. Hesitantly, as though she wasn't sure if her legs would respond, she took a step towards the bed and sank down onto it. Her body felt brittle, her breath leaden.

It hardly seemed possible, but Max had walked out on her. Not just out of the room, or even the villa, but out of her life. He hadn't actually said as much. But he hadn't needed to. She had seen it in his eyes. Something had happened between that phone call out on the terrace and her walking into the bedroom—some insight or decision that had turned him away from her, away from their marriage.

Curling her knees up to her chest, she hugged them against her body. Shock gave way to misery, and tears began sliding down over her cheeks, and then the shock returned and her heartbeat started to shake. Her body started shaking too, and she was glad suddenly that she was sitting down, for she knew that her legs were definitely not capable of holding her up, or of supporting the weight of misery in her chest.

She took a deep breath, striving for calm, but the pain in her chest was too loud, too demanding.

He'd left her. Max had left her.

After everything they'd been through, she'd thought for one brief, blissful moment that they had a chance, that maybe her love would be enough for the two of them to make their marriage work. But now it was all over before it had even got started.

She covered her mouth with her hand.

Was it really that surprising, though? The pull between them had only ever been sexual on his side, and what couple had ever managed to build a future on great sex?

Thinking about her parents' marriage, she felt her pulse quiver. Not a happy or healthy marriage, anyway.

Remembering his question, she felt her shoulders tighten. Would it have been any different if she'd told him the truth? That at first she'd told herself that she was marrying him for money, but that even then the real reason she'd agreed to his proposal was because she loved him, had never stopped loving him.

Love had been the reason she'd let him back into her life. And the reason why she had agreed to turn her life upside down.

Only now he was gone, and the idea of his not being there was unimaginable. Agonising.

Suddenly she felt exhausted. Her eyes were blurry with tears again and her head was aching. But the pain would pass. Maybe not today, or tomorrow, or even in a year... or five. Sometime in the future, though, it would be just a dull ache above her heart, like the pain of losing her mother and her grandmother and Yves.

She had survived losing Max once, and she would do it again. But first she needed to sleep, for she was just so tired.

Crawling up towards the pillows, she pulled the sheet over her body and closed her eyes. Soothed by the steady, soporific sound of the rain striking the ground, she fell asleep.

* * *

It was the sound of the birds that woke her. Not right away.
At first their cries were just background noise to the confused and unfinished dream she was having about Emile
and Max and that boat she had seen on the second day of
their honeymoon.

Opening her eyes, she gazed groggily around the room.
It was still daylight and, grabbing her phone, she realised
with shock that she had slept for nearly two hours. Judging
by the fact that the sky was no longer dark, but streaked
with palest pink and yellow, she had slept through the
storm too. Outside, the surf sounded reassuringly soft and
regular, and the air felt warm but fresh, as though it had
just come out of a tumble drier.

She felt fresher too—less tired and less desperate, both
her body and her mind revived by sleep. It wasn't that she
felt any better about Max's rejection, just that she could see
past it. Her heart might be in pieces, but that didn't mean
her life had to be too. She had recovered from breaking up
with him before, and the House of Duvernay had survived
wars and recessions. It would survive Max Montigny.

Only somehow she didn't think that he was going to
hang around anyway. He had walked out for a reason. Had
the company been prosperous, then perhaps it might be
different, but it was clear that he didn't want anything to
do with her, and she felt sure that his feelings would ex-
tend to their business relationship.

Her mouth twisted. Obviously he would feel that way.
To Max, all of this—including their marriage—had only
ever been about business. She had been the one to start
weaving fantasy through fact, letting the intimacy and intensity of the last few days sweep her away.

Perhaps for a short time it had swept him away too.
Only when it had come to returning to reality, to leav-

ing the perfect little self-contained bubble of their honeymoon, he'd come to his senses. And that was when he'd decided to walk.

Tears burned behind her eyes and she breathed out shakily. Even though accepting that fact felt like a knife being driven through her heart, in some ways she was glad of the pain, for it made her focus on herself in a way that she never had.

Before, there had always been a long list of people and problems: Colette, Emile, her grandparents, Yves, Louis, Duvernay. And each time she had put her own life on hold in order to find a solution.

But from this moment on that was going to change. *She* had changed.

Her heart might be broken, but her brain was working just fine, and she knew that it was time to stop fixing other people's lives. Even though she wasn't quite sure how she was going to do it, she was going to start living *her* life— not the life decided by those around her.

A life on her own...without Max.

She might have wed in haste, like her parents, but that was where the similarity between their marriage and hers would end. Right now a life without Max felt like a life without warmth and sunlight, but however agonising it was to imagine, she was going to divorce him.

If she was going to make good on this promise to change then she needed her name and her business back. And that meant divorcing Max—although she would leave the details to the lawyers. She might have found the strength to deal with the concept theoretically, but it would be a long time before she would be willing or able to speak to him again—if ever.

First things first, though. She needed to go home.

She packed methodically, the rhythm of folding and

layering her clothes helping her stay calm. Changing out
of her bikini, she found a pair of skinny-fit jeans that she'd
brought with her in case of a freakish cold spell, and a
loose tobacco-coloured linen jumper. Her face was pale,
and her eyes were slightly pink and swollen, and for a moment she wondered whether mascara and lipstick would
make things better or worse. Deciding it would be easier
just to wear dark glasses, she left her hair loose, picked up
her bag and shoes and walked towards the door.

All that was left to do was thank the staff and make
her way to the airport. But first she wanted one last walk
along the beach.

Walking through the villa, she felt some of her self-
control start to slip away, and suddenly she was fighting
tears again. She had loved being here with Max, getting
to know him, getting to know herself, but there was no
point in thinking that way.

Swiping at her eyes, grateful that she hadn't bothered
to apply mascara, she stepped out onto the terrace—and
froze.

Max was sitting on the curved steps leading down to
the pool. He was hunched over, his head in his hands, an
empty glass lying on its side beside him.

She stared at him in stunned silence. What was he still
doing here? Had the storm delayed his flight? And what
exactly was she supposed to say to him now?

Glancing down, she felt her heartbeat skip erratically.
He was still wearing the same charcoal-coloured suit, only
it was soaking wet. She could see water dripping from
the jacket, and the fabric was dark and swollen-looking.
With shock, she realised that he must have been sitting
out in the storm.

Carefully setting down her bag and shoes, she walked
towards him. 'Max…?'

He looked up at her and she felt her heart twist, for his eyes were dull and colourless.

'I didn't know you were still here,' she said quietly.

He nodded. 'I couldn't leave.'

She bit her lip. 'Was it the storm?'

'The storm?' He frowned, as though he didn't understand her question.

'Did they close the airport?' Obviously they had. What other reason would he have for still being here? Although she wasn't sure why he hadn't sheltered from the rain.

His eyes fixed on her face, and then slowly he shook his head. 'I didn't go the airport. I couldn't—'

His voice cracked and, glancing down at his hands, she saw that they were shaking. Suddenly she was shaking too.

Forcing herself to lift her chin, she said stiffly, 'Why not? Why couldn't you go?'

Her heart was beating so hard that she felt light-headed. It didn't mean anything, him being here. There was probably some logical and simple reason. But—

She drew a breath, trying to calm herself.

Why else would he still be at the villa?

Don't even go there, she thought desperately.

But she couldn't help herself. From the moment she had walked out onto the terrace and seen him it had been there, hidden beneath the surface but still there, a longing and a hope that she knew was stupid and senseless. And yet she couldn't stop herself from feeling it.

'I couldn't leave you,' he said slowly.

She stared at him mutely, not daring to ask any of the questions milling around inside her head, not willing to have her hopes crushed again.

Suddenly she knew that she couldn't stay standing up. With legs that shook slightly, she sat down beside him. Up close, she could see that his shirt was drier than his suit, but still damp. She felt her throat swell.

Reaching over, she carefully righted the glass. 'Did you stay out here in the storm?'

Max shrugged, then nodded. 'I tried to leave, but I just couldn't.'

'What about your mother?'

Hearing the concern in her voice, he flinched inwardly. Even now she was thinking about someone other than herself.

'My lawyers got an emergency injunction so the photographers can't go within fifty metres of her house, so she's doing okay.'

He watched the tension in her beautiful face ease a little, and then she reached out and touched his jacket.

'And what about you? You're soaked through. Why didn't you come inside?'

For a moment he couldn't speak past the ache in his throat. And then he said, 'Because I knew if I saw you that I'd never be able to do it. I'd never be able to leave you. And I have to leave, Margot. I can't do this to you any more.' Clenching his jaw, he breathed out unsteadily.

'Do what?' Her brown eyes were searching his.

'All of this. Everything. I've treated you so badly, and I don't want to *be* that person.' He ran a hand over his face, suddenly struggling for words. 'I don't want to hurt you.'

Margot felt suddenly close to tears. 'So why are you leaving me, then?' She stared at him, frustration overriding her fear. 'If you don't want to hurt me then why are you doing this?'

He hesitated, his expression stricken. 'You did all this to protect your family. You're such a good person, Margot. And I'm not. You deserve better than me.'

Her chest tightened. 'Max—'

He shook his head. 'I want to be with you. That's all I want—all I've ever wanted.' His mouth twisted. 'That's why I came back to France. Why I bought the shares. Why I offered to marry you. For a long time I didn't want to admit it to myself, let alone you, but I need you to understand why we can't be together.'

Margot couldn't look at him. 'And why *is* that, Max?' Her voice split, the hurt and the longing rising to the surface. 'Why can't we be together?'

His hand slid over hers, and reluctantly she turned to face him.

'Because I love you,' he said softly. 'But I know you don't love me. I know you only married me because you love your family, and I'm sorry for making you do that. Sorry for everything else I've done and said.'

She gazed at him, feeling hot and dazed, as though she'd been sitting in the sun all morning, too stunned with shock and happiness to speak.

'You love me?' she croaked.

He nodded, his fingers tightening around hers.

'And what about if I love you?' she said shakily.

He stared down into her face. 'But you don't, do you?'

She couldn't reply, but she knew that she must be nodding, and smiling, because suddenly he breathed out raggedly and then he was pulling her onto his lap, wrapping his arms around her, holding her close, then closer still, as though he never wanted to let her go.

'You're such an idiot,' she whispered. 'Of *course* I love you, Max. I've loved you since I was nineteen years old.'

Lifting her face, she saw that his face was damp now too—but with tears, not rain.

'It nearly broke me, losing you,' he said, and his voice was hoarse with the emotions he was no longer trying to hide. 'I need you like I need air and water and food. Without you, nothing matters. Without you, I have nothing. I *am* nothing.'

Searching his face, she knew that he was telling the truth. 'Not to me,' she said softly. 'You're my husband, and my heart belongs to you.' She smiled up at him. 'And now I think we should get you out of that suit.'

He gazed down at her, his eyes gleaming in the sunlight, and she felt a rush of pure love for him as his mouth curved upwards.

'That has to be your most transparent attempt yet to get my clothes off.'

Reaching up, she curled her arm around his neck. 'Did it work?'

In answer to her question he scooped her into his arms and stood up, the burn of his gaze melting her bones and searing her skin.

'I think so. But you know I never like to leave anything to chance. So let's go and make certain.'

And, turning, he carried her back into the villa.

* * * * *